BEFORE & AFTER
YOU & ME

"Before & After You & Me is gut-wrenching, raw and real. If it's possible for a book to break your heart and mend it at the same time, Dallas Woodburn's story does just that. Lyrically written, the novel takes the reader on Emma's inward journey as she struggles to piece her life back together after a tragic accident she blames on herself. The book isn't written in chronological order but takes the reader back and forth between the "before"— the time leading up to the accident, and the "after," where Emma must deal with the repercussions of her actions and decisions. Emma's inner struggles are beautifully portrayed in a manner that is relatable and thought-provoking, while the story's details that the author reveals bit by bit weave together like a colorful tapestry, leading to a satisfying ending that's bittersweet but filled with hope. Highly recommended!"

—REBECCA BISCHOFF, *Hole in the Rock*

BEFORE & AFTER YOU & ME

DALLAS WOODBURN

OWL HOLLOW PRESS

Owl Hollow Press, LLC, Springville, UT 84663

Before and After You and Me

Library of Congress Cataloging-in-Publication Data
Before and After You and Me / D. Woodburn. — First edition.

Summary:
Emma blames herself when a freak accident at a pool party leaves Hunter, the town's rising track star and her former boyfriend, paralyzed from the waist down.

Cover Design by Jen Marie Hawkins
Cover Image from Pexels

ISBN 978-1-958109-48-9 (paperback)
ISBN 978-1-958109-49-6 (e-book)

*For Maya and Auden, who split my life into
Before & After in the very best way.*

PROLOGUE

IT HAPPENS AT A PARTY.

The week before Christmas. Robbie Zwick's house. A cloudy California night absent of stars.

In the months to come, I will examine and reexamine my memory of this night, trying to find the exact moment the party veered off course. Because at some point—some moment before The Moment—there must have been a fork in the road, like in that famous Robert Frost poem we read in freshman English class, and somehow this party took the wrong path. And that made all the difference.

I cling to this belief, because it means that somewhere out there, in some other universe, this party took the other path—the right path—the one leading to normal and expected outcomes. In some other universe, another version of me had cheap wine spilled on her shoes, woke up with a dull hangover, and met other-universe Céline for coffee the next morning to compare and dissect every ordinary detail.

But in this universe, the party routed itself toward nightmare. Again and again, the moment that sticks out in my memory is this: someone had the idea to go skinny-dipping.

That moment changed everything. That moment ruptured my normal, average life.

And Hunter's life too, of course. Hunter's most of all.

Nobody except me will remember whose idea it was to go skinny-dipping in Robbie's bright blue pool.

The reason I remember?

It was my idea.

1

THE ACCIDENT

"YOU CAN'T MOPE around and avoid Hunter forever," Céline says.

"Why not?" That is, in fact, exactly what I plan to do the rest of winter break.

"Because you can't." In the background, there is a rustling sound; I picture Céline standing in front of her open closet, rifling through her thrift-store gems, trying to decide what to wear tonight. It doesn't matter what she decides. Whatever she wears, she will look effortlessly chic and put-together.

I flop backwards onto my bed. "You didn't see his face. It was like… like he'd been slapped." A snake of guilt coils around and around my stomach. Still, I don't regret breaking up with him.

"Don't worry about Hunter. It'll be a huge party. You can avoid him."

I laugh. "That's even weirder! Being at the same party and not even acknowledging each other? Besides, I bet he'll come over and talk to you. Just to show me he still can."

"What does that mean?"

"He'll want to rub it in. Even though we broke up, you two are still friends. It's like he stole you from me."

"Nobody stole anybody. And who knows, he might not show up."

"Did he text you? Have you talked to him?"

Céline sighs. "No. But c'mon, Em!" Her tone shifts into pleading. "All I want is to go to a party with my best friend. That's all I've wanted all semester long. Is that too much to ask?"

It has always been hard for me to say no to Céline. And now? Now that she's played the "all semester long" card? Now there's no way I can beg out of Robbie Zwick's party.

"Okay, okay," I surrender. "Can I raid your closet for something to wear?"

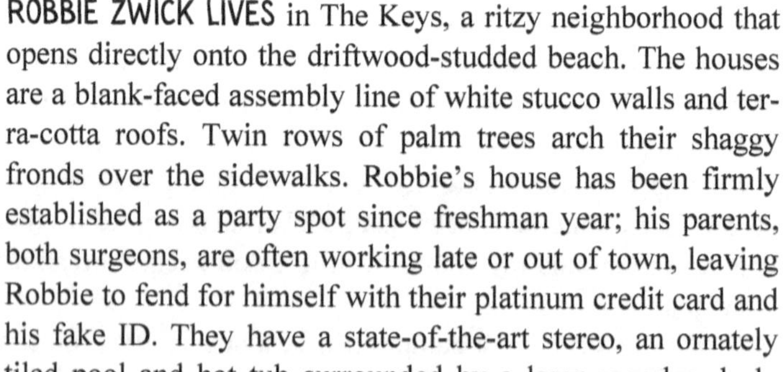

ROBBIE ZWICK LIVES in The Keys, a ritzy neighborhood that opens directly onto the driftwood-studded beach. The houses are a blank-faced assembly line of white stucco walls and terra-cotta roofs. Twin rows of palm trees arch their shaggy fronds over the sidewalks. Robbie's house has been firmly established as a party spot since freshman year; his parents, both surgeons, are often working late or out of town, leaving Robbie to fend for himself with their platinum credit card and his fake ID. They have a state-of-the-art stereo, an ornately tiled pool and hot tub surrounded by a large wooden deck, and neighbors who never call the police to complain about the noise.

I gaze around the pool deck, enjoying the hazy film settling over my thoughts. Lizzo thumps from the stereo and a dance floor is slowly forming over by the barbeque grill, under the potted palms. I bob my head to the beat, taking sips from my red plastic cup, surprisingly glad to be here. *Something* is going to happen tonight. I can sense it. I'm home for the holidays, buzzed from rum-and-Cokes, and the air feels charged with possibility, and there is Mark Sampson, taller than I remember, and he's lost his acne, and I could flirt with him, if I wanted to. I'm single now. I could even kiss him in some dark corner of Robbie's house.

But I won't kiss Mark Sampson. I won't even flirt with him. Maybe if I were a different type of person, the type of person who likes to cause a scene and be the center of drama, maybe then I would kiss him. Anabelle would kiss him, simply to prove she could. But my breakup with Hunter happened mere hours ago, and I don't particularly want to kiss anyone else. David's face flashes into my brain—my treacherous brain—but I push the thought away. He is thousands of miles away. And he is Anabelle's.

Hunter would inevitably find out if I kissed someone else at Robbie Zwick's party. At a party like this, no matter how discreet two people try to be, someone will stumble on them looking for the bathroom, or notice their disheveled hair or misbuttoned shirts or creeping blush when they glance at each other, and word will travel around the party and pop up the next morning on social media and pretty soon everyone will be talking about it. If Hunter had been the one to break up with me, then maybe I could rebound with someone else tonight. But as the Dumper, the only acceptable post-breakup hookup is to reconcile and make out with the Dumpee. And I am *not* going to do that, no matter how drunk I get.

I glance around for Céline, who is supposed to keep me from doing anything that will be gossiped about tomorrow. Almost as soon as we arrived, she slipped her hand out of mine, saying she would get us both drinks. But she didn't come back. I eventually gave up and poured my own rum-and-Coke, and now I can't find Céline anywhere. I'm willing to bet the real reason she dragged me here tonight is that she's hoping Hunter and I will get back together. She was my friend first, but now she's Hunter's friend too—and the two of them have gotten closer all semester, while I've been thousands of miles away. Instead of a Venn diagram with me in the middle, the three of us morphed into an equilateral triangle. It must be awkward for her now, with us broken up. Now we'll go back to a Venn diagram again, only instead of me in the middle, it will be Céline in the middle.

Someone bumps into me from behind and I nearly stumble into a bush.

"Oh crap, sorry," a familiar voice says. I regain my balance and look up into Matt Hayward's kind brown eyes.

"Hey Emma," he says, a smile in his voice. As if everything is normal. As if I didn't just smash his best friend's heart to smithereens. "You're home."

"Yep." *Home.* I thought Wabash was starting to feel like home, but then I arrived in Buenaventura for winter break and my whole body loosened up. There's something nice about relaxing back into my old self, like slipping on a comfy pair of well-worn jeans.

I expect Matt to nod goodbye and continue on his way, but he doesn't seem in a rush. "How's art school?" he asks. "Where is it, again? Ohio?"

"Indiana." Wabash Academy for the Arts is a small private boarding school tucked amid the quilted cornfields between Indianapolis and Chicago. I still can't believe I got the scholarship—when I applied last spring, it felt like throwing glitter at the stars. Like blowing out the candles on your birthday cake and making an outrageous wish.

And then my outrageous wish came true, and I learned that wishes can be complicated beneath the surface.

"So you're happy there?" Matt asks.

"Yeah," I answer automatically. "I am." My tone comes out more defensive than I mean it to be. When I received the scholarship, it seemed like the decision was already made for me. Like there wasn't even a choice. Of course I would go. It's the opportunity of a lifetime.

"I mean, Indiana is super cold," I continue. "But I like the snow. And art school is great." Because in a lot of ways, it is great. But also it is frustrating, and scary, and exhilarating, and lonely.

Matt's looking at me with that same openness I recognize from that afternoon we sat in his car together, parked in my driveway, as the sunlight slanted toward dusk. Like he knows there is more for me to say and is patiently waiting for me to say it.

But while I did unload my thoughts and fears to him six months ago, tonight I take a sip of my drink, swallowing down my words. I don't know how to capture the layers of my life in Wabash, how to explain it to someone on the outside.

"I couldn't live somewhere that cold," Matt says when it's clear I'm not going to elaborate. "We're spoiled here. Beach life."

"You get used to it," I tell him. Which is true. And also not.

Yesterday, I had boarded my flight home in the middle of an Indiana winter: gray and brown and barren. Salt-crunched roads, dirty snow hulking along the curbs. Icy winds that slam your face whenever you turn a corner, making your eyes water and your eyelashes freeze. When I exited the airport terminal into the warm smog of Los Angeles, it was like I'd time-traveled back to summer. Everyone is wearing T-shirts and flip-flops even though it's a week before Christmas. Here in Southern California, you can even skinny-dip in the winter, thanks to heated pools.

"Well, I'll see you around, Emma," Matt says, heading toward the keg. "Welcome home."

"Thanks." He must have heard from Hunter that we broke up, but he's still being nice to me. That's Matt for you. I think of his small warm car, the way he handed me the box of tissues. *A girl like you.*

I watch the back of Matt's head until he disappears into the crowd. A cool breeze sweeps in from the ocean, smelling of salt. My bare arms break out in goosebumps. The salt air smells both fresh and rank, both cleansing and decayed, in a way I can't fully explain to my Wabash friends who have never lived by the ocean.

I breathe in deeply. Once, after a day at the beach, Hunter buried his face in my hopelessly tangled, windblown hair and called me a goddess.

I push the thought away, crossing my arms over my chest even though my mom says crossed arms make me look unapproachable and Céline once tipsily admitted that, yes, some people do think I'm a little aloof. I gaze around the backyard, searching for Céline. Across the pool, Hunter casually rubs the back of his neck, a gesture that sends a pang through my chest. He is talking to Siggy Taylor, who everyone knows is a huge flirt.

The thing is, I hadn't planned to break up with Hunter this morning. I was hoping to arrive back in Buenaventura and realize that my growing doubts all semester were just flimsy ghosts, and that when I saw Hunter again in person, I would not want to break up with him at all. Or, at the very least, I was going to wait and break up with him in January, right before catching a plane back to Indianapolis for the spring semester. That way Hunter and I could have one last hurrah, one final nostalgic run-through of all our favorite hangouts and hookup spots around town. I would have someone to keep me company during the three p.m. Christmas Eve dinner at my grandmother's nursing home, a place that always makes me sad. And I would be invited to the Murray family's annual cookie-decorating party, an afternoon I've genuinely been looking forward to since last Christmas, when Hunter's mom gushed over my detailed precision with sugar icing and food coloring.

But when Hunter came over this morning, all of my careful plans fell to pieces. I knew I couldn't make it through winter break pretending everything was fine between us. I desperately wished I had stuck with my decision to break up with him over the summer. That was when we were meant to break up. All this time we've been prolonging the inevitable.

I glance back. Hunter leans against a palm tree, alone. The tree is strung with white Christmas lights that sway erratically in the breeze, casting shadows on his face. Siggy must have gone off to flirt with someone else. Hunter is wearing a faded cross-country T-shirt, the one I'd borrowed and worn it to school when we first started dating, a badge of ownership announcing to the world that we were together.

That seems so long ago. Another life.

Hunter alternates between staring gloomily into his beer can and gazing around the pool deck. Is he deliberately looking at everyone except for me? He's refused to meet my eyes since this morning, when the breakup words came spilling out of me.

I feel terrible for hurting him. I want to tell him that. Later, maybe. I sip my rum-and-Coke. Later, maybe I'll walk over and tell him, *I'm so sorry, Hunter. I'm sorry for the way things ended.* Maybe he'll turn and stalk away, maybe he'll splash beer in my face, maybe he'll push me into the pool. But no matter what his reaction is, I know things will be better once the words are out.

Because this morning everything was so abrupt, so messy and unfinished. I want Hunter to know that I do care about him. I always will. I wish things could have been different. I wish—

"Is that Emma Mason?!"

Siggy Taylor sways a little in her heeled sandals and string bikini, silver starfish necklace dangling into her cleavage. Siggy does not talk much to me out in the real world, but for some reason drunk Siggy is one of my loudest admirers.

I push my thoughts away from Hunter. I'll wait to apologize. I'll give him space. Who knows where Céline disappeared to; for now, at least, I've got Siggy to distract me.

"Oh my godddd!" Siggy yells, squeezing her bony arms around my shoulders. "It's so good to see you!!"

"You too." I pat Siggy on the back gently. Once, at a previous Robbie Zwick party, Siggy spent twenty minutes holding both of my hands in her own, marveling at my "artistic fingers" and pretending to read my fortune. "You have great love in your future, and great sadness also," Siggy had intoned, her eyes momentarily looking quite sober as they latched onto mine, and I remember feeling a shiver down my spine as I pulled my hands away from her grasp.

Now, Siggy steps back but keeps her hands on my shoulders. Her fingers are surprisingly strong and her silver rings are cold against my skin.

"Oh my god, Emma," Siggy says, each word a sour alcoholic burst of breath upon my face. "Are you okay? I heard what happened."

"You mean me and Hunter?" I flick a strand of hair away from my eyes, trying to seem nonchalant.

Siggy nods, her movements exaggerated and slow. "He told me what happened. I'm here for you. I'm *here* for you, Emma."

"Thanks, but it's really okay. I'm fine. We grew apart, you know?"

Siggy's eyes are watery. "I can't believe he would do that to you."

"No, it's my fault," I clarify. "*I'm* the one who broke up with *him*."

"That's *right*, you broke up with him!" Siggy exclaims, waving her arms wildly. "Of course you broke up with him! I mean, how could you not, after what he did?"

My throat tightens. "Wait, what? What are you talking about?"

"I can't believe he would cheat on you with some slut from Roosevelt." Siggy clasps my hand, her fingers squeezing mine in a way that is probably meant to be reassuring. But I am not reassured. A wave of nausea rolls through my gut.

"What?" I ask. "Where did you hear that?" Blood pounds in my ears.

Siggy bends forward and rests her forehead on my shoulder, as if the weight of her bleached hair is suddenly too much. "Everyone's talking about it," she mumbles.

I remember watching Siggy and Hunter across the pool, how Hunter rubbed his hand across the back of his neck, the way he does when he is nervous. "Did Hunter tell you that?" I ask. My voice is soft and hollow, an echo of itself.

Siggy nods, her head still resting on my shoulder. Her hair grazes my arm, tickling unpleasantly. Her head is heavy and I want to push her away. My heartbeat quickens. Doubt settles in, even as I try to disarm it. *Who does Hunter even know at Roosevelt? Is it that Ashley girl, from the concert?*

"I'm sorry," Siggy murmurs.

"Hunter wouldn't cheat on me," I insist. "He wouldn't. He's only saying that because he's pissed I ended things." Even to myself, the words are not convincing. *Had* Hunter cheated on me? Is *that* why he can't even look at me? Maybe he's not heartbroken after all—maybe he's guilt-ridden.

Or maybe he's proud. Why else would he tell Siggy, unless he wanted word to get around the party and back to me? He must want me to know. He must want this sickening suspicion to wind its way through my memories, tainting every kiss and phone call and "I love you" we shared. He must want to hurt me.

I hate him. I'm furious. *It's a mistake. There must be some mistake.*

Siggy lifts up her head and looks at me, her eyes filled with drunken tears. Mascara clumps her lashes and trails of black leak from the corners of her eyes.

"You two seemed so perfect together," Siggy says. Then she leans back and shouts, "Guys suck!"

"Amen, sister!" someone yells in reply. Laughter, a few whoops and hisses.

I gulp my drink. Despite myself, I'm thinking about the first time Hunter and I slept together, squeezing ourselves into the backseat of his mom's car. His palms sweaty on my thighs. Formal dress hiked up around my ribcage. He groaned my name, then collapsed on top of me and kissed my hair.

I want to smash something. I want to get drunk. I want to get drunk and then smash Hunter in the face with my purse, which would likely deliver a pretty solid blow because I'm not only carrying my cell phone and wallet, but also Céline's cell phone and wallet. Céline hates carrying a purse, so when we go out together, I take care of Céline's stuff. Because we're best friends, and that's what best friends do for each other.

I scan the pool deck. Where is Céline? Does she know about Hunter and some other girl? People are congregating around a new case of beer—maybe Céline is over there? I step forward, then stop. Hunter is no longer leaning against the palm tree across the pool. What if he is getting another beer? The last thing I want right now is to bump into Hunter Murray.

I am thinking all of this, feeling Mark Sampson's eyes on me from a few feet away and Hunter's eyes not on me from wherever he is at this damn party, downing the last of my rum-and-Coke as I half listen to Siggy speculate about Elliot Escoval's relationship status, the stereo blasting Justin Timberlake and—*Oh!* my heart leaps with relief—there is Céline, grinding with Matt on the makeshift dance floor—thinking all of this, my heart pounding dizzily with anger and alcohol, I say to no one and to everyone, "Let's go skinny-dipping!" and peel off my T-shirt in one fluid motion and leap into the pool, as if I am born to play this role, as if everything is pre-destined. It feels fated, this moment.

Because the reality is, I hate pools and I hate swimming and I hate my bony hips and A-cup boobs.

Before this moment, I've never skinny-dipped in my life.

Other people whip off their clothes and race onto the pool deck with whoops and shouts, jumping in and pushing each other in. I eggbeater in the deep end, the water not as warm as

I expected it to be. Goosebumps fan out over my breasts and stomach. A group of boys splash each other and water gets into my eyes. There is shouting, and laughter, and then everything narrows, a camera lens focusing, zooming in. A beat, two beats, of silence.

Screams and panic erupt from the shallow end.

A body, floating there.

Hunter's red hair.

In that moment, my life splits: there is Before, and there is After.

2

BEFORE

JUNIOR YEAR, DECEMBER 18

ON MY FLIGHT home to California for winter break, I can't
stop thinking about my recurring dream. In it, Hunter's mom
repeatedly slaps me in the face, *smack smack smack*, telling
me to stay away from Hunter, that I'm going to ruin his life.
Each time I awaken nauseous and ashamed. In real life, I like
Hunter's mom a lot. And she likes me (or is excellent at pretending that she does). She makes me proud of the skill
embedded in my hands, the hours upon hours my fingers have
spent poised with a paintbrush, trying to get a certain cast of
light just right.

Annabelle insists the dream is nothing to worry about.
She thinks it's a sign that I'm feeling "premature guilt" over
my decision to break up with Hunter at the end of winter
break.

I gaze out the airplane window and try to push the dream
away. I'm excited to see Hunter, a genuine and untempered
excitement. Maybe I don't want to break up with him after

all? Maybe all that angst, all those late-night conversations with myself that wound around and around in my mind, wondering, *Do I really love him? Is this what love is? If I really loved him, would I even be asking this question?*—maybe all of that was simply the result of stress and distance. Maybe Hunter and I haven't grown apart; maybe it's only temporary, the short-term result of trying to forge a whole new life for myself in a whole new place. Maybe I'm not attracted to David, not really; maybe I've only been lonely, and when I see Hunter again I'll realize like a bolt of lightning: *I don't want anyone else. Hunter is the one I love. Hunter is the one I want.* And then maybe I'll change all my careful plans, and instead of breaking up with Hunter before heading back to Wabash, the two of us will be closer and more in love than ever before.

The flight attendant comes by to take drink orders. I ask for a ginger ale, then pull down the shade and turn away from the window. The rest of the flight I play solitaire on my phone, licking peanut salt from my fingers and trying to focus on how excited I am to see Hunter. Because I *am* excited. That must mean something, right?

***

"EMM-MA!" MOM CALLS from downstairs.

"Com-ING!" I shout. Is it Hunter already? He's early. My stomach flutters with nerves. I've spent the past month obsessing about what it will be like when we see each other again, and still I'm not ready.

I study myself in the mirror above my dresser, smoothing a few wisps of hair that float up around my face. I'm wearing a sleeveless blue dress that Céline says makes my eyes pop.

I wish Hunter were whisking me away for a romantic day together. But he's not.

He's coming over for brunch.

With his parents. And my parents.

Apparently my mom made the plans months ago, when Hunter and his parents came over to watch football. No one bothered to tell me about this brunch until last week.

"Doesn't it weird you out sometimes?" I remember asking Hunter on the phone. "That our families are, like, so close?"

"I dunno, I think it's kind of nice," he answered. "Your parents are great. And they miss you. We all miss you, Em."

Just like that, a pit opened up in my stomach, and I ended up apologizing. I wasn't even sure what I was apologizing for.

None of this used to annoy me. But since I moved away, Hunter's closeness to my parents has started to get under my skin. Maybe it's because I'm trying so hard to create my own path, to twist free from my parents' plans and desires for my life. Meanwhile, Hunter is dropping by my house even though I'm not there. He's yelling at the referees with my dad and devouring my mom's chocolate-chip cookies.

It's no wonder my parents adore my boyfriend. He is the son they never had. Their affection for him has hardened like a protective shell, and now it seems unbreakable.

"A fine young man," my dad says whenever Hunter comes up in conversation. "A hard worker. Driven." Even though I don't go to Buenaventura High anymore, my dad still attends all of Hunter's races and cheers him on.

"A very nice boy," my mom always agrees. "Handsome too," she'll add softly, winking at me. When Hunter and I first started dating, this wink would cause a fierce blush to flood my cheeks as I thought about all the things Hunter and I might do together, all the things I wanted to do with him. After the Spring Formal, I would blush remembering the things Hunter and I had done. But now, my mom's obvious winking embarrasses me.

"Em-MA!" Mom calls again.

"Be down in a minute!" I am not ready to go downstairs. Not yet. I've only been home for thirteen hours, ten of which I spent passed out in bed. I haven't even seen or talked to Céline yet. She doesn't know that I'm planning to break up with Hunter. Even though she's *my* best friend—not his—there is a tiny part of me that worries she will take his side in the breakup. I mean, she spends every day at school with him, in real life. I am merely a voice on her speakerphone, an image on Face Time, thousands of miles away.

If I tell Céline that I'm planning to break up with Hunter at the end of winter break, she'll try to talk me out of it. And I don't want to be talked out of anything. It's hard enough to hear the whispers from my own heart, telling me what it wants.

What does it want? What do I want?

I'm not sure.

Outside, the sun slips from behind a cloud and light floods my room. I open the window and press my nose to the screen to breathe in the fresh air. The bright sunshine smell of home. We live too far from the ocean to smell its salty tang, but I imagine I can.

When I close my eyes and try to picture Hunter's face, it is blurry. Fragmented. Nose, eyes, mouth—I can do each feature separately—but I can't construct a whole face. Not Hunter, whole.

On my dresser rests the delicate beaded bracelet and silver wishbone necklace he gave me for my birthday and Valentine's Day. On my bookshelf are yearbooks with dog-eared pages, hearts drawn around his photo. Under my bed, there is a shoebox filled with notes he passed to me in fifth-period Calculus. In my closet, my old racing flats are still covered in sand from our cool-down run after our final track meet last season.

I pick up the framed photo on my nightstand. The two of us at the Spring Formal, Hunter's crimson tie perfectly matching my gauzy dress. His arm is around my waist and I am leaning into him, our bodies pressed close. We are beaming. We look so happy together.

Here's the thing: when I'm away at Wabash Academy, the memories I share with Hunter seem so far away. Almost like they don't even exist, or like they happened to someone else. But now, back at home, everything from my past is alive and close. I look at my giddy smile—six hours after that photograph was taken, Hunter and I had sex for the first time, parked in his mom's car at Fisherman's Point—and I look at Hunter's arm around my waist, anchoring me to him.

I don't know what to do.

Am I still that girl in the Spring Formal photo? Or have I become someone else?

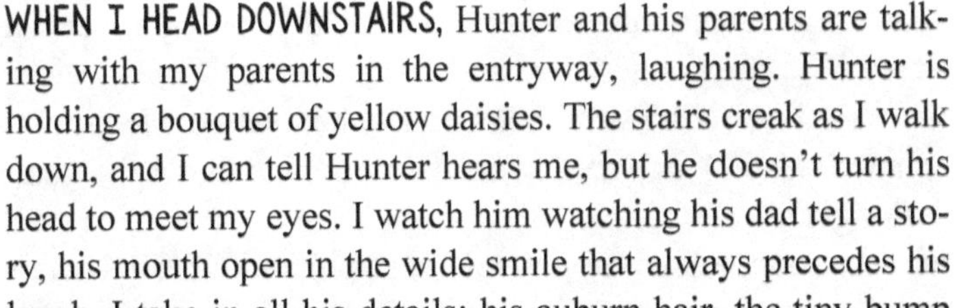

WHEN I HEAD DOWNSTAIRS, Hunter and his parents are talking with my parents in the entryway, laughing. Hunter is holding a bouquet of yellow daisies. The stairs creak as I walk down, and I can tell Hunter hears me, but he doesn't turn his head to meet my eyes. I watch him watching his dad tell a story, his mouth open in the wide smile that always precedes his laugh. I take in all his details: his auburn hair, the tiny bump on his profiled nose, his freckled cheeks, his muscled arms. *I love him. Do I love him?* He still hasn't looked at me.

"And that's when we knew we'd never go back there again!" Hunter's dad says in a booming voice, and everyone laughs.

I leap off the bottom stair and reach for the daisies.

"Emma!" Hunter's mom exclaims. "How lovely you look!"

"Hi, Mrs. Murray. Thank you." I lean into her hug and wave hello to Hunter's dad. Then I bring the daisies to my nose. "These are beautiful," I murmur to Hunter.

He looks at me, finally. "So are you," he says with a grin.

Quietly, our two sets of parents step away, like actors slipping offstage.

"We'll be getting breakfast ready," my mom says. "Only a few more minutes on the French toast."

"What'll you kids have to drink?" my dad asks. "Milk? Orange juice? Coffee?"

"Coffee would be great," Hunter says, sliding an arm around my waist.

"Emma?"

"Me too, please. With room for cream." I started drinking coffee because everyone at Wabash drinks coffee. I don't actually like the taste all that much, but I like pouring in the cream and sugar and stirring it around with a spoon. And I like bringing the cup to my mouth and inhaling its coffee scent.

"Right-o," Dad says, heading for the kitchen. He turns to Hunter's dad. "So, Steve, what did you think about the game last night?"

As soon as they're gone, Hunter pulls me to him, wrapping both arms around my waist. "Hey, you," he says softly. It's our thing—*Hey, you*—and I smile.

"I missed you," I say, and it's the truth. I wish we could press Rewind and go back to last year, even for a day or two. Things were so much simpler then. I was so sure of everything then.

"I missed you, too, Pea," Hunter says. He leans in and kisses me. It is not complicated as I feared it might be. I haven't forgotten how to kiss him. I haven't forgotten the taste and texture of his lips, or the sandpaper roughness of his two-day-old stubble against my chin. It is the same kiss he gave me at the airport when we said goodbye, and at his birthday party in front of all his friends, and in the middle of the dance floor at the Spring Formal, and our very first kiss in the sweltering track shed as we put away our floatie belts after a pool workout.

Hunter pulls away. "Guess what?" he whispers.

"What?"

"I drove here separately from my parents. How about after brunch we go to the orchards and find a place to park?"

"Um, yeah. Okay."

He leans in and kisses me again. I was wrong before—this is not the same kiss from the track shed and the Spring Formal and his birthday party and the airport. Those kisses electrified me. But here, now, kissing him feels flat. Fizzled out.

Or maybe this is the same kiss he has always given me, and I have changed.

I pull away, my heart sinking with the realization that I don't really want to be making out in a car with him. Is this what it means to fall out of love? I try to summon my giddy elation from back in October, when I surprised him for his birthday, but it's not there.

What I love most about Hunter is that he is comfortable and familiar. But comfort and familiarity are not reasons enough to stay together.

"And then tonight we have Robbie's party," Hunter says, hands anchored to my hips.

I blink, pulled out of my thoughts. "What?"

"Robbie Zwick's party. Didn't I mention it before? Everyone's gonna be there. You'll come with me, right?"

"Oh, right. Sure, of course I'll come." For some reason, the thought of seeing all my old classmates from Buenaventura High at the same old Robbie Zwick party from last year makes a wave of sadness crash through me. The past few months, my life has expanded enormously. Meanwhile, everything here at home has kept cruising along on autopilot, the same as if I had never left. It's disorienting.

"You okay, Emma?"

"Yeah, I'm fine. Why?"

"You seem… different, somehow." He leans back, studying me like I am a painting in a gallery.

All semester, Hunter's been saying I've changed. And he's right. I have. But aren't people allowed to change?

With every passing second, my certainty congeals and solidifies into something rock-hard, unshakeable. *This is not what I want anymore.*

"Em-MA!" Mom sings from the kitchen. I pull away from Hunter, swatting his roving hand away. He grins. I smile back, but my stomach is churning.

I need to break up with him.

And it can't wait until January.

THERE ARE MANY things I'm *not* thinking about as I sit down across the table from Hunter Murray, my boyfriend of the past one year and six weeks:

I'm not thinking about decorating holiday cookies at the party Hunter's mom hosts every year, the trays of golden-brown sugar cookies like miniature blank canvases, the bowls of M&Ms and Sno-caps, the frosting glistening in plastic sandwich bags with the corners carefully cut off into make-shift pastry bags. I'm not thinking of the cookie I made for Hunter last year, two candy-canes with our initials on them, fitting together into a heart shape.

I'm not thinking about what it will be like to face Christmas Eve dinner without Hunter as my buffer. I'm not remembering how it was before I started dating Hunter: stifling yawns as I sat between my parents in the dining room of my grandmother's nursing home, the sad smell of antiseptic and floral air freshener, using plastic utensils to cut into a fatty slab of roast beef.

I'm not thinking about driving down a rutted dirt road and parking in the middle of an orange grove and climbing over the center console onto Hunter's lap, the night outside the half-open car windows humming with crickets and other creatures I don't know the names of, only the particular cadence of their chirps and calls that make the world feel weighted with anticipatory energy and make my pulse quicken with aliveness.

As I sit down across the table from my boyfriend of the past one year and six weeks and touch the tines of my fork against the southwestern egg scramble and cinnamon-apple French toast on my plate, I'm not thinking about any of the plans I had for winter break with Hunter.

Because Hunter Murray no longer fits into my plans.

I focus my attention on cutting my French toast into small bites. My mind wanders to an article we read in science class last year, during the unit on earthquakes. The article described the San Andreas fault, the boundary between the Pacific tectonic plate and the North American tectonic plate, stretching from Mexico to Canada along the California coast. On the map, Buenaventura was a small dot, only half an inch away from the alarmingly red fault line.

"Here you go, honey," Mom says, passing me the syrup.

The article warned that the San Andreas fault is stressed enough for the next Big One: an earthquake with a magnitude of at least 7.0. Now, I imagine the ground beginning to shake under the kitchen table. I swear I can feel it stirring beneath my feet. Around the room, I imagine bookshelves toppling, dishes falling off their shelves, pictures crashing to the floor. Then the ground will begin to rock more violently, like a capsizing ship. Windows will shatter. Outside, sidewalks will ripple and roads will buckle.

I take the syrup from my mom. "Thanks," I say, tipping the bottle so syrup floods my plate like water from a burst hydrant. I stab a bite of sticky-wet toast with my fork.

Across from me, Hunter is flecking his eggs with Tabasco sauce, his brow furrowed. I imagine tall office buildings crumbling like sandcastles in a surge of ocean water. I set my fork down without taking a bite.

"Hunter?" I ask. "Can I talk to you in the other room for a minute?"

3

AFTER

"I'LL GO WITH YOU, sweetheart," Mom says. "I know it's hard and scary, but we really should go visit him today."

It's 10 a.m. two days after Christmas—eight days after The Accident—and I'm standing at the kitchen counter, eating—trying to eat—a slice of apple pie for breakfast. With the tines of my fork I mash up a piece of apple and bits of crumbly crust, then bring the small bite to my lips.

"Céline's going with me," I mumble with pie in my mouth. "She wants to see him too."

"Oh. Okay." I can tell my mom is hurt because she doesn't look me in the face. Instead, she frowns and uses a dishtowel to attack a permanent coffee stain on the counter. Years of sloshed coffee has seeped into the grout between the tiles, but still my mom attacks the brown stain as if one more attempt will finally wipe it away for good.

I take another bite, then carry my half-eaten pie to the sink and wash it down the garbage disposal. My plate and fork clatter into the dishwasher.

"Do you girls need someone to drive you?" Mom asks. "I can wait out in the car if you don't want me to come inside."

No, Mom. You absolutely cannot drive us. Which is selfish of me. She wants to visit Hunter, to hold his hand and tell him she is thinking of him and praying for him. But I don't think I can bear the sight of my mom's tears, her pained posture hovering above Hunter's hospital bed. I don't want to remember the way she stroked my hair right after the breakup and said everything would be all right, even though I knew—in a deep inner place, I knew—that she thought breaking up with Hunter was a terrible mistake.

Later, when she learned about Hunter's accident, her eyes flashed with accusation. Like my big mistake had caused an even bigger mistake, and now none of it can be undone.

I think back to my conversation with David and Anabelle at Eggs 'N' Toast a couple weeks ago—a lifetime ago—about serendipity. How proudly I'd proclaimed my love for that word, my staunch belief that we should make meaning out of life's accidents and tragedies. How stupid I was then. How painfully naïve. David was right—things don't happen for a reason. Serendipity is bullshit.

"It's okay," I tell Mom. "I already talked to Céline. She's gonna pick me up in, like, half an hour. I better go shower."

I slip out of the kitchen before Mom can say more.

"I'm here if you need to talk," she calls after me, but her voice is faint, so faint I can almost convince myself that I didn't hear anything as I flee up the stairs to my room.

I LAST SAW CÉLINE a week ago, the morning after The Accident. She came over and the two of us sat on my bed not looking at each other, our fingers twisting the yarn ties on my quilt. "Do you wanna talk about it?" Céline asked, and I said, "No, not really." So we sat on my bed and listened to a random Top 40 station on Spotify. Céline slumped against the pillows and cried a little. I slumped beside her, too shocked for tears. I kept thinking about the way Hunter's hair spread out in the water, dark red, the closest thing there was to blood. It seemed wrong, somehow—such a terrible accident but no visible blood.

Were it a normal day, Céline would beep the horn and idle alongside the curb, waiting for me to come out of the house. But today Céline parks in the driveway and walks up to our front door, ringing the bell like a salesperson. She's dressed up like she's going to church, in a white blouse and long, flowered skirt. I immediately feel too casual in my jeans and camisole.

I shout a goodbye to Mom and close the door quickly behind me. I don't want to invite Céline inside. I just want to get going, to get this over with.

"Thanks for picking me up, C."

She leans in and hugs me tightly. For as long as we've been friends, we've rarely hugged like this—at most we give each other a quick squeeze hello or goodbye—because Céline is not the touchy-feely type. I know this is a big deal for Céline, this tight, long hug, meant to say: *I'm here for you. I love you. I'm devastated, too.*

I hug her back and try to lock myself into this moment, to not think any further forwards or backwards than this small fragment of time. I mentally document little details: the boniness of Céline's shoulders, the cool metal of her bracelet against my arm, the citrus tang of her deodorant.

After a few more seconds, Céline pulls away. "We don't have to stay long," she announces.

"Yeah," I agree. We walk across the front lawn and climb into her car.

We don't speak much during the ten-minute drive to the hospital. Céline turns up the radio and I stare out the bug-flecked windshield at the familiar trees and houses. It is a beautiful day, sun-warmed with a faint breeze drifting in from the ocean. The sky is a cloudless blue that makes me think of a child's crayon drawing: a pure blue, a simple blue-blue.

If we kept driving straight, instead of turning off to the hospital, we'd eventually run into Buenaventura High; this street literally bisects the campus. It is a sprawling campus, open and airy, with outdoor hallways and lots of palm trees, beige walls with sea-green trim. Students eat lunch outside in the grassy quad—nobody eats in the cafeteria. During the school day, the street is closed to traffic with a yellow gate at both ends, but since school is out for winter break the road is open now. We could drive right through campus and I could point out my old locker, facing the street, green paint worn off a little by the salty air.

Almost as soon as I arrived at Wabash Academy, I missed the open hallways of my old high school, the palm trees and birds of paradise, the ivy-obscured bench behind the English wing that Céline and I had claimed as our own. Now, I spend my school days cooped up in the same stuffy building for the majority of my classes. This closed-in feeling got worse in the weeks leading up to finals, as the veil of winter slowly overtook the world and I spent less and less time outdoors.

Céline turns left onto a side street, winding her way toward the hospital nestled at the bottom of the hill. My anxiety heightens, and I suddenly regret not letting my mom drive us.

As a kid, I dreaded getting vaccination shots at the doctor's office more than anything and my mom would always sit beside me, squeezing my hand. I wish I had her hand to hold. I squeeze the car cushion with my fingers, but it's not remotely the same.

Céline easily finds a spot in the half-empty parking garage. As we walk toward the hospital's rear entrance, she reaches over and links her pinky with mine. "We don't have to stay long," she says again.

A giant Christmas wreath hangs above the automatic entrance doors that slide open as we approach. Inside, the hallways are decorated with red-and-green garlands and blue-and-white twinkle lights. Paper cutouts of Santa and angels are taped to the walls, and every so often a menorah or a dreidel. I pretend the decorations were put up for Hunter, whose mom is Christian and dad is Jewish. One year in elementary school Hunter was my seat partner, and after winter break he bragged for weeks about getting to celebrate both Christmas and Hanukkah. He described in detail all the gifts he received; I specifically remember a remote-controlled racecar that could do flips and drive upside-down. I had no desire for a remote-controlled racecar, but picturing his room overflowing with presents made me fiercely jealous.

I brought up the memory once, after we started dating, and Hunter laughed and waved it away. "I never got more presents than anyone else," he said. "I just wanted you all to feel bad." He leaned back in his chair, smiling at some memory, and then added, "Man, I was an annoying little kid back then, huh?"

Céline strides purposefully down the tiled hallway. I follow, my sneakers squeaking loudly. I keep waiting for someone to give me a dirty look, to come over and say,

"Shhh! This is a hospital!" But no one, not even Céline, seems to notice my squeaky shoes.

We sign in at the front desk, where they give us "Visitor" nametags and tell us Hunter's room number. Mechanically, I stick the nametag to my shirt and follow Céline to the bank of elevators. It is like I'm viewing the world through a thick, blurry lens. Or maybe I'm underwater, because sounds seem muted, too. My ears are filled with the drumming of my own nervous heartbeat. The elevator dings and I follow Céline inside. The tug upwards makes my stomach lurch.

At the fourth floor, Céline steps off the elevator. I follow, looking down at my feet, watching them take one step after another. My sneakers are gray, the shoelaces frayed at the ends. This winter break, Hunter and I were supposed to pick out new trainers together at Ray's Running Plus, the local running store. I can't go there now—I can't face the owner, an accomplished marathoner named Ray who always cheered loudly for Hunter at our high school meets. Ray knew Hunter since he was a little kid and used to tell me stories about the road races "little Huntie" would run. "People would go, *Look at the little guy*!" Ray would say, chuckling. "This eight-year-old boy zipping past all these grown-ups. Amazing!" And Hunter, grinning, would duck his head slightly as if embarrassed.

Hunter has always loved running more than I do. I can go weeks without lacing up my trainers, but even two days without running drives Hunter crazy. He once explained that running for him is like art for me. "I need to run," he told me. "It's not a choice, it's a *need*." I got it—that drive inside you, like an itch under your skin. I can't imagine my life without painting. Just thinking about it makes me feel claustrophobic.

What will Hunter do if he can't run anymore? How will he survive?

"Here we are," Céline says, her voice barely above a whisper. "Room 414." The door is ajar. The only noise emanating from the dimly lit room is the low murmur of the television.

"Should we knock?" Céline asks.

I nod. She knocks softly. We stand there together, waiting. My chest is tight. Hard to breathe. I think of Hunter's body floating facedown in the pool. How his lungs filled with water.

"I don't think anyone heard," Céline says after a moment. "Maybe we should go in." She gently pushes open the door and ventures inside.

I watch my feet take one step forward, then another, into the shadowed room.

I'm not sure what I was expecting. I prepared myself—at least, I thought I did—but I obviously didn't do it well.

The sight of Hunter makes my breath catch.

His eyes are closed. I can't tell whether he is sleeping or unconscious. He looks so fragile, lying there in the hospital bed, tubes and wires sticking out of him like tentacles. A large bandage covers most of his head. His skin is ghostly pale and his face looks bloated. Beeping machines surround his bed like anxious, pestering relatives.

I keep telling myself, *This is Hunter,* but my brain refuses to accept the information. *Not Hunter, not Hunter,* my brain insists. *This cannot be Hunter.*

"Emma! Céline!" Hunter's mom says in a loud whisper. She gets up from her chair and crosses the room to hug us. It seems she has aged twenty years in the past week. Her eyes are bloodshot and puffy. "It's so nice of you girls to come by."

"Of course," Céline says. "We won't stay long, just wanted to see him."

"Hello, girls," Hunter's dad says, rising out of his chair to shake our hands. He's a lawyer and has always been formal around me, even last summer when I was having dinner at their house multiple times a week.

"How's he doing?" I ask, then immediately bite my lip, unsure if I've said the wrong thing. Are we not supposed to ask that question? But Hunter's dad steps in right away.

"His vitals are good," he reports in a clinical tone. "Lungs are strong. It appears his brain was pretty much unaffected, which is very fortunate. That's often a danger with pool accidents—lack of oxygen to the brain can cause permanent damage."

"We have a lot to be grateful for," Hunter's mom says with a watery smile. "And you girls know Hunter—he's a fighter."

"He sure is," Céline says.

"He needs to fight now like never before," his dad says. "With a complete spinal cord injury, recovery is going to be a long road."

Celine bites her lip. "What does that mean? Complete spinal cord injury?"

Hunter's dad clears his throat. His own spine straightens, as if steeling himself to say the words. "Hunter's spinal cord was severed. He's never going to walk again."

No. No. No.

My brain pushes back against the words. I picture Hunter's earnest, serious face. *Running is my life.*

My mouth is dry. I'm in the middle of a movie scene, acting out a part I don't know how to play. I've forgotten all my lines.

Hunter's parents urge us to each take a private moment with him. "He can hear you," Hunter's mom asserts. "I firmly believe that. He knows you are here."

Céline goes first. She leans down and whispers into Hunter's ear for a long time. I can't hear what she says. At one point she starts to cry, but she quickly gathers her composure and wipes away her tears. Then it's my turn.

My heart pounds as I walk to Hunter's bedside. I am numb. These feet are not my feet. These hands are not my hands. I awkwardly touch the hospital blanket. I am afraid that if I touch him, I'll only break him more than I already have. I shouldn't be here. I have no right to be here. I lean in close to his ear, but I can't think of anything to say other than, "I'm sorry." I whisper it again and again, until it begins to lose its meaning. Then I tell him, "I love you." This too feels meaningless. *I love you*—hollow husks of words that I have no right to say.

Later, as we're leaving the hospital, my phone beeps. A text message from Anabelle.

Did you break up with him yet?

I don't reply. My stomach roils. My skin flushes.

My fault. My fault.

"You okay, Em?" Céline asks, unlocking her car. Her voice sounds far away.

All I can think of is Hunter, comatose in that hospital bed. Hunter, paralyzed from the waist down. Hunter, telling me, "I need to run. It's not a choice, it's a *need*."

I stumble over to a trash can and throw up, flashing back to that time I got sick on Hunter's lucky racing flats. Hands on my knees, I look down at my old shoes. I imagine wearing these shoes until I break them down. Until the rubber soles erode away completely, until I wear through the foam and the fabric, until I am left with nothing but my bare, bleeding feet.

4

BEFORE

I CAN'T BELIEVE my first semester at Wabash Academy is nearly over. Saturday before the last week of classes, campus is abuzz with festive energy. Christmas lights adorn my dorm hallway and most every window. I struggle into my snow boots, pull on my poufy coat over my T-shirt and pajama bottoms, and head outside to meet Anabelle. Most Saturday mornings, we snub the Dining Commons, sign out with our Dorm Mothers, and walk the couple blocks downtown to our favorite breakfast spot, Eggs 'N' Toast. Sometimes you need to leave campus or else you'll go completely stir-crazy.

A light snow falls. The ground gleams crystalline white. I love the sound of my boots crunching through the snow. I love how the world is hushed, muted, peaceful. I wave to Anabelle, trudging toward me across the quad.

"God, I hate the snow," Anabelle says, breathing hard. She links her gloved pinkie with mine as we walk off campus. The gesture reminds me, with a pang, of Céline. We usually talk every few days, but we've both been busy and haven't spoken in nearly two weeks.

I suddenly ache for Céline's laugh, which, alarmingly, I can't quite hear in my head. But I can envision the crinkle Céline gets above her left eyebrow when she is worried. I can picture Céline's facial expressions from her tone of voice, like Céline can infer all the things I'm not saying from the things I do say. Céline always knows if I am upset about something, even if I say I'm not, and even if we are talking on a staticky cell phone connection two-thousand miles and three time zones away from each other. That's what being best friends means.

Céline is the one person in my life who I can never lose or bullshit.

"Ohmygod," Anabelle whispers, tugging on my arm.

"What?" I resolve to call Céline as soon as I get back to my dorm room. For now, I surrender my thoughts to Anabelle's drama at hand.

"It's David," she says.

"Where?" I ask.

"Up ahead."

"In the red beanie? You sure that's him?"

"Yeah—c'mon! If we walk fast, we can casually bump into him." Anabelle unlinks her pinkie from mine and strides ahead.

I crouch down and pack a fistful of snow in my two gloved hands. Then I hurl it toward the figure in the red beanie. I aim high on his back, but the snowball loses momentum and sinks, hitting him in the butt.

He whirls around. Anabelle is right, it *is* David—wide eyes, strong cheekbones, stubble shadowing his jaw. I make an innocent face and point at Anabelle, who looks from David to me with eyebrows raised.

David grins. "You don't want to get in a snowball fight with me," he says. "You have no idea what you're getting into." Instantly he reaches down, expertly packs snow into a ball, and fires it at Anabelle. It explodes against her chest in a spray of white powder. Anabelle shrieks.

Mission accomplished.

David takes off down the sidewalk and Anabelle chases after him. I follow slowly, trying to give them space, enjoying the cold touch of the snowflakes on my face.

"Em-MA! Hurry up, slowpoke!"

Across the street, at the café entrance, Anabelle waves frantically while David stamps his boots. As much as Anabelle is dying to snag a booth with David, I know she won't rush inside with him on her own. "Friends above boys. That's my motto," she says, usually when I step out into the dorm hallway to take a call from Hunter. Still, she is not above sulking. If David gets impatient waiting and Anabelle loses her chance to flirt with him over breakfast, there will be repercussions. The last thing I need right now is a sulky Anabelle in addition to a guilt-tripping Hunter and the looming pressure of final exams.

"Get a table!" I yell. "I'll meet you inside!"

Anabelle waves, beaming. David holds the door open and she touches his arm as she brushes past.

I remember feeling that way about Hunter. Infatuated. Animated. A special kind of light-headedness, where every detail of the world seems more beautiful. When Hunter visited in September, I took him to the Dining Commons and we held hands under the table as we ate. The plain white walls seemed brighter. The veggie lasagna tasted less bland than usual. When you are in love, everything has more spice. Life makes more sense. All the building blocks of your existence stack up in stunning alignment.

But lately, our relationship has felt strained and off-kilter. When I think of Hunter, I think of weight. Steel and concrete. Boulders and bricks.

Things will fall back into place when we see each other. I'm sure they will. Long distance is the problem. It's tough being apart for so long.

A bell on the door jingles as I step inside the warm café. Country music plays on the radio. Blue-checkered tablecloths and daisy-filled vases add to the homey charm. The walls are decorated with cross-stitched quotations, watercolors of cornfields, and sepia-toned photographs. One time I tried to count all the ceramic ducks and pigs; eventually I gave up because I kept losing track.

I spot Anabelle and David crammed into a booth in the far corner—they're sitting on the same side. David's closer to the wall; I wonder if he slid in first and Anabelle followed. That would be just like her, to brazenly sit on the same side instead of sliding in across from him. For the hundredth time, I wonder what David's deal is. He must know that Anabelle has a massive crush on him. I mean, she isn't exactly subtle. He flirts with her enough to keep her on the hook, but never does anything to actually move things forward. Does he simply like the attention? Or is he genuinely clueless? When I floated the idea of Anabelle asking him out instead of waiting and waiting for him, she rolled her eyes and said, "Oh, Emma. That would ruin all the fun."

"Hey guys," I say as I slide into the other side of the red vinyl booth.

"Emma, hey!" David flashes me a grin and I smile back.

"Fancy meeting you here," I say, using a British accent for no reason.

But David and Anabelle don't seem to notice my weirdness. Anabelle says, "I know, right?" in a giddy voice, and

David explains that he's meeting his friend Jayden to study. Like Anabelle, David is a "townie" who grew up here, as opposed to someone like me who came to Wabash Academy from far away.

"Jayden?" Anabelle says. "Your best friend from middle school? He doesn't go to Wabash, does he?"

"No, he's at the public high school. But we're still tight." He rips open a sugar packet and pours some into his coffee. "If I only hung out with Wabash kids I'd go insane."

"Um, hello!" Anabelle says. "Look who you're sitting with!"

"Present company excluded," David says. "Well, Emma at least. She's not like other pretentious Wabash girls. I don't know about you, Belle. Jury's still out." He winks.

Anabelle gasps, pretending to be offended, but it's obvious she is thrilled.

"Bottomless coffee and chocolate-chip pancakes," David says. "The secret to surviving finals." He looks up and waves both his arms. "Yo, Jay! Back here!"

A short guy with scruffy brown hair and hipster glasses approaches our booth, nodding a hello to me.

"Jayden Charleston," Anabelle declares dramatically, as if delivering lines in a play. "I can't believe it. I haven't seen you since, what, eighth grade?"

"Hey Anabelle." Jayden seems wary. "Yeah, it's been a while. I guess I'm pretty much the same."

"Your glasses are much more fashionable now," Anabelle says. "You look like that actor. What's his name? Ugh, I can't remember. You know who I mean, don't you Emma?"

I shrug helplessly.

"Well, you look like him, Jayden. I bet you have, like, a million girlfriends. I bet you're a total player these days."

Jayden blushes. Can he tell that Anabelle doesn't mean anything she's saying? She's flirting with him in such an over-the-top way, trying to make David jealous. I hate when Anabelle gets like this. As if she is the only person who matters, and everyone else is merely a distant planet in her orbit.

"Take a seat, man!" David gestures across the booth.

Jayden meets my eyes, asking permission, like we are allies in this strange drama of David and Anabelle. I smile and scoot over, and he sits down just as the waitress comes over. She takes our order—we all opt for the chocolate-chip pancakes, except for Jayden, who gets blueberry—and refills our coffee mugs.

"Chocolate, sugar, and caffeine," David ticks off on his fingers. "My three main food groups."

Anabelle laughs, hitting him on the arm.

"So how do you guys have a study group if you don't go to the same school?" I ask.

"That's the genius of it!" David laughs. "I could never have a study group with you and Anabelle for, like, Art History. We'd just talk about the class the whole time and never do any work."

"Yeah, it actually helps that we're studying for different classes," Jayden says. "We don't get sidetracked because we don't have the same reference points. And I get way more work done here than when I'm trying to study at home by myself, you know?"

Across the booth, Anabelle murmurs to David, "I could never study with you. I would get way too distracted."

I focus my attention on Jayden. "So what class are you studying for?" I ask.

"U.S. History," he says. "The teacher is awesome—like, we're learning a lot, and she actually makes it interesting—

but all of the tests have been super hard. I'm nervous for the final."

"You'll be great," David cuts in. "Dude has basically a photographic memory."

"Who's the teacher?" Anabelle asks.

"The legendary Mrs. Brug," Jayden says.

Anabelle sighs. "I'm so jealous! She's the main reason I regret transferring to Wabash. I've heard her class is *life changing*."

Before long they're reminiscing about middle school, laughing about inside jokes I don't understand. I flash back to Hunter's birthday party, listening to my friends from home swap stories and references that were completely meaningless to me. Even though I'd only been gone for a couple months, I felt so out of the loop. I guess a couple months is an eternity in the soap opera of high school. What else has changed since then? I'll be even more of an outsider now when I go home for winter break.

The waitress brings our pancakes. I lick syrup from my fork and glance out the window at the falling snowflakes. Hunter's words from Thanksgiving flit into my mind: *It feels like you're slipping away. Like you've changed.*

Is it true? Have I changed?

"What about you, Emma?" David says, breaking me out of my thoughts.

"Sorry, zoning out. What are you guys talking about?"

"The idea that everything happens for a reason. Do you agree?"

"Hmmm, I don't know," I hedge, smearing more butter onto my pancakes. "I mean, I would like to think so. One of my favorite words is serendipity."

"Ooh, mine too!" Anabelle exclaims. "I love that word! I'm thinking of getting it as a tattoo."

David raises an eyebrow. "Where?" he asks her.

Anabelle smirks. "Wouldn't you like to know."

On the table, Jayden's cell phone buzzes. He glances at it, then ignores it. "I've never heard of that word," he says, turning his body toward me and away from the two lovebirds across the table. "What does it mean?"

I mirror his body language, giving Anabelle and David space to branch off into their own conversation. "Serendipity means a fortunate accident."

"Like, a coincidence?"

"Sort of, but even better. It's more like a mistake that ends up being a good thing after all, when you look back on it."

Jayden cocks his head, considering. "I think that's really cool."

"I think it's total bullshit," David interrupts.

Anabelle opens her mouth wide and hits him on the arm. "Rude!"

David shrugs. "Emma can take it. I'm only being honest. All of those rainbows and roses are bullshit. Serendipity is merely a nice idea we use to feel better about our screw-ups and disappointments. Nothing happens for a reason. Life is meaningless. It's one big chaotic mess." He polishes off the final bite of pancake on his plate, like a period at the end of his statement.

Anabelle laughs, but I am not amused. Does David realize how condescending he sounds? What's his deal? Why ask me what I think, and then shoot down what I say?

"It's not bullshit." My voice is louder than I intend. "It's the truth. Fortunate accidents happen all the time."

"Senseless accidents happen far more often. How do you explain car crashes? Gun violence? Poverty, disease, war? I could go on and on. How can you say those things happen for a reason?"

I swallow. "Okay, I'll agree with you there. Sometimes, things happen and there's no logic or reason at all."

David pumps his fist in the air.

"But," I continue, "that means it's up to us to find a reason. We make a reason. We can turn the heartache and tragedy into something meaningful, if we choose to. That's what I mean by serendipity."

"Exactly!" Anabelle chimes in. "Emma: one. David: zero."

I expect David to brush my earnestness aside with a wisecrack, but instead he gazes straight into my eyes, as if searching for some hidden answers there. "Emma Mason. I have to say, you've given me something to think about."

Despite myself, my cheeks flush under the intensity of his attention. Yes, David can be annoying and condescending at times. But I understand why Anabelle hasn't been able to let her crush go. There's something about the way David narrows his focus on you that makes it seem like you're the only person in the entire room.

Jayden's phone buzzes again. "It's my mom," he says, sighing. "She keeps texting me. Sorry, guys, I gotta go pick up my little brother."

"Dude!" David says. "We haven't even studied."

"I know. His practice was canceled because of the snow. I'll catch you later."

We say goodbye as Jayden downs the rest of his coffee, leaves some bills on the table, and heads for the door.

"Em and I should probably be going, too," Anabelle says abruptly. "We only signed out of the dorms for an hour."

I'm shocked—Anabelle has never cared about following rules—but then she leans close to David and adds, "Do you want to come hang out? We can sneak you into my dorm."

"Sure. That sounds much better than studying by myself."

Leaving the café, the dynamic is different with David along. The sidewalk is only wide enough for two, so I let Anabelle and David go ahead. I trail a few steps behind, like an awkward chaperone. When we get back to campus, I try to peel off toward my dorm, but David notices and says, "Where you going, Emma? You promised you'd hang out."

"C'mon, Emma!" Anabelle says, waving me toward them, her eyes frantic. Maybe she's worried that David will bail if I do.

So I tag along to Anabelle's room. Her Dorm Mother is rarely around during the day, and her roommate, Hannah, spends a lot of time at home—like Anabelle, she is "a townie" who grew up a few minutes from campus. Wabash Academy technically requires all students to board in. They say it helps foster "a unified and intensive learning community." (Anabelle says it helps foster the high tuition.) But your parents can sign you out whenever they want to. At the beginning of the semester, Hannah was around all the time, but now she spends most nights at home. She says it is quieter and easier to study there. I wonder if she simply gets homesick. Homesickness is definitely something I can understand.

Anabelle has gradually taken over their entire dorm room, her things creeping over onto Hannah's side: a pile of library books on Hannah's desk; sweaters drying on a towel laid out on Hannah's bed; Anabelle's favorite brand of Greek yogurt amassed in the supposedly shared mini fridge. Hannah—sweet, quiet—never complains. "She doesn't care,"

Anabelle says, waving her hand dismissively. "She's never here, anyway."

Sometimes I worry, being friends with Anabelle. What happens if one day she gets tired of me? What if she casually tosses me aside?

Anabelle has decorated the walls with classic movie posters and Salvador Dali prints and strands of twinkle lights shaped like stars. I love spending time here. It's more of a sanctuary than my own dorm room, which could be invaded at any moment by Nora's loud drama posse, talking over each other and wanting me to weigh in on some passionate debate. Still, sometimes I leave Anabelle's room feeling restless and insecure, intensely aware of all that I don't know and all that I am lacking. She is so worldly, so sure of herself. I am indecisive, unsure of what I want.

David's presence shifts the atmosphere in the room. I'm conscious of my faded T-shirt and pajama bottoms. Earlier, when I slipped on my coat without changing out of my PJs, I felt empowered and free—a young woman, out on my own, thousands of miles from home—why *shouldn't* I go out in my pajamas? I would appear cool by how little I cared about appearing cool. But over breakfast my buzz faded, and now I just feel ridiculous. I sit in Anabelle's desk chair, fiddling with her Rubik's Cube. Is high school like this for everyone? Surges of carefree confidence that crash into anxious self-doubt? Does everyone feel uncertain sometimes, or is it just me?

Across the room, David looks alternately bored and pensive. He and Anabelle are sitting on her raised bed, leaning back against the handmade pillows Anabelle says came from "the *best* vintage store." Anabelle laughs at everything David says and touches his arm when she talks. She's telling a story about a girl she met at summer camp who was on some reality show. I've heard the story three or four times already. I zone out and admire the pillows, decorated with intricate, colorful bead designs. My favorite has a cartoon duck stitched with real feathers.

Eventually Anabelle finishes her story and the conversation dips into a lull, so I try to extricate myself. "I've got the worst headache." I rub my forehead for effect. "I'm going back to my room to lie down."

As I expect, Anabelle does not object. "Oh, honey, I'm sorry," she says. "That's a good idea to get some rest." Her voice is two octaves higher than normal.

I stand up and pull on my coat. To my surprise, David hops off Anabelle's raised bed and says, "Yeah, I should probably get going too." He wraps his scarf around his neck and steps toward me. "I can walk you back to your dorm."

One glance at Anabelle's panicked eyes, and I backpedal fast. "Oh wait, I just remembered my roommate's girlfriend is in town this weekend. I should probably give them some more alone time." It sounds like the blatant lie it is. Nora and her girlfriend broke up weeks ago. But David doesn't know that—right?

"Why don't you take an aspirin?" Anabelle offers, rummaging in her purse and pulling out a small pill bottle.

I am aware of David, his hand on the doorknob.

"Thanks," I say, placing the pill in my mouth and dry swallowing. David unwinds his scarf. Anabelle brightens like a flower in a windowsill, stretching toward the sunlight, pressing hopefully against the glass pane.

Two hours later we are still there, playing a meandering game of two-truths-and-a-lie that we keep dropping and picking up again. Anabelle and David are scrolling through her phone for more music when my phone buzzes in my pocket. I eagerly pull it out. Hunter's name blinks on the caller ID.

"Is that *the boyfriend*?" Anabelle says.

I nod as I answer the phone. "Hi, babe," I say to Hunter, struggling to get up from the beanbag chair. My legs are sprawled awkwardly in front of me, and I can't manage to push myself up to my feet. I briefly consider rolling over onto my hands and knees, but that would be way too embarrassing.

"Here." I look up and there is David, helping hand extended. I slide mine into his. Across the room, Anabelle is intensely focused on her phone.

"Thanks," I say, allowing David to hoist me up.

"No problem."

"Who's that?" Hunter says.

"Oh, no one." I duck out into the hallway and shut the door behind me. "That's just Anabelle."

"I swear I heard a guy in the background."

"That's just David."

Hunter snorts. "Of course. I should have guessed."

I slump down against the wall. Lately, every conversation with Hunter is a minefield. He never got jealous like this before I moved away.

Does he somehow sense the tiny flicker in my heart when I'm around David? How does he know, when he's thousands of miles from here?

Besides, everyone has stupid little crushes. My feelings for David are fickle and easy to push away. It's not like I would ever act on them.

As if on cue, Hunter says, "I don't get why you're always hanging out with David. You two are practically joined at the hip."

I laugh. "We are not."

"He's all over your socials, Em."

"He's my *friend*! The only reason we hang out is because Anabelle has a massive crush on him."

"Don't be naïve. David doesn't like Anabelle. He likes you."

My cheeks grow hot. "No he doesn't."

"Why's he over in *your* room, then?"

I sigh. "We're in Anabelle's room."

"Just the three of you?"

"Um… yeah."

"Isn't that kind of weird? Why don't you give the two of them some alone time if they're so into each other?"

"I tried, but then he wanted to leave, too—"

"And that doesn't sound suspicious."

"—and Anabelle was freaking out. Look, I don't even know why we're still talking about this. It doesn't matter."

"Fine, I see how it is. You're too busy to talk to your lame boyfriend."

"Hunter! You're being ridiculous."

"Whatever, Emma."

"Listen, I'm here. Okay? I'm out in the hallway, talking to you. What do you want to talk about?"

"Nothing," Hunter says. "Go back to your friends. Later."

He hangs up.

I lean against the wall, staring at my cell phone and trying to decide whether to call him back. My sinuses burn with tears. He probably won't answer, and I don't want to leave some rambling voicemail that will only perpetuate whatever argument this is we're having.

Maybe it's better to do nothing. Later he'll call to apologize and whatever he is upset about will disappear and we can have a nice, rational conversation.

Lately it seems like Hunter is constantly interrogating me—where I am, what I'm doing, who I'm with. Anabelle's words run through my mind: *Do you ever feel like you're wasting so much energy trying to hold onto something that isn't working anymore?* Maybe she's right. Maybe most relationships do run their course eventually. Maybe Hunter is holding me back from fully experiencing my life here at Wabash. Always-opinionated Anabelle has been surprisingly reserved on the subject of Hunter. She's a good listener, and she doesn't know Hunter the way Céline does; her distance from our relationship gives me freedom to spill what I'm truly thinking. And how do I describe him? *Clingy. Possessive. Jealous.* While Anabelle has never said it explicitly, her disapproval of Hunter seeps through her tight-lipped smiles and encouragement to "spread my wings." I know she thinks Hunter isn't good enough for me.

I'm grateful to have Anabelle to process with. When I try to talk to Céline about Hunter, she doesn't really hear me. "He cares so much about you, Emma," she'll say. "These are growing pains. I'm sure you guys can work through it."

I hadn't expected Céline—the whispering wise-ass, the stealthy note-passer, the brainiac with spot-on bullshit detector—to be so utterly charmed by Hunter. But she is. She's always saying how lucky I am to have found him. "It's obvious you guys have a real connection," she said once, blowing into the foam of her chai latte. "That's rare, Em. You have no idea how rare that is."

It's not that rare, I almost said, but didn't. *You could have it too, if you wanted.*

Guys gravitate toward Céline. She often gets asked out on dates by random strangers. Her guy friends are always confessing their love and making things awkward. She's dated a series of guys on and off throughout high school but has yet to meet anyone she's crazy about. For whatever reason, she likes to keep boys at an arm's distance. Hunter is the only guy I've truly seen her relax and be herself around. Before I moved to Indiana, Céline and Hunter planned a surprise going-away party for me. And she routinely helps him pick out gifts I would like: a lucky silver wishbone necklace for Valentine's Day, a peony corsage for the Spring Formal, a dozen miniature sunflowers for our one-month anniversary.

Our one-month anniversary. Hunter made reservations at Ferraro's, the fancy Italian restaurant by the beach, and we both got dressed up. I felt certain it was the first of many anniversaries we would celebrate. That we would both keep choosing each other and choosing each other. At the time, I didn't even know Wabash Academy existed.

I slide my phone into my pocket and touch the doorknob of Anabelle's room. What if I walk in on her and David making out? Nope. Don't need to see that.

Instead, I turn and flee down the hall toward the stairwell. Halfway there, I remember my coat is in Anabelle's room. Oh well—I'll get it later.

Outside, the cold air slaps my face. It is no longer snowing, but the wind has picked up. My T-shirt is a thin veil; the wind bites into my skin as if I'm wearing nothing at all. Everything is gray. The sidewalk is puddled with gray and the clouds hang low and gray in the sky. The buildings press around me, staunch gray towers. Crossing my arms against my chest, I hurry across the quad, back to my empty dorm room. When I get there, I tug off my snow boots and fall into bed. It's still early in the evening, but sleep comes easily.

When I wake up, I am panting, coated in sweat. If I had a nightmare, I can't remember it. Outside my window, night has fallen. My reflection is a hollowed-out shadow.

The clock reads 1:22, but some inner force propels me to pull on a sweatshirt and lace up my running shoes. It is as though I am still half-asleep, still dreaming. I haven't worn my running shoes in weeks, but they hold my feet with a familiar grip. I sneak down the hallway and slip out into the night like a ghost.

The campus is blanketed with quiet. Christmas lights glow in windows, blinking colors onto the white snow. I jog slowly, more of a shuffle to keep from slipping on the icy sidewalk. Soon I abandon the shoveled sidewalk for the snow-covered grass. My body feels good. I pick up the pace. Snow flies up behind my feet like icy sparks. I am a pulsating heart. I am cold, damp skin. Not sure if I am running away from something or running toward something.

I am simply running—a blur of motion, frozen hands and pumping lungs, steamy clouds of breath, and the irrational nagging unease that something bad is going to happen.

5

AFTER

MOM CRIES AT the airport. She tries to hide it by rubbing her nose with a tissue and claiming allergies. Dad hugs me and slips two twenties into my palm "for emergencies." I wipe away pretend tears, wave goodbye, and flee into the security line. Part of me will miss my parents, of course—but right now that part is eclipsed by my longing for escape.

Soon I am seated on the plane. I gaze out the window as we lift off into the smoggy air of Los Angeles. My limbs are lighter, buoyed by hope and relief.

In Buenaventura, it is impossible to be anyone but Hunter Murray's ex-girlfriend. Everyone must assume I broke up with him *after* the accident. Everyone must think I'm a terrible person. Returning to Indiana, I am a snake shedding its skin, surging forward anew, leaving my old self behind.

Nobody at Wabash Academy knows what happened over winter break.

Nobody has to know.

MY DORM ROOM is dark and cold and quiet. I flick on a light. Nora's vintage movie posters are thumb-tacked to the walls. A photo collage I made hangs above my bed. I wheel my suitcase across the room, drawn to our smiling faces. The floorboards creak softly under my snow boots. The collage's centerpiece is a photo of me, Nora, Rachel and Anabelle on Halloween, a litter of kittens in high heels and tiny skirts, pointy black ears taped to headbands, whiskers drawn on our cheeks with eyeliner pencil. I peer at my own frozen, wide smile. *Who is that girl?* She seems like a stranger now.

Outside, an icicle plunges from the eaves and smashes onto the sidewalk. The noise makes me jump. Nora's side of the room is quiet, waiting—she isn't coming back until to-morrow. For a little while, I have our room to myself.

For the past few weeks, all I have wanted is to escape Buenaventura and to be alone. Suddenly, I've been granted both wishes.

It's only five p.m.—two in California—but I'm exhaust-ed. I slip off my boots and cocoon under the covers. Before I drift off, my cell phone buzzes: Anabelle is calling. I let it go to voicemail. I'm not ready to talk to Anabelle yet. She texted me a few times over winter break and I responded with quick canned phrases, sentiment inserted with exclamation points: *merry xmas!! hope ur break is amazing!! miss u xoxoxo!!* I never responded to her text asking if I broke up with Hunter. I should delete it—many times I almost have—but something keeps stopping me. Maybe I want to punish myself. Every time I see Anabelle's text, I remember the last time I saw Hunter happy and whole. How I smiled across the breakfast table at that person and then shattered him.

Outside, the wind picks up and tree branches tap against the windowpane, like someone knocking to get in. Night is falling quickly. With the lights off, my room is a timeless dark. It could be midnight. It could be three a.m. I turn toward the wall and tug the covers over my head. Sleep comes upon me like a slowly unwrapped gift.

When I wake up, morning light streams in through the window accompanied by the *ping-ping-ping* of melting snow. As I pull on fresh clothes, I listen to the voicemail Anabelle left. "Hey girl, it's me! I haven't heard from you in ages. Call me when you get this so I know you're still alive?" She laughs, her tone light and sarcasm-laced as usual, but there is something else underneath. Something quiet and serious. "Can't wait to see you," she adds. I can picture her eyes, flashing with earnestness. And then the message ends.

I listen to it once more. Then I press Delete. I'm not ready to see Anabelle or any of my friends here. I can't tell them about Hunter's accident—I want to pretend it never happened. Wabash Academy is an unscathed, safe place where I can push the guilt away. But my armor is still too thin. My friends, especially Anabelle, will sense something is wrong. I need more time.

I stuff a couple books, a sketchpad, and pencils into my backpack and magnet a note to the mini fridge:

AT THE LIBRARY. SEE YOU TONIGHT. WELCOME HOME! –E

But as soon as I get outside, I don't want to go to the library. I'm worried I'll run into someone I know. I want to be alone, for at least a little while longer.

My car, parked in the gravel lot behind the dorm, is a bread loaf of snow. I hack at the icy crust with an ice scraper. My gloves quickly soak through and clumps of snow fall into my boots, cold and wet against my jeans. But it is a release, my mind focused only on the rhythmic scraping of plastic blade against ice. I quickly warm up with the physical effort;

by the time I wrench open the frozen-shut car door and collapse into the driver's seat, sweat has gathered under my armpits and at the small of my back. It takes a couple tries, but eventually the car's dormant engine stutters to life.

I drive slowly through the town's historic district, wary of black ice. Right before winter break, I hit black ice and skidded sideways, almost crashing into an oncoming car. All I could do was grip the wheel, screeching in panic, "What do I *do*?" Fortunately, Rachel—calm, dependable, Indiana raised—was in the passenger seat and grabbed the wheel, helping me guide the car to the curb. It was Rachel who drove us back to the dorm, chattering about her upcoming art history exam, reciting the terms she had memorized. By the time we arrived home my frayed nerves were more or less mollified, and Anabelle soon repackaged the experience into another anecdote featuring California Girl Emma, Braving the Midwest. The punchline: "We don't *have* icy roads in *California*!" Anabelle delivered the line with intense surprise, turning me into an alien hailing from a comically foreign planet. "You mean it *snows* here in the *winter*?" And everyone laughed. Even I laughed.

But I remember the way every muscle in my body tightened when I felt the car's wheels begin to slide on the ice, control slipping from my grasp in an instant. Now I always drive slowly, nerves on alert.

I pass wide-porched houses and old brick warehouses, faded American flags hanging limp and frozen. Giant sycamore trees loom over the street, bare limbs reaching upward into the gray sky. I cross the river that separates the working-class part of town from the wealthier, newer neighborhoods surrounding campus. In the summer, the river sparkles a picturesque blue-green and you can sometimes spot people fishing as you drive over the bridge. But in the winter, the river is a roiling brown mass littered with chunks of ice. Rumor has it the river is severely polluted—students pass around stories of two-headed frogs and fish with legs—and in the winter, I believe every word. The river looks sickly, toxic.

I keep driving, past the strip mall with fast food joints and dive bars, past the bronze statue of a lion, past the street where David rescued me from that freezing cold walk on Thanksgiving a lifetime ago.

I circle back to the highway and drive north. The farther I get from town, the emptier the highway becomes. I am the last person alive after the apocalypse. Nothing to either side of the salt-crusted highway but dead scrub and furrows of frozen dirt. Occasionally, a lonely farmhouse flanked by a weathered gray barn. Before moving to the Midwest, I always imagined cheerful barns painted a bright red, surrounded by shoulder-high green fields of corn. But in real life, I have yet to see a barn painted red.

About thirty minutes from town, I glimpse something strange in the distance. Rows of giant, graceful steel windmills, gleaming white, stretching over the flat dirt fields. Gazing at them through my ice-specked windshield, I almost start to laugh. They look so out of place, so ridiculous. Science fiction. My impulse is to call Hunter—the windmills are something he would appreciate.

But I can't call Hunter. I pull over to the side of the road and park. I rummage in my backpack, slide out my sketchbook and least-dull pencil, and begin to draw. As the windmills slowly take shape on the page, the pressure inside me eases a little. I focus on the curve of lines, the texture of shading, the sharp angle of the blades as they slowly rotate through the January air. Everything else seeps to the edges of my consciousness. I keep sketching until the light has bled completely from the sky. In perfect synchrony, the windmills blink red warning lights into the darkness.

By the time I venture back to the dorm, it is late. I missed dinner. I say goodnight to Mrs. Jenkins, who scolds me lightly for staying out at the library so late.

"I got wrapped up in my book and totally lost track of time!" I lie. "I'm so sorry!"

"It's okay. That's happened to me many times." She gives me a little smile and waves me on down the hall.

My room is quiet and still when I unlock the door. Part of me hopes Nora is still awake, watching one of her favorite courtroom dramas on her laptop, waiting up for me. But the light is off, the blackout curtains pulled shut. Nora is snoring softly, white noise machine emitting the sound of gentle rain. Over winter break, she texted me that her New Year's resolution is to "take control" of her insomnia with a carefully constructed bedtime routine and sleep schedule.

The raindrops transition to the sound of ocean waves rhythmically crashing on the beach. Even in the middle of Indiana, I can't escape home.

6

BEFORE

THANKSGIVING MORNING, I wake up to bright sunlight knifing through cracks in Nora's blackout curtains. Pushing them aside, I'm blinded by the dazzling white of a fresh snowfall. My breath catches—it's so beautiful.

As a California girl who grew up watching Christmas movies and dreaming of snow, I gleefully anticipated my first Indiana winter. I couldn't wait to go sledding, to ice-skate, to build snowpeople. I stocked my small dorm cupboard with hot cocoa mix and marshmallows and imagined curling up in a blanket and doing my homework with the snow falling peacefully outside the window. Before moving to Wabash, I had never even seen real snow before, unless you counted the time I went camping with Céline's family. On a cold morning hike in the mountains, we came across a patch of hardened snow, more like ice really, melting into the muddy ground. Even that pitiful snow excited me—I insisted Céline take a photo as I touched it delicately with one finger. I can remember the moment vividly, how I sucked in my breath when the tip of my finger pressed into the dirty granules of ice. "It's cold!" I said, and Céline, who grew up visiting snow because her grandmother lives in Toronto, laughed and said, "Duh, Em. It's snow."

Like Céline, my new friends—most of them born and raised in snowy places—do not share my enthusiasm for snow. I've learned to join in when they complain about the slippery sidewalks and the shapeless bulk of winter gear. But there are moments—walking to class through a swirl of snowflakes; trudging through fresh snow, unexpectedly soft under my boots; looking out the window at the pure, hopeful expanse of a snow-covered lawn and white-dusted tree branches—that my childlike elation is impossible to hide.

Behind me, my door opens. "Isn't this great?" Anabelle says, door clicking shut behind her.

I turn, surprised. I've never known Anabelle to praise anything about winter, not even a fresh snowfall. "It's stunning," I agree.

"What are you looking at?" Anabelle flounces to the window, pressing her cheek against mine as she peers around the dark curtain. Her hair smells of vanilla and mint. "Yuck, it snowed last night?"

I let the curtain fall back down. "Yep."

"Whatever," Anabelle says. "Nothing is going to ruin today. Not the snow. Not stupid David bailing. Nothing."

"David's not coming?" My heart sinks a little.

"Nope. He texted me last night. He's being lame. Whatever!" Anabelle licks the wrapper of a peanut-butter cup. "This is the best Thanksgiving meal I've ever had."

"What do you mean? It's only ten in the morning."

"This Thanksgiving is going to be an all-day affair." She hands me a king-sized Milky Way. "Here, I brought you breakfast."

"Thanks." I slowly tear off the wrapper. I don't particularly want to eat a candy bar, but if I decline Anabelle will think I'm sulking, and I don't want to start off the day on a sour note. I want this Thanksgiving to be great. So I bite down hard, a large bite. The caramel sticks to my teeth and the chocolate tastes almost painfully sweet.

A month ago, I was touched when Anabelle invited me to stay with her for Thanksgiving. Fresh after a fight with Hunter, I said yes. I only found out two days ago that Anabelle is planning an "untraditional Thanksgiving" with nothing but junk food and booze. Her parents aren't going to be home—her dad is on a business trip to China and her mom, a flight attendant, couldn't get the holiday off. It was too late for me to change plans; flights are impossibly expensive.

So it is that I find myself sitting on the living room floor of Anabelle's house. It's me, Anabelle, Rachel, Nora, and two girls from Anabelle's poetry class. We pass around potato chips and stream old episodes of *The O.C.*

"God, Em, how could you stand to move away from California?" Rachel says. "You used to live in paradise!"

"It isn't as glamorous as they make it seem on TV," I explain. "My family isn't rich and we don't get invited to fancy parties on the beach."

"Emma's being modest," Anabelle tells her poet friends, two sleepy-eyed girls with braided hair and chunky-knit sweaters. I can't tell whether they're sisters or simply dressed alike. "She grew up right by the ocean—like that." Anabelle points to the screen, where the characters are walking along the beach against a stunning backdrop of orange and purple sunset and the dark glittering ocean. "Didn't you, Emma?"

"Well, yeah, I lived close to the beach, just not… never mind." I wish I could rewind time and portray myself honestly from the very beginning. At the beginning of the semester, I wanted to seem fashionable and sophisticated, and California was the unusual, shining thing about me. It was my opportunity to be distinct, the center of a circle of friends rather than just another nameless student melting into the crowd. So I had channeled Siggy Taylor, shifting California front and center, pushing everything else about myself to the background. Over the weeks and months my persona gradually expanded until I resembled a carefree beachy girl, reminiscing about surfing even though I'd only surfed twice in my life and was horrible at it, complaining about the snow even though I secretly found it thrilling. My wish was granted—now, more than anything else, it is my California roots that define me among my Wabash friends. The problem is, I sometimes feel like an actress playing a part.

Onscreen, a fistfight erupts at the fancy dinner party, upsetting the hors d'oeuvres table. One of the poets complains about how expensive everything is in California. "I went there a few years ago," she says. "My family took a trip to Disneyland."

"But it's worth it," Anabelle says. "Part of what you're paying for is the weather."

"Hey, I have an idea." Nora nudges my slippered foot with hers. "We should spend next Thanksgiving at your house, Emma!"

I smile vaguely, trying to imagine what it would be like if my Wabash Academy world and my Buenaventura world collided.

I can't even imagine it.

I am a different person here at school than I am at home. Maybe that's why things have been so off with Hunter lately. Maybe he's not changing—maybe I am.

"Earth to Em! Earth to Em!" Nora says. "You're such a space cadet sometimes."

"Sorry." I didn't anticipate missing my parents with such an intense ache. What a stupid, impulsive decision to stay at school for Thanksgiving instead of flying home. I keep waiting for my phone to ring—Mom and Dad saying hello, wishing me a happy holiday—but they haven't called yet. I could cave and call them, but somehow that seems like failure. I want to be Independent Emma, happy in my life here.

They'll call soon. Mom's probably busy baking pies. For as long as I can remember, I've helped Mom make three Thanksgiving pies: pumpkin, pecan, and apple. Mom believes you can never have too much pie. On this we are in full agreement. Holidays in our family are not a single day, but rather a series of days punctuated by pie. I love eating a large slice for breakfast, whipped cream giving me a sugar rush that carries through the morning. Whenever my friends drop by, the first thing Mom does is slide a pie out of the fridge and cut everyone a slice.

Which gives me an idea. I push myself up off the floor.

"Can you bring me another can of pop?" Rachel asks.

"Sure." I grab a soda from the fridge and toss it to her. Then I pull on my snow boots. "Hey guys, I'll see you in a bit. I'm going for a walk."

"It's freezing outside!"

I shrug into my coat. "I want some fresh air. I won't be long."

I slip out the front door and into the frigid wind, stepping carefully down the slope of snow. The street has been plowed, but the sidewalks are mounds of white. I trudge down the block, my boots sinking into the snow with each step. On the drive here, I noticed a grocery store not too far away. The frozen tree branches creak in the wind and snowflakes melt on my cheeks, wetting my face.

Ever since the year's first snowfall in early November, I've been dreaming of the beach nearly every night. Not a summer beach, but a winter beach—quiet, desolate, only the waves and the seagulls and me, running. In real life, I don't run much at all anymore. But in my dreams, I run barefoot in the sand for miles and miles. I wake up with drool puddling on my pillow, the sheets tangled around my legs, my heart beating rapidly. I'm chasing something that is retreating from me, like waves receding up the shoreline. The dreams give me a weird sense of panic that time is running out.

At the store, I buy two cans of pumpkin, sweetened condensed milk, lemon juice, a box of pie crust mix, a bag of apples. Eggs, vanilla, brown sugar. At the last minute, I remember whipped cream.

The walk back seems much further with the heavy grocery bags taut in my fingers. I'm almost to Anabelle's street, my nose running from the cold, my clenched fingers frozen in my gloves, when a red pickup truck stops at the curb. The driver honks once, in a friendly way. I squint into the window. *David?*

He waves. "Emma! Hey!"

The wind blows strands of hair across my face. I don't know what to do. I'm torn between loyalty to Anabelle and a pressing desire to get out of the numbing cold.

David reaches over and opens the passenger door. "You must be freezing. Can I give you a lift?"

A stubborn part of me wants to keep walking. But the wind is biting, only growing colder as the sun sinks blearily toward the horizon, and my arms ache and my toes are wet in my boots. Anabelle's house is another half mile away.

"You sure?" I ask him. "It's not out of your way?"

"Get in here!" David grins and there is a dangerous fluttering in my chest.

I collapse into the passenger seat, settling the grocery bags around my feet and slamming the door shut. The heater is on full blast, a glorious rush of warmth against my face and hands.

"Thanks," I say.

"No problem."

David turns the radio down. Guns N' Roses gives way to the Rolling Stones. I stare out the passenger window at the mounds of grimy snow. A plastic grocery bag flaps in the wind, caught in a tree branch. Already, the fresh snowfall has been disheveled, its beauty wiped away.

"What you got there?" David asks, nodding at my grocery bags.

"Pie ingredients," I say.

"You're making pie? You better save a piece for me."

"And why is that?"

"For gallantly showing up to give you a lift. You do realize that makes me your knight in shining armor." His eyes flash at me, a challenge. *Is he like this with everyone? Or does his flirting mean something?*

"You could have had all the pie you wanted," I retort. "But you turned down Anabelle's invitation. So no pie for you."

"That's not fair."

"Yes it is."

"No it's not. She didn't tell me there would be pie—or that you would be there."

I fiddle with the heating vents, shifting the hot air away from my face. "Why wouldn't I be there? Anabelle's my best friend."

"I assumed you'd be going home for Thanksgiving."

"Flights are expensive. I'll be heading home soon enough for winter break."

David pulls up in front of Anabelle's house. It crosses my mind that he didn't need directions—he knows which house is Anabelle's. We sit there for a few moments in silence, watching the tree branches thrash in the wind. Then he clears his throat. "So I guess it's too late for me to change my mind and join you guys?"

"Anabelle's pretty mad at you. I think she felt snubbed."

He laughs. "Hell hath no fury like Anabelle scorned. Or something like that."

"Something like that." I know I should thank David for the ride, gather up my grocery bags, and trudge up the snowdrift to the front door. But I can't bring myself to unbuckle my seatbelt. I want to stay in the warmth a little longer, talking with David, our breath fogging up the windows.

"What kinds of pie are you making?" he asks.

"Pumpkin. And apple with cinnamon crumble on top."

"Omph. You're killing me. Apple pie is my favorite."

My favorite. The way he says it, his eyes sweeping from my hair to my eyes to my lips, makes it sound like he's no longer talking about pie. He's talking about me.

I think of that day when Hunter sort of broke up with me, when Matt drove me home and we sat like this in front of my house, and I almost tried to kiss him. What if I had? It would have ruined everything. And yet... maybe all this time, I've been trying to make things work with Hunter when we aren't supposed to be together anymore. Maybe this is the universe, nudging me forward.

I shift slightly in my seat. David inches closer. His face is so close. Dangerously close. My brain is locked into this moment, here in the warm cab of this pick-up truck with this delicious dizzy feeling in my chest. Not thinking of Hunter, not thinking of Anabelle, not thinking of anything past right now…

My phone rings, shattering the silence. David leans away. After a bit of fumbling, I retrieve the phone from my purse.

"Happy Thanksgiving!" Mom says. At the sound of her voice, the moment dissolves. "Emma? Are you there?"

"Yeah, I'm here," I tell her, flooded with shame. I can't get out of David's truck fast enough. I open the door, grab my groceries off the floor and smile goodbye. David smiles back, but it is a tight smile.

"Thanks for the ride," I whisper to him, then slam the door behind me.

"What was that?" Mom asks.

"Oh, nothing." I watch David's muddy red truck rumble off down the street.

If I dump Hunter, what will my parents think? No one I date in the future would come close to measuring up.

As if on cue, Mom asks, "Have you talked to Hunter today?"

"No."

"You should call him. He misses you so much." Mom tells me she is making two pumpkin pies this year, because pumpkin is Hunter's favorite, and she is going to send an extra one home with him. "Linda doesn't like pumpkin pie, can you believe it?" Linda is Hunter's mom. "She's not even making one this year. Said Hunter likes mine best anyway."

An hour later, I slide my own pies into the oven and then join my friends, who are still sprawled out in front of *The O.C.*, candy wrappers and empty soda cans strewn around them. Onscreen, Ryan races up the stairs to meet Marissa at the New Year's Eve party. I've already seen the episode, so I know he makes it there in time. In television shows, the characters always make it there in time.

Before long, Anabelle busts into her parents' liquor cabinet and the soda becomes mixers. The poetry twins pass out on the couch. I completely forget about my pies and they burn beyond repair. I don't tell Anabelle about David giving me a ride home.

Late at night, head spinning from the alcohol and sugar, I crawl into my sleeping bag on the living room floor. I dream again of running along a lonely winter beach. Only this time, I turn and run into the waves. The cold water engulfs my ankles, my knees, my thighs, my waist. I slosh deeper and deeper into the ocean, the waves pulling me further in—breasts, shoulders, neck—until my lips and nose and eyes are below the surface. My nose fills with water. My eyes burn and my lips taste salt. I dream of drowning, and then I dream of nothing.

7

AFTER

JUNIOR YEAR, LATE JANUARY

EVERY SUNDAY AFTERNOON, I call my parents and we talk for a few minutes. I usually pretend to be in a hurry, rushing off to a study session or a group hangout. The less my parents know about my daily life, the better. I don't want them to worry. I tell Mom that yes, I let Mrs. Jenkins know about the "situation" that happened over winter break and yes, I scheduled an appointment with a counselor to "talk through things." In reality, I couldn't bring myself to do either.

I want distance—from Buenaventura, from Mom and Dad, from Hunter, from everything that's happened. I want to forget.

But Céline won't let me forget. She's visiting Hunter every day at the hospital and texts me frequent updates:

Hunter smiled today. We watched the last Harry Potter movie. Remember in elementary school when we'd run around the backyard with brooms, pretending we were playing Quidditch?

Hunter's appetite is improving. He doesn't really like hospital food (who does?) but he loves the strawberry Jell-O.

Hunter is beginning to speak in full sentences. His energy is improving.

Whenever I visit I bring the newspaper and we do the Sudoku puzzle and the crossword. His mind is sharp—he's the same brainiac he always was. He tells me what to write and I fill in the letters.

We were talking about you today, remembering all the fun times we used to get into.

That last sentence makes me smile because it sounds like the old Céline, the real Céline, who is always slightly off when quoting popular sayings or lines from movies. I consider writing back, *It should be "all the trouble we used to get into" or "all the fun times we used to have." You mixed up the two sayings, sillypants.* The old Céline would understand this as a challenge and shoot back a message combining all the phrases she could possibly think of, probably with a smattering of GIFs thrown in for good measure. But I'm not sure how this new Céline in this new reality would react. Are jokes still allowed now that Hunter is paralyzed? It's like The Accident has bleached all sarcasm away so everyone is left communicating only in sincere, hopeful statements.

I don't know how to respond to Céline's earnest messages cataloging her daily interactions with Hunter. Each time, I click Reply and stare at the blank message box. After a few minutes, I begin stringing meaningless letters together. Gobbledygook. I never press Send.

MY FIRST WORKSHOP of the new semester goes pretty much the same as my workshops last semester. This painting is one I've been toiling over for weeks, since before winter break. It depicts a lonely diving board suspended over a pool, hovering in midair as if by magic. The colors are oversaturated, extreme; I wanted the viewer to look at the painting and *feel* the heat of the midsummer scene. But when I came back after break and looked at it with fresh eyes, the painting seemed cartoonish and flat.

"Your technique is strong," Mrs. Post says in her critique. "But I feel that something essential is… missing. Keep at it."

Frustration burns in my chest. What am I even doing here at Wabash? Do I honestly think I can be an artist? I'm not an artist. I'm a striver, a poser, a wannabe. Ever since Hunter's accident, it feels like something essential is missing not only in my art, but in the core of my self. And I worry that no matter how hard I try, I won't ever be able to find it.

The walk back to the dorm after Painting class is a blur. I unlock my door and stand for a few moments in the darkness, dripping snow onto the mud-strained carpet. My whole body burns with a deep chill. I rummage around under my bed and find a package of crackers, only half stale. My stomach growls at the first taste of salt. I am so frazzled that when my phone rings, I answer without thinking. "Hello?"

"Emma?" Céline says. "Is that you?"

"Yeah." Guilt and loneliness fill me like warm steam. I swallow a spit-gluey mass of cracker crumbs.

"I got so used to your voicemail, I wasn't actually expecting to get a hold of you."

"I know. I'm sorry. It's been crazy busy." My words sound pathetic even to my own ears.

"I've been worried about you, Em. How are you?"

It is so good to hear Céline's voice. I try to keep my voice steady. "I'm fine. Just, you know, busy. Like I said."

"Have you gotten my texts?"

"Yeah, I have. Thanks. I'm sorry I haven't written back—things have been so crazy here…"

"It's okay. I know you must be thinking about Hunter a lot and I wanted to keep you posted. He's doing better each day. The doctors are saying he might be discharged from the hospital and moved into a rehab facility within a week."

"That's great news."

"It's not at all like it was when we went to see him that first time," Céline continues. "I know that first visit was kind of scary, but I wish you could see him now. I sent you a couple photos, did you see them?"

"Oh, yeah—thanks."

"He's regained a lot of the use of his right hand. And his left is getting better, too."

A tiny bud of hope announces itself in my chest. "What about his legs?"

The line hums quietly for a moment. Finally Céline says softly, "No, Emma. Remember what his dad told us? Hunter is never going to walk again."

I picture Hunter flying around the curve of the track into the homestretch, that single-minded look of determination on his face, his feet barely seeming to hit the ground between strides.

"How is he doing, really?" I ask. "Be honest."

"Good," Céline says, her voice loud and upbeat again. "Really, really good. His brain was unaffected. He's smart and funny as ever. He's got all the nurses wrapped around his finger. It's hilarious. He's the prince of the hospital, getting extra Jell-O cups all the time. I'm always teasing him about it."

The fondness in her voice cuts me—I feel jealous and left out, which is stupid. This is not about me at all. "It's nice of you to visit him," I say.

"It's no big deal," Céline says. "I have the time. I like keeping him company."

I am flooded by a rush of emotion—homesickness, sadness, guilt, anger. I don't know how to deal with this complicated mess swirling around inside me. I would give anything to burst out of my own skin. To escape myself.

I thought that if anyone would understand how I'm feeling, it would be Céline. But I have never felt further from her than I do right now. She doesn't even seem like my best friend anymore. She belongs to Hunter. The only reason she's calling is to update me on his life.

An old insecurity sweeps in, fresh and raw. "Did I ever tell you that when Hunter and I first got together, his friends said he was dating me to get closer to you?"

"What?" Céline asks. "That's ridiculous. Why didn't you tell me when it happened?"

"I thought it was Robbie and Brett being stupid and trying to cause drama."

"Yes. That sounds like exactly what it was."

I sigh. "I don't know, C. I've always had an inkling that there's something between you and Hunter. Some spark." It is the first time I have said these words aloud. I thought I would feel lighter, freer, after giving voice to these doubts that have wound around my brain for so long. But I don't.

"There's no spark," Céline insists. "Hunter and I are just friends."

"Are you sure?"

"Of course I'm sure. Where is this all coming from?"

I sigh. "I'm sorry. I don't know. At Robbie's party, Siggy told me that Hunter cheated on me before we broke up. And it made me remember what his friends said last year, and it just—I mean, all the guys always like you, Céline. Why would Hunter choose me instead of you?"

"Emma. Listen to me. First off, guys do not always like me. But we can talk about that later. More importantly—Hunter loved *you*. He still does. You're the one who broke up with him, remember? Whatever Siggy told you is a total lie. Hunter would never have cheated on you."

Relief courses through me. Céline sounds so certain that it brings back my own trust in Hunter. In what we had.

"You're right. I'm being stupid. It's just—you promise me, C? You swear on all the waves in the ocean that there's never been anything between you and Hunter?"

A pause.

The silence stretches, longer and longer.

I pull the phone away from my ear and look at it, thinking the call dropped. But it didn't. "Céline, are you still there?"

She says quietly, "Yeah, I'm here. I guess... there's something I should tell you, Emma. It's not a big deal—and I don't want you to freak out—which is why I never said anything before..."

Dread fills my stomach. Maybe this knowledge has been buried inside me for a long time. But nothing can stay buried forever. "Tell me. I want to know."

Céline sighs heavily. When she finally speaks, her voice is quiet and strained. "It was back in November. I drove Hunter home from a party, and he was pretty drunk. He'd had a bad race that morning, and he was upset that you weren't coming home for Thanksgiving."

She pauses again. I don't say anything. I look down; my left hand, flecked with paint, is shaking.

"Which isn't an excuse or anything," Céline adds. "But when I dropped him off at his house, he gave me a hug and then he kissed me. We both pulled away so fast—it was bare-ly a peck, I swear Emma—and he knew right away it was wrong. We both did. It was a drunken mistake, and it didn't mean anything. He didn't know what he was doing."

My voice sounds cool even though my heart is hammer-ing. "I think he knew exactly what he was doing. He always wanted you, C. He settled for me, but he wanted you. And you always wanted him. Admit it."

Céline's voice is high and pleading. "That's not true, Emma. This is why I didn't tell you about it—it wasn't a big deal, honestly—"

"It's a big deal to me." My voice grows louder. My breath is raggedy bursts. I want a place to funnel this ava-lanche of pain. "It makes me look back and doubt all my memories with him. With both of you."

"I'm so sorry. I shouldn't have told you."

"No, I'm glad you did. Thank you for telling me. At least now I know the truth. Bye, Céline."

"Em, please. Don't push me away. We've been best friends forever."

I still vividly remember the day I met Céline. The first day of kindergarten, morning recess. I sat alone on the swings. She was wearing a rainbow jumper, her hair in pigtail braids, an effortless confidence in her demeanor even at six years old. She marched right up to me and asked if I wanted to be friends. Simple as that. I said yes, of course. She plopped down onto the swing next to me, and I wasn't alone anymore.

"If you want me to stop visiting him, I will," Céline of-fers. Her voice is desperate. "Whatever you want me to do, just tell me."

I've always wondered what drew Céline to me that day in kindergarten. Why did she choose me to be her best friend?

Maybe she could tell that in the galaxy of our school, I was only a faint, hazy star. She must have known that next to me, she would shine all the brighter.

I remember Hunter gazing at Céline with pure awe at the birthday party we had thrown for him. I nearly choke on my words, spitting them out like bile. "No, please, go ahead, Céline. Hunter is all yours. I broke up with him and then I broke him forever. Go on, take my sloppy seconds and live happily ever after."

I hang up.

I have never hung up on Céline before.

Just then, Anabelle barges into my room without knocking—typical Anabelle style. "Are you wearing that?" she says incredulously.

I look down at my faded overalls and long-sleeve striped shirt. "What's wrong with this?"

"I mean, it's cute, Em, but it's not really dance attire."

Oh yeah. The back-to-school dance. "That's tonight?"

"In an hour. C'mon—" She grabs my hand and yanks me up off my bed. "I've got a dress that will look killer on you."

My phone rings, Céline's wide grin filling the screen, a photo I took of her when we went to the beach last summer. I press "Ignore" and shove the phone into my purse.

"Hey Anabelle," I say. "You know how you're always wanting to give me a makeover? Tonight's the night. I'm all yours."

"Really?" She squeals and squeezes my hand. There's nothing in the world that Anabelle loves more than a no-holds-barred makeover. "By the time I'm done with you, Emma Mason, you won't even recognize yourself."

Perfect. I could use a costume tonight. An escape.

8

BEFORE

DURING A LAZY Sunday Netflix binge in Anabelle's room, she suggests that we all stay in town and celebrate Thanksgiving together, at her parents' house.

My heart leaps. Growing up, Thanksgiving was an occasion that made me envious. Other families celebrated with large, extravagant meals, their kitchens and dinner tables crowded with relatives and cheerful noise. My family has always been small. Just me, my parents, and my grandmother who talks in looping circles about people I don't know.

Even before my grandmother was diagnosed with dementia and moved into a nursing home, Thanksgiving has always seemed a little sad to me. Mom has no siblings; Dad had one much older brother who died of a stroke when I was seven. Uncle Fred. What I remember most about him is that he raised chickens. As a kid, I loved following him around, helping scatter feed. We'd traipse around the vegetable garden, bending down to check the leaves for hornworms.

Mom brings up Uncle Fred whenever she's trying to convince Dad to get a check-up at the doctor. "High blood pressure runs in your family," she says. "Think of your poor brother." But Dad always insists he is fine. He doesn't like doctors or hospitals.

Now, I envision Thanksgiving at Anabelle's house. I imagine all my Wabash friends around a huge table, laughing and celebrating together. I could offer to make some California-style dish: stuffing topped with avocado, or sautéed fruit kebabs, or some recipe I'll find in a chic food magazine. (In reality, my mom makes the most traditional of Thanksgiving dishes: mashed potatoes, peas, cornbread, gravy from a can… but my friends don't need to know that.)

Anabelle nudges me. "What do you say, Em—are you in?"

"Yeah!" I say. "I mean, I hope so. I have to check with my parents first."

Mom and Dad are surprisingly okay with me spending Thanksgiving in Indiana. "If that's what you want, sweetie," Mom says over Face Time, her brow slightly wrinkled above her round-rimmed eyeglasses.

"I guess you're right, Em," Dad puts in. "Flights are expensive, and you'll be home soon for Christmas anyway."

I had been braced for conflict. I look down at the pad of paper on my lap, a list of reasons for staying at school outlined in embarrassing detail. In the face of my parents' approval, my prepared arguments dissolve into a bewildering ache of homesickness.

"We'll miss you," Mom says, as if sensing my thoughts. "The Murrays have invited us over for Thanksgiving dinner, and they'll be sad to hear you won't be there."

"Wait, what?" I stand up and my notepad slides to the floor. I can hear the gentle chanting of Rachel's yoga video next door. "You're having Thanksgiving with Hunter's family? Why didn't anyone tell me?"

"I guess we assumed you and Hunter had talked about it," Dad answers.

"Does that change your plans at all, sweetie?" Mom asks in a teasing voice.

"No, sorry. I already promised Anabelle." Outside, the tornado siren blares. "What about Grandma?"

"Oh, she's coming, too. Your father will drive over to the nursing home and pick her up in the afternoon. She actually seems excited, huh, Larry?" Dad murmurs his assent.

I know I should be happy that my parents and Hunter's parents have become friends, but over the past few months their friendship has knitted tighter and tighter until it now seems a little too close for comfort. For my comfort, anyway. I mean, they have inside jokes. They send each other text messages with annoyingly proper grammar. Once, I called my own house and Hunter's mom answered the phone. In a strange way it almost feels like Hunter and I are married, our families hopelessly enmeshed.

"What's that noise in the background?" Mom asks.

"Nothing," I tell her. "The tornado siren. It's only a test."

I'm not actually sure whether it's a test or the real thing, but I'm no longer scared of tornados like I was when I first moved here. Nobody else is worried when the siren sounds. I've trekked down to the basement enough times alone, waiting by myself amid the dank mess of dirt-encrusted garden tools and dilapidated lawn furniture for the warning to cease, to learn that tornados aren't like earthquakes. Back home in California, I don't know a single person who doesn't have some sort of Earthquake Story. But here in Indiana, many people live for years and years without actually witnessing a tornado.

"It's nothing to worry about," I explain to my parents. After a few more minutes of conversation, we say goodbye.

I pull on a jacket and head across The Quad to Anabelle's dorm. Her door is ajar; I knock and she says, "Come in!" Anabelle looks up at me from her desk—for once, she's actually studying.

"You okay?" she asks.

I flop backwards onto Hannah's cold bedcovers. "My parents are having Thanksgiving with *Hunter's family*. Can you believe it?"

Anabelle doesn't reply. I cross my arms behind my head and stare at the ceiling. "My parents are so gaga over Hunter," I say. "I mean, he's amazing, and I love him—but it's like he can do no wrong. He has flaws, too, you know?"

Anabelle eyes me over her textbook. "You sound jealous," she says evenly. "Hunter is stealing your parents' attention, and you don't like it."

"I'm not jealous. It's just… weird, that's all. Parents aren't supposed to love their daughter's boyfriend so much. It's unnatural."

"Uh-huh." Anabelle raises one eyebrow.

I stick out my tongue at her. "Don't psycho-analyze me."

Anabelle sticks out her tongue at me. Then she smiles and puts down her book. "We can talk about it if you want."

But I don't even know what else to say. "No, that's okay. I'll let you get back to studying. See you later."

When I step out of the dorm lobby, the cold wind instantly bites through my coat. I won't last outside very long. I trudge to the parking lot and climb into my car, start the engine, and crank up the heater. A James Taylor song plays softly on the radio—one of my dad's favorites. I remember dancing with him to this song as a little girl, at someone's wedding, my stocking feet balanced on top of his dress shoes.

Now, staring out the window at the bare-limbed trees, I know Anabelle is right. Deep down, I am jealous. Because I can't compete with Hunter. He is so funny and interesting, with the sort of easy charm that completely eludes me. He is the son my parents never had. They will be devastated if we ever break up.

When the music gives way to commercials, I turn the volume down and pull out my phone. If I don't tell Hunter soon, he'll hear it from his parents, and I want the news to come from me. The phone rings four times, five times. I hate leaving voicemails. I always feel awkward, rambling on. I almost hang up, but then he answers.

"What's up, Pea?" I hear shuffling, voices, laughter in the background. "Sorry, I'm with the guys. We're heading into Pasta Roma to carb load."

"Oh, that's right—you've got a race tomorrow. We can talk later."

"No, no, I have a minute. Hey Ben, will you order me spaghetti and meatballs?" Laughter. "Shut up. I'm not going to dignify that with a response." More shuffling, and then Hunter's voice, warm and close. "Em, hey. How's it going?"

I don't want to upset Hunter before a race. But maybe this won't even upset him. Things have been so distant between us lately; our only conversations are these brief snatches when one of us is in a rush, en route to something else. I take a deep breath and come out with it: "I wanted to let you know that I'm thinking of staying here for Thanksgiving."

Silence.

After a few moments I ask, "Hunter? You still there?"

"Yeah, I'm here." His tone is icy. For a moment, I am relieved—so he *does* care! He *does* miss me!—but my buoyancy quickly deflates when I realize how upset he is. "So you'd rather stay there than come home," he says. "Wow. I don't know what to say."

A heavy stone drops into my gut. "I'm sorry. It's not that I don't want to come home, it's just—flights are so expensive, you know? And I'll be home soon for winter break."

"That's still six weeks away."

"I know. But the time will fly by," I insist. "We're both so busy with school and finals…" I pause, waiting for Hunter to chime in and agree, to say he understands. But he doesn't.

I hear wind in the background. I picture Hunter standing outside Pasta Roma in the quickly descending darkness, but then I remind myself that it's three hours earlier where he is. It's not getting dark there yet. I picture slush on the ground, but then I remind myself that it's not freezing where he is. It's probably seventy degrees out. He's probably in a T-shirt. Sometimes it seems we're not only in different time zones— we're in different seasons entirely. Hunter exists in perpetual summer, while I'm bracing myself for winter.

When Hunter speaks, his voice is a whisper. "I miss you, Pea. I really miss you."

My heart aches. It's been a long time since I've heard this raw vulnerability in his voice. "I miss you too."

"Do you?"

"Of course I do!"

"You've got all these new friends and activities—you've got this whole new life—and I'm glad you're happy there, Em. I really am. But I worry sometimes. It feels like you're slipping away. Like you've changed."

"I haven't changed, Hunter. You know that. I'm still me."

"It seems, lately, like—I don't know. Different than how it used to be. Remember when I came out to visit you? Remember how hard it was when I had to leave? I know it was hard for you, too, not only for me. I could tell that you hated to be apart."

"I did—I *do*. I still hate being apart."

"Then why aren't you coming home for Thanksgiving? I thought we were both counting down the days."

I swallow. "I'm trying to be practical. Save money. It's not *that* much longer until I'll be home for almost a whole month."

Another long pause, and then Hunter sighs. "Yeah. I guess you're right. Winter break is around the corner. Promise you won't bail on coming home then?"

I laugh. "Of course not! You won't be able to get rid of me. I'll be, like, stalking your house."

I can hear him grinning. "I'll wake up and you'll be standing outside my window watching me sleep."

"You'll be like, *When do you go back to Indiana again?*"

"Never."

"We'll see. You might get tired of me."

"I could never get tired of you, Pea." His voice has relaxed. I wish, suddenly and fiercely, that I *was* going home for Thanksgiving. I wish I could snap my fingers and teleport to Pasta Roma right now and sit next to him eating slightly overcooked pasta drowning in sauce. I wish I had never left Buenaventura at all.

"So what are you doing out there for Thanksgiving?" Hunter asks. "Is one of the teachers hosting a dinner for the students?"

"I'm actually going to Anabelle's. She lives—I mean, her parents live—in town and she's having a bunch of us over. It won't be the same as being at home, but at least I won't be alone."

"Who's going to be there?" Hunter says. He's trying to sound casual, but tension lurks in his tone.

"I don't know. The usual crew."

"David?"

I almost lie. But what if Hunter sees a photo on social media and David is in it? "Yeah, I think so."

Hunter laughs, but it is sad, resigned laughter. "I should have known. That's the real reason you want to stay there, isn't it? You'd rather hang out with David than with me."

"Hunter, how many times do I have to tell you? David and I are just friends."

"Okay, Em," he says. "Fine. Whatever. Have a great Thanksgiving. Have fun with all your new kitten friends."

This is the first time Hunter has mentioned my Halloween costume, which he would have seen on Instagram. Céline commented, "Wowzers!" to our heeled boots and cleavage-baring shirts and kitten-ear headbands, and I told her I liked our costume better the year before, when we dressed up as Thing One and Thing Two from *The Cat in the Hat*. But the truth is, a secret part of me liked being a sexy kitten. There is something powerful in the way I can reinvent myself here at Wabash Academy. Back home, everybody knows me and no one really sees me anymore. They see what they expect to see. Emma Mason: Céline Ziza's best friend. Hunter Murray's girlfriend. The AP art kid; the JV track runner. Average and ordinary.

At Wabash, even when I'm not dressed up as a kitten for Halloween, I sometimes feel like I'm wearing a costume. Pretending to be a sophisticated, confident artist with Big Ideas.

"Have fun with *David*," Hunter continues. "See if I care!"

"That's real mature, Hunter. Real understanding of you."

He hangs up without a goodbye. My hand is shaking as I set the phone down in the plastic cup holder. I turn off the car engine and sit for a little while in the darkness as the heat slowly seeps away. Outside, the wind howls like the sound of something dying.

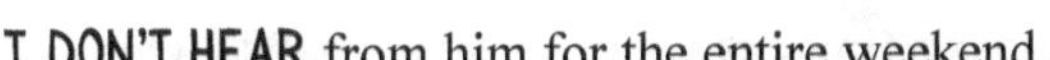

I DON'T HEAR from him for the entire weekend.

"Are we broken up?" I ask my friends. We are sprawled in Anabelle's room, painting our nails. Anabelle did laundry earlier and her sweaters are draped all around the room, drying, making the air feel close and damp.

"I don't think you're officially broken up," Anabelle says. "You're in the murky gray area. You need to break up with him definitively, if that's what you want."

"I think you should wait out the weekend and then call him," Rachel says.

Later that night I lie facedown on my bed, mentally practicing what I will say. With help from my friends I have written out a script: *I really care about you, but I don't think this is working anymore. Long distance is too hard. It's nothing you did wrong, it's me. I need to focus on myself right now. I need my independence.* I'm preparing for battle, wrapping myself in an armor of clichés.

I close my eyes, pressing my cheek against the bed and breathing in. A faint smell of incense is embedded in the worn quilt, which I found at a thrift store back in August. The quilt is made from fabric scraps, a hodge-podge of colors and patterns—so different from the quilt in my childhood bedroom, with its orderly rows of blue. I fall asleep quickly, without even changing into my pajamas.

Early the next morning, my phone rings.

Hunter.

Watching my phone's lit-up vibrating on the bedside table, my heart pounds wildly. I quickly calculate the time difference—it's four a.m. in California. *Has he been up all night? Is this it? Are we breaking up?* After hesitating for a couple seconds, I answer.

"Hello?" I try to adopt the icy tone I'd practiced.

"Emma, listen—I'm sorry. I'm so, so sorry." Hunter says he overreacted—the stress and distance are getting to him. Cross-country practices have been hell lately and his last race went horribly. He is fighting a sore hip, worried his old injury will flare up again, but also trying not to lose his scoring spot on the team roster. And final exams are looming.

"I took it out on you. I'm sorry. I just miss you so much."

I sit in silence, the phone hot against my ear. I'm not sure what I feel—relief, happiness, anger, disappointment, some swirling combination of everything?

"I'd be lost if we broke up," Hunter continues. "I couldn't make it without you."

"Don't say that," I tell him.

"Seriously. You're my girl, Pea." His voice is solemn, intense.

I look at my carefully written script. The paper is sweat-damp in my hand. Pricks of blue ink bleed through from my to-do list on the other side.

"Hunter," I begin. "I really care about you."

But I can't get the rest of the words out.

After few beats of silence I say I miss him, too, of course I miss him, I can't wait to see him for winter break. We stay on the phone until I have to leave for class, listing all the things we'll do when we're reunited back home. Driving out to Fisherman's Point. Walking along the pier. Tacos from our favorite food truck. Long runs down the beach. Dancing all night at a Robbie Zwick party.

"I really love you," Hunter says, right before we hang up.

"I love you, too," I say, and the confusing thing is that, despite everything, I still mean it.

9

AFTER

AS WE GET ready for the back-to-school dance, Anabelle puts on an old Olivia Wilde movie. Céline and I saw this movie in theaters when we were in middle school. We loved it so much that after the credits played we remained in our seats, chewing on cold popcorn kernels at the bottom of the bag, and watched the entire movie straight through again.

I remember how Céline swooned over the theme song, a romantic piano number with a slow, graceful beat. "I'm going to dance to that song at my wedding," she declared. I diligently stored this information away in the correct file folder of my mind—I needed to keep track of these things because I was going to be Céline's maid of honor and Céline, of course, would be mine. It was something we established early in our friendship, since I am an only child and Céline has only a brother. Growing up, we often pretended we were sisters. "Hey, sis," Céline would say, and I would respond, "What?"

in a bored voice, feigning nonchalance but feeling a secret joy expand in my chest.

Pushing Céline from my mind, I turn my attention to the mirror and watch Anabelle finish tying my hair up into a sleek topknot. I'm wearing Anabelle's extremely short, bright red dress. She's paired it with sheer black tights and my black boots. The girl staring at me in the mirror is a stranger. Charcoal-rimmed eyes. Raspberry-stained lips. Flushed pink cheeks.

"Ta-da!" Anabelle exclaims. "What do you think?

"Perfect."

"Good, because you look *smokin'*." She gives me a squeeze, then leans past me to touch up her own eyeliner in the mirror. "Remember—you're a single lady tonight! Let's find you a rebound!"

I choke out a laugh. Part of me can't imagine kissing anyone else besides Hunter. It seems impossible that I'll ever kiss anyone again. Another part of me wants to hurl myself at the nearest body, lose myself in adrenalin and heat.

We flee the warmth of the dorm into the icy black night. The cold hits my skin like a slap. Neither of us is wearing coats. Anabelle grabs my hand and we run across The Quad. The Great Hall looms closer and closer. We fling ourselves through the entrance, gasping for breath, and quickly push forward into the crowd before any teachers see us. Wabash Academy supposedly has a dress code, but no one really follows it—especially at school dances. Still, I don't want to take any chances that Anabelle's short red dress is deemed too short and I'm sent back to the dorm to change.

Inside the Great Hall it is stuffy and hot, filled with thumping bass music and laughter. Instantly I am transported back to winter break. Thumping bass music, cool night air. Slipping into Robbie Zwick's backyard, Céline at my side, laughing together at something random and stupid and ours. Anabelle links her pinky with mine and I exhale.

We dance for a little bit, and then we drink some punch that Anabelle spikes with a tiny flask she'd tucked into her boot, and then we dance some more. I'm not much of a drinker. The alcohol floods my brain and the knots wound up inside me relax and everything becomes less serious. It seems like this is all pretend. Like I've transcended the realm of actions and consequences.

"I'm getting more punch," Anabelle says into my ear. "Want some?"

"Hell yes!" I laugh and kiss her on the cheek.

"Woo!" she says, slapping my butt. "I like drunk Emma! Don't do anything crazy until I get back. Promise?"

"Promise."

But as soon as Anabelle leaves the mass of dancing bodies, I feel alone. It's no fun dancing by myself. I nudge and sidestep my way out of the crowd and lean against the back wall. I imagine myself as a bright red balloon, happily adrift from my real life. I remember that I was upset earlier—of course I remember that sick feeling in my gut—but for the moment, it is a pet dog on a leash that I'm observing with detachment.

Across the room, David is talking to one of his friends, laughing. He lifts a plastic cup to his lips.

I think of Hunter as he was that night, shortly before The Accident. In my mind he is frozen, eternally safe on the pool deck, leaning against a palm tree. I hate remembering the way he scanned around in all directions, restless and drunk. Looking everywhere but at me.

David glances my way and smiles. At first, I'm not sure if it is a smile directed at me or just a general smile in a general direction. Am I staring? I'm probably staring. I look away, but then I can't help it. I look back at him.

He nods a goodbye to his friend, drains his cup and sets it down on the ledge behind him, and walks over to me.

"Hey Emma," David says. Even in the dim lighting, his teeth gleam.

"Hi," I say, matching David's smile. "Anabelle went off somewhere…" I look around but don't see her in the dark mess of bodies around us.

"I didn't come over here to talk to Anabelle. I came over to talk to you."

"Oh." I don't know what to say. My drunken thoughts swirl together like a little kid's finger painting.

His eyes trace me up and down. "Wow. You look… different."

I tug at the hem of my dress. "Good different or bad different?"

"Good different. Definitely good different."

I am an actress playing a part. Anabelle's makeover has worked its magic. Or maybe that's the alcohol. I never drink this much.

"I heard you broke up with your boyfriend," he says. "I'm sorry."

No you're not, I think, and I surprise myself by saying the words out loud.

David's smile spreads slowly across his face, making me think of butter melting slowly in a pan. "Okay, you're right," he says. "I was glad to hear it, actually."

My heart is hammering. The Accident flashes through my thoughts. Launching myself through the water, splashing past people to get to Hunter's body. He was floating there, motionless, like a dumb kid playing dead. Two of the brawny waterpolo guys dragged Hunter from the pool and laid him out on the pool deck. He looked so thin and pale. I climbed out of the water, dripping, shaking, not even aware of my own nakedness. I stood next to Matt and watched a suddenly sober Céline perform CPR.

The relief I felt when Céline announced, "He's breathing." The relief—and, yes, love—that swelled in my chest. I don't want to think about it.

I think instead of Thanksgiving, when David gave me a ride back to Anabelle's from the grocery store. His sly glance as we talked about pie. Heat whooshing from the vents. My face warms from the alcohol, or the memory, or maybe both.

"So how are you?" David asks. "Are you holding up all right?"

"I'm fine," I say. "Well, actually not fine. I lost my favorite lip balm."

"That sucks," David says, mock-serious. "We should get a search party together. I can make LOST signs."

I play along. "Missing: tube of lip balm. Peppermint flavored. Reward offered."

"Oh, a reward? Now it's getting interesting. What would the reward be?"

"I don't know," I say. "Chocolate?"

David drops his head, disappointed. *Wait, I can do better!* I'm surprised by how desperately I want him to keep gazing at me with that electric smile.

"Oh wait, I've got it," I say. David looks at me expectantly.

I'm not thinking of Anabelle. I'm not thinking of Hunter. I'm not thinking of anything past this moment.

I know exactly what path I'm heading down, and yet I do it anyway. Like taking a deep breath and diving into a pool. I lean closer to him and say, "The reward would be a kiss."

David grins. "Oh yeah?" he says. "A pepperminty kiss?"

"Definitely."

I'm not sure if he steps toward me first, or if I step toward him. All I know is that he reaches out and it feels natural to slip my hand into his warm, waiting palm.

As David curls his fingers around mine, I'm struck by a thought: *This is what was meant to happen. This is what should have happened last semester.* I should have broken up with Hunter last summer. I should have been free and single when I met David. I should have gone to Robbie Zwick's party as David's girlfriend, and maybe Hunter would have been dating someone else, too—that Foothill girl, or maybe even Céline. I would have been okay with that if I was with David. (Deep down, I know I would definitely *not* have been okay with that, but I let myself pretend.) In my fantasy, I am dating David and Hunter is still running, captain of the track team, and we are friendly toward each other. And Céline is still the old Céline, my Céline, sending me handwritten letters with fart jokes and silly doodles in the margins. And everything is right with the world.

"Your hand's cold," David says, interrupting my thoughts.

"My hands are always cold. Poor circulation."

"You know what my mom says?" David asks. He squeezes my hand gently.

"What?"

"Cold hands, warm heart." He brings my hand up to his lips and blows warm air onto my fingers. It feels nice. For the first time since The Accident, I think that maybe, one day, I could learn to forget the whole guilty mess of that night. Maybe I could shove all of that into a little corner of my heart and lock it away.

"You want to go somewhere quiet?" David asks.

I know what he is really asking.

And I nod. I do want to go somewhere quiet with him. My head is pounding. My limbs are floaty. All my thoughts coalesce into a single desire. *I want I want I want.*

David leads me to the other side of the Great Hall. My legs are a little wobbly. I'm not sure if it's because I'm drunk or because of the flashing lights, the stuffy heat, the booming music. Probably a combination of everything. We slip through a door and down a hallway. Before I know it, we are stumbling into a dark space. A closet? My back presses against something hard. He kicks the door shut behind him, and then his lips are on mine. He pulls out my topknot and threads his fingers through my hair. My body is nothing but nerve endings and electricity. When he unzips the back of my dress, I don't resist. It feels so good to sink into this nothingness, to let my thoughts and emotions turn off for a little while. Wrapped up in David's arms, I lose myself. My mind is swept blank and time falls away and the only thing that matters is his heartbeat and mine, his hands and mine, his mouth and mine.

Eventually, our frantic kissing slows. He pulls away. We are both breathing heavily. A shiver winds its way down my spine. I clutch my dress against me, feeling exposed. Ashamed.

"We should do this again sometime," David whispers in my ear.

All of my desire has leached away and I feel sick and spent. I'm a used tissue, tossed in the trash. "Please," I say, my voice desperate. "Don't tell Anabelle."

David winks and reaches behind me to zip my dress back up. "Don't worry. This can be our little secret."

Five minutes later, I'm back in the stuffy Great Hall with the pounding bass music, snaking my way through the crowd of bodies. In my mind, I reach back and clasp Anabelle's hand, holding on tight so we won't lose each other. In the present, I reach back for no one. Voices murmur around me like buzzing insects. I pass through the crowd unnoticed and alone.

Stumbling out into the frigid air is like snapping my fingers and coming back to myself. Like waking up from a fever dream.

What have I done? What have I done?

My mouth tastes sour and my bloated stomach is combustible. I can't go back to the dorm. I can't. Instead I trudge across the snow to the painting studio. I crave my solitary corner, my orderly row of colors.

The studio is quiet, empty, smelling thickly of paint. I flick on the florescent lights and they buzz softly to life. Last week, I bought a blank canvas for the midterm assignment, a still life. I know I should save it for the midterm. But I don't want to paint a still life. Not right now. Not when everything inside me is the opposite of still.

I prop up the canvas on my easel and stand there for a few minutes, studying it.

Ever since I came to Wabash, I spend my painting sessions glancing over my shoulder, afraid someone might be watching and judging my hesitant brushstrokes. But tonight, the empty canvas sucks me in like an ocean riptide. As soon as I touch color to the bristles of my paintbrush, the chaos inside me grows still.

My sense of self drops away. Time drops away. Thought drops away. I watch my fingers hold the paintbrush, watch my arm sweep from here to there across the canvas. Slowly, shapes begin to emerge. When I finally step back, my forehead is damp with sweat.

Gazing at what I have painted makes me want to cry. But I am too tired to cry. I am too tired to do anything but stand here. Shame flushes my ears and neck. I painted this?

Feet. Giant, pale, slightly hairy feet. Man feet. No—boy feet.

Man-boy feet.

The skin is a nearly translucent blue, wrinkled from being underwater. Tufts of dark hair drift up from each toe. The left big toenail is a deadened purple-black and there is a small blister, taut with blood, on the right pinky toe.

Hunter's feet.

I turn away. My head pounds and my stomach churns. I must paint over this to erase it. But first—

I dash out of the studio, down the hallway, and into the empty bathroom, where I crouch in a toilet stall and try to slow my breathing. There is no one to hold my hair back as I vomit.

Afterwards, flooded with exhaustion, I can't summon the energy to return to the studio and face the larger-than-life, intricate detail of Hunter's feet. Instead, I retreat to the dorm. I fall asleep aching for Céline, for Anabelle, my stomach in tight double-knots.

I have ruined everything.

10

BEFORE

JUNIOR YEAR, LATE SEPTEMBER

CÉLINE GIVES ME the idea. She starts talking about Hunter's birthday in September, even though his birthday isn't until October. But Céline has always been a planner, especially when it comes to holidays and birthdays.

"It'd be fun to throw him a party," she says. "A surprise party. What do you think, would Hunter like that?"

"Are you kidding? He'd love that." It's raining outside and I'm sprawled on my bed, wearing shorts and a T-shirt because this is a humid late-summer rain, not the cold rain we get in Buenaventura. Nora's out somewhere, but our room still smells of the popcorn she made for breakfast.

"Awesome." Céline's tone turns business. "I'll ask his teammates to take Hunter somewhere for the day, to get him out of the house. Or do you think having it at a restaurant would be better?" I can tell she's going through a mental checklist. *First step: ask Emma's opinion. Check. Next step: secure a venue.*

"Having it at his house would be easiest," I say. "No need for a reservation, and you don't have to worry about being too loud."

"Good point," Céline says. "And I'm sure his parents will be fine with letting us take over their house for a few hours."

"They'll probably want to escape. They'll go over to my house and hang out with my parents." I laugh, even though I'm not really joking—I'm pretty certain that is, in fact, what the Murrays will do.

"I wish I could be there," I say with a sigh, rolling over onto my stomach.

Which gives me an idea. I glance at the wall calendar above my desk. Maybe I *can* be there…

"Hey Céline, when are you thinking of holding this party?"

"Well, as close to his birthday as possible, but not on a weekday. Maybe the Friday after his birthday?"

"Perfect!" I say excitedly. "I'll be done with all my midterms by then. What if I fly home for a long weekend?"

"Oh Emma, that would be amazing! A bonus surprise at his surprise party! Hunter won't know what hit him."

"Like me at my surprise party," I say.

Céline laughs. "You were the cutest deer in the headlights I've ever seen." She mimics my stupefied voice when everyone leapt out from behind the couches in my parents' living room: "Oh my god. Oh. My. God."

"I was totally clueless. I didn't even know surprise going-away parties were a thing."

"They're not!" Céline says. "That's why it was so perfect! We had to do something to show how much we'd miss you."

"I miss you so much."

We chat some more about Hunter's party, but soon Céline has to leave for her babysitting job. "Catch some rays at the park for me!" I say. In California, September still feels like summer.

"Will do!" Céline says. "Wish you were here to go on the swings with me."

"I do too," I say, but she's already hung up.

CÉLINE WASTES NO TIME in planning the party, full steam ahead. I help her find a photo of Hunter to use for the invitation. We choose one where he's eating a piece of French toast, powdered sugar everywhere. His eyes are wide, his eyebrows raised—I remember taking that picture, and he was trying to make me laugh—but it looks like his expression is one of surprise.

Within twenty-four hours, there's a detailed event page with more than fifty people invited. I recognize most of the names, but some are unfamiliar. New friends? Céline has always been outgoing, making friends quickly and easily. She has an aura that makes people comfortable. I'm lucky that Céline and I became friends in kindergarten—I scored the jackpot by claiming her as my best friend in such an early round. If we were to meet for the first time today, I wonder if I would stand out enough from the crowd to be her friend, much less her *best* friend. Would she still pick me?

Céline puts my name on the event invite like we are co-planning this party. But she's the one doing most of the work. She's the one people are sending their RSVPs to. She's the one getting in touch with Hunter's parents and teammates. She's the one buying decorations and brainstorming food and drink options. Which makes sense—she's good at it, plus she's just down the street instead of halfway across the country.

I try to help out as much as possible, but most of my suggestions come too late—things Céline has already taken care of. So I gradually stop making suggestions. It seems easier to step back and let Céline work her magic without interruptions from me.

———

A WEEK BEFORE I'm scheduled to fly home for the surprise, Hunter and I get into a huge fight. It starts with something small and stupid, as most of our fights do. He's upset that I haven't responded to his texts all day; I explain that I've been busy with midterms. "You're not as busy yet because you guys are on a later schedule," I remind him. "Remember how crazy midterms were last year?"

"Yeah, but I'm busy too, Emma. I'm a student-athlete! I have three hours of practice every day, but I still find time to call you. Sometimes it's like you don't even miss me at all."

"Of course I do!"

"Well, I'd appreciate feeling like I was more of a priority in your life."

"You are!" *I'm coming home to surprise you for your birthday!* But, of course, I can't tell him that.

Hunter sighs. "You've changed, Pea."

"What do you mean? How have I changed?"

"It's like—you feel so far away. Not just the physical distance, but more than that—it's like we're on different wavelengths. Maybe long distance is too hard."

My pulse quickens. "Are you suggesting what I think you are?"

"I don't know. Maybe."

"Look, I have an exam tomorrow, so I can't do this right now. I'll talk to you later."

"Em, wait—"

I hang up before we can go any further down that path. I almost call Céline, but for some reason I can't bring myself to hit her number on my speed dial. I don't want her to know that Hunter and I are fighting.

I head to the Dining Commons even though I've already had dinner. At first I think I'm looking for Anabelle. But when I see her, my heart sinks a little, and I realize that David is the real reason I came here. He is the one I was hoping to bump into.

But he's not here.

"Hey!" Anabelle says when I sit down. "I thought you were studying."

"I needed a break. And some fro yo."

"Everything okay?" Anabelle studies my face.

I look away, pretending to dig in my bag for something as I say brightly, "Yeah, I'm fine. Just, you know, Art History is ruining my life, but what's new?" I'm tired of talking about Hunter to Anabelle. Tired of talking in circles around the same damn question—*should I break up with him?*—while she listens with a serene smile, as if any moment I'll be struck by a brand-new epiphany. I'm tired of myself. "Be right back."

Walking across the Dining Commons, I feel wound up and restless. I want to break something. I yank down the handle of the soft-serve machine, hard, but it doesn't do any harm. The machine steadily spits out the frozen yogurt like it always does.

When I return to the table, Anabelle and Rachel are earnestly discussing the merits of leggings versus yoga pants. I listen without listening. After a few minutes, during a lull in the conversation, I ask, "Is David around?" Trying to sound casual.

Anabelle wipes ketchup from her mouth. "Haven't seen him. Why?"

"I was thinking that since he took this class last semester, maybe he could give me some tips for the midterm." I chew on a gummy bear, rock-hard from the cold fro yo.

"Do you want me to text him?" Anabelle asks.

"No, it's okay."

When I get back to my room, I have three missed calls from Céline. I call her back, expecting to hear about plans related to the surprise party, like a last-minute change in the menu (currently sliders and sweet potato fries catered from Study Hall Café, Hunter's favorite local restaurant) or maybe a guest-list update. Instead, Céline says, "Don't worry, Emma. I talked some sense into him. Everything is all right."

"What?"

"Your fight with Hunter. He called me after you hung up because he was so upset. I was able to calm him down and show him how ridiculous he was being."

"Thanks," I say quietly. I should probably be grateful, but mostly I feel annoyed. *Why did Hunter call Céline? Céline is my friend, not his. I'm his girlfriend. I'm the one he should have called to talk things out.*

"He misses you, Em. That's what all this is about. He sees photos of you with other guys and he gets jealous."

"David is my friend, Céline! Since when am I not allowed to have guy friends?"

"Whoa, calm down. All I'm saying is, Hunter's worries are going to vanish the moment he sees you at his surprise party. He's going to realize that you do make him a priority and what an idiot he was to suggest otherwise."

"Okay," I say. "You're right." I want to get off the phone as quickly as possible.

"I should probably let you go," Céline says. "Hunter's going to call you, I'm sure."

We hang up. Hunter doesn't call. I don't call him, either.

THE FINAL DAYS leading up to the surprise party are a whirlwind of exams, papers, and painting. Then, suddenly, it is the day of my flight. Anabelle drives me to the airport so I don't have to take the shuttle-bus or pay the high rates to park my car there over the long weekend.

"Have fun!" she tells me at the entrance to security. "I'm sure he'll be super surprised."

"I hope so!" I say. "I hope he's happy to see me."

"If he's not, then he's an idiot," she says, hugging me. "You're awesome. I'll hold down the state of Indiana while you're gone."

"You do that."

We smile at each other. Even though I'll only be gone for a long weekend, I already miss Anabelle. I wish I could fold her up in my suitcase and take her home to California with me. I wave goodbye and join the snaking line of passengers waiting to go through Security. Maybe growing up means that no matter where you go, you're always missing someone.

THE TIME CHANGE and flight time from Indiana to California pretty much cancel each other out, so when I arrive at LAX, the local time is only half an hour later than when my flight took off in Indianapolis. It's kind of trippy.

Céline meets me at baggage claim. As soon as I see her, I start skip-running toward her like a little kid. I can't help myself.

"Céline!"

"Em!"

I skid to a stop and stand before her, smiling so fully my cheeks hurt. I'm bouncing up and down with happy energy, but I don't lean in for a hug until she opens her arms wide and embraces me tightly.

"It's so great to see you!" Céline says. She smells exactly as I remember—floral shampoo, the citrus tang of her deodorant.

"I missed you!" I say. Somehow, it never fully hits me how much I've missed her until I see her again after being separated, and an absent piece of me settles into place, and I think, *How did I ever manage to be so far away from this person for even a few days?*

After a moment, Céline pulls away. "We should probably get your bags," she says, making a beeline toward the baggage carousel. This is Céline: productive, efficient, methodical. I follow in her wake and stand beside her at Carousel 3, eying the stream of suitcases for mine. I can tell from the crinkle in Céline's forehead that while she is happy to see me, she is simmering with stress underneath the surface. There is definitely a to-do list scrolling through her mind.

"So, what's left to do for the party?" I ask.

Céline immediately launches into a monologue about balloons, cupcakes, whether she got enough paper plates and napkins, and if I've seen those little poppers that people use on New Year's Eve—would Hunter like those?

"Um, yeah," I say, hoisting my suitcase off the carousel.

"I was thinking everyone could pop those when we yell, 'Surprise!' Is it okay if we stop by a party store on the way home to see if they have any?"

"Sure," I say. "But could we grab In'N'Out first? I'm starving!"

Before long we're driving in Céline's car, our windows open to the warm breeze. When you look out the airplane window, descending into Los Angeles, it's impossible to ignore the layer of smog blanketing the city—but when you're on the ground, the haze seems to disappear. I breathe in deeply. Home. It's hard to believe that I'm really here. I can relax. Settle back into this comfortable life, surrounded by people I've known for years and years. Already, as we start and stop down congested Sepulveda Boulevard, my life in Indiana seems like something I read about in a book—not real, not mine.

At the party store we find the poppers Céline wants, plus shiny balloons and blue streamers. Next we stop at a bakery to pick up cupcakes, and then we go to Study Hall Café to get the sliders and sweet potato fries. By the time we pull into Hunter's driveway, I'm ready for a nap. But Céline is a tautly pulled wire, sparking with energy. She thrives off this kind of thing. The day she and Hunter threw the going-away surprise party for me, she was in charge of keeping me occupied for most of the day. I kept thinking she must have downed espresso instead of a chai latte at our Starbucks pit stop because she was so hyped up.

As we walk up to the front door, Céline explains that Hunter is out at a movie with his teammates. I'm surprised when Céline walks in without knocking. "Hi, Mrs. Murray!" she calls out. "Look who I brought with me!"

Hunter's house. I practically lived here all summer—Hunter and I were constantly back and forth at each other's houses—but now I feel shy. I study my surroundings like I'm on set in a movie. Comfy gray couch. Matching recliners. Brick fireplace with framed school photos of Hunter and his brother on the mantel. The house smells of mint and lavender from Hunter's mom's diffuser. Hunter gave it to her for Christmas last year, and she is obsessed with trying new scents, but she always comes back to her favorite two.

Mrs. Murray sweeps out of the kitchen. She has Hunter's tall, lean frame and almost always wears yoga pants and strappy athletic tops, her hair up in a ponytail. Today is no exception. When she sees me, her eyes widen with surprise and her face breaks into a smile. "Maureen!" she shouts, as I was pretty sure she would. "Maureen, get in here!"

My mom hurries in from the kitchen, her brow furrowed in concern. I didn't tell her I was coming home for the weekend. I guessed that she would be hanging out with Hunter's mom, helping prep for the party, and I figured I would get in multiple surprises at once.

Mom. When I see her, tears spring to my eyes. I've missed her more than I realized. Her hair hangs in loose waves around her face. She's wearing jeans and a patterned blouse I helped her pick out. Right now, glimpsing her in person for the first time in two months, she is both familiar and new. I can see our resemblance. I've always loved when people say I look like my mother.

"Emma?!" she exclaims, both hands on her heart. "Emma! What are you doing here? I can't believe it!" She runs past Mrs. Murray and embraces me in a tight hug.

"Surprise!" I squeak out, and then Mom is crying and I am crying, too.

"What are you doing here? When did you get in?"

I explain about helping Céline plan the surprise party for Hunter and hatching my plan to fly out for the weekend as a bonus surprise.

Mom gives me another squeeze. "I feel like it's my birthday too!" she says, laughing. "Just wait till your father sees you!" She promises not to give anything away—I'll surprise him tonight when I come home after Hunter's party.

"He might be in bed when you get home," Mom says. "He's been so tired lately. They're really busy at the office, and he's been working hard. You'll surprise him in the morning."

"That will be even better!" I imagine nonchalantly walking downstairs, sitting next to him at the kitchen table, and pouring myself a bowl of cereal—like I used to do every weekend. My heart lurches with a strange homesickness. Even though I am home, I feel removed from my old life here. This weekend is so fleeting, so temporary. I hug my mom tighter.

As Céline and I help my mom and Mrs. Murray with finishing touches for the party—hanging up streamers and balloons, filling a cooler with ice and sodas, setting out napkins and paper plates—I keep glancing around for Hunter. It is strange to be at his house without him. I am dying to see him, but I'm a little nervous, too. We never talked about our argument; he called me the next morning, part of our usual routine, and we both acted like nothing happened. But things have been strained between us all week. I'm hoping that as soon as he sees me, everything will go back to normal. No, better than normal—perfect. I'm hoping everything will be perfect.

There's a knock on the door and Céline rushes over to answer. A guy I don't recognize stands at the threshold, lugging a cornhole board. "Hey, it's the queen!" he says, giving

Céline a hug. *The queen?* "Where do you want these?" he asks her.

"Out in the backyard would be great!" she says, following him around back.

A few minutes later, when they come inside, Céline introduces us. "This is Henry," she says. "He's new on the cross-county team. He moved here from Oregon."

"Oh, of course," I say. "Hi Henry." In truth, I have no idea who he is. Hunter hasn't mentioned him. Maybe they aren't that close. Or maybe it's a sign of the many ways my life and Hunter's life are out of sync.

I push my worries away and shake Henry's hand. Behind his smile I can tell he's studying me, gauging all the differences between me and Céline. It's obvious that Henry is fond of Céline, and that they're comfortable around each other. Do I measure up? Am I what he expected? Does Hunter talk about me very much? So many questions I yearn to ask but can't.

Soon, guests begin to arrive. My mom heads home and Hunter's parents escape up to their bedroom. The lights dim; dance music swells from the speakers. Céline keeps telling people not to eat the cupcakes yet, that the cupcakes are waiting for Hunter. I'm wearing a pink lace dress I bought especially for this occasion, but it feels wrong now—like I'm trying too hard. I keep checking my phone, but there are no texts from Hunter. *He's at the movies,* I remind myself. *His phone is off.* And as far as he knows, I'm working diligently on my midterms right now. I haven't heard from him since early this morning, but that's probably because he's trying to be a good boyfriend. He doesn't want to distract me.

Céline is racing around, playing DJ and chatting to people. It's like she's forgotten all about me. I find myself standing in the corner chatting with a group of girls including

Siggy Taylor, who arrived at the party tipsy and loud. She does a double take when she sees me. "Emma Mason! I thought you were lost in a cornfield somewhere!"

I force a laugh. I can't tell if she's making fun of me or not.

"How's art school?" asks Briana Faden, who was in AP Art with me last year.

"Great. It's really great. I'm learning a lot." I sound so boring. How can I explain to people here what life is like at Wabash Academy? I can't capture it, not truly. Not beneath the surface. Hopelessness washes over me, like I'm painting a still life that isn't working. No matter how many times I paint over the canvas with white and resketch the shapes, the perspective remains off—the separate parts refuse to come together to capture the whole. I have this same feeling when trying to describe Buenaventura to my Wabash friends.

"What's it like living in the dorms?" Siggy asks. "I'm so jealous. Do you feel like you're at college already?"

"Um, sort of. We have Dorm Mothers, though. And curfews. You're not supposed to bring guys up to your room, rules like that."

"Emma wants to bring guys up to her room!" Siggy screeches. "I'm telling Hunter on you!"

"No, no—I'm not talking about me..." I stammer, my cheeks burning.

Siggy laughs harder. "Look how red she is. I'm just messing with you, Emma. I know nothing could break up Buenaventura High's perfect couple." She smirks.

Briana launches into a story about some freshmen girls on the dance team, and then everyone is laughing about something Mr. Gallo, the science teacher, said in class last week. They try to explain it to me, and I laugh along, but I don't really get why it's so funny.

After a while, Céline shouts, "Okay, people! He'll be here in five!" The room buzzes with anticipation. Céline comes over and grabs my arm. "Here, Emma, wait in the kitchen. When Hunter comes in, everyone jumps out and says, 'Surprise!' and then you bring out a cupcake and sing 'Happy Birthday.' That way you're making a grand entrance. Okay?"

"I don't need a grand entrance. Shouldn't I jump out with the rest of you?"

"No, this is better. Believe me." Céline is radiant, glowing. She arranges a cupcake on a plate, a candle poked into the frosting. She hands me a lighter and tells me to light the candle when I hear him come in.

Suddenly, she pulls her phone out of her pocket and yelps, "They just turned onto this street! They'll be here in less than a minute! Okay, I'm gonna hide." She squeezes my arms. "You'll be great. Love you."

"Love you too." Why do I feel so nervous? This is Hunter. My boyfriend. I should be bursting with excitement to see the thrilled expression on his face.

I hear the front door open. The mumble of voices and footsteps. Then all of a sudden, a roar: "SURPRISE!" The popping of poppers.

My hand shakes as I light the candle on the cupcake.

Hunter's voice: "Whoa! Hey, everyone!"

Laughter and cheers. The swell of many voices, all talking at once.

My footsteps click on the tiled kitchen floor. My heart pounds. Cupping a hand to shield the candle's flame, I walk carefully around the corner into the living room.

Hunter is half hidden in the crowd of people. Robbie Zwick's arm is slung around his shoulders. Céline is standing right beside them, looking for me. When our eyes meet, she smiles excitedly.

But Hunter is the one I'm focused on.

And Hunter is focused on Céline.

He's gazing at her so intently, with an expression of pure awe on his face. I've never seen him look at anything that way before.

At my surprise going-away party, Hunter and Céline jumped up from behind the couch in perfect unison. A perfect team. A perfect couple. I immediately noticed the way their hands touched on the back of the couch. They were smiling so cheerfully that I couldn't do anything but smile back. After a couple seconds, Hunter hopped over the couch and wrapped me in his arms. And the pit that had yawned open in my stomach—the seed of doubt—the flicker of suspicion—I locked it away.

"To Céline!" someone shouts now.

"Oh, this was a joint effort," she says loudly, nodding in my direction. I know this is my cue to start singing, "Happy Birthday," but my throat is dry and I can't seem to form the words. I walk forward slowly, still cupping my hand around the candle, hunched over slightly like an old lady. The crowd parts for me. I feel strangely afraid to meet Hunter's eyes.

Céline starts singing, "Happy Birthday," and everyone else joins in, and then I hear Hunter say incredulously, "Emma?"

That's when I peek up at him.

He looks shocked.

"Happy birthday, dear Hunter," I sing softly. I don't even know if he can hear me.

"Oh my god, Emma. What are you doing here?"

I'm standing right in front of him now. Hunter stares at me like he can't quite process what he is seeing. Finally he reaches out and touches my hair, a huge smile spreading across his face. "Emma," he says simply.

I hold up the plate, a sweet offering. "Happy birthday," I tell him. "Make a wish."

"My wish has already come true," he says. In one swift motion, he blows out the candle, grabs me around the waist, and pulls me to him. The crowd whoops and hollers.

He kisses me in front of everyone.

We both get cupcake frosting on us.

"Céline did most of it," I tell Hunter when we emerge for air. My cheeks are warm. My mouth tastes of his peppermint gum. Just like that, all my insecurity has melted away. "It was Céline's idea to throw you a surprise party in the first place."

"But it was Emma's idea to turn in her midterms early," Céline shares. "And she's the one who flew all the way out here to surprise you. All I did was blow up some balloons." There's something in her tone that reminds me of when I lost her seashell necklace at the Spring Formal. Self-deprecating, almost martyr-ish.

"No, you did all the work," I tell her. The more she deflects praise, the more I want to push to give it. "Really, Hunter. Céline is amazing."0

"You're both amazing," Hunter says, squeezing my hand. "Thanks so much for all of this, both of you. I can't believe it."

Céline seems happy, buoyed with the success of the surprise. She flirts with Henry for most of the night, and at one point they're out in the backyard together, just the two of them. I make a mental note to ask her for all the details tomorrow.

As for Hunter, he doesn't let go of my hand the entire night.

11

AFTER

I PURPOSEFULLY ARRIVE late to Painting because Anabelle is in my class and I don't want to talk to her. I'm not ready. I managed to successfully avoid her yesterday—I spent all day hunkered down in a study room of the library—but it's only a matter of time. I still don't know what I'm going to do when I see her. Paste on a smile and cheerfully lie to her face? Or confess my traitorous drunken hookup and accept the end of our friendship?

When I enter the studio, the room is abuzz. Everyone is talking about the mysterious painting that was waiting when Mrs. Post came in this morning to set up for class. The painting is propped up against the whiteboard at the front of the room, even more stark and chilling than I remember from Saturday night. Hunter's giant, pale, underwater feet. There's a rawness in the painting that is difficult for me to look at. It's too honest. Too exposed.

"It's stunning," says Sabrina Nichols, the talented watercolor artist who sits to my right. "I've never seen that shade of blue before."

"I can't stop staring at it," chimes in Blake Nishioka, whose landscape paintings are as detailed and precise as photographs. "It's haunting. In, like, a brilliant way."

"Yeah," I say, willing my voice to sound normal. "It's, um, really good." I wonder if my cheeks are red. Is it obvious that I'm sweating? I want Hunter's feet to disappear. Better yet, *I* want to disappear.

Mrs. Post makes a big deal about the painting, too. "There is an emotional core to this painting that we should all strive for in our work," she says. "It is clear these are not just any old feet to the artist. There is a relationship here between the painter and his or her subject. That intensity thrums beneath the surface. I challenge all of you to dig deep inside yourselves and approach your own art with this same brave outpouring of self."

This is the kind of praise I've been yearning for since I came to Wabash Academy. Mrs. Post has never been very complimentary about my paintings. She is always telling me to do exactly what she is describing—to dig deep, to be brave, to unleash my emotions onto the canvas—but there's no way I can stand up and claim this painting as mine. I broke up with Hunter and he is paralyzed and now I'm turning his pain into art? What kind of heartless jerk does that?

"The only criticism I have about this painting is that the artist neglected to sign it," Mrs. Post says, staring out at us with her discerning gaze. "Is the artist here with us in the room?"

Silence.

I cross my arms, tucking my hands into my armpits so they won't rebel against me and rise of their own accord.

If I'm honest with myself, deep down, I do feel proud of my painting. It is a breakthrough for me. For my art. I can't help but feel proud. But that pride makes me sick. I shouldn't even be allowed to paint Hunter. It's wrong for me to paint him. Isn't it? Because The Accident didn't happen to me. It happened to him.

"I really wish our artist would come forward," Mrs. Post pleads. "It is important to be acknowledged for your work."

Is it my imagination, or is she looking directly at me when she says it?

I'm debating with myself about whether I should let my guard down and claim the painting, claim my pain, claim my messed-up, guilt-ridden heart—when Mrs. Post shifts her attention to the other side of the room.

Anabelle is raising her hand.

My pulse races. Does she know I painted those feet? How could she know?

"Yes, Anabelle?" Mrs. Post says, beaming. "Are you our mystery artist?"

Anabelle hesitates. I wait for her to point at me, to say, "Emma painted it! She is my best friend and I would know her style anywhere!"

Instead, she smiles and nods, her head held high. "Yes, I painted it," she says. "I guess I was so caught up in the process that I forgot to sign my name when I was done."

I watch in numb disbelief as Anabelle calmly stands from her seat, walks up to the front of the room, and leans in with a Sharpie to sign her name across the corner of my artwork. Everyone but me applauds.

AFTER CLASS, as I trudge across The Quad, I hear Anabelle shout my name. I brace myself and turn, forcing a smile even though I am seething inside.

"Emma, hey!" Anabelle exclaims, grabbing my arm. She's wearing sparkly purple eyeliner and her cheeks are rosy from the cold. "What happened on Saturday at the dance? You disappeared on me."

"I'm sorry. I started feeling sick, so I went back to the dorm."

Her eyebrows pinch in concern. "You should have texted me. I was worried about you. I came by yesterday and knocked on your door, but no one answered."

"I know. I'm sorry. I wasn't thinking." *I'm so sorry, Anabelle. You have no idea how sorry I am. But still, it doesn't give you any right—why did you lie and say that the painting was yours?*

She smiles, linking her arm through mine. "It's okay. Just don't do it again, all right?"

"All right." I remember David's whisper: *We should do this again sometime.* I wish desperately I could reach back through time and yank myself away from him. How could I have been so selfish and reckless?

The guilt is overpowering. I can't do this. I can't simply go on pretending I'm her friend when I totally betrayed her.

And yet at the same time, I'm furious with her. She betrayed me, too—although she doesn't know it was me who painted the feet. She must know the real artist will come forward eventually, right? Or maybe she assumes that if no one has claimed the painting yet, no one will. Especially not now that she has claimed it. Who would dare speak up against the fiery strength of Anabelle's convictions?

"That painting you did—it's amazing," I say, testing the waters.

Her smile lights up her face. "Mrs. Post really liked it, huh?" There is no hint of shame or apology in her voice. It's almost as if she has convinced herself that she really did paint those giant ghostly feet.

Maybe it's better this way. If people knew the painting was mine, they would obviously want to know whose feet they are. They would ask so many questions, trying to get to the root of all the haunting emotion that Mrs. Post was going on and on about. This way, I don't have to explain what inspired the painting. I don't have to give voice to my regret and shame. I don't have to tell anyone here what happened to Hunter over winter break. (*All your fault*, the voice inside me whispers. *All your fault*.) Meanwhile, Anabelle gets to claim the painting without experiencing any of the pain herself. Maybe the painting can be my penance—my gift to her.

"I've never seen you drink like that before," Anabelle says, changing the subject back to Saturday night. "No wonder you got sick! And that makeover I gave you. It was like you were a different person."

"I know. I didn't like it."

"Me neither," Anabelle says, surprising me. "I like regular Emma best."

I feel a surge of tenderness toward her—my only close friend here. What would life be like at Wabash if I weren't Anabelle's sidekick? A lot lonelier, that's for sure. A lot less glamorous and exciting.

"Hey Anabelle!" Sabrina falls into step on Anabelle's other side. "Oh my gosh, your painting. It's incredible. You should totally enter it in the spring competition."

"Really, you think so?" Anabelle unlinks her arm from mine and sweeps her curls back into a bun. "I dunno, I might wait and see how the rest of the semester goes."

"If you enter that painting, you'll totally win," Sabrina says. "It's so… mature. You know? It doesn't look like a student painted it."

"Aww, thanks Sabrina," Anabelle says. "I worked really hard on it." Her voice sounds completely genuine. How can she lie so effortlessly?

No. We can't remain friends like we were before. There's too much baggage between us now. Too many secrets and lies. David. Hunter. The painting. When I remember the calm way Anabelle raised her hand and accepted everyone's astonished praise over "her" work, I feel like a pot on the verge of boiling over. Almost like Anabelle is trying to claim Hunter too. And I realize that the anger I'm feeling is not only about Anabelle—it's aimed at Céline as well.

I can't bring myself to forgive Céline for kissing Hunter. For being her irresistible self. For letting Hunter love her all this time, when he was supposed to love me. I wish Céline had never told me that she and Hunter kissed. I wish I didn't know. Because now I can never dig up these weeds of doubt about our entire relationship that have overtaken my memories.

Is that what I'm most angry at Céline about? For telling me the truth?

"You okay, Em?" Anabelle asks, nudging me.

Anabelle, I need to tell you something.

But I can't bring myself to say it. I can't tell Anabelle the truth. She'll be devastated. And for what purpose? I can't ask for her forgiveness. How can I expect Anabelle to forgive me for what I did with David if I can't forgive Céline for kissing Hunter?

"Yeah, I'm fine," I say. "Just tired."

David promised he wouldn't tell her. So if I don't tell her, she won't ever find out.

The best thing is for me to just slip away slowly. Let a distance naturally grow between us. She'll find a new best friend. She's Anabelle, after all. She doesn't need me.

Dear Mrs. Muna,

Have you ever created a painting that you wonder, Where did that come from? And not necessarily in a good way?

How do you know what is okay—what is yours—to create art about?

Do you think it's possible to create good art that still feels safe?

I don't know if my questions are making any sense. But you were the only one I could think to reach out to. The teachers here don't really get my work. Sometimes I feel like I have no clue what I'm doing here.

Anyway, thank you for reading this.

-Emma

Tomorrow morning, a hot swell of embarrassment will flood my cheeks that I actually sent Mrs. Muna this email. But right now, it's 2:14 a.m. and I can't sleep and I don't really think about it. I just click Send.

IT IS SURPRISINGLY EASY to avoid Anabelle.

The new semester means new classes, and other than Painting, we don't have any classes together. Wabash Academy is a sprawling campus, with many different walkways and veering paths. I explore new circuitous routes, pulling my faux-fur-lined hood down near my eyes and hunkering through the cold. I look downward and wrap my scarf around my mouth. In my snow boots and poufy down jacket, I am anonymous. Just another student trudging to class.

I start going to the Dining Commons for dinner at 5:30, right when it opens, because it's mostly empty then. I sit at a table by myself, reading a book or reviewing notes from class. Then I go to the studio and paint until my fingers ache and my head whirls from paint fumes.

Eggs 'N' Toast? Anabelle texts me on Saturday morning.

Sorry, too much work, I text back, then head straight to the painting studio. When I get back to my dorm hours later, there's a take-out box waiting on my desk. I open the lid. Cold chocolate-chip pancakes and a small container of slightly congealed syrup.

Thanks, I text Anabelle. But I can't imagine sitting across a booth from her like normal, pretending that everything is the same between us.

One night, I arrive back at the dorm late. I got swept into painting and completely lost track of time. I breathe a sigh of relief when I sneak past Mrs. Jenkins' half-open door without her noticing me. The last thing I need right now is a lecture about curfew.

Nora is away at a weekend drama camp, but when I open the door to our room I can sense a presence. My heart pounds and my palms are instantly clammy.

"Hello?" I say, flicking on the light. I jump. "Shit, you scared me! What are you doing here?"

Anabelle sits cross-legged on my bed. "Hey, stranger," she says, unapologetic as always. "Just thinking. Waiting for you to get home."

"I was at the studio."

"You're always at the studio these days."

"Yeah—I mean, it's why I came to Wabash. To work on my art."

Anabelle sits quietly, hugging a pillow and picking at the hem of her jeans. The mini fridge hums.

My stomach is hollow. I've been waiting for something like this, but I've also been hoping I could evade it, slip through the days and weeks of the semester like a ghost.

"What's going on with you?" Anabelle says. "Ever since we got back from break, you've been acting different. Why are you avoiding me?"

"I'm not avoiding you," I lie. "We've got different schedules this semester. And my course load is awful. I'm already drowning in homework."

"That's crap and you know it."

"It's true! I'm super busy with school."

Anabelle rubs her eyes and blinks at me. "We're all busy, Emma. But I'm not stupid. I can tell when my best friend is acting weird. I wish you'd tell me why so we could fix this. Did something happen at the dance?"

"No, no! Of course not." Tears well up behind my eyes. *My best friend.* If Anabelle keeps pushing, I'll cave and tell her about hooking up with David. And then our friendship will most definitely be over. For good. Guilt burns in my chest. I don't know why I hooked up with the one guy who is off-limits, the one guy Anabelle has been in love with for years. In some twisted way, it was because of Hunter—our breakup, his terrible accident, the hospital visit with all the beeping and wheezing machines. But how can I explain to Anabelle what I can't even explain to myself?

"I'm not avoiding you," I repeat quietly. As if saying the words enough times will turn them into truth.

I want to ask her about my painting. Why did she say it was hers? But I have no right to be upset about her stealing my artwork—I stole David. I guess that makes us even.

Anabelle studies my face for a long moment. Then she decisively leaps off my bed, her boots hitting the floor with a *thump*. "I thought we were friends," she says with a shrug. "I guess I was wrong."

I look down at my snow boots. My throat is clogged with tears and all the words I can't bring myself to say.

Anabelle sets something down on my desk. Then she walks out of the room without a backward glance. I almost run after her, but my feet are rooted to the ground. Instead, I shut the door, feeling numb.

On my desk, on top of my Art History textbook, glints a metal key.

The spare key to my dorm room. Anabelle gave it back.

I dig my key ring out of my pocket and find the spare key to her room. The keys we copied and gave each other last semester—like friendship bracelets, only more practical.

The key ring pinches my fingers as I painstakingly wrestle off Anabelle's dorm room key. I set it on top of the spare key to my room. Then I take both keys and shove them in my bottom dresser drawer, all the way to the back, where I can almost forget they exist.

THE NEXT DAY in Painting class, Mrs. Post tells us to put away our paints and easels and take out our laptops. *Wait, what?*

"Today is the beginning of an exciting endeavor in your lives as young artists," Mrs. Post says. "We are launching an Art in the Community project here at Wabash Academy, and you are its inaugural class." She explains how we will be spending the rest of the semester coming up with an original project to engage the local community in an artistic endeavor of some sort. "I don't have to tell all of you this," she says, a sparkle in her eyes. "But I'll say it anyway: don't be afraid to be creative!"

My mind is whirling. This isn't what I signed up for. I didn't come to Wabash to engage with the outside world. I came here to paint. All I want to do is retreat to my little corner of the studio, hide behind a huge canvas, and lose myself in colors and brushstrokes.

"This is a big project—too big to do alone," Mrs. Post continues. "Besides, to paraphrase John Donne, no artist is an island. My goal with this project is not only for you to engage with the outside community, but also to collaborate with each other. So I will be putting you into pairs. Listen for your names as I call them out. You will have the rest of the class period to meet with each other and begin brainstorming!"

A paired project? Oh god, please don't make me partners with Anabelle. Please no...

It takes eons for Mrs. Post to call my name. The number of us left unpaired dwindles down and down. Anabelle's name hasn't been called yet, either.

"Emma Mason," Mrs. Post says.

I steel myself.

"And Kevin Daniels."

Relief courses through me. I wonder if Anabelle feels relieved, too. I look around the room and find Kevin, who gives me a thumbs-up. I don't know him very well, but he seems nice. He defended my painting in my very first workshop—looking back now, I can see how the painting might have been a failure, yet Kevin understood what I was trying to do. He was one of the few people who saw the potential through the imperfection.

I grab my backpack off the floor and head over to Kevin's desk.

"Hey, partner," he says, pulling over a chair so I can sit beside him. He has a genuine, effortless smile. "I'm glad we're paired up together."

I smile back. "Thanks. Me too."

Kevin doesn't look like an artist. At least, not what the stereotypes say artists should look like. He doesn't have any visible piercings or tattoos. His light-brown hair is cut short and parted on the side. He's wearing a long-sleeved T-shirt, jeans, and sensible boots. Maybe Kevin doesn't dress like a stereotypical artist because he doesn't need to. His art speaks for itself. From what I've seen of his work, he is majorly talented. He did a series of paintings of trees that were vibrantly full of life—it was as if the trees had personalities, as if they were able to speak through the canvases.

"So, Emma Mason," he says, leaning in close and dropping his voice. "There's something I need to tell you."

My heart quickens. "Um, okay. Shoot."

"We're going to be working together closely this semester, and I think we need to be transparent with each other from the get-go." He pauses, then drops his voice to a whisper. "Now, be honest with me. Promise?"

I nod, scooting even closer to hear him better.

"What toppings do you like on your pizza? Because I foresee a lot of late nights refueling with pizza, and I have strong beliefs against pineapple as a topping."

I burst out laughing. My first real laugh since The Accident.

"Well, that's unfortunate," I say, trying my best to sound serious. "Because my favorite pizza is… Hawaiian."

"No! Dagger through the heart!" Kevin leans back, holding his chest like I've literally stabbed him with a dagger. He's goofy and easy to be with and—most importantly—he doesn't know me. Joking around with him like this, I feel… normal. Like I can pretend, for the rest of class at least, that I'm the same girl I was before winter break.

Maybe this assignment will be okay after all.

12

BEFORE

IT IS HARD for me to pin down exactly what, or why, but after Hunter visits me, something changes. On the surface, everything resumes as before: our morning text messages, nightly phone calls, yearnings and plans and purple X's drawn through each day of my calendar.

But also, this: I often find myself smiling as I fit my key into my dorm-room lock, hearing Nora shout my name in greeting. After school, I explore the running trails along the river, running to the beat of my playlist rather than trying to match my body rhythms and pace with Hunter's. He is so much taller than I am—two of my strides equal one of his. He only left a week ago, but I no longer reach for his hand or instinctually look for him around every curve and building of campus.

ONE MORNING IN PAINTING CLASS, as Mrs. Post talks about our upcoming still life assignment, a girl with curly dark hair and cat-eye glasses asks to borrow a pen. I find one at the bottom of my backpack and hand it to her. A couple minutes later, the girl takes out some gum and silently offers the pack to me as if we're already friends. I take a piece even though I don't really like gum. It's a citrus flavor. Sour.

After class, we walk out together like this is something we do every week. She asks, "Wanna get coffee?"

"Sure," I say, slightly bewildered yet excited. We stroll across The Quad toward the Student Union. At the café inside, we grab a seat at a small round table with uneven legs that tilts whenever weight is put on it.

Her name is Anabelle and she lives in the other upperclassman dorm, across The Quad from my own. The café is a popular gathering spot for students, noisy with the murmur of voices and the whir of the blenders. I keep leaning across the table to hear Anabelle better, forgetting about the rickety table until it shifts sharply under the weight of my elbow, threatening to topple our drinks.

"I never thought I'd come to Wabash," she admits, stirring soymilk into her coffee. "I'm a townie—I grew up literally three miles away from here. Wabash Academy always seemed like this snooty private school, closed off from the outside world." She sighs. "I went to the public high school my freshman year. Sometimes I wish I had stayed there."

"Really? Why did you decide to come to Wabash?" I take a small sip of my coffee, willing myself not to make a face. How do people drink this stuff? I tear open another sugar packet and dump it in.

Anabelle glances out the window, then back at me. "Well, I had a sort of falling out with my friend group. I wanted a fresh start. And I've always liked poetry. It seemed like a good opportunity to focus on my creative self."

"That makes sense." I chance another sip of coffee. The sugar helps.

"Anyway, what about you?" she asks. "What brought you here from LA?"

I told Anabelle I'm from LA because nobody outside of California knows where Buenaventura is. Besides, LA sounds more glamorous, and Anabelle seems like a person who appreciates glamour.

I shrug. "I love painting, and this will give me the best shot at getting into an art program in college. Plus, I wanted to live somewhere new."

Anabelle points her finger at me. "I call bullshit. You grew up in LA! Why would you want to move to the middle of these boring-ass cornfields?" She gestures wildly with her hands when she talks, flinging her coffee cup this way and that. I sense people looking at us.

My cheeks grow hot. I'm not even lying, but it feels like I am. "To be honest," I say, "I wanted a break from California. To experience the seasons. I thought it would be like a sitcom—pep rallies and hayrides and, I don't know, friendly people? Everyone always says that people are friendlier in the Midwest."

Anabelle laughs. "Really?"

"Yeah," I say, flustered. "But I mean—I don't know, it's been a lot harder to settle in than I expected. I miss home more than I thought I would."

Anabelle reaches over and touches my hand. "This is about a guy," she says, her eyes suddenly serious. "Am I right?"

"Well, yeah, I have a boyfriend back home. Hunter."

Anabelle nods, her eyebrows cinched in concern, looking at me straight on. It is the same way Mom and Céline look at me. When I talk to someone, my eyes usually dart around, to their forehead, chin, cheeks, the tabletop, a picture across the room. Now, my fingers trace the ridges in the sleeve around my coffee cup. I force myself to meet Anabelle's eyes.

"I don't know if I love him anymore."

I'm shocked to hear the words leave my lips, but Anabelle nods along, *Yes, yes*, her eyes magnified behind her glasses, filled with interest and empathy. I've only just met her, but somehow she feels like a safe refuge for my innermost thoughts. I find myself telling her all about my history with Hunter, confessing my doubts, how we almost broke up twice, how I've been trying to convince myself that everything is fine between us. Misgivings about our relationship only make me want to cling tighter, worrying that Hunter wants to be with someone else. I am terrified to lose him even though I'm not sure I love him anymore. Sometimes he makes me feel claustrophobic.

"You know what I think?" Anabelle says. "Sometimes there isn't any right decision. If you're meant to stay together, you will. And if you're meant to break up, you'll know."

"Really?" I ask, not even caring that I sound like a child yearning for answers. Her attentive listening, without seeming to judge me or Hunter at all, makes me feel like I've been truly *seen* for the first time since I've come to Wabash.

"Of course. I can tell you've got a great intuition, Emma. Plus, give yourself a break. Love is complicated. Especially when you have a lot of history." She squeezes my hand. "You know what? I'm going to a poetry reading tonight. You should come."

"Okay," I say, polishing off the rest of my coffee. I haven't clicked like this with anyone I've met at Wabash yet.

Anabelle points across the table at me. "I bet he said 'I love you,' first. Am I right?"

"Yeah."

"Did you say it back right away?"

"Well, yeah. I mean, how could I not?"

"You've got to be true to yourself, always. Don't just say what someone wants to hear. Never tell a guy you love him when you're not sure, because then your whole relationship becomes a lie."

Before I can respond, Anabelle leaps up out of her chair. "David!" she shrieks, waving to a well-built guy in a polo shirt and jeans. "David!"

People look our way, but this time I'm not embarrassed. *Let them look.* I feel proud to be friends with someone as vibrant and self-assured as Anabelle, filled with her own strong opinions, her own inner light.

Anabelle winks at me. "Be right back." I watch her saunter up to David and throw her arms around him in a hug. David's smile is enormous.

I think of Hunter and am flooded with guilt. I remember the joy that filled my heart when he first told me, *I love you Pea.* Actually, he texted it first, and then he came right over. When he got to my house, he parked crookedly at the curb and ran up the driveway to where I was waiting for him on the front steps. His eyes were so focused. So certain. "I love you, Pea." The reason I said it back right away was because I meant it.

Do I still love Hunter? Do I want to break up? I don't know. I'm too afraid to delve further into those questions. My life has changed so much in the past few weeks that I can't bear any more changes. I am a boat sailing away from the harbor; Hunter is the compass back to my old life. I can't throw him overboard.

SLOWLY, MY DAILY SCHEDULE MELDS with Anabelle's. We meet in the library and study together. We grab coffee after class. We go to the gym and run on the elliptical machines side by side. We make each other spare keys to our dorm rooms. Sometimes I come home from class and there is Anabelle, sitting in my desk chair and writing in her journal. Sometimes I sleep over in Anabelle's room because her roommate is rarely there. On these nights, I don't call Hunter. The next morning, I tell him I'm sorry, I fell asleep at my desk.

Both Hunter and I are busy with schoolwork, so we talk less often. I forget to put the cap on the purple marker and it dries up, so I throw it out. I stop marking a countdown of Xs on my calendar.

I am independent, autonomous. The homesickness in my throat quietly erodes until one day I notice myself swallowing easily. I am on my own in a vast open place, hours away from the tidal pull of any ocean—and I am happy.

Céline and Hunter and Buenaventura High seem so far away, they could be another universe. Here in this universe, I have Anabelle. And I am so grateful to have her. It is like she reached out and chose me—me, out of the hundreds of students swarming campus—to be her best friend. She must see a glint of the things in me that I see in her. Vibrancy, self-assurance, strength. Inner light.

I am giddy with the possibilities of the person I might become.

IN PAINTING CLASS, Mrs. Post announces that we'll be doing our first round of workshop. "*Workshop* is a fancy term that basically means giving feedback on each other's work," she says. "The only way we can grow as artists is to hear constructive criticism from our peers. No artist exists in a bubble."

We spend twenty minutes at the beginning of each class discussing two or three paintings in progress. The artist isn't allowed to comment or explain their painting. "The work must speak for itself," Mrs. Post says. "When your painting is hanging in a gallery, you aren't there whispering explanations into the viewer's ear, right? This is your chance to hear what others' impressions and thoughts are about your work, based solely on the work itself. And who knows? You might be surprised what new ideas come forth through this process!"

Now every day at the beginning of class, my stomach is a pit of roiling snakes. Finally—all too soon—Mrs. Post calls my name as one of the workshopped artists.

For my still life painting, I zoomed in on single ear of husked corn. I painted the corn huge, so it spills off the edges of the canvas. Instead of yellow, I used varying shades of purple for the kernels. Other than that, the still life is hyper-realistic. But I was interested to see what the viewer's experience of corn would be if the color is unexpected. I'm planning to do a whole series like this: vibrant orange apples; blue bananas; a bowl of hot pink lemons.

Mrs. Post asks everyone to begin with aspects they like about my painting. People comment on the composition, the way I use negative space and shape, the precision of my shading. But soon, the discussion veers into criticism.

"I don't really get the purple?" says Sabrina Nichols, scrunching up her nose. "Why purple? What are we supposed to read into this color choice?"

"It sort of feels like the artist is trying too hard to be edgy," adds Blake Nishioka. "Like she is using color to get attention, instead of letting her painting skills speak for themselves."

Even Anabelle chimes in. "I agree that the purple is a little distracting. Emma obviously has talent—why not depict the corn realistically? It's like my brain can't even compute that the image is corn because the color is so distant from reality."

"But that's exactly the point," a strong voice interjects from the other side of the room. I look over with a surge of hope. Maybe *somebody* understands what I was trying to do!

"Sorry, Mrs. Post." Kevin Daniels raises his hand. We are supposed to wait for Mrs. Post to call on us, so the discussion doesn't descend into chaotic arguing.

"Yes, Kevin. Go ahead," Mrs. Post says with a smile.

"I'm passionate about this," he says, gesturing earnestly with his hands. "Yes, if Emma had painted the corn yellow, it would have been a very good painting. Her skills are strong and the corn would have looked so realistic, it would have seemed like you could lean in and take a bite out of it. But, to me, it would have been a sort of..." He smiles apologetically at me. "A sort of, forgettable painting, you know? The type of painting you glance at for a couple moments and then continue on your merry way."

Mrs. Post nods. I doodle in the margins of my notebook. I can't even bear to look at my painting anymore. I can't look at anyone in the room. This workshop experience is awkward and uncomfortable, like eavesdropping on other people gossiping about you.

"But by painting the corn purple," Kevin continues, "the piece all of a sudden becomes captivating. It grabs your attention and holds your memory. The color disassociates you from the subject of the painting in a really cool way. I mean, look at us—we're spending all this time debating about *an ear of corn!*"

He laughs, and some other people join in. The energy in the room has shifted and I can exhale a little.

"I guess what I'm trying to say is…" Kevin runs a hand through his hair. "I feel like the artist—like Emma—took a risk here. And I would hate for our advice to her to be *play smaller*. No. I think she should take this crazy color impulse and run with it!"

I look up from my doodling long enough to catch his eye and smile. *Thank you.*

"Thank you, Kevin," Mrs. Post says. "I have to say I agree. With all of you. I agree with Kevin that Emma has taken a daring risk here, and I love it." She pushes her bangs to the side of her face and stares at me with her piercing, serious eyes. "Emma, please—continue to do this in your work. Continue to mine those parts of your creativity that are unique and arresting. At the same time, I can also understand some of the confusion people have about your piece. I think this stems from a lack of identity here. Why an ear of corn? What does this mean to you as an artist? I feel we are only getting access to the surface of you. There is no emotion on the canvas—you rely on your skill and talent to carry the load. I know you can dig deeper. Be brave, Emma. Take the risk of letting your artistic self be your authentic self."

I nod, on the verge of tears. Even though I know she is not saying that I am a horrible painter, that I totally failed, that my painting sucks—it *feels* like that is what she is saying. And I have no idea how to do what she is asking me to do. I thought that I did put emotion into my work. I mean, I tried to paint the best ear of corn I could. I put a ton of effort into getting the shading and shadowing just right. I care a lot about my art. Doesn't that count for something?

After class, I tell Anabelle I have a headache and need to skip out on our coffee date.

"You're not mad at me, are you?" she says. "You know it was just workshop. It doesn't really mean anything."

"It means something to me," I murmur.

"Oh, Emma. Don't worry about it. Workshop is just a bunch of people pretending they're art critics. You don't really say what you think about a piece. You follow where the discussion leads and make up shit as you go." She throws an arm around my shoulder and kisses my cheek. "You know I love your purple corn, *dah*-ling. It's brilliant."

"Then why didn't you say so in class?"

"Because that's not the way the discussion was headed. It's okay, Emma—when my piece comes up for workshop, you can rip it to shreds. I won't care."

But I don't want to rip it to shreds. "I like your artwork, Anabelle."

"And I like your work, Em. You're an amazing artist!" She stops in her tracks. Her arm is still around my shoulders, so I have to stop walking, too.

"Fine," she says. "I promise, next time you are work-shopped, I will stick up for you. You're probably right. It's what friends do for each other."

"I didn't say that. You don't have to stick up for me. I want you to be honest."

"I will be honest. For you—not for anyone else." She winks. "Okay? Are we good? Do you want me to bring a latte to your room?"

"No, it's okay. We're good." I smile, forgiving her even though I still feel a lingering annoyance. It's hard to stay up-set at Anabelle for long. She's like her own weather system, constantly changing, constantly moving on to something else. I've heard people described as *a force of nature*—I never understood what that meant until I met Anabelle. To stay angry at her would be like staying angry at the wind or the rain. Pointless.

Plus, it's obvious she didn't mean to hurt my feelings. And she's my only real friend here. If I get in a fight with her, I'll have no one. I need her more than she needs me. I can't afford to lose her.

Back at the dorm, I'm relieved that Nora isn't in our room. I shut the door behind me and dial Hunter's number. If I'm lucky, I'll catch him during his lunch period.

He picks up on the second ring. "Hey Pea, what's up?" His voice is so warm and familiar. I ache to be there with him. I can picture it so clearly in my mind, the way it was last year. Sitting on the grass in the sunny quad with our circle of friends. Sprawled out next to Hunter, our hips touching. His hand on my knee.

"Pea, you there? Is everything okay?"

When I manage to get the words out, tears leak out too. "I had my first workshop today." My voice sounds strained and sniffly.

"I'm guessing it didn't go that great?" he asks gently.

"It was horrible. I don't know what I'm doing here. Maybe I was stupid to come. I don't know if I have what it takes—if I'm good enough—"

"Emma." Hunter's voice is serious. "Don't let anyone make you doubt yourself. You deserve to be there. You're more of an artist than anyone I've ever met. You have to keep painting. It's what you were born to do." I can tell from his tone that he means it. He's not just saying this to make me feel better.

"What about when we went to Chicago?" I ask. "And we saw that chalk artist? And you said—"

"I remember what I said," Hunter interjects. "And I was being an idiot. I was jealous of your art—of your talent. I felt like it took you away from me. But that was the stupid, selfish part of me talking. Because you wouldn't be *you* without your art, Pea. And the world would be a worse place if you stopped painting. So don't. Don't ever stop. Okay?"

"Okay," I manage to choke out. "Thank you."

"You don't need to thank me. I'm just stating the truth."

These are the exact same words he said on our first date, at the giraffe exhibit, when he called me dazzling. I'm sobbing now, and it's not about the workshop any longer. I'm sobbing because I miss Hunter so much I can barely breathe. I feel guiltier than ever that I said those things to Anabelle. How could I ever have doubts about our relationship? He is the one for me. He understands me. He supports me. He loves me. And I love him. I really, truly do.

"I'm sorry," I say when my tears finally slow.

"What are you sorry for? You have nothing to be sorry for."

A moment later, across the phone connection I hear the bell ring. Lunch at Buenaventura High is over, but Hunter stays on with me for a few more minutes, until I force him to hang up. "You'll be late to class! Gallo gives detentions if you're late!"

"Okay, okay. I'm on my way. Call me later?"

I tell him yes, of course I will. I miss him so much. I can't wait to see him when I come home for Thanksgiving.

"Me too, Em," he says. "I'm counting down the days."

13

AFTER

MRS. MUNA DOESN'T REPLY to my email. I wonder if she regrets nominating me for the scholarship.

It's another sleepless night, but I force myself to stay away from my phone. No sending any emails or texts that I'll be embarrassed about tomorrow.

The thing is, I can't stop imagining Céline and Hunter, together. I picture him brushing her hair away from her face and leaning in to kiss her. I imagine him laughing, telling her, "I never really loved Emma. I always loved you." I remember when we visited Hunter in the hospital, the way Céline leaned in and whispered in his ear for a long time. What did she say?

Céline no longer texts me updates on Hunter's progress. We haven't spoken since our terrible fight. I miss her. I have dreams where I'm wandering through a maze, looking for her. I always wake up before we find each other.

The guilt bares its teeth, digs into my ribs. Memories sneak their way into my thoughts: camping with Céline's family at Lake Tahoe every summer; the hundreds of sleepovers we had at each other's houses, falling asleep turned toward each other, knees almost touching; the first time Hunter kissed me, his mouth tasting of chlorine; the vanilla smell of his mom's car that he borrowed for dates; the giddy Starbucks session I had with Céline after the Spring Formal, recounting every detail, sipping our chai lattes and feeling impossibly grown-up. The swishing fronds of the palm trees and the lapping of the water in my ears as I floated beside Hunter during a pool workout. Céline's arms clenched around me in a hug: the cool metal of her bracelets on my bare arms, the bony strength in her shoulders. The going-away party they planned together for me, yelling "SURPRISE!" in perfect unison, their faces earnest and glowing.

Had a part of me suspected, even then, that there was something between them?

I don't know. I can no longer pinpoint what was simmering on a low burn in the back of my mind for a long while, and what was merely anger, grief, a lashing out at whomever was nearest.

It doesn't matter. I lost them both.

I wind up staying awake the entire night. The next morning, a Saturday, I lace up my sneakers and run and run and run. I run until my legs quiver and my whole body is chilled with sweat.

Morning frost glitters on the grass. A Midwestern winter no longer seems magical. No, winter is long and bleak and gray. I do not build snowpeople or make snow angels or daydream of snowball fights. Snow is merely cold. Winter is something to hunker down and get through.

My long, slow walk back to the dorm takes me downtown, as if my feet lead me here by muscle memory. Eggs 'N' Toast. Chocolate chip pancakes sound heavenly right now. I step inside, pausing in the entryway to stomp mud off my shoes. When I look up, I freeze. Across the room, at a table by the window, sit Anabelle and David.

Anabelle's curly brown hair shines in the morning sunlight. She laughs at something David says, touching his arm, leaning so close that her forehead almost rests on his shoulder. She is radiant. They both are.

The knot that has wound itself tighter and tighter in my gut cinches closed. I turn and flee.

The decisions I made in that brief fragment of time during winter break—breaking up with Hunter, suggesting we all go skinny-dipping—were the first rumblings of an earthquake. Without warning, the destruction expanded outward until the landscape of my life was irrevocably changed.

And I am helpless to get it back to the way it was.

I GRAB FOOD at the Dining Commons and head back to the dorm, where I shower and change into a paint-splattered T-shirt. Nora should be gone most of the day at play rehearsal. I have the room to myself. I put down newspaper on the carpet, set up my portable easel, and drag my half-finished painting of Hunter's left leg out from underneath my bed. If I get to work, I can maybe finish it today.

Ever since that first painting I did of Hunter's feet, I've become obsessed. I've suddenly gained access to a part of myself I never knew existed. When I'm painting now, I don't agonize over colors or shadows or textures. I don't sketch, erase, re-sketch, re-erase, in an endless loop. I simply dip my brush into the paint and let my thoughts fall away, watching my arm and hand move across the canvas as if they belong to someone else.

At the same time, my emotions are heightened. When I paint, all my anger and sadness and regret, all the pain I'm continually trying to tamp down, rises up within my veins and explodes across the canvas in a flurry of brushstrokes. Completing a painting session is like waking up from a dream—or maybe from a nightmare. I am exhausted and disoriented, and sometimes my right hand is shaking. But there's a strange exhilaration, too.

That first painting I did of Hunter's feet, the one I left on the easel the night of the back-to-school dance, remains on display in the painting studio with Anabelle's signature scrawled across the bottom right corner. Even when I try not to look at it, my eye is drawn to it like a beacon. The studio isn't my safe space anymore. So I've taken to holing up and painting in my room when I know Nora will be gone for a while.

I didn't intend to do more paintings of Hunter's feet and legs, but the images keep flowing out of me, unstoppable. One painting turned into two, into three, and now it has become a whole series—what I think of as "The Hunter Series." I haven't shown these paintings to anyone. In class, I paint quiet pastoral scenes and intricate, layered abstracts. Mrs. Post will pause beside my easel, nod her head, pat my shoulder, compliment my technique. But I never hear genuine excitement in her voice when she talks about my artwork. Her eyes don't light up like they did when she looked at that first painting I did of Hunter's feet.

I save my authentic painting sessions for my bedroom. After the canvases dry, I stack them under my bed. Hunter's feet, hips, thighs, calves. His muscles and tendons and bones. They pile up beneath my mattress like a graveyard.

I don't know how much time has passed when I become dimly aware of a knocking sound. I am coming up for air after being underwater—the edges of the world are blurred. It takes me a moment to realize that the knocking is someone at my door.

I consider just ignoring it. But then I think, *Anabelle*. And even though it's stupid—even though it is surely not Anabelle—after I have that thought, I can't *not* answer the door.

I set my paintbrush down, undo the lock, and yank open the door.

"Hey," David says.

He's wearing a collared shirt and jeans and his hair is just the right amount of mussed. Objectively, I know he is handsome. He is very handsome. But he doesn't seem handsome to me anymore.

"What are you doing here?" I ask. My voice sounds accusatory.

David shrugs. "I wanted to see you." His eyes survey my body and one side of his mouth lifts in a smirk.

I look down at my pajama bottoms—old, faded, baggy from years of wearing and washing—and my gray T-shirt smeared with dried paint, an XL size that I won in a raffle at a road race with Hunter, RAY'S RUNNING PLUS emblazoned on the front in neon green. My hair is tied up in a messy ponytail. David probably thinks I look like a total mess. Who cares. I am a mess.

"How did you even get in here?" I say. "You're not supposed to be in the girls dorm."

"Your Dorm Mother let me come up. I told her I was your partner for the Community Art Project."

"But you're not my partner. Kevin is."

"She doesn't know that." Again, that grin. The grin I used to think was so charming.

I cross my arms, blocking the doorway. "She will soon. Kevin is coming over this weekend to work on our project."

David lifts an eyebrow. "Kevin, huh? Should I be jealous?"

You have no right to be jealous. But I don't say it. David is only trying to push my buttons. "I barely know him—we're just partners for this project. But you can't go around lying to Mrs. Jenkins. You're going to get me in trouble."

I'm not thinking about the wet canvas behind me until David says, "Whoa." I turn, and I see what he sees: my painting of Hunter's left leg, about three-quarters of the way finished. The leg is enormous, filling the canvas, the muscles straining. Color bursts from the canvas, loud shades of red and purple. It's a pulsating wound, a screaming bruise. At the very top the leg is cut off, like a mannequin limb.

"That's a painting I'm working on," I say, trying to sound casual. "It's part of a series I'm doing. Paintings of legs and feet."

"Legs and feet? Do you have a fetish or something?" David laughs. He's trying to make a joke out of this. A joke out of my paintings. My cheeks flush.

"It's not funny, David. It's art."

"Sorry, sorry. I was just kidding."

I can't believe I ever let him kiss me. I think back to what Hunter said about my art—*You have to keep painting. It's what you were born to do*—and I want to cry.

It's not that I regret breaking up with Hunter, or that I want to get back together. But I feel terrible that he ever felt insecure about David. That I ever let David come between us.

I make my tone hard. "You should leave."

"Jeez, Emma, you don't have to be so sensitive. I told you, I was kidding. Your paintings are good, okay?"

"It's not about the paintings. You shouldn't be here, peri-od. Aren't you with Anabelle now?"

David smirks. "Who told you that?"

"I saw you this morning, at Eggs 'N' Toast. You two looked like a cou0ple." Now I'm the one who sounds jealous.

David leans against the door frame. "I mean, Anabelle's great, we're friends and everything—but we're not together." He reaches out and touches my hair. "You don't have to wor-ry. I didn't tell her anything."

I step away from him. "*Never* tell her, okay? I'm serious. It's our secret. It was a mistake."

"Are you sure you don't want to make that mistake again?" The vulnerability in his eyes catches me off guard.

My voice softens. "I don't think it would be a good idea."

David straightens up, his face shielded again. "Okay. I get it. I'm not going to keep trying to convince you. See you around, Emma."

After David leaves, I can't get into painting the way I did before. I stand there, poised with my paintbrush, but instead of feeling detached from myself, I am hyper aware of my own body. My arm, my hand, my fingers. My body and its traitor-ous desires. My body, betraying Anabelle like it was nothing.

When I look at Hunter's three-quarters-finished left leg, all I feel is shame. My paintings are too intense, too painful, too much. Nobody else will understand them.

Best to keep my real artwork in the graveyard under my bed, where it belongs.

———

I SHOVE EVERYTHING AWAY, back under my bed, not even caring if the wet paint smears. I need to escape this dorm. I need to escape myself. I grab my purse and barrel out of my room, storming down the hallway, not even sure where I am headed.

"Emma?" Mrs. Jenkins pokes her head out of her room at the end of the hall. "Are you okay?"

Reluctantly, I pause beside her door. "Oh, yeah, I'm fine." My knee jiggles with pent-up energy. "Just, you know—schoolwork can be stressful."

Mrs. Jenkins holds up her hand. "Wait here a moment." She disappears inside her room.

I bite my fingernail, wondering for the hundredth time what it would be like to unburden myself to Mrs. Jenkins. She has kind eyes and a gentle aura, and seems like a good listener. But I couldn't tell her everything—most certainly not about hooking up with David—and besides, I wouldn't know where to begin.

"Here you go, sweetie." Mrs. Jenkins returns, placing a box into my hands. I look down, confused. It's a tea box. Chamomile.

"Your mother gave this to me before she left for home," Mrs. Jenkins says. "She asked me to surprise you with it when I could tell you were having a rough day. Oh, and there's this too." She slides a white envelope on top of the tea box. At the sight of my name in my mom's looping handwriting, tears spring to my eyes. I blink them away.

"Thank you." My voice wobbles.

"I hope this was the right time to give it to you."

"It's the perfect time. I needed this today."

Mrs. Jenkins pats my shoulder. "I'm here if you want to talk. Try not to stress too much. This too shall pass."

This too shall pass. It's exactly the kind of thing my mom would say. The kind of thing I used to believe was true, before The Accident. But there are some things that never pass. Some things that are never made right.

I can't tell my messy, complicated truth to Mrs. Jenkins.

"Thank you," I say again, giving her a little wave goodbye. But instead of heading back down the hall to my room, I continue out the door, tea box and card in hand.

When I get to my car, I rip open the envelope. Inside there's a card with a silly drawing of two cats playing checkers and the words, *King me!* Mom has crossed it out and written: *Queen me!* What we used to say when I was a kid and she taught me to play checkers.

I open the card. Out falls a gift certificate to Sweet Treat Cupcakes.

EMMA–

I WISH I WERE THERE RIGHT NOW TO MAKE YOU A CUP OF TEA AND SURPRISE YOU WITH A CHOCOLATE CUPCAKE, BECAUSE FROSTING AND SPRINKLES MAKE EVERYTHING BETTER. ☺ BUT EVEN WHEN I'M NOT PHYSICALLY WITH YOU, I'M THERE IN SPIRIT. I LOVE YOU. CALL ME ANYTIME, OKAY?

XOXO, MOM

I try calling, but her phone rings and rings—likely on silent. So I drive. I grip the steering wheel tightly as I look out the windshield at the shadows of the buildings, the winter tree branches nearly stripped bare of leaves. Sweet Treat Cupcakes is in the cute downtown district, right across the street from the hotel where Mom stayed. I circle the block, pull up to the curb, turn off the headlights. Mom and I discovered Sweet Treat Cupcakes, and then I took Hunter here during his visit last semester. I haven't been back since.

I get out of the car and beep the doors locked. The bakery sign blinks CLOSED, but the lights are still on inside. I stand in front of the lit window, shivering in my thin coat. My fingers are numb.

A bell jingles as the bakery door opens. I look up into the face of a young woman, her eyes filled with concern. "Excuse me, are you okay?"

"Oh, yeah, thanks—I'm fine." I wipe my nose with the back of my hand.

"Here, why don't you come inside?"

I allow myself to be ushered into the warmth and light of the bakery, which smells like our kitchen during the holidays, when Mom and I bake pies. The woman pulls out a chair for me to sit down. Then she disappears into the back. The bakery is the same as I remember—same polka-dot wallpaper, same display of hand-sewn potholders and aprons for sale, same cheerful yellow tablecloths. I wipe under my eyes with the pads of my fingers and dig through my purse for a tissue. I blow my nose. Of course the bakery looks the same—it hasn't been that long since I last came here with Hunter.

The young woman returns. "Something to make you feel better," she says, setting down a cupcake, napkin, and fork onto the table. The plate is bright pink and the cupcake wrapper is polka-dotted. "It's our bestseller, Chocolate Heaven."

"Thank you," I say. "How did you know chocolate's my favorite?"

"A wild guess." She winks. "I have a sixth sense for these things."

"Um, I have a gift certificate." I open my purse, dig around for the card.

"That's okay." She waves me off. "This one's on the house. You can use the certificate the next time you come in."

"Wow, that's really nice of you. This looks delicious."

The young woman smiles and returns to the display case, which she wipes down with a paper towel. I bite into the cupcake. The thick frosting makes my teeth ache.

When I finish, I crumple up the polka-dot wrapper and set it in the center of the pink plate, alongside the frosting-crusted fork. When I came here with Hunter, I chose a red velvet cupcake, and crumbs got lodged underneath my fingernails. Hunter joked that it looked like blood. Before we left the bakery I escaped to the bathroom—right there, tucked away in the far corner—and washed my hands, but it was no use. My fingertips remained red-tinged for the rest of the evening. Now, I think of Hunter's red hair fanning out in the water of Robbie Zwick's pool—the closest thing there was to blood.

I can't remember what flavor cupcake Hunter got that day. Peanut butter? Strawberry?

My stomach churns with sweet frosting and chocolate.

"If you want to talk about it," the woman says, her attention still focused on wiping down the display case, "I am happy to listen. I know from personal experience that talking to the people you love can be hard. Sometimes it helps to talk about your problems to a total stranger."

"Oh… um, thanks. I don't know. I mean… I don't really know where to begin."

"It's okay if you're not ready," she says. "I understand. When my father died, it was months before I wanted to talk about him. It was like I wanted to hoard all my memories of him, like I was afraid that talking about him would lessen him somehow. It's so hard to capture people in words, you know?"

"Yeah, it is," I agree. "I'm not good with words. That's why I paint."

"You're an artist?" She visibly brightens. "My father was an artist too! A painter! He was going to paint a mural for me on that wall there." She gestures toward the blank white wall behind me. "But the cancer came back before he could get started."

My throat tightens. "I'm so sorry."

"In May it will be a year since he passed, and I still haven't managed to do anything with that wall. It makes me sad to look at it, to be honest."

"What was he going to paint a mural of?"

"I have no idea! I'm clueless about painting. My art form is baking."

"Well, you're an amazing baker. That cupcake was out of this world. Thank you."

"It was my pleasure. I'm glad you enjoyed it." She ducks down behind the case again.

I stealthily pull out my wallet, wedge a five-dollar bill half under my plate, and stand up to leave. When I open the door, the bell jingles.

"My name is Dana," she calls after me. "It was nice to meet you. Come back anytime."

"I'm Emma. And thanks—I will."

Driving home, I can't stop thinking about our conversation. Even if I wanted to talk about my problems, where would I begin? What would I say to Dana? Would I confess that sometimes, I worry that I'll never again be truly happy because of my role in Hunter's accident? Because of me, a life was ruined, so it's only fair that my life be ruined, too. *I broke up with my boyfriend. I didn't even talk to him at the party. I was the one who jumped into the pool first. The Accident was my fault. And now he's paralyzed. And I'm...* What am I, exactly? I don't know. Damaged. Broken. Frozen.

Back in my dorm room, collapsing into bed, I close my eyes and wonder for the millionth time what Hunter thought when his face hit the water—that last thought before his spine cracked and everything went black.

14

BEFORE

IN THE WEEKS leading up to Hunter's visit, he and I talk of little else. Every morning, I use a thick purple marker to draw a big X through another day on my Yosemite wall calendar. The days march out across the calendar like a row of ducks in a carnival game; I want to use an air rifle to shoot down every one, *pop pop pop*. The waiting is tortuous. Before I leave for my morning class, I always send Hunter a quick text: *10 days... 9 days... 8 days ...*

And every night, Hunter texts his version of our countdown: *Only 7 more sleeps... 6 more sleeps... 5 more sleeps ...*

When we talk on the phone, I run through the list of all the things I'm excited to do with him, all the places I want to take him: the Indianapolis Zoo (even though I don't really like zoos) where we can reenact our first date; the Art Institute of Chicago and Millennium Park; Golden Spoon, the ice cream place I found near campus, that has the best Rocky Road I've ever tasted. Rocky Road is Hunter's favorite and he slowly convinced me of its merits over a summer of sharing double-scoop sundaes from The Coastal Cone.

Then one day, I wake up and there are no more Xs to draw on my calendar.

I make my bed, tidy up my stacks of books and art supplies. Our mini fridge is stocked with Hunter's favorite flavor of Gatorade that I've been steadily swiping from the Dining Commons, hiding small bottles under my sweatshirt because students aren't supposed to take food or drinks out with us. I do my hair and carefully apply makeup. I'm wearing a thin flowered sundress I borrowed from Nora. I spritz on the perfume Hunter gave me for my birthday.

It's only been twenty-seven days since we last saw each other, but my life is completely new. Have I changed? I study my eyes in the mirror, the same eyes I've stared into countless times in countless mirrors. Will Hunter think I look different? Will Hunter look different?

As soon as my final class lets out, I speed-walk across campus to the parking lot. At the airport, I park carefully and hurry to the arrivals gate. Even though it's still an hour before Hunter's flight is scheduled to get in, I can't seem to slow down my excited pace.

I brought along my art history textbook, planning to read the chapter we've been assigned for this weekend. I sit on a bench within clear view of the arrivals gate and dutifully open the book. I read three pages without any comprehension whatsoever, turn back to the beginning of the chapter, and read them again with no greater success.

I close the book.

Twelve minutes have passed.

I get up, go to the restroom even though I don't really have to go. I wash and dry my hands, check my makeup. I buy a soft pretzel and nibble off the salt.

Twenty-one minutes have passed.

I open my book again, skip forward a few pages, and try again.

Screw it. I dig around in my purse for a pen, and fill the margins of page 26 with inky blue doodles. A looping curlicue that spirals into an ocean wave. A voluptuous flower dotted with stars. A mosaic of heart shapes, shaded with cross-hatched lines. In this way, the minutes creak along.

And then, suddenly, there he is—familiar lopsided smile, familiar green eyes, familiar arms wrapped around me in a hug. A living, breathing relic of home, here in this new place. I'm surprised to find myself sobbing, snot trailing onto Hunter's gray sweatshirt.

"Hey, you," Hunter says, stroking my hair. "It's okay. It's okay."

"I'm just so happy to see you!" I choke out, struggling to regain my breath. I rummage in my purse and find a rumpled paper napkin to blow my nose. When I look up at Hunter, the tears threaten to well up again. Seeing him is like traveling back in time, back to my old life in Buenaventura that for the past month has felt unreachably far away. Right now, the two of us could be standing outside Mr. Gallo's classroom, squeezing out the last thirty seconds of lunch before the bell rings. We could be waiting in line to order fish tacos at Snapper Jack's, our favorite Mexican restaurant. We could be sprawled across the couch in my living room, watching a vampire movie on Netflix, my mom poking her head in to ask if we want popcorn.

I blow my nose again. Homesickness lodges in my throat. These are the kind of stubborn tears that remain no matter how many times I try to swallow them away. Like when you're bodysurfing and accidentally swallow a mouthful of ocean water, and it takes forever to get rid of the saltwater taste.

I forgot how large Hunter's hands are. He reaches for my hand and it disappears inside his. It's comforting.

"So," I say after we retrieve Hunter's duffel from baggage claim and make our way across the parking garage; after I beep open the locks and Hunter throws his duffel into the trunk; after I settle into the driver's seat and Hunter slides into the passenger seat, and the confined space between us makes me suddenly nervous, shy. "What should we do first?"

"I don't know. What do you want to do?" His smile reminds me of some sly animal in a children's book, a fox or maybe a wolf. His fingers graze the back of my neck, trailing goosebumps.

I shiver. In the pit of my stomach is a delicious-sick feeling I nearly forgot existed.

We spend the entire weekend reveling in being together. We drive around town. We eat Ethiopian food and gourmet cupcakes. We walk along the river and sit on the grass underneath the sycamore trees. Families and couples trundle by in paddleboats, their wakes rippling across the glassy water. The leaves on the trees are just starting to change color, bursting with flaming branches of red and orange and gold into the blue bowl of the sky.

On Sunday, we make the two-hour journey up to Chicago. I'm driving, Hunter is in the passenger seat scrolling through my phone for "good music"—"All my music is good!" I tell him, but he playfully rolls his eyes—when all out of nowhere the car gets wobbly. At sixty-five miles per hour, it feels like I'm trying to steer a boat through choppy water.

"Something's wrong!" I say. "Hunter, what's going on?"

"Pull over!" he says urgently.

I manage to maneuver the car to the shoulder of the freeway. I turn off the engine. Hunter finds the hazard lights. My heart is racing and I'm almost hyperventilating. Hunter gets out to take a look.

Seconds later he gives me the report: "Flat tire. Back right one."

I let out a long breath. "Okay. Not the end of the world. Do you know how to change a flat?"

"Not really," Hunter says. He seems embarrassed. "I could try, but…"

"I don't either." Last year, Céline asked me to take a "life skills workshop" with her at the community center, but I begged out because I had plans with Hunter. Now, I'm kicking myself. I'm sure they would have taught us how to change a flat tire. All I can do is sit here uselessly and call my parents for help.

"It's okay, Em," Dad says. "Things like this are why we signed up for that roadside assistance plan. I'm just glad you two are safe." He says to hang tight, a tow truck should arrive before too long.

With the sun beating down, it soon becomes ridiculously hot in the car, so Hunter and I wait outside on the pavement. The grass at the side of the road is shriveled and brown. There aren't any trees to provide even a hint of shade.

"Man, it's crazy hot out here," Hunter says. I expect him to follow up with some comment about *me* being crazy hot— usually he does—but he falls silent.

"I know it is. I'm sorry." Dad said the flat tire was not my fault, that it was simply bad luck—but the thing is, it *feels* like my fault. I can't help but think that if Hunter had been the one driving, the flat tire never would have happened. He would have avoided the pothole or nail or whatever I drove over that caused the damage, and we'd be halfway to Chicago right now, laughing and singing along to my "good music."

Eventually, the tow truck arrives. The driver, a burly man with a handlebar mustache, glances at us skeptically. "You kids even old enough to drive?" he asks.

Hunter stands up taller. The driver laughs. "I was kidding ya," he says, bending down to inspect the tire. When I tell him we're on our way to Chicago for the day, he shakes his head. "There's no use putting on the spare then," he says.

"Why?" I ask.

"Because it won't last all that way and back. You two kids need a new tire."

After he gets my car onto the bed of the tow truck, we join him in the cab—me squeezed into the middle, Hunter by the passenger door—and Mr. Handlebar Mustache starts the engine. He chews on a toothpick the way my dad does sometimes, deep in thought. The radio plays a Beach Boys tune. Mr. Handlebar Mustache tows us to a repair shop, where he carefully lowers and unhooks my car. I watch anxiously, as if I'm a parent and my child is getting a booster shot at the doctor.

Thankfully, Al's Auto Repair isn't busy and we don't have to wait long for assistance. A man with JIMMY on his nametag helps me pick out a new tire. I ask if I can watch while he changes it, but Jimmy says customers are required to stay in the front office waiting room for safety's sake. Hunter slumps in a hard plastic seat, ballcap pulled low over his eyes.

It's past noon by the time we get back on the road. I nibble on pretzels as I drive. Hunter rolls down the windows and cranks up the stereo. Between the wind and the music, it's too loud to talk even if we wanted to. But I don't particularly want to.

If we were talking, here's what I might say to Hunter: *You know what's weird? How you can be sitting six inches away from someone and feel like you're on entirely different planets.*

And: *You know what else is weird? How you can feel so close to another human being it's almost like you're intrinsically connected, but then just a couple hours later it seems like that same person is a stranger.*

By the time we reach Chicago, we're both starving. I find a parking lot downtown, sighing in relief when I cut the engine. *We made it. Safe and sound.*

"Great job, Emma," Hunter says with sincerity.

I laugh.

"No, really. You were so calm during the whole drive. I never could have handled it that well. You're amazing."

I look over at him. He's wearing a button-down collared shirt, and his hair is burnished copper, and he is so handsome. Sometimes, even though we have been together for a long time, I can't believe he is really *my* boyfriend. He stares at me like he wants to memorize me forever.

"I love you, Hunter Murray," I say.

"And I love you, Emma Mason."

We wander downtown, holding hands and strolling through the humid sunshine. I pause in front of a small Italian restaurant, a place my parents would fondly refer to as a "hole in the wall"—it looks romantic. The type of restaurant with candles on the tables and menus like little books. "How about this place?" I ask.

"Sure," Hunter says.

My favorite thing about the restaurant is the accordion player who wanders around, playing songs for each table. He is an elderly man with a warm smile revealing two gold teeth. In a lilting foreign accent, he introduces himself as Gordy.

"Where are you lovebirds from?" Gordy asks.

"She goes to school at Wabash Academy," Hunter says, pointing at me.

"In Indiana," I clarify. "About two hours from here. But I'm originally from California."

"We both are. San Buenaventura. I'm visiting for the weekend."

"Aha!" Gordy says. "I have the perfect song for you!" He sings us a wonderfully off-key rendition of "California, Here I Come." Afterwards, we applaud and I give him a five-dollar tip.

Gordy reaches for my hand, brings it up to his lips, and kisses it gently. "Listen to me, you take care of this beautiful lady," he tells Hunter. "You treat her right. Okay?"

Hunter smiles. "That's easy to do. She's the best thing in my life."

We go to Navy Pier and Millennium Park, where we take photos of our distorted reflections in the shiny silver bean sculpture. I post it on Instagram: me and Hunter, our faces magnified over our tiny cartoon bodies, like looking into a funhouse mirror. Our cheeks are pressed together. Our smiles are immense.

AT THE END OF THE DAY, on our way back to the parking garage, we pass by a middle-aged woman who is drawing with chalk on the sidewalk. Colorful, intricate scenes: a rainbow pastel tiger with bared teeth; a go-go dancer with a tasseled headdress; a bouquet of vibrant blue roses, dripping with diamonds. There is a bucket beside her with a sign: WE ARE

ALL EPHEMERAL. SUPPORT AN ARTIST AT WORK, CREATING EPHEMERAL ART.

I drop a dollar bill into the bucket and tell her, "What beautiful work."

"Thank you," she says, smiling at me.

As we continue walking, Hunter says, "That was nice of you."

I shake my hair out of its ponytail, enjoying the slight breeze. "She's talented. Plus, it's good karma for me to tip other artists."

Hunter chuckles, squeezing my hand.

"What?" I say. "I'm an artist."

"I know that. But, I mean, you're a student. You're not doing it as a career." He pauses. "Are you?"

"I don't know. I haven't really decided yet. But I definitely respect people who try to make a living doing what they love."

"But don't you think there's lots of different things you could love?" Hunter asks.

"Not the way I love art."

"I get it, but you have to be practical, Emma. For most people, art is a hobby. I mean, I love to run, but I don't plan on being an Olympic athlete. You don't honestly think you can make art into a career, do you?"

I am stunned. I've never heard anything like this from him before. "Um, I guess I haven't really thought about it."

"Even Vincent van Gogh thought he was a total failure his entire life," Hunter continues. "He would have starved if not for his brother… what was his name?"

"Theo," I say numbly. I always thought Hunter supported my art. Last year he came to all my art shows, and he seemed proud. Was he pretending? Humoring me? Saying what I wanted to hear? Now it seems he doesn't actually believe I am good enough.

We walk in silence. If Hunter notices that I'm upset, he doesn't acknowledge it.

The thing is, I don't even know if I want to make art my career. Maybe I'll end up working in the business world like my dad hopes I will. Or maybe I'll pursue a career where art is a component, like graphic design. Or maybe I'll teach art. What I do know, beneath it all, is that I want to be with someone who respects me instead of acting like I'm some naïve child who doesn't understand the real world.

"What does ephemeral mean?" Hunter asks eventually.

"Temporary. Not lasting."

The sun is sinking toward the horizon when we climb into my car to head back to Wabash. Hunter yawns and stretches, leaning back in his seat. Soon he begins to snore. I stare out the windshield, thinking of that chalk artist, what it must be like to abandon her drawings on the sidewalk every night, knowing they will be washed away by the next rain. I imagine her taking one last look at them before she leaves. Mrs. Muna was always saying that the *process* of creating art is what matters, not the end result. Still, I don't know if I could be like that chalk artist. I don't know if I could continually create something that matters to me, knowing it will only disappear to nothing.

***

I LEAN AGAINST HUNTER as we walk back to the dorm from the parking lot. Maybe I've packed too much into this long weekend. It's not even nine p.m., but I am exhausted. "My sleepy lady," Hunter says, an arm slung around my shoulders.

Unfortunately, the door to my room is partway open. Noise bleeds out into the hallway. A dizzy pop song, bursts of laughter, voices clamoring over each other. When I push the door fully open and enter the room, Nora and Rachel and a couple other girls from the hall are sprawled across our two beds. They wave hello. Nora turns down the music.

I push my tiredness aside and wedge a smile onto my face. "Hi everyone!" I introduce Hunter to the other girls who haven't met him yet.

"How was Chicago?" Rachel asks.

"It was a blast. There's so much to do there! I already can't wait to go back." I climb up onto my bed and make room for Hunter beside me.

"We'll have to take a girls trip up there sometime. Maybe catch a show or something," Nora says.

The conversation meanders from summer travel adventures to school-related gossip to hook-up stories. Nora asks how Hunter and I met, even though she already knows. She's probably just being nice because she knows I like telling this story.

"It was freshman year of high school," I begin, resting my hand on Hunter's knee. He puts his hand on top of mine. "Cross-country season. Poor Hunter developed a stress fracture in his hip."

"What's a stress fracture?" one of the other girls asks.

"It's a tiny hairline crack in the bone," Hunter says.

"Ouch."

"It's caused from running too hard and too much," I explain. "The only remedy is rest. So he was forced to sit out the season."

"It sucked," Hunter says.

"But he still went to every race to cheer on his teammates. I remember him pacing around the finish chute like a caged tiger. His job was to mark down final times on a clip-board Coach Bill gave him."

"And he started flirting with Emma," Rachel interrupts. "Ahh. How cute." She also has heard this story before.

"Not quite," Hunter says. "I mean, I wasn't that smooth." He grins at me.

"Even though he couldn't run," I continue, "he could work out in the pool, where his hip wouldn't feel any im-pact."

"Every single afternoon, I spent hours in that damn pool!" Hunter says. "Swimming laps, running with a flotation belt. When Emma got shin splints, Coach Bill prescribed pool workouts for her too."

I squeeze his hand. "And that was how we got to know each other."

"Yep. Nothing much else to do but talk to each other, stuck in that pool every afternoon. And then at some point, I guess we just started dating."

The way he says it bothers me—like we didn't have any choice in the matter, like it only happened because of proxim-ity. "Remember the giraffe?" I want to ask him, but now Nora is talking about her ex-girlfriend, who she still hooks up with occasionally when she's drunk.

Hunter disentangles his hand from mine to scratch his nose. He spoke with such disdain for those pool workouts, but for me they are a treasured memory. We never would have gotten together if not for those hours we spent bobbing side by side and swimming laps, back and forth and back and forth across the pool.

Later, alone with Hunter while the others watch a TV show in the common room, I can't help but bring it up again. I use the term *serendipity*, one of my favorite words. A fortunate accident. "Don't you think?" I say. "It's good we both got injured, or else we never would have started dating."

Hunter's eyes narrow and darken slightly. "Getting injured is never a good thing."

"That's not what I'm saying." I reach for his hand, but he pretends not to notice and picks at a scab on his knee.

"Not being able to run was torture for me," Hunter says.

I sigh, frustration expanding in my chest like popcorn in a microwave. "All I'm saying is, it happened for a reason. It brought us together."

"We would have gotten together anyway."

The air in the room is close and stale, the tension flickering between us like thousands of tiny hot wires. Any words I can think to say will only come out sounding jagged and barbed. I look down at my hands, holding each other.

Then, something in Hunter's manner shifts. He snakes his arm around my waist and pulls me to him, and the gloom evaporates as if I had been imagining it. He kisses my neck, my ear, my lips. "I had my eye on you, Emma Mason," he murmurs.

"Oh you did, did you?" I tease, kissing him back.

"Yoo-hoo in here!" Mrs. Jenkins knocks on my mostly closed door, pushing it all the way open.

Hunter and I leap away from each other.

"Emma, remember to keep the door open, please," Mrs. Jenkins says. "Especially when you have a gentleman visitor."

"Sorry," I mumble. Hunter snorts a laugh but tries to turn it into a cough.

"Curfew is in thirty minutes." Mrs. Jenkins raps on the door once more, her eyes doing a quick sweep of my room, before she gives us a nod and continues down the hall.

"Gentleman visitor," Hunter says, waggling his eyebrows. We collapse into laughter.

But later—when Hunter is back in the boys dorm and I'm trying to fall asleep—I still feel unsettled. Because in the back of my mind, I know Hunter is lying. He didn't have his eye on me. Maybe he had his eye on one of the fast gazelle girls—Stacy Carmichael, or Mariah Quinn. But otherwise, he only had eyes for running. Before our pool workouts together, he never said two words to me during practice or at track meets. I know, without a doubt, that we never would have started dating if not for both of us getting injured at the same time.

THE NEXT MORNING, our visit is already over. I can't believe the weekend flew by so fast. Hunter offers to book an airport shuttle—he doesn't want me to have to drive back to the dorm alone. But I insist. "Every extra minute with you is worth it," I say, which is the truth. He smiles and kisses my forehead.

We don't speak much during the drive. Hunter stares out the window, as if trying to memorize every row of every cornfield. I turn up the radio, some old Katy Perry song I recognize from Buenaventura High dances. Sadness festers inside me. Why did I even apply to Wabash Academy? Why did I choose to move thousands of miles away from my boyfriend, from my best friend, from my family?

I don't feel independent or grown-up or self-confident. I only feel homesick and unsure. I wish, more than anything, that I could board the airplane with Hunter and fly back into my old life.

I start to say something to Hunter about it: "Hey, do you ever think—"

"Isn't that the exit?" he interrupts, pointing.

"Yep," I mutter, turning the steering wheel hard to the right and veering across the lane and onto the exit ramp. Hunter reaches over and turns down the radio.

The GPS voice announces in its robotic monotone, "Continue onto Colonel H. Weir Cook Memorial Drive."

"Colonel H. Weir Cook Memorial Drive?" Hunter repeats. "That's the longest freaking street name I've ever heard." He meets my eyes and cracks a wry smile.

I smile back, recognizing this as his attempt to lighten the mood. I'm not the only one who is feeling nostalgic. Right now, we both wish that things were different—that we were back to last year, holding hands through the halls of Buenaventura High.

But this is the path I've chosen, and I need to see where it goes.

"I'm proud of you, Pea," Hunter says softly, as if reading my mind. "You're the bravest person I know. It's been really cool to see this whole new life that you've created for yourself."

"Not wholly new. You are still a huge part of my life," I remind him. "You know that, right?"

"Yeah," Hunter says, squeezing my knee. "I do."

And just like that, despite the pain of having to say goodbye to him, it also seems like everything is right in the world. I *know* that Hunter and I can survive long distance. I'll be home in a couple months for Thanksgiving, then again for winter break, when we'll have practically an entire month together.

I walk with Hunter as far through the airport as I'm allowed. He holds his duffel bag in one hand, my hand in the other. Now I can't imagine what it will be like to once again walk around not holding Hunter's hand. How do people walk around by themselves, arms hanging lonely at both sides? How do people stand it? I squeeze his hand, and he squeezes mine back.

Too soon, we reach the security line entrance. I cry as we kiss goodbye. Hunter is not the crying type, but his lips taste of salt from my tears. He walks backwards through the security line, waving. I blow kisses until he passes through the metal detectors and disappears into the mass of travelers. Then, he is gone.

I stand there watching a while longer—five minutes, ten minutes, or maybe only two or three minutes, maybe time has slowed down again without Hunter here beside me—until my purse begins to feel heavy on my shoulder. The metal buckle on the strap bites my bare skin. I turn and head back to the parking garage, my empty hands awkward at my sides.
Driving back to campus, Hunter's absence is a heavy weight in my chest. The seat beside me is an empty space where a body should be.

15

AFTER

I THROW MYSELF into schoolwork, staying late at the library, trying to keep myself distracted from thoughts of David and Anabelle, Hunter and Céline. I stay away from the art studio, where Hunter lingers in the brushes and paints. My half-finished feet and leg paintings languish beneath my bed.

I call my parents every Sunday—Dad's phone, because Mom puts hers on silent as she efficiently marches through a list of virtual assistant tasks for clients but then forgets to turn her ringer back on when she's done working.

As usual, on this Sunday, Dad answers. He sounds happy to hear my voice.

"How are things with my favorite girl?"

"Great!" I lie.

"You're still liking your classes?"

"Yeah, they're really interesting."

Dad starts to say something else, but Mom has joined him on speakerphone and starts talking at the same time.

"What?" I ask.

"We were wondering if you're still planning to come home for Easter," Mom says. "I want to book your flight soon, before it gets too expensive."

I try to imagine what it will be like to return home to the ghosts of winter break. To a Céline I haven't spoken to in weeks. To a Hunter who is paralyzed.

I imagine bumping into people I know at the supermarket, people who will politely say hello and ask me about school and the Midwest and my parents, nodding and smiling in a fake-pleasant way while behind their smiles a name is scrolling by on repeat, *Hunter Hunter Hunter,* and when they get home they'll call their friends and say, *You'll never guess who I ran into at the grocery store today. Emma Mason! So sad, what happened between her and Hunter Murray. I can't believe she broke up with him after he got paralyzed in that horrible accident.*

I'm sure that's what everyone thinks: that I ended things with Hunter not before, but *after* he got paralyzed. That I broke up with him *because* he got paralyzed. Céline knows the truth, of course. And I told Siggy, but she was so drunk at Robbie's party that she may not remember.

For the most part, news of our breakup was immediately eclipsed by news of Hunter's accident. Timing links the two incidents, one seemingly a direct result of the other.

But nobody, not even Céline, knows the *real* truth: that I caused The Accident. And not just because I was the one who suggested skinny-dipping. The Accident never would have happened if Hunter hadn't been drunk. Why did he drink so much at Robbie Zwick's party? Because he'd just been dumped. By me. *My fault. My fault.* Was it even an accident, or did Hunter dive into the shallow end on purpose, because I broke up with him?

"Emma?" Mom says. "Are you still there, honey?"

"Yeah. Sorry. I'm not sure if I can come home for Easter—things are so busy with school projects—can I let you know later?"

"Of course," Mom says, but she isn't able to hide the disappointment in her tone. "Don't wait too long, though, okay? I want to book your flight."

"Listen, I've got to get off the phone now," Dad says. "It was wonderful talking to you, sweetheart. Makes my day to hear your voice. Love you."

"Bye, Dad. Love you too."

"He's not feeling very well," Mom murmurs.

Alarm jolts through my body. "What's wrong? Is Daddy okay?"

"Oh yes, I'm sure he's fine. Just a little stomach bug. If he's not better in a couple days I'll make him go to the doctor."

"Okay." The alarm recedes in a gentle wave. "Keep me posted."

Mom is quiet.

After a long pause, I say, "I'm wearing your sweater today. The yellow one you gave me, with the pearl buttons."

"That is a nice sweater, isn't it?" Mom says, her voice brighter.

"It is. I get so many compliments whenever I wear it."

"I'm glad." I can picture my mom smiling, but for some reason the image is a sad one. A bittersweet smile.

"I want you to be happy, sweetheart," she says softly.

"I'm fine, Mom. Really. You don't need to worry about me."

Outside my dorm window, the trees are barren of leaves. In the wind, their skeletal limbs bump against the thick glass pane, a melancholy drumming. It's already dark enough outside that I can see the ghost of my reflection in the window-pane, hair hanging limply around my face, my eyes hollow smudges. The tree branches dance in and out of the reflection so it looks like I am a lost girl hiding out in the wilderness.

"I ran into Linda at the grocery store," Mom says. "She told me Hunter is doing really well. He's back at school, even. It's amazing."

"Wow. That's great. I'm really glad."

After I broke up with Hunter and the Murrays left, Mom sat beside me on the couch and pulled my head onto her shoulder. She stroked my hair as she said, "I know it hurts now. But believe me, honey: it will get better. Time heals all things."

Time heals all things were Mom's words of comfort throughout my childhood, soothing everything from skinned knees to hurt feelings to middle-school heartache over the boy who liked Céline instead. I used to confide in Mom about everything, seeking her guidance on problems and decisions I was struggling over. Mom has a way of slicing up the world into clear, manageable pieces, of shining a light on a problem until a solution appears in the brightness.

"I'm here if you need to talk," she'd said the night of The Accident, and the day after that, and the day after that. At first, I felt too shocked for words, and then it seemed too late. Now all my words have dried up, calcified in my throat.

Time heals all things. After The Accident, her favorite phrase lost its potency. Hunter's crushed vertebrae and sliced spinal cord are something that time cannot—will not—heal. Ever.

Now, I yearn to tell Mom about my Hunter Series. I want to describe how it feels to channel my anger and grief into something beautiful. I want to tell her how Mrs. Post lit up when she saw my first painting of Hunter's feet—how, even though she didn't know whose artwork it was, she stopped the entire class to rave about the energy and emotion in the brushstrokes.

I want to ask her what I should do about Anabelle. About David. About Céline. But these problems are so much bigger than those old middle-school dramas. There are no simple solutions. Unburdening myself to Mom would only make her worry about me. It's possible she would even insist that I leave Wabash Academy, transfer back to Buenaventura High.

So instead, I tell Mom I have to go. "I have a meeting for this Community Art Project."

"Okay, honey, have fun. Are you eating enough? Real meals, not just cereal all the time?"

"Yes, I promise. I'll talk to you later, okay?"

"I love you," Mom says.

"Love you, too." I hang up, grab my coat and keys, and shut the door behind me, rushing down the two flights of stairs and outside into the cold. The air bites my cheeks. My features shrink inward, like a video I saw once of a sea anemone seeking protection within itself. I shove my hands in my coat pockets and trudge through the snow to the Student Union.

Kevin is there already, sitting at a table in the corner. His head is bent in concentration as he draws in a notebook, headphones jammed into his ears. I say his name, but he doesn't hear me. I tap him on the shoulder and he jumps a little, then takes out his earbuds.

"Sorry," I say, giving an awkward little wave hello. "Didn't mean to startle you. What are you working on?"

"Oh, nothing. Doodling helps me clear my head. Sometimes it's so chaotic in there."

"I know exactly what you mean." I sit down heavily into the seat across from him. "Don't you wish our brains came with volume knobs, so we could turn down our thoughts? That voice inside my head can be so loud."

"What does it say?" Kevin asks, kindness in his eyes.

"Oh, you know. Just the usual stuff. I get stressed about school, and my paintings, and this project... speaking of which, we should probably start brainstorming."

Kevin takes my cue to change the subject, and the conversation turns to potential topics for our Community Art Project. Maybe we could do some sort of painting class for elementary schoolers? Although neither of us has much experience teaching. And we'd have to buy materials for all the kids—that could get expensive. Could we apply for a grant to purchase materials? That's getting more and more complicated, and we're on a tight deadline. What if instead of teaching kids, we teach a class for senior citizens? Something like... photography... using their smartphones? Assuming they all have smartphones. And is that artistic enough, or is it more of a technology class?

Kevin suggests we scrap the teaching component and do something off the beaten path, like chalk art on the sidewalks around the city. Which sounds really fun... but is it engaging the community enough? One of the main requirements is to involve members of the community.

An hour later, we still haven't found a promising idea. We decide to take a break and sleep on it. Maybe the right idea will spring up in our dreams.

"Are you headed back to the dorms? I'll walk with you," Kevin says, draining the last dregs of his tea.

"No, I've got a lot of painting to do. I'm off to the studio." I try to plan my painting sessions for when the studio should be empty; I don't like to work with anyone else around.

Kevin doesn't seem surprised that I'm going to the studio an hour before curfew. He props his chin in his hand, smiling at me. "So when do I get to see your artwork?"

"What do you mean? You've seen plenty of my paintings."

"I mean your underground art. Not the stuff you do for class—I'm talking about the stuff you create purely for *you*."

I lean my elbows on the tabletop and it shifts beneath my weight, reminding me of when I came here with Anabelle, that first day we became friends.

"Don't you have art like that?" Kevin asks. "Or am I the only one?"

I find myself telling him the truth. "No, I do, too. I keep those paintings under my bed, where no one knows they exist. What about you?"

"My underground art is right here." Kevin opens his notebook and slides it across the table to me. I stare down at… cartoon drawings. Most seem to be of a boxer dog, with a lolling tongue and smiling eyes, doing a variety of human activities: reading a book, flying a kite, sunbathing on a lounge chair. The latest one is unfinished—a cartoon bubble extending from the dog's mouth, waiting for words.

I don't know what I was expecting, exactly. But it wasn't this.

Kevin's artwork that I've seen in class is deep and serene, intricately layered and exquisite. His series of trees is filled with emotion, as if each tree has a personality, a history, a story. These cartoon drawings are light and airy. Playful. Like cotton candy.

"Wow, Kevin. These are really cool. So different from your paintings in class."

"Thanks. I've always loved cartoons. Paintings can seem so weighty and serious. These doodles are pure fun. The truth is that when I first moved here from Colorado, my freshman year, I was really homesick."

"I get that."

"Oh yeah, you're from California, right? Yeah, it's a big change, moving to Wabash. And personally, it was the first time I really lived away from my family. That was real tough at first. I especially missed my dog, Gar." He points at the cartoon boxer dog with the big grin.

"He's adorable. His personality jumps off the page."

"He was a character, that's for sure. I miss that guy."

Was—past tense. My heart sinks.

"He died last year," Kevin continues, as if sensing my thoughts. "He was really old, and he got sick. My parents had to put him to sleep. I hate that I wasn't there to say goodbye." He wipes his eyes. "Shit. This is embarrassing. Crying over my dog."

"No, don't be embarrassed. Pets are part of your family."

"Do you have any pets?"

"Sadly, none. My dad's allergic. But my best friend back home has a beagle named Benny. I know it's not the same—I mean, Benny's not *my* dog—but I really love him. I'd be wrecked if he died."

Kevin gathers up his used napkins, stuffs them in his empty paper cup. "Well, thank you Emma. For not making me feel like a sentimental idiot."

We smile at each other.

"So when do I get to see them?" Kevin asks.

"See what?"

"The paintings under your bed."

"Sometime, maybe. I don't know—you might think they're weird."

I'm surprised to see hurt wash over his face. "I wouldn't think they're weird," he says. "I would be honored to see your underground artwork."

I turn away, shrugging into my coat. "Thanks," I say softly.

"Whenever you're ready, I'm here," Kevin says. And somehow, I feel like he's talking about more than my paintings.

A FLYER IS TAPED TO THE ART STUDIO DOOR.

STUDENT COMPETITION IN THE CREATIVE ARTS! PAINITNG. SCULPTURE. ANIMATION. WRITING. APPLICATION FORMS AVAILABLE IN THE MAIN OFFICE.

I shut the door behind me, pushing the flyer out of my mind. To enter my work—my *real* work—in a competition would mean admitting that I painted it.

I'm not ready for that.

As usual at this time of night, the studio is empty. I pull out a new blank canvas from my locker, organize my oils and brushes and palette. I'm planning to paint a landscape of a lemon grove. I begin by lightly sketching the outline with a charcoal pencil. But the buzzing need inside me is not eased—it only grows more insistent.

This is not what I need to paint right now.

What I need to paint is Hunter. Not his toes, or his feet, or his legs. Him. His chest and torso and neck and face. His smile. His wholeness. I want Hunter to be more than his feet or his legs. More than his running. More than his paralysis.

I sweep away the charcoal outline, dip brush to paint, and stand before the empty canvas. I am poised. I am ready to create something new. I am ready to paint without an outline, fearlessly. Not locked in my dorm room. I am ready to paint bravely right here, in the light of the art studio.

Across the room, propped against the wall, my first painting of Hunter's feet blares with vibrant life.

I wait for that feeling to wash over me, that mix of inspiration and shame and anger and passion, that sense of overflowing from my deepest self onto the canvas. I close my eyes and try to summon Hunter's face, but I can't quite capture it. He is wavy lines, blurred edges. A smudge of a smile, a twinkle of an eye, but nothing I can grasp onto. Nothing I can capture with my paint and brushes.

I pull my phone from my pocket. Take a deep breath. Press number 2 on speed-dial. Listen to the hollow ringing. My heartbeat echoes in my head. Then the call clicks over to voicemail. I hang up without leaving a message.

I alone know the truth: The Accident would not have happened if someone had been looking out for Hunter that night. That person was supposed to be me. I was always the one by his side, the one who kept him from getting so drunk. But that night, I kept my distance. That night, I yelled, "Let's go skinny-dipping!"

My paintbrush clatters to the floor. I bury my face in my hands. My tears smell of paint and charcoal.

Will I ever be able to paint again without thinking of him?

16

BEFORE

JUNIOR YEAR, EARLY AUGUST

WHAT PEOPLE DON'T tell you about a road trip is that it's exhausting. The monotony is what gets to you. Mile after mile, road sign after road sign, gas station after gas station. After a while, the hours blur together. There's a reason road trips look so fun in the movies: they're montages. Scenes spliced together, like pushing fast-forward. In real life, a road trip is like pushing a slow-motion button. No matter how fast you drive, it still seems you're not making much progress.

Utah is a landscape of red rock formations that gradually lose their novelty after hours of driving. Colorado is steep mountain roads, pouring rain, getting passed by lumbering eighteen-wheelers because my car can't go faster than sixty uphill. Kansas is a flat, flat expanse of pastures and crops stretching as far as I can see in any direction. Missouri is humidity and mosquitoes and damp gray sky.

We listen to Mom's classic rock. We listen to my indie pop. We listen to the radio. We listen to a murder mystery audiobook, but I have a hard time following the plot and Mom gets tired of me asking her to explain what just happened, so we only make it through three chapters.

At night, we stay at featureless motels because bed-and-breakfasts are too far from the highway, not to mention too expensive. We collapse into bed and promptly fall asleep because we're so exhausted. We set our alarm clocks early so that we can eat our complimentary continental breakfast and hit the road to get a jump on the hot weather. Soggy bacon and oversalted eggs and dry white toast.

Four days after we leave California, when I finally glimpse the WELCOME TO INDIANA sign on the side of the highway, I am so happy that I could cry. Almost there. We're almost there. Only two more hours and we'll be there.

WE TURN OFF the main road and drive through a wrought-iron archway that spells out WABASH ACADEMY FOR THE ARTS. Tall, shady trees line the road. My first impression of my new home is a trim expanse of green lawn, surrounded by tall stone buildings. I spot the clock tower from the brochure Mrs. Muna gave me.

It is not yet noon. The campus seems empty, quiet. Mom turns into a lot marked GUEST PARKING. I unfold myself from the passenger seat and stumble out of the car on cramped legs, stretching my fingers up toward the sky. The air is dense, humid—an entirely different sort of heat than we get in California. Cicadas hum from the trees.

"We made it," Mom says, wrapping one arm around my shoulders. "Wow, Emma. This place is beautiful. It looks like a fancy liberal-arts college."

"I can't believe I'm actually going to *live* here."

"Me neither," Mom says. "Gosh, I'm going to miss you. But I'm not going to let myself think about that right now. C'mon, let's get out of this heat!"

We head across the parking lot, toward the Admissions Office, to start my new life.

"HERE YOU ARE. Emma Mason. Room 202," says Mrs. Jenkins, my new Dorm Mother. She looks to be about my mom's age, with short brown hair and friendly blue eyes. Her dangly silver earrings are shaped like open-faced books.

"Are you an artist, too?" my mom asks her.

"I dabble around. Sculpture is my favorite. I sub for classes here at Wabash occasionally. But my professional training is in adolescent counseling. I've been a Dorm Mother here for almost ten years now."

"That's wonderful," Mom says. Her shoulders relax a little.

Room 202 is smaller than I expected—smaller than my room back home. It is furnished simply with two twin beds, two wooden dressers, and two matching wooden desks.

"Looks like you beat your roommate here," Mrs. Jenkins says, handing me the key to my new room. "That means you get first pick of the beds." She winks. "I'll be down the hall if you have any questions."

Mom and I thank her, and I cross the thin blue carpet to the window, pulling back the curtains. We are on the second floor, looking out onto the green lawn—The Quad, Mrs. Jenkins called it during her brief tour. Across The Quad is the clock tower, which apparently is the Dining Commons. The painting studio and other classrooms are scattered around campus. Later, Mom and I plan on doing an extensive tour ourselves.

I lay down on both beds, but they feel the same to me. So I set down my backpack on the bed on the right. It's where my bed is situated in my room back home.

Mom and I unpack the car, bringing load after load up the two flights of stairs to my new room. When all my stuff was piled in the car it seemed like a lot, but once we unpack everything, the room still seems bare. I guess I'm used to my room back home, crammed with knick-knacks from all the years of my life.

Mom pulls something from her purse and sets it onto my dresser. I lean forward to look. A silver heart-shaped necklace with a red gemstone in the center.

"My necklace! Oh my gosh, where was it?"

"Stuck between my car cushions," Mom says. "It must have fallen out of my purse after we bought it. I found it a couple weeks ago, but I was waiting until now to give it to you."

Stuck between my car cushions. I imagine Céline's seashell necklace, still wedged somewhere in Hunter's mom's car. But I quickly push the thought away.

"It's perfect," I say, hugging her. "Thank you." I reach behind my neck to do the clasp, looking at myself in the mirror. The necklace is a gentle weight against my breastbone.

Just then, a soft knock on the open door. A girl stands in the doorway, wearing cut-off jeans and a pink tank top, her dark blonde hair in pigtail braids. She smiles and says, "Hi, I'm Nora, your roommate!"

Mom sneaks into the hallway to chat with Nora's parents, giving us time to get to know each other. We quickly discover we have the same taste in music (Taylor Swift and Billie Eilish) and movies (pretty much anything with Emma Stone). She's a drama student from a suburb of Chicago, cheerful and organized, and generous with sharing her things—she puts her TV on top of the mini fridge between our beds, so we both can watch it. We hang twinkle lights all around the room and discuss ideas to maximize space in our tiny closets. I imagine us becoming close friends, swapping clothes and whispering secrets across the room as we lay in our beds at night. By dinnertime—Mom and I join Nora and her parents at a nearby Italian restaurant, right down the street from Mom's hotel—hope is rising in my chest like a shiny balloon.

THE WEEKEND IS A WHIRLWIND of meetings and seminars and tours and welcomes. Mom and I are apart sometimes, when there are separate events for the new students and for the parents, but we meet up again for meals and free time. We spend an afternoon wandering the sycamore-lined downtown streets, as if we are tourists on vacation. We duck into an air-conditioned cupcake shop to escape the heat, splitting a vanilla cupcake with rainbow sprinkles.

"So do you like it here, Em?" Mom asks. "Is it what you imagined?"

"Even better." The campus is strikingly beautiful, the teachers are super accomplished, and the painting studio is like one of my daydreams come to life—elegant wooden easels, fancy paint sets and brushes, huge windows pouring in natural light. "I can't believe I'm going to school here. It doesn't seem real."

Mom sighs. "I didn't expect to have to say goodbye to you already. I thought I still had two more years before you went off to college."

"I know. I'm sorry."

"You don't have to be sorry." She spears a bite of cake with her fork. "You really *love* it, don't you? Painting?"

Mom is so practical and efficient. She is probably baffled by her daughter's desire to spend hours upon hours cooped up with paint and brushes, wandering around inside the wild jungle of imagination. I've tried to explain why I love to paint, but words seem insubstantial. Like trying to explain why I need to breathe.

I try again. "I do. It feels like… like part of me. Like, if I'm not making art, I'm not truly myself. Or at least, I'm not my best self. You know?"

Mom nods, waiting for me to continue.

"Painting feels like this gift I've been given, and I don't really know where it came from—"

"Certainly not from me or your dad," Mom interjects with a smile. "Remember that time the power went out and we played Pictionary?"

I laugh. "Dad still insists it was clearly a turtle."

"It was definitely a donut."

"Anyway, I guess I just… I feel like if I don't give it my all, I might always regret it. And I don't want to live with regret, wondering, *What if?* Does that make any sense?"

"Perfect sense. I don't know when my baby got so grown-up," she says, brushing a strand of hair off my forehead.

"Mo-om." I duck my head away.

"I guess you're never too old for your mom to embarrass you, huh?" she says, laughing.

Still, even when she embarrasses me, it is comforting to have my mom around. I am a little kid trying out a new bike, and she is my training wheels, keeping me safe, preventing me from falling flat on my face. With Mom here, I'm not alone.

But everyone knows you can't keep training wheels on forever. Sunday night, we go out to dinner again with Nora's family, and then Mom and I pop into Sweet Treat Cupcakes just the two of us. Mom treats me to a chocolate cupcake— my favorite—but I can't eat much. There's a giant lump in my throat. Mom is catching a flight early tomorrow morning. This is goodbye, until Thanksgiving. More than three months from now. I've never been apart from my mom for longer than a week.

We linger at our table by the window, chatting about people back at home and my new class schedule. Outside, the sunset fades to night, the streetlamps blink on, the fireflies spark to life in the grass.

Eventually, Mom looks at her watch and says, "I think it's time, sweetie."

Tears fill my eyes. "Already?"

"You start classes tomorrow. You need to be well rested."

"Let me drop you off at your hotel on the way."

"No," she says. "I'd rather go back to your dorm with you."

"What? Why?"

"It's a mom thing. I like knowing you're at your dorm safe and sound. I can get a rideshare from there."

All too soon, we are back in my car, retracing our route to Wabash Academy. Parking in the student lot. Walking to my dorm.

"You don't have to go up with me," I say outside the dorm entrance. I open the app on her phone and help her order a rideshare. "I'll wait with you until your car comes."

"Are you sure, Em?"

"Yeah. This is better."

When her ride pulls up, she wraps me in a long, tight hug. "I love you, Emma," she whispers in my ear. "I'm so proud of you. Remember, your dad and I are only a phone call away. Your home will always be there, waiting for your return." She gives me one last squeeze and then pulls away, slipping into the backseat of the waiting car.

I wave as her car drives away, turns a corner, and disappears.

She is gone.

The tears threaten to overwhelm me. I can't go up to my room yet. I don't want Nora to see me like this.

I walk through campus blindly, my head down. After a little while, I stumble across a well-kept grove of flowers and trees, surrounded by a short metal gate and softly lit by ground lights. A sign reads WABASH ACADEMY ALUMNI GARDEN. The gate is open, so I wander inside. Crape myrtles drop purple flowers onto the grass. Rose bushes stretch their thorny limbs up to the stars. In the back corner, a small wooden shed is nestled among the trees. The door is unlocked; it squeaks a little when I push it open. I fumble on the wall until my fingers find a light switch. Light floods the little room: it's a garden shed, neatly organized with landscaping tools. Spare pots and soil rest on a large metal table. Brooms and rakes lean against the wall. For a garden shed, it is remarkably clean. I sit down on the floor, fold my face into my bent knees, and let myself cry. Tonight, I mourn my old life in Buenaventura.

Tomorrow morning, I begin my new life at Wabash Academy.

ONE WEEK INTO THE SCHOOL YEAR, Nora gets a part in the fall play, and things between us shift. She's hardly around anymore, always out at rehearsals. She's still cheerful and friendly, but there is a subtle barrier between us. It's like her friend roster is all filled up with drama kids, so I've been downgraded to ROOMMATE. More than an acquaintance, but less than a real friend.

Hunter and I talk every day, multiple times a day. We text each other constantly. At night I drift to sleep with my cell phone's warmth pressed against my ear. Hunter's murmurings wind their way through my dreams.

Weekend mornings, the time difference between us means I can sleep in and still call him before he heads out on his long run. I listen to the phone ring once, twice—and then there he is, his familiar voice a tether to my old life. He says groggily, "Good morning, sunshine" as, two-thousand miles away, I slide a mug into the dorm-room microwave to heat water for tea.

"Good morning," I murmur softly, trying not to wake Nora, sleeping in the twin bed across the room. If I didn't know she was there, it would be easy to forget—she sleeps like a rock, flowered pink comforter pulled up above her head. All I can see of her is a few tufts of blonde hair poking out from the top.

"What do you have going on today?" Hunter asks.

"Not much. Studying, painting, the usual. You?"

"Track practice and a boatload of homework. And then some of us are going to a concert tonight."

"A concert? That sounds great!" I try to keep envy from seeping into my voice. I'm happy for Hunter that he's doing fun things. "Who's performing?" I ask.

"A bunch of bands. Ashley scored tickets for us."

Ashley. Who's Ashley? But all I say is, "That's cool." I don't want to be one of those clingy, possessive girlfriends who are suspicious of every girl their boyfriend comes into contact with. I want to be open, calm, trusting. And I do trust Hunter. I just hate the wide gulf of physical distance between us. Sometimes I try to comprehend all the miles between Indiana and California, and it makes my head ache.

You chose this, I remind myself. *You wanted to come here. You wanted to forge a new life off on your own.*

Sometimes I can't remember why I ever wanted those things.

"Well, I should get going," I tell Hunter. Tears are building behind my eyes, and I better hang up before he hears them in my voice. "I'll talk to you later?"

"Okay," Hunter says. "I'll text you from the concert."

And he does, sending me a photo of the brightly lit stage before the bands come on. Later he sends me a selfie of the group: three guys from the track team, two girls, and him. I don't recognize either of the girls, but they look nice—like we would be friends if I knew them. I wonder if Ashley is the blonde one or the brunette?

I try to focus on my homework, but I'm having a hard time retaining any information. My mind keeps drifting to the concert. I wish so badly that I was there.

Hunter is like Céline—naturally outgoing—whereas I've always been a bit shy. Neither of them has trouble making friends. Neither of them understands what it's like to move somewhere totally different, somewhere you don't know a single person.

"Everyone here is a stranger," I tried to explain to Hunter.

He brushed it off. "Go introduce yourself to people. Then they won't be strangers anymore."

He makes it sound so easy. But it's not easy for me. I get butterflies and sweaty palms and even if I summon the courage to say hello to someone, my brain sometimes goes blank and I can't think of anything else to say.

Eventually I give up on my homework and crawl into bed. I glance at the time on my phone—10:30—and do the conversion to West Coast time—7:30, so Hunter is still at the concert. I won't text him; I don't want to bother him.

I press number 2 on my speed dial, but Céline doesn't pick up.

Right before I drift off to sleep, my phone beeps. A text from Hunter. *Miss you.* And I feel better. I thank the stars over and over that I changed my mind after I tried to break up with him before.

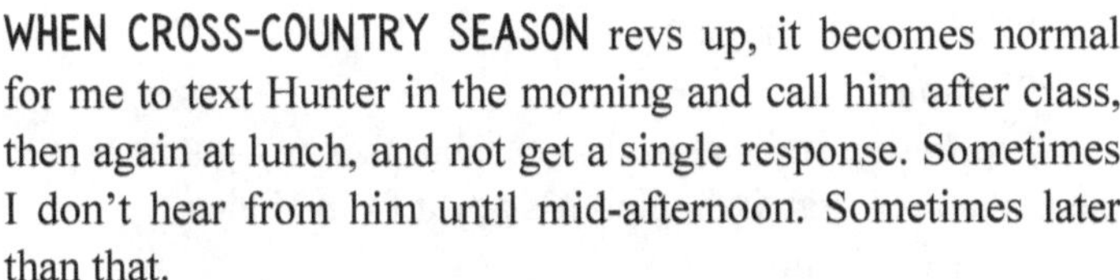

WHEN CROSS-COUNTRY SEASON revs up, it becomes normal for me to text Hunter in the morning and call him after class, then again at lunch, and not get a single response. Sometimes I don't hear from him until mid-afternoon. Sometimes later than that.

What's he doing all this time?
Does he not think of me at all?
Has he met somebody else?
Does he have a crush on that Ashley girl?

I'm too afraid to ask him.

Our first big argument happens when I'm already having a crummy day. In my art history seminar, Mr. Marsh calls on me and even though I admit that I don't know the answer, he keeps asking follow-up questions, trying to push me to come up with something. But I can't. I shrink further down into my seat, blushing and flustered, until he sighs and moves on.

Throughout the day, I keep calling Hunter, again and again, but all I get is his voicemail.

Nora and I had planned to meet for dinner, but at the last minute she bails. Eating alone at one of the big round tables in the Dining Commons is like having a spotlight shining directly on you, with a lit-up arrow and the word LOSER. I sit there, awkwardly chewing rubbery chicken parmesan and reading random BuzzFeed articles on my phone to avoid people's eyes. I text Hunter, but he doesn't reply.

I sense a presence to my right and look up. A guy stands there holding a tray. He's what Céline would call "understated cute," with a calm, quiet aura. He's wearing a baseball cap, jeans, and a CU Boulder T-shirt. "Is anyone sitting here?" he asks.

"No, it's yours."

"Thanks." He sits down, politely leaving an empty seat between us, as if he doesn't want to crowd me.

"I'm Kevin," he says.

"Emma."

We flash a smile at each other, but then my phone buzzes on the table. I grab it, hoping it's a text from Hunter.

It's from Céline.

Mrs. Lindy caught Siggy and Jason making out in the stairwell and went on an EPIC rant, it was awesome, we could all hear her from the classroom because she left the door open. I quote: *"I have a Magic 8 Ball that says you are getting detention!"*

I smile. Mrs. Lindy is famous around campus for keeping a Magic 8 Ball on her desk and consulting it at opportune moments.

Omg I'm dead, I text back with a laughing emoji.

Wish you were here.

Me too.

When I glance up from my phone, Kevin has his notebook out, doodling with one hand while he eats with the other. I want to ask what he's drawing, but I'm too shy.

I wonder if the teachers at Wabash Academy will ever feel familiar like the teachers back home at Buenaventura High. All my teachers here are professional artists. I want to impress them, to prove I belong here. My painting teacher, Mrs. Post, is my favorite—but even she intimidates me.

I should go clock in more time at the painting studio before curfew. I tuck my phone into my pocket and push back my chair from the table. Kevin looks up.

"I'm heading out," I say. "See you around."

"I think we have painting class together. Fourth period?"

"Mrs. Post?"

"Yeah, same. I remember that painting you did of the beach. You're from California, right?"

"Yep. It's my first year here."

"Hang in there," Kevin says. "It can be a rough transition, at the beginning. But it gets better."

"Thanks." His kindness has me suddenly on the verge of tears. I duck my head, embarrassed. "Well, I'll see you in class, then."

"See you, Emma."

On my way to the studio, I press 2 on my speed dial.

Céline answers on the first ring. "Hey Em!" Her voice makes the anxiety in my chest ease a little, while at the same time homesickness lodges in my throat.

"Hey! I miss you."

"I miss you more."

"I miss you most." Crossing The Quad, it's like I've stepped into the brochure Mrs. Muna handed me that day in art class. Grand stone buildings, ivy-covered walls, the clock tower rising above it all like a proud sentinel. It still feels surreal that I'm actually here.

"What are you up to?" Céline asks.

"On my way to the painting studio. You?"

"Boring homework. Hunter's coming over later to watch the new Last of Us, but I'm sure you already knew that."

No, I didn't know. But I don't want to confess to Céline that I haven't heard from Hunter all day. *Is he mad at me? What did I do?*

Back when I lived at home, it didn't bother me that Hunter and Céline watched The Last of Us together. I never really got into the show—it gave me nightmares, to be honest—but the two of them are obsessed.

But now, I get this sinking feeling in my stomach to imagine the two of them hanging out without me. Sitting close on the couch. Sharing popcorn.

Why hasn't Hunter texted me back all day?

"We'll Face Time you later," Céline says. "When we're together. It'll be fun."

"No, that's okay." The last thing I need right now is to feel like a third wheel with my boyfriend and my best friend. And I don't want to get in a fight with Hunter in front of Céline. "I'll probably still be at the studio."

"You're always at the studio."

"It's why I'm here, C." I climb the steps to the art building. "Speaking of which, I better go. Tell Hunter not to hog all the popcorn."

She laughs, and love for her balloons inside me. It's so easy to love Céline. No wonder everyone does.

When Hunter finally calls me back, it's close to eleven p.m. Indiana time—hours past curfew. I've been trying to write a lit analysis for English but can't focus. I'm so angry at him that I just watch my phone vibrating on the desk until it clicks over to voicemail. *Give him a taste of his own medicine.*

But I can't hold out for more than forty seconds before calling him back.

"I miss you so much," I say. "Why haven't you texted me back all day?"

"I've been busy. Got a big test in history."

Not too busy to hang out with Céline, I think. But what comes out is: "I'm so lonely here."

"Well, you could have stayed in Buenaventura," Hunter replies coolly. "You chose to be all by yourself."

Hurt and frustration blisters in his voice. Anger, too. When I first told Hunter I was moving to Indiana, he was upset that I was choosing to live so far away. He took it personally. He thought I was leaving *him*.

How can I explain that transferring to Wabash Academy wasn't about him? The decision was bigger than our relationship. Accepting the scholarship to come here was about taking a chance and being brave. Going after my art. My dreams. My future.

"You know what, Hunter?" I say. "I'm really not in the mood for this tonight—"

"Why didn't you stay here with me?" Hunter interrupts. It is the first time he has ever asked this outright.

"You know why," I say. "This was a great opportunity." My head throbs, from the base of my neck all the way up to my temples. My shoulders are knotty wood.

"You could change your mind," Hunter says. "You could come back. School's barely started. Tell your parents you made a mistake. Come home."

But I don't want to come home. Even though things are hard here, even though I'm lonely and homesick, I know that leaving Wabash with my tail between my legs is not the answer. At least, not yet.

"I can't give up, Hunter," I say quietly. "I have to give this a chance."

"Why? Why do you have to? Maybe it's ironic that I'm saying this, but life isn't meant to be an endurance race you power through. If something isn't the right fit, you don't need to stick it out to prove a point."

"I'm not trying to prove a point."

"Remember how great the summer was? Hanging out every day, going for runs together on the beach?"

"Mm-hmm," I murmur noncommittally. The truth is that all summer, I felt a quiet tension simmering between us. Even at the Spring Formal, it lurked quietly beneath the surface. It was there in the car at Fisherman's Point, when Hunter yanked down my underwear with an urgency akin to anger. I kissed him fiercely, trying to turn his anger into passion, but I didn't fully succeed. That was why I cried, tears blurring my eyes and snot dripping from my nose, as Hunter grunted my name into my disheveled hair. Afterwards, when he kissed my face gently and asked what was wrong, I choked out, "I love you so much." I remember how his eyes softened. How he held me tightly. And I did love him. I *do* love him. But it can be a painful love, sometimes.

"Things could still be like the summer was," Hunter continues. "If you were here, we could study together and eat lunch together and, like, go on actual dates. I'm tired of dating a person on a screen."

He stops abruptly. I picture him biting his lip.

His words ring in my ears. *I'm tired of dating a person on a screen.* "Wow, um. I don't really know what to say. Are you implying—I mean, do you want to—"

"No!" he interrupts. "I don't know why I said that. I didn't mean it like that."

"Really?"

"Really. I was talking without thinking. I just miss you, Pea."

"I miss you too."

The silence between us is heavy.

"Listen," I say after a few moments. "I should probably go. I've got some homework to finish up. And I should let you get back to studying."

"Okay," Hunter says. His voice is uncertain and far away. "I'll call you before bed?"

"Sure," I say. "Bye." Hanging up is like severing a cord between us.

I stay up past midnight, sitting in my uncomfortable desk chair with my laptop open in front of me, my cell phone on the desk. I wait for it to vibrate and light up with Hunter's face.

But it remains silent.

I can't call him. I won't call him. It is his turn to call me. He promised he would.

Nora snores softly in her bed across the room. I wait up past one, two a.m., my eyelids drooping. Eventually, I switch off my desk lamp. Soon my chin falls against my chest and I succumb to sleep. Hunter never calls.

17

AFTER

IT'S A WEDNESDAY evening and I'm at the painting studio, trying to paint a close-up of a spider crawling on a window-sill. It's not working. My brushstrokes look simultaneously cartoonish and lifeless. If I turn this in, Mrs. Post will give me one of her disappointed looks.

But I'm tired of thinking about Hunter. I'm tired of painting him. I'm tired.

I've been working on safe, pleasant paintings to fulfill the assignments: beach landscape; abstract of a stained-glass window in a church down the street; still life of a bowl of apples and grapes, painted the proper colors. I tell myself I am improving my technique, working on shadow and light, tone and depth, the nuances of shading.

But really, I am hiding.

During workshop, Mrs. Post tells me the same thing she always has: it's apparent I have technical skills and an eye for color, but my artwork is still missing something—vibrancy, grit, passion. Heart.

I always nod in agreement, promising to keep searching, to dig deeper, to work harder. I don't tell her the reason I paint now is to *ignore* my heart. Ever since David laughed at my painting, I've stopped working on my Hunter Series. I've lost touch with the work. Or maybe I'm avoiding it. Why pry open my heart on purpose? Why make myself vulnerable? Why bare all of my giant, ugly pain on the canvas? I am afraid of my pain. I am afraid that it is too big, too unwieldy, too much. I don't think I'm brave enough to show my true paintings to the world. In the studio, working on banal landscapes and safe portraits, I can focus on something other than my own problems while I get lost in the contours of lines and shapes in front of me.

My phone buzzes. Dad's photo lights up the screen.

"Hi sweetheart," he says when I answer. "Are you busy? I don't want to interrupt your schoolwork."

"No, I can talk. What's up?"

"Nothing in particular. Just wanted to check in." I can tell from his voice that he's worried about me. "Do you need anything?"

"No, I'm good, but thanks."

"Okay. Well, you'll let me know, right? If you need anything. I'm always here."

"Thanks, Dad. I will."

He tells me about playing golf with Hunter's dad. How Hunter is doing really well—everyone has been so impressed by his recovery, his strength, his determination. He's lifting weights every day after school. Still making top grades. I can hear the pride in my dad's voice when he talks about Hunter, and it makes me slump inside. Why is my dad telling me all of this, anyway?

"Well, I better get going," I say when there's a break in the conversation. "Give everyone a hug from me."

"I love you, sweetheart."

"Love you too."

Three days later, I receive a check in the mail, along with a note scrawled on the back of a grocery list. *Don't need to tell your mother. Treat yourself to something nice. Love, Dad*

There is a blank space, and then at the bottom he's written in smaller letters, *We miss you.*

The grocery list is in Mom's handwriting, but I can tell Dad was the one who actually went to the store because the directions are so detailed:

- ½ gallon nonfat milk

- organic eggs (make sure to check the carton that none are broken)

- 1 lb low-sodium turkey breast & ½ lb provolone

- apple-cinnamon oatmeal (comes in a green box)

- 3-4 yellow peaches (not too ripe!)

Something about the grocery list makes me teary. I fold the slip of paper into a small square and slide it into the zippered pocket of my wallet.

The next day after class, I cash the check and drive to the mall. There's an art supply store tucked away somewhere—Anabelle took me here last semester.

It's strange to be at the mall on a weekday, as if I'm playing hooky from real life. The stores beckon with loud dance music and bright lighting. It's like walking around inside a TV commercial. Eventually, I find my refuge: Peggy's Art Supply Plus.

It's a narrow store that stretches back surprisingly far. Twinkle lights hang down from the ceiling and prints of famous paintings adorn the walls. I could spend all day here, wandering the cramped aisles bursting with pens and pastels, easels and chalk, paper and more paper.

Today, I'm one of the only customers here. After meandering through the rest of the store, I make my way over to the paint section. Standing in front of the orderly rows of vibrant colors, hope wells up in my chest. *Maybe there's a way I can make things right. Maybe... Maybe...*

I purchase three paintbrushes and a new acrylic paint set, plus an 8 x 8 canvas. I normally gravitate toward the big canvases—especially lately—but something about the small square of blank white draws my attention. I buy it, even though I have no idea what I'm going to use it for.

I thank the cashier, pick up my bag of purchases and turn toward the exit—and there she is. She sees me the same instant I see her. She doesn't break her stride, just continues walking right toward me, her brown curls twisted away from her face with polka-dot barrettes. She stops a couple feet away, as if it's dangerous to come too close.

"Hey, Emma," Anabelle says. Cordial, but making it obvious there is a wall between us, and I am only getting access to the surface of her.

"Hi," I say. It is all I can say.

"What'd you get?" She gestures toward my bag.

"Oh—some new paints. And, um, brushes. What are you here for?"

"Need to get supplies for that Community Art Project. I got paired up with Courtney, who isn't doing shit. Hey, listen," she says, one hand on her hip. "I'm just going to come out and ask you straight: are you hooking up with David?"

"What? No! Why would you think that?" I try to keep my tone even, although I'm sure my face gives me away.

"Rachel saw him leaving your room the other day." Her eyes briefly flash onto mine, and underneath her façade of nonchalance there is surprise. And confusion. And hurt.

I can imagine what she's thinking: *David? Out of all the guys in the world, you had to go after David?* Because David was always hers. David was always the one she wanted.

My skin is hot all over, as if I am a firecracker and someone has lit the fuse.

"He stopped by to say hi the other day," I tell her, which isn't technically a lie. "I hadn't seen him in a while." Also technically true.

Her brow creases. "So nothing's going on between you two?"

I must pause a little too long, or maybe my face gives something away, because Anabelle holds up her palm in a gesture that screams STOP.

"Wait," she says. "Never mind. I don't want to know." She smiles at me, but it is a brittle, hard-edged smile. Her eyes are shards of broken glass. "Bye, Emma."

"Bye." It is all I can say.

Anabelle steps past me and walks further into the store. I half turn and watch her for a few moments. She doesn't look back.

I almost run after her. Instead, the coward inside me wins out and I escape to my car.

When I think about everything that's happened, spiraling outward from that night at Robbie Zwick's party, it is a heavy weight pressing down on my chest. Maybe talking about it would ease the pressure. But I can't imagine where I would even begin.

Plus, I doubt Anabelle would listen to anything I have to say.

Not that I blame her. Right now, I don't want to listen to me either. I'm tired of hearing myself think. I want to escape my own thoughts.

The chilly winter air smells of car exhaust and sour garbage. The bright red sun peeks out from behind a strip of tall office buildings, sinking toward the horizon. It reminds me of the red lights blinking in the sea of windmills I discovered a few weeks ago.

Climbing into my car, I almost decide to drive to the windmills again. But then my stomach growls, and I realize I haven't eaten since breakfast—I used the lunch period to paint that dumb spider. No matter how many hours I log, my safe studio paintings don't seem to be improving. If anything, they're getting worse—more stilted, quiet, drained of life. Just like me.

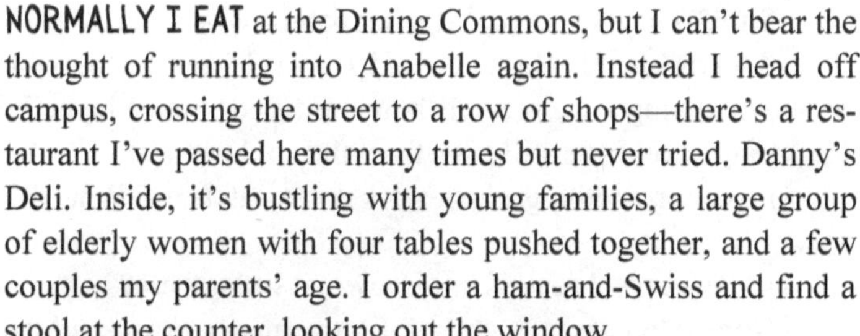

NORMALLY I EAT at the Dining Commons, but I can't bear the thought of running into Anabelle again. Instead I head off campus, crossing the street to a row of shops—there's a restaurant I've passed here many times but never tried. Danny's Deli. Inside, it's bustling with young families, a large group of elderly women with four tables pushed together, and a few couples my parents' age. I order a ham-and-Swiss and find a stool at the counter, looking out the window.

I unwrap the sandwich and pull a book from my backpack. Restaurants are lonely when you're alone, and I always bring a book so I can have "company" while I eat. But instead of reading, I stare out the window at the gray clouds threatening snow.

"Hey, Emma?"

Kevin is standing next to me, holding out a sandwich wrapped in brown paper. He's wearing a striped green-and-blue shirt and his green eyes leap out at me. "Um," he says, thrusting the sandwich in my direction. "I think this is yours."

"What? No, I've got mine—" I say, displaying my ham-and-Swiss, which I suddenly realize is not a ham-and-Swiss at all but rather a turkey-bacon-tomato club. "Oh," I say, staring at it in disbelief. I've already eaten half of it.

"The lady at the counter switched our orders by mistake," Kevin says, his tone apologetic.

I'm embarrassed and don't know what to do. I swat the air with my hand like I'm shooing a fly. "Keep it—it's yours," I say, forcing a close-lipped smile as I picture a strand of tomato clinging to my teeth.

But Kevin doesn't move. He must want *his* sandwich, not mine. I use a plastic knife to try cutting away the part I've eaten, sawing futilely at the thick bread.

"It's okay," Kevin says after a moment. "I mean, can I have yours?"

"Sure," I say, relieved. "It's ham-and-Swiss."

"Sounds good." He nods, and I swivel back to the window, wondering if he can tell how mortified I am. Maybe he thinks my cheeks are still pink from the cold outside.

He says something else, but I don't catch it. "What?" I ask.

He clears his throat. "Um, is anyone sitting here?"

"Nope. Here, be my guest." I move my backpack a little to make more room. He sits down at the stool beside me. I open my book and stare down at the words, but I am flustered, unable to concentrate. I'm hyper-aware of him next to me, paper crinkling as he unwraps the sandwich. He takes a bite at the same time I do. His elbow brushes mine, just barely. I let my book fall closed and stare out the window, listening to our chewing.

I feel him looking at me and I keep my focus out the window for as long as I can stand it. When I finally turn toward him, he smiles. "Delicious sandwich!" he says. "I'm glad you have better taste in sandwiches than you do in pizza."

I roll my eyes, relaxing a little. "Yours isn't bad, either," I say. "I pretty much devoured the whole thing before you could wrestle it away from me."

"Best thing that's happened to me all week," he says, taking a sip from his drink.

"What?" I laugh in surprise. "Why?"

"Because after I finish eating this delicious sandwich, I'm driving to the Indianapolis Museum of Art. I was going to ask you in class if you wanted to go with me, but I chickened out. Now I get a second chance. To ask you, I mean."

Inwardly, I stiffen. "Oh. That's really nice of you to think of me, but I don't know…"

"There's a temporary exhibit of Basquiat's work," Kevin explains. "Something about your work reminds me of his. That's why I thought of you."

"Wow. Um, thank you. I don't even know what to say. That's a huge compliment!" I fell in love with Basquiat's work last year, after Mrs. Muna showed us a video about contemporary artists. His paintings are frantic, vividly alive. I think I recognized some destructive, obsessive impulse in his work that was—still is?—beating within my own heart and fingertips.

I hook my ankles around the stool. "It's just, that, you know—I'm kind of busy tonight. Lots of work to do."

"That's too bad. But I get it."

"Maybe some other time," I offer.

"Yeah. Except… this is the final week of the Basquiat exhibit."

A moment ago, I wasn't even sure I wanted to go to the exhibit. But if this is my only chance? Now I'm dying to go.

I hear myself say, "I really like you, Kevin—I like spending time with you and working on our project—I just, um… I'm not in the right place to, like, date right now? If that's, um, what you're asking?" I stare down at my greasy napkin.

"I like you too, Emma. A lot. I have to admit, that was what I was hoping. But I get it."

I brave a glance at him.

He smiles. "How about this? Will you come to the Basquiat exhibit with me on a non-date?"

Even though I don't know him that well, I have a strong sense that he will respect my wishes. He won't push me. He won't try for more. He will be my friend. And god, how I need a friend right now.

"Okay," I say. "A non-date. I can do that."

EVEN THOUGH THIS IS THE FINAL WEEK of the exhibit, the gallery is deserted. Maybe because it's a weeknight. The hardwood floors echo our footsteps as we wander, alone together, from room to room. Security guards nod greetings but remain stationed at their posts. One guard, an elderly man with yellow-white hair and a wrinkled uniform, sleeps in a chair near the exit, his mouth hanging open.

Basquiat's paintings remind me of graffiti art, splashes of bright color and bold, shaky lines. Kevin and I stand quietly in front of a fevered angel, wings protruding erratically from its tilted body. I've seen a print of this painting before, in a textbook. It is surreal to be standing here before it, so close I can see the texture of the brushstrokes.

"This one's called *Fallen Angel*," Kevin reads from the placard on the wall. "It says here that Basquiat was commenting on how beauty and darkness coexist."

"Hmm." I lean in closer, studying the smears and ridges of paint. After a few moments, I step away. "Kinda sounds like crap to me."

Kevin laughs, a surprised laugh. He holds up his hands in surrender. "You can come read it for yourself if you'd like."

"No, no—I believe that's what the sign says. I mean the whole thing about beauty and darkness coexisting. That's crap."

Kevin takes a step back from the painting, closer to me. "Don't you think darkness can be beautiful?" he asks.

"I think people over-romanticize darkness." I remember my freshman self, reading gothic novels and yearning for drama. "What's beautiful about pain?"

Kevin doesn't respond. I gaze at the painting. The angel has a red slash for a mouth that could be a smile or a grimace; it's difficult to tell. Its halo is sharp and pointy, as if fashioned from barbed wire.

"What I love about this painting is the color palate," I say, to change the subject. "What a striking blue that is." It is a bright, robin's egg blue.

"It is a nice blue," Kevin agrees.

I'm surprised by how much I like standing here next to him. When I breathe in, he smells like aftershave and minty shampoo. Across the room, the security guard snores loudly, startling himself awake. He looks over at us with a dazed expression, then consults his watch. "Okay, kids. We close in twenty minutes."

"Thanks," Kevin says.

We wander through the remainder of the exhibit. A sign at the exit states that Basquiat was twenty-seven when he died of a heroin overdose on August 12, 1988.

August 12 is Hunter's birthday.

The date settles painfully in my gut like I've swallowed a rock. No matter where I go, no matter what I do, I won't ever be able to escape the past.

ON THE DRIVE BACK to Wabash Academy, Kevin tells me about the windmills he stumbled across one day, driving the side roads up to Chicago through Benton County.

"Me too!" I tell him about discovering the same windmills myself, sketching them in my notebook when I first arrived back at Wabash after winter break.

"Seriously? They're cool, right?"

"Oh my gosh, so cool. And weird. They're like science fiction."

"Exactly! This fleet of futuristic windmills plopped down in the middle of nowhere."

"You sort of expect that you'll go back and try to find them, and they'll be gone. Like they were never there."

"Emma, you're the only person I've met who has seen them. Everyone else looks at me like I'm crazy when I mention them." He describes how, in autumn, the tall stalks of corn ripple beneath the windmills like waves along a shoreline. I close my eyes and try to picture it. Everything stirred by the same gentle force.

"I wish I could touch a windmill," I say. "I don't know why. I guess it's a strange wish." I fiddle with a loose button on my sweater. "We should find them again. Paint them."

"That would be awesome! Maybe this weekend?" He glances at me, hesitating, and then he says, "Another non-date?"

I sit up straight, drumming the dashboard excitedly. "Or project research. Kevin, I just got the best idea!"

18

BEFORE

LATE SUMMER, BEFORE JUNIOR YEAR

I SIT ON the edge of my bed and look around my room, trying to notice and soak in all the details that have become invisible in their familiarity. The precise shade of the walls, soft yellow like the outer edge of a sunflower's petals. A framed illustration of my name, outlined by Disney princesses—a souvenir from a trip to Disneyland when I was nine, at the peak of my princess obsession. A cross-stitched picture of daisies that I made in sixth grade, my fingers stinging from the point of the needle as I pressed it through the fabric again and again.

Tonight is the night I've been dimly focused on all summer. My stomach is equal parts nervous trepidation and shivery excitement.

In the morning, I will break away from the only home I've ever known.

I will hug and kiss Dad goodbye, and then Mom and I will hit the road in the six a.m. darkness, before traffic gets too bad. A couple weeks ago, Mom and Dad bought a new car and gave me their old one. Previously, I thought it was a total clunker. I yearned for a sleek Prius or an all-electric Volt: the efficient, environmentally conscious cars popular in California. But as soon as Mom and Dad handed over the keys, the car transformed from a frog into a princess. Sure, it's ten years old, with a scratched paint job and funky-smelling upholstery. But to me, it is beautiful. My very own car!

I've grown to love this car over the years. We've been through a lot together: my driving exam (twice—I failed the first time when I nearly sideswiped a UPS truck double-parked on the street); early morning rides to track practice; countless In'N'Out runs with Céline; trips to the beach with Hunter. Sand is now buried in the cracks between the seat cushions and soda stains decorate the carpet floor pads. I am comforted that I will be traveling all the way to Indiana behind this wheel. Even after Mom leaves, this black four-door sedan will be parked in the lot outside my dorm, like a touchstone or a time machine. I could hop in, turn the key, and drive all the way back home if I need to.

When I think of the journey ahead, I picture a list of items—a neat row of boxes waiting for checkmarks. We will wind our way through Nevada, then Utah, then Colorado and Kansas. We'll cross the Missouri River and drive through Illinois to Indianapolis, then head another sixty miles east to Wabash Academy, where I will spend the next two years of my life.

The last item on the checklist is saying goodbye to my mom, who will fly home to Buenaventura on Monday after a weekend of move-in and orientation activities. I can, in theory, imagine the moment: after all, I have said goodbye to Mom countless times before. I can imagine her soft arms wrapped around me in a hug; the floral smell of her freshly shampooed hair; the way she will turn away, fiddling with her purse or jacket buttons, looking everywhere but at my face in an attempt to mask her tears. I can imagine the sting of tears in my eyes. I can hear Mom say, "Take care, sweetie," her voice breaking. I can imagine the hollow clopping of her heeled boots growing fainter, receding to silence.

And after that, what? What comes next? My imagination runs dry. The tidy row of checkmarks morph into a blank page.

Nothing.

Anything.

"Hey, you."

I look up. Hunter smiles, arms crossed, leaning against my bedroom doorframe. His sunburned nose is peeling and his red hair has lightened from a summer of running ten-milers on the beach. He's training for a half marathon, planning to work his way up to a marathon next.

"How long have you been standing there?" I ask.

"Hours."

"Sorry. I was spacing out."

"You looked pretty deep in thought," Hunter says. He crosses the room and sits beside me. His hand is a warm anchor on my back. "You okay?"

"Yep. I'm all packed up."

"Looks like you hijacked your mom's suitcases, too."

"There's a lot of stuff to take!"

"I can see that," Hunter says in a teasing tone.

"I'm not just going on vacation." If I don't keep talking, I will lose my composure and dissolve into tears. "I'm *moving*, Hunter! I'm moving halfway across the country!"

"I know," Hunter says. His voice has lost its playful edge. "But this is what you want, right? This is your dream."

"Yeah." I sigh. "It is. And I'm excited. I am. But I'm also scared. In reality, everything is so much more complicated than when it only exists in your head."

Hunter nods, quiet.

"Do you get nervous before a big race?" I ask.

"Of course I do."

"You never seem nervous. You always seem so calm and confident."

"It's all for show," he says with a wry smile. "I've got you fooled."

I pick at a dried splotch of paint on my jeans.

"You want to know the truth?" Hunter asks. "I think you're always going to be nervous about something that matters to you. It's a good thing, actually, because it means you care. Like, I'm nervous about you leaving. Because I care about you, Pea. A lot."

"I care about you, too." I wipe my sweaty palms on my thighs. "Don't be nervous. We're gonna be fine."

"You don't sound very convincing."

"I guess I'm a little nervous, too."

"I'll come visit you. And you'll be home for Thanksgiving. It's not *that* far away."

Here in the late summer sunlight of my bedroom, Thanksgiving is an impossibly distant glimmer in the future. It almost seems unreachable.

"Plenty of couples make long distance work," Hunter says.

I imagine being at Wabash Academy, trying to make new friends and dive into my new roster of classes while constantly calculating the time where Hunter is and wondering what he is doing. I imagine myself turning down invitations and opportunities, staying in at night so I can talk to him on the phone. I imagine myself wobbling, out of balance: planting one foot in the soil of Indiana while trying to keep my other foot firmly in the halls of Buenaventura High.

Coach Bill says that during a race, you need to focus your gaze ahead of you and pursue the horizon. You might be tempted to keep turning and glancing back over your shoulder. But doing so will only slow you down.

How will I fully immerse myself in my new life at Wabash Academy if I'm always looking back at Buenaventura High?

How will I grow and evolve as an artist if I'm scared to let go?

My heart hammers. I push my sweater sleeves up. "It's so hot in here," I say.

"Yeah, you are," Hunter quips. He leans over and kisses my neck. I turn and kiss him back, but my mind is whirling. *I can't, I can't, I can't, I can't.* I pull away.

"I can't do this," I say softly.

Hunter's eyebrows knit together. "We don't have to go out tonight. We can stay in. Watch a movie or something." Our plans for this night, my last night, are to drive around town to all our favorite spots: the orange grove, the high school track, Coastal Cone for some ice cream, the parking lot at Fisherman's Point that looks out at the ocean waves.

"No," I say. My chest is going to crack wide open. I imagine my heart spilling out in a gush of blood. I imagine it falling onto the carpet. I can picture it clearly: pumping and pumping, like some crazed wild animal, uncaged on the floor.

"What I mean is," I say. "What I mean is, I don't think I can do this. Any of this. Anymore."

Hunter's face is pale. His freckles are pinpricks of shadow. "What are you saying, Emma?"

"I'm saying, I'm going to be far away. It's going to be really hard. Maybe it's best if we just, you know…"

"No, I don't know. You're going to have to tell me." Hunter's eyes bore into me: hard, sharp, hurt.

I am aware of breathing in, breathing out. In, out. "Maybe we should take this as a natural ending point. Let things go. Stop pushing so hard to make this into something it's not."

"Stop," Hunter says. He takes my hands in his. His grip is tight, hurting my fingers. "You don't really mean this. You're scared about leaving, and you're lashing out. It's okay. This is your nerves talking."

"No." I pull my hands out of his. "I'm serious. I think it would be for the best. I mean, really, how many high school couples stay together in the long run? How many long-distance relationships work? Almost zero."

"Emma, don't—"

"We've been kidding ourselves. Long distance sucks. If we stay together now, we'll just awkwardly limp along, growing more and more distant from each other, and then we'll break up at Thanksgiving. Staying together only draws this out longer and makes everything more painful in the end. Band-Aids hurt less if you rip them off fast."

"Shit, Emma! How can you be saying this? How can you sound so detached about us?" He taps his knuckle against my head. "Is Emma still in there? Where's Emma?"

"I'm sorry, Hunter. I know this seems sudden—"

"I don't get it," he interrupts. "How long have you been having these doubts?"

"A little while. I've just been thinking about things."

Hunter rises from the bed and steps away from me. "Is that really all I am to you—all we are to you—some meaningless high school relationship?"

Tears spring to my eyes. "Don't say that. You mean so much to me."

"I love you, Pea."

"I love you, too," I say, my voice breaking.

"You're the one who is choosing to move halfway across the country. But I've supported you. We can make it work. I mean, we've got something special here. Don't you think?"

I look up at him. He towers over me. He's run his hands through his sun-bleached hair and now it is sticking up in all directions. His cheeks are flushed. He looks as if we've just had an intense makeout session in the backseat of his mom's car, except there is anger flashing in his eyes. Anger seeping from his pores.

I've broken us. I've broken everything. Even if I try, I can never take back what I've said. Everything between us will always be different, from this moment forward.

"Don't you think we're special?" Hunter repeats, desperation in his voice.

"I don't know," I admit. I bury my face in my hands. I hear Hunter's footsteps leave my bedroom. I hear him thump down the stairs. I hear the front door open and close. It is not a slam—Hunter would never slam the door of my parents' house—but it is a decisive sound nonetheless. A firm shutting of what, a moment before, was open.

I spend the night, my last night, curled up in my childhood bed, surrounded by the zoo of stuffed animals I've accumulated over the years, none of which I am bringing with me. Mom knocks and comes in once, bearing chamomile tea, to ask if everything is okay.

"Yeah," I lie. "It's just, you know—hard saying goodbye to Hunter." I let Mom assume I mean saying goodbye to him for the semester, not for good. Because I don't want to talk about it. Not yet. I will clarify tomorrow, during the first leg of our drive, and Mom will spend the next three days listening as I talk things through. By the time we arrive at Wabash

Academy, I will feel wrung out. Clean. Ready for new beginnings.

"Aw, sweetie. Goodbyes are always hard. Do you want some company?"

"It's okay," I say. "I think I'll go to bed soon."

Mom kisses me on the forehead. I squeeze my eyes shut to keep tears from leaking out.

Instead of going to sleep, I binge-watch *Stranger Things* on my laptop with my earbuds plugged in. My eyes are swollen. The tears keep coming and coming. My nose leaks watery snot. I cry about Hunter, and I cry about leaving home, and then I keep crying until I don't know what I am crying about anymore.

Past midnight, I creep down the darkened hallway to the bathroom and wash my face. The cold water stings my pores. In the mirror, my eyes look afraid.

A little after three a.m., I call.

He answers on the second ring. I can tell he wasn't sleeping, either, because his voice doesn't sound groggy.

"I'm an idiot," I say. "I'm so sorry. I made a huge mistake." That's all I can get out before tears completely overwhelm my voice.

"It's okay," Hunter whispers. "Don't cry. Shhh, it's okay."

"You were right," I say, hiccupping. "I'm scared. I lashed out at you. I'm sorry."

"It's okay," he says.

"So we're still together, right? I don't want to break up. I love you."

"I love you, too, Em."

"It was stupid, what I said. I didn't mean it." I listen to the silence for two, three moments. Four, five, six. "Hunter? Are you still there?"

"Yeah," he finally says.

"I didn't mean any of it. Really."

He exhales. "I know."

"I don't want to leave you. I'm going to miss you so much."

"I'll miss you, too."

"Will you come over?" I ask. "Please? I need to see you."

Ten minutes later, I'm crossing the dewy grass in my bare feet toward Hunter's waiting figure, leaning against the crooked jacaranda tree on my front lawn. There is a damp chill in the air and Hunter is wearing his cross-country sweatshirt. When he sees me, he opens his arms. I run to him.

Kissing him, my throat feels thick with glue. His arms are a comforting weight around me, tethering me to the earth, to my front lawn, to this familiar life.

He kisses my lips and my cheeks and my neck, renewing his claim on me.

This is right. He's the one I'm supposed to be with. But deep inside, a smaller voice says, *It's only a matter of time.* The brave part of me knows that this moment, right now, is the lie. What I said this afternoon in my bedroom: that was the truth.

My own words clang through my mind, loud as cymbals: *If we stay together now, we'll just awkwardly limp along, growing more and more distant from each other, and then we'll break up at Thanksgiving.*

"It's cold out here," Hunter whispers, nipping my ear. "Let's go to my car."

Staying together only draws this out longer and makes everything more painful in the end.

"Okay, for a minute." I let Hunter take my hand and lead me to his mom's car, to the backseat.

The fog huddles around us. I breathe it in, cold and wet, like I am inhaling sadness. I can keep breathing, or I can hold my breath.

It is easier to just keep breathing.

19

AFTER

AT THE BASQUIAT EXHIBIT, an ember inside me sparks to life. I wake up early the next morning—before my alarm even goes off—and my whole body is buzzing, wide awake. Awareness flashes through me: *I want to paint. I want to paint. I want to paint.*

Coming face-to-canvas with Basquiat's artwork—brave, intense, frantic, bold—has reminded me why I fell in love with painting in the first place. It wasn't to be safe. It wasn't to hide. It wasn't to perfect the details of my technique. It was to express something meaningful. To create something that would stir emotion in the heart of another person. In that beautifully chaotic and hodge-podge art room at Buenaventura High School, with art prints covering the walls and mobiles hanging from the ceiling and classical music emanating from Mrs. Muna's ancient paint-streaked boom-box, my skin felt like it would burst open from the jumble of emotions bottled up inside of me unless I was able to release them onto the canvas. And when I did—when I painted something that I put my heart and soul into—it was the greatest satisfaction I could imagine.

I want to feel that again. I want to push myself, scare myself, strip down to nothing but my naked, unadorned inner self and shine a light on all the shadows I've kept hidden for so long.

The problem is, I need a place to paint where I feel unencumbered and safe. In the painting studio, no matter how much I try to loosen up and be free, I am confined by the weight of workshops, of my peers' criticism, of Mrs. Post's expectations. My dorm room has been tainted ever since David made fun of my painting. Plus, even when I think she'll be gone for a while, Nora could barge in at any moment—it's her room, too.

I need a secret place. Somewhere I don't have to worry about being discovered.

I pull on an old sweatshirt and jeans and meander across campus. I don't even realize where my feet are leading me until I am standing there at the gate.

The Alumni Garden.

The shed.

Inside, it is exactly as I remember from the last time I was here, when I escaped here to cry after telling Mom goodbye. The metal table is the perfect height for my portable easel. I race back to my dorm room and gather my supplies. Excitement courses through my veins. Back in the shed, I set my latest painting on the easel—a half-finished, lifeless landscape of a yellow field and a red barn—and paint over it with white. A fresh start. Then I close my eyes, take a deep breath, and dive in.

THE DAYS PASS IN A BLUR. I fidget through my classes, taking notes diligently, reading the assigned chapters in my textbooks each afternoon. Sometimes I catch myself staring out the windows of the library, thinking about brushstrokes and color, the shadows of hair on a bare calf muscle, the delicate ridges on a toenail. Nights, I escape to my garden shed studio and paint until my eyes sting and my fingers cramp.

I prop my latest painting on my easel. It is a large canvas, dominated by two disembodied legs floating in a crimson background. I tie my hair back and get to work.

Time slows and then ceases to exist at all. This is one of my favorite things about creating art—when I lose myself in the process, forgetting where I am, losing my sense of self. The best kind of disappearing.

___

THE DOOR TO SWEET TREAT CUPCAKES jingles as I step inside. The warm air smells of sugar and butter. The shop is bustling, with a line of people waiting to order. A little girl sits with her mom at one of the tables, frosting smeared all over her face as she takes a giant bite.

When I reach the front of the line, Dana smiles. "Hi, Emma! So nice to see you again."

"You too! Wow, it smells amazing in here." I order a sampling of mini cupcakes and grab an open table next to the large blank wall.

The bell jingles. Kevin enters the stop with a girl I don't recognize, who seems around our age. She has short curly hair, glowing golden skin, and a radiant smile. She unwinds her colorful scarf and slides off her coat to reveal a patterned jumpsuit that would look ridiculous if I wore it. On her, it looks both trendy and artistic. *She's the type of girl for Kevin. Not me. He deserves someone like her: magnetic, cool, happy.* But watching them stand in the entryway together, wholly wrapped up in conversation, I feel… jealous.

Stop it, I chide myself. *He already asked you out. You turned him down. You're friends, nothing more.*

Eventually Kevin spots me, hugs the girl goodbye, and heads across the room to my table while the girl joins the end of the line.

"This place is great!" Kevin says, plopping down across from me. "Even better than I had imagined. I could really see this being a community gathering spot. Cupcakes and coffee, what more could you need?"

"And you haven't even tried the cupcakes yet!" I push the plate toward him. "Here, I got us a wide variety. I didn't know what your favorite flavor is."

"Definitely anything chocolate."

"Me too!"

Kevin slaps his forehead. "So this means we'll argue over pizza toppings and then fight over the last cupcake. I knew you were trouble, Miss Mason."

"I'm just relieved your terrible taste in pizza doesn't extend to desserts. Here, try this one. Chocolate Heaven."

He bites into it, closing his eyes. "Wow."

"Amazing, right?"

"Yes. Okay, I'm sold. Let's do our project here."

I laugh. "You haven't even met the owner yet!"

"I don't care. All I want to do is eat more of these cupcakes and make artwork with you."

"That's all I want, too," I say, before I think to stop myself.

Kevin smiles at me, and I blush, feeling exposed. I need to change the subject. "Who's that?" I ask, nodding across the room to where Patterned Jumpsuit Girl sits alone, typing on her laptop.

"Oh, that's Megha. Why?"

"Does she go to Wabash? I don't think I've seen her around."

"No, she goes to the public high school. We met a while back, at the art festival downtown. Have you gone?"

I shake my head. "Must have missed it somehow."

"They have it every summer, right before school starts. Last year Megha had a booth there. She does awesome calligraphy."

"Wow, that's great." I was the one who asked about her, but now I can't remember why. I don't want to be talking about Patterned Jumpsuit Girl and her awesome calligraphy.

"Hey," Kevin says, unwrapping a red velvet mini-cupcake. "Maybe Megha can help with our project. She knows a ton of people in the community, especially artsy kids at the high school. She can help us spread the word."

I cross my arms, kicking myself that I even asked about that girl. I don't want to bring in someone else. I like things the way they are—the two of us. I thought he did, too.

But The Accident should have taught me to expect this. Everything can change in a heartbeat. Anything can disappear.

I open my notebook, smooth flat a blank page. "First, we need to figure out what we're doing."

"A mural, right? On that blank wall?" He points.

"Well, yeah. I mean, that's the idea. But we still need to talk to Dana and get her permission."

"I'm sure she'll be stoked. Didn't you say she wished for a mural?"

"Yeah. But we need a plan. She'll want to know what the mural is going to be about."

"The windmills, right?"

"As a starting point. But what else? Right now, we have no clue."

Kevin waves his hand. "Details, schmetails. We'll figure it out."

Anxiety rises inside of me, like I am pot on the verge of boiling. I don't even know why I'm getting so upset.

"Megha?" Dana calls from the counter. "Your tea is ready, sweetheart."

Scratch that. Of course I know why I'm upset. Because of Megha. Because Kevin thinks she is an amazing artist and has probably asked her out on a date, too. Because I stupidly thought that I was special to him—that our friendship was about more than being assigned to work together on this project—but it turns out, I'm only a small sliver of his life. I thought that I knew him because I feel so effortlessly comfortable around him. But what do I know about him, really? He doesn't like pineapple on his pizza. Chocolate is his favorite cupcake flavor. He thinks Basquiat is a genius and he draws cartoon doodles of his dog. Which doesn't add up to much. I only know the surface of him.

Not that I blame him. He only knows the surface of me too. I've presented him a carefully curated version of myself, revealing the details that seem charming or amusing or quirky, but I haven't shared anything that matters. Not really. None of the messy, murky, raw or painful parts.

"Kevin, we can't figure it out as we go. That sounds like a disaster waiting to happen."

"It sounds like art to me. Creativity isn't inspired by a checklist. Maybe this project will help you let loose a bit."

"What's that supposed to mean?"

"What Mrs. Post is always saying in workshop. You're an incredibly talented artist, Emma. Your skills are superb.

But it's almost like… your paintings are *too* precise. Too perfect."

Not you too! I remember my first workshop at Wabash, when Kevin stuck up for me. He was the only one who actually understood what I was trying to do.

As if reading my mind, he says, "Like remember those pieces you used to do? The purple corn? There was something so intense and vibrant there. You took a risk as an artist. That painting had a heartbeat."

I try to keep my face impassive. "So you're saying my recent work is lifeless. Thanks for your brutal honesty."

"No, Emma, you're missing my point."

"Please, continue. The whole reason I came here today was to hear you criticize my art."

Kevin sighs. "All I'm saying is, sometimes you need to close your eyes and dive in, you know? Not overthink things. Have you ever done that?"

My heart pounding dizzily with anger and alcohol, I said to no one and to everyone, "Let's go skinny-dipping!" and peeled off my T-shirt in one fluid motion, diving into the water without thinking twice.

I push back my chair. The warm air in the shop is stifling. The sugary taste in my mouth is too sweet.

Screams and panic erupting from the shallow end.

A body, floating there.

Hunter's red hair.

I stand up, grab my purse. I need to get out of here.

"Emma? Are you okay? Look, I'm sorry—I didn't mean—"

"I need to go," I choke out. "I'll talk to you later."

And I flee.

"**EMMA!**" Kevin catches up to me halfway down the block. He touches my arm. I stop, but I don't turn around. I wipe at my eyes with cold fingers. My gloves are still tucked away, in my coat pockets.

I don't want to tell him about The Accident. I'm not ready.

Why am I still trapped inside that terrible night? How will I ever find the words to explain the regret and grief that have settled in my stomach like heavy stones?

"Hey, I'm really sorry," Kevin says. "I don't know what got into me. That was out of line, to criticize your artwork like that. I was trying to be helpful, but it came out all wrong."

"It's fine," I say softly. "Let's forget about it."

"So we're okay?" he asks. "Come back to the shop with me, so we can talk to Dana?"

"No. I mean, yes, we're okay. But no—I should get back to the dorm. I'm exhausted. I need to lie down."

"Let me walk with you."

"You don't need to. I'll be fine, really."

Beneath my boots, thin tendrils of green poke up between the sidewalk cracks. Spring is coming.

"Emma, there's something I need to tell you," Kevin says, his tone serious. He said these exact same words in this exact same tone the day we were paired up to work together on this project, and then he asked me that silly question about pizza toppings. He does this, I'm learning: tries to break down tension with humor.

"You know what I said at the Basquiat exhibit? About darkness being beautiful?"

I nod.

"That was a load of crap. I was only trying to impress you by sounding smart. I'm not a dark person, actually. I'm not a fan of drama. I don't like playing games. And I want you to know that I like you, Emma. A lot. I like hanging out with you, talking with you, simply being around you. I hope I didn't do anything to ruin that."

Surprised, I tilt my face up and meet his eyes. Hazel green, with flecks of gold, as if Kevin is illuminated from the inside with golden light.

I rise onto my toes and brush my lips against his. Only for a moment. Long enough to feel it—a different sort of earthquake. Not a breakup earthquake. A good kind of earthquake. That world-tilting, legs-shaking, head-spinning heart rush.

But Kevin doesn't know me. Not really. If he knew me— if he knew what type of person I am, what I did to Hunter, to Anabelle, to Céline—would he still *like me, a lot?*

I doubt it.

"I'm sorry," I mumble, stepping back. "I don't know why I did that."

"Don't apologize." His smile is wide. "I've been wanting to kiss you for a long time. I—"

I shake my head. "No, Kevin. We can't. It was a mistake. I'm sorry."

"Didn't seem like a mistake to me."

"Let's just focus on the project, okay? I'll see you in class on Monday. We can figure out our next steps then."

I expect to see hurt in Kevin's eyes. Or anger. Or frustration. But I don't see any of those emotions. He studies me with patience, like I am a puzzle and he is trying to sort through my pieces. Figure out which ones fit together. Not force anything.

"Let me walk you back to your dorm," he says, following me down the street.

I wave him off. "I'm fine."

"Please."

"Okay. If you insist."

Spring may be coming, but the chilly air still belongs to winter. We stand huddled next to each other at a stoplight, waiting for the pedestrian signal to change. The clouds press down around us, smothering the buildings and the concrete with gray. The light changes, and we walk together into the biting wind.

20

BEFORE

SOPHOMORE YEAR, MAY

"I CAN'T BELIEVE the Spring Formal is finally here!" Céline squeals.

"I know!" I wonder if she can tell how nervous I am.

The Spring Formal is a tradition at Buenaventura High—basically, it's Prom for underclassmen. Last year, I didn't go. Céline went with this guy Steve, who she dated for a couple weeks before deciding she just liked him as a friend. Céline is ridiculously excited that this year, we are double-dating to the dance.

We're at a nail salon in the mall, lounging in matching cushioned recliners with our bare feet soaking in warm soapy water. The room is brightly lit and smells strongly of nail polish and other chemicals I can't identify.

Céline leans her head back against the headrest and sighs happily. I try to do the same, but I can't quell a vague discomfort. Someone shouldn't have to crouch at my feet, smoothing my calluses and clipping my toenails.

"I can't believe this is, like, your first time getting a pedicure," Céline says.

"I always have blisters from running. And, I mean, I can paint my own nails. I paint everything else!"

Céline laughs. "Well, I'm glad I could guilt-trip you into getting your nails done with me."

"You were right. This is a special occasion."

"I'm gonna be guilt-tripping you all summer, you know."

"I know."

"It's what you get for moving away."

The woman paints my toenails and fingernails with precise, efficient strokes. She squints at my cuticles as if she is studying directions on a medicine bottle. *It's okay*, I want to assure her. *You don't need to worry about my cuticles.*

Afterwards, walking through the parking garage to Céline's car, I inhale the fresh air, which seems cleaner than usual after the harsh chemical smell of the salon.

Céline chatters nonstop about the dance—what flowers the guys are getting us, what she's heard about the restaurant we're going to for dinner, what are the chances that Robbie Zwick will get busted for sneaking in alcohol. She opens her car door with exaggerated caution, and reaches over to unlock the passenger side for me. "You okay, Em?" she asks, as we carefully use the pads of our fingers to buckle our seatbelts.

"What? Oh, yeah—just a little tired, all of a sudden."

"You should power-nap when you get home. Be ready to par-tay tonight!"

Tonight, tonight, tonight. Butterflies fill my stomach.

A pop song comes on and Céline turns up the volume. In the past few months, she has become more and more of a weekend partier. I usually go with her to the parties at Robbie's house, serving as designated driver while Céline gets tipsy. Hunter never comes along because he has long training runs early on Saturday mornings. But he says as soon as the season ends, he'll join us.

Céline's hands tap along to the beat on the steering wheel. Her fingernails are painted lavender to match her formal dress. She's going with Matt Hayward, who she insists is "just a friend," though I can't see why. Matt is nice, friendly, handsome. He's on the track team with Hunter, and they've been good friends for as long as Hunter and I have been together, so I know him pretty well, too. I can tell Matt has a thing for Céline. He's always dipping his head a little when he talks to her, a smile lighting up his face, color in his cheeks. I hope he and Céline get together at the dance. Then maybe we can be a foursome—Céline and Matt, me and Hunter—and go on double dates all summer, until I leave for Wabash.

Céline drops me off, and I head straight upstairs to my room. I lay down on top of the covers, palms down on the bedspread. My fingernails are painted a light pink with white French tips. For my toenails I chose a deep red, which I'm now regretting because it looks like my toes are bleeding. I chose the red polish to match my dress. I found the perfect dress—long and hip-hugging, with a sweetheart neckline and cap sleeves. "Oooh," Céline said when I tried it on. "That's a dress to get *laid* in."

I try to take a nap but end up merely lying there with my eyes closed, thoughts racing around and around inside my skull. I wonder what my first time will feel like. I wonder if it will hurt a lot. *What if I cry? Will Hunter freak out?*

What if the time comes and I can't go through with it?

What if I'm bad at it?

What if the condom breaks?

Oh god, I can't think about that.

After a while, I get up and shower and put on my dress. I rarely paint my nails and my fingers feel different, the tips weighed down ever so slightly by the shiny polish. I tear apart my room looking for my new necklace but can't find it anywhere.

"Mom! Do you know where my necklace is?" I call down the stairs.

No response.

"Mom!" I run downstairs in my bare feet. The necklace is silver, heart-shaped, with a red gemstone in the middle. Mom and I found it in a jewelry boutique downtown. It was expensive, but she insisted on buying it for me. A gift to celebrate my scholarship to Wabash Academy. The store clerk wrapped the necklace in white tissue paper and Mom carefully placed it inside her purse. And that is the last memory I have of the necklace.

Mom is in the kitchen, her back to me. The radio plays a Beatles song. She's chopping an onion for meatloaf, a dish Dad loves but I don't really care for. I know she's making it for dinner because I'll be out of the house tonight. Little kindnesses like this make me ache for my mom even though we are standing in the same room. I wonder how I'll ever manage, in just a few short months, to live so far away from her.

Paul McCartney croons about a raccoon and Mom hums along. I've never understood this song, but I love the melody. And my mom has a pretty singing voice. I stand for a moment, unnoticed in the doorway, listening to her voice weave in and out of the music.

After a moment I say, "Hey."

Mom jumps a little but keeps chopping, not turning around, pretending she wasn't startled. "Hi, sweetie."

I lean against the counter. The fresh-cut onion makes my eyes sting. "Do you know where my necklace is? The one we got for the dance?"

"I'm not sure. Where was the last place you had it?"

"I remember you put it in your purse after we bought it."

"Hmmm." Mom sets down her knife and turns to face me fully. Her face brightens like a light switch has been flicked on. "Wow, honey, look at you. Absolutely beautiful."

"Thanks."

"I'm serious." She turns on the faucet and washes her hands. "Hunter is going to flip his lid when he sees you."

My throat tightens. Usually, I talk to Mom openly about Hunter. About everything. She's always said she wants me to be honest and tell her when I'm ready to have sex, and to promise I'll be safe. I've imagined having a calm, rational, brief conversation, after which my mom will take me to the doctor to get a prescription for birth control pills. That's what other girls at school do. Siggy Taylor keeps her birth control pack in the front pocket of her backpack, visible whenever she unzips the pocket for a piece of gum or a pen. One time, her birth control pills fell out onto the floor in the middle of class. Siggy calmly reached down and picked up the small pink disk without batting an eyelash.

I've been planning to channel Siggy—unflustered, un-afraid, rationally talking to my mom about sex like an adult. But now that the time has come, I can't go through with it. I keep chickening out and diverting the conversation to other topics. Mom has no idea that Hunter and I are planning to have sex tonight.

Or what if she does know? Maybe it's obvious? My mom has an uncanny ability to know what I'm thinking. Sometimes it seems like my forehead is transparent, a clean windowpane.

Like all my mom has to do is look at me, and she can read all the thoughts swirling around inside.

I glance down at my nails. The problem with trying not to think about sex? Suddenly it's the *only* thing I can think about.

"Let's check my purse. Maybe it's still in there," Mom says, drying her hands on the rooster towel above the sink. The radio station switches to a commercial break.

The necklace isn't in Mom's purse. It isn't in my backpack. It isn't in the downstairs bathroom or the upstairs bathroom or my bedroom. Mom and I search and search to no avail, and then all of a sudden it's time for me to go to Céline's house for pictures, and we still haven't found it.

Céline lets me borrow a silver seashell necklace. We pose for photos in her backyard. All the parents sigh and chatter about how grown-up we look, how it seems like just yesterday we were running around in diapers. Mom takes a photo of me and Hunter. He wraps his arm around my waist and pulls me close. My smile is taut. We haven't spoken about tonight, but in my mind every event is a checkmark on a countdown.

Getting ready: check.

Pictures: check.

Dinner at the Nautilus Bistro: check.

Car ride to the dance: check.

The ballroom is packed by the time we get there. Matt immediately leads Céline onto the dance floor. Hunter and I follow. We move together, bodies pressed close, his hands on my hips. I wrap my arms around his neck, nestle my face against his. *I'm ready. I'm ready.* Though a part of me wishes we could stay like this, dancing forever.

Dozens of songs later, the dance floor is hot and stuffy. My feet ache and my forehead is sweaty. I'm not sure what time it is when Hunter leans down to my ear between songs and whispers, "You ready to get out of here?"

I find Céline and tell her we are leaving. She pauses from grinding with Matt so she can hug me goodbye. "You better call me tomorrow!" she says, playfully smacking my butt.

The dance: check.

Still fifty-eight minutes until my curfew. Hunter drives to Fisherman's Point and parks. We gaze out at the dark water. The parking lot is deserted. He leans in toward me and we start to kiss, like we've done so many nights before. But this time seems different. This time my heart is pounding like a jackhammer and there is a nervous lump lodged in my throat. But also, it's like my body is totally separate from my mind, craving him, aching for more of him. My body knows what it wants. My body is not having any second thoughts. *I'm ready. I'm ready.* I mean, it is a special night. We are prepared. Committed. We love each other. I've known for a while that he is the person I want to take this step with.

I'mreadyI'mreadyreadyready.

I reach down and tug at his belt buckle.

Hunter pulls away and looks at me, his eyes huge and serious in the dark of the car. "Are you sure?" he asks.

"Yeah, like we talked about. I'm ready."

We climb into the backseat. Hunter reaches down and unbuckles my sparkly silver heels, slipping them gently off my feet. The moment is so tender and loving that I wish I could press a "pause" button and freeze us, right here. But then my shoes thump to the floor and Hunter unbuckles his belt and presses against me, kissing my lips, my cheeks, my neck, fumbling to tug down the straps of my dress and undo the clasp of my bra. I end up reaching back and unclasping it for him. He keeps asking if I'm comfortable, if it's okay, if it hurts. It does a little, but I tell him I'm fine. Mostly, it is strange and new. The whole thing only lasts a few minutes. I thought I would feel closer than ever to Hunter, but he seems detached, his eyes closed. At the end, he groans my name and grabs my hair, but he accidentally yanks the necklace, too, breaking the clasp.

"I'm so sorry, Em," he murmurs, stroking my cheeks, thinking I'm crying about the necklace. "I'll pay for it. I'll buy you a new one."

"No, it's not that." I wipe my eyes. My mascara is running. I don't really know why I'm crying. It's not regret, exactly, or fear, or sadness—it's more of a supreme awareness that I just crossed a threshold, and now I can never go back. And in a few months, I'll be crossing another threshold and moving halfway across the country. And even if Hunter and I stay together, it won't be like this anymore. Things will change. Things are always changing. I bury my face in Hunter's shoulder.

"I love you so much," I say, tears leaking from my eyes.

"Oh, Pea," he says, squeezing me tightly. "I'll always love you."

I FORGET ABOUT THE NECKLACE until the next week, when Céline asks for it back. I don't know why, but I can't bring myself to tell her the truth—the memory of Hunter yanking it off feels intensely private. So I say the necklace must have fallen off at the dance. "I lost it. I'm so sorry, C."

"No worries," Céline says, but I can tell she's annoyed. I offer to pay for it, but she won't accept any money.

Months later, when I leave for Indiana, Céline's necklace remains wedged somewhere between the seats of Hunter's mom's car. Something about that bothers me, but I can't put my finger on exactly what it is.

21

AFTER

AFTER WE TALK to Dana about our idea to paint a mural for her shop, the project comes together quickly. We describe the windmills and Dana claps her hands giddily.

"That's perfect!" she says. "My dad would have loved something like that."

"Really?" I ask. I want so badly to get this right for Dana and her dad.

"You know," Dana says, "my dad lived here in town pretty much his whole life. He loved this place. He would tell you about all the hidden gems and tucked-away beauty in small towns like this, if you only take the time to look."

"Hey!" Kevin says, eyes sparking. "That gives me an idea. What if we painted a mural that's, like, a collage of this town?"

"Fantastic!" Dana squeals. "We can have the windmills, and the old clock tower, and the lion statue, and the river…"

I pull out my sketch pad, jotting down ideas. "What if the river winds down the entire length of the mural, and also we make it into a border on the other walls, too?"

"Ooh, I love that idea. See, that's why you two are the artists, not me."

"And don't forget the shop," Kevin puts in, biting into a Campfire S'mores cupcake. "Sweet Treat Cupcakes needs to be front and center."

"This is a great list." I read back through everything we have down. "Anything else?"

"The town cemetery," Dana says softly. She gives me a watery smile. "It's where Dad is buried. I visit him there every Friday. Bring him his favorite cupcake—Lemon Sunshine."

"Yes, of course we'll add the cemetery in there." I put down my pencil, my mind already brimming with images and ideas. "Kevin and I will draw up a rough draft and get back to you."

"Oh, you don't need to do that," Dana says. "In fact, I'd rather you surprise me with the finished artwork."

"Are you sure?" Kevin asks. "I mean, this is your shop. Do you really want to give us free rein over that entire wall?"

"That is exactly what I want," Dana says. "I trust you both. I can't wait to see what you do to that boring white wall." She leans closer across the table. "It's like when I'm developing a new cupcake flavor. Sometimes I get an idea for a combination, and to other people it might sound a little wacky, like my Green Tea cupcake. But you need to give it a try and see what happens, or else you'll never know what you're missing."

"I agree completely," Kevin says. I can sense his eyes on me, and I wonder if he is also thinking about our kiss the other day.

Dana slaps the table. "Guess what? Green Tea is now one of my most popular flavors! Sometimes you gotta take a risk and dive in. You know what I mean?"

"Yes," I say, meeting Kevin's eyes. "I do."

***

"EMMA? YOU OKAY?"

With a jolt, I look up and there he is. Hunter. His tall, lean form moves toward me, hair sticking up like a wild bush. My chest is hollow. My heartbeat is a lonely, frantic echo.

The last time I saw him walking, he was hurrying away from me, nearly running down the driveway to his car parked at the curb. I stood alone in the doorway; our parents chatted over breakfast in the dining room, oblivious. I watched Hunter slip into his car. As quickly as he could shove the key in the ignition, he started the engine and drove away. Then he was gone.

"Emma?"

I blink. Kevin is standing there. He touches my shoulder, his face pinched with concern. His eyes are a similar green as Hunter's eyes, but there is no anger in them, only kindness.

"You look spooked," he says.

"Oh—I'm tired, I guess. You looked like a ghost for a second, coming at me."

Kevin puts his arms out in front of him and makes zombie noises. I laugh. Slowly, Hunter evaporates like mist in sunlight.

Kevin and I are camped out by ourselves in Sweet Treat Cupcakes. It is eight p.m., after the shop has closed. Before she left, Dana supplied us with fresh, steaming coffee and more cupcakes than two people could possibly eat. (Especially because I'm already full from the pizza Kevin brought along: half Hawaiian, half pepperoni.)

We are sketching out the design for the mural in pencil along the wall. When we're finished, the plan is to paint the whole mural in a single day. That's going to be the tricky part. The risky part. The "have a little faith and dive in" part. Because in order to get this project done by the deadline, we need other people to help. We're going to invite the community to come in, pick up paintbrushes, and co-create this artwork with us.

If it works out the way we hope it will, it's going to be a magical day.

But it could also be a total disaster.

I resume sketching the Wabash clock tower while Kevin gets back to work on the windmill section. After a little while he pauses, stepping away from the wall and stretching his back. "Can I ask you something, Emma?"

I wipe a strand of hair away from my forehead. "If this is about pizza toppings, I swear for the hundredth time that my love for Hawaiian is forever. You can't sway me away from pineapple."

He laughs. "I wouldn't dare try." Then his tone gets serious. "I've been wanting to ask you—and it's okay if you don't want to answer, but I can't stop wondering about it…"

My heartbeat quickens. *He's going to bring up the kiss.* I brace myself. "Sure, what is it?"

"Why did you let Anabelle take credit for your painting?"

My pencil stills. My breathing seems loud. I don't say anything.

"It *is* your painting, right? The giant legs and feet, underwater?"

I almost lie and say no it's not my painting, of course not, it's Anabelle's painting. But for some reason, I never want to lie to Kevin. Maybe because he seems so honest. Maybe because he never judges me. Maybe because... I trust him. I trust him a lot.

I clear my throat. "How did you know?"

"Your style is so distinct. I knew, as soon as I glimpsed the painting, that it was yours. I'm pretty sure Mrs. Post does, too. It looks nothing like Anabelle's other work. How come you let her take credit?"

I sigh. "It's complicated."

"It's not right. That's your artwork."

I give him a sideways glance. "I guess I wanted to keep it underground."

"Ahh... so that's your underground artwork? You have more paintings like that? Wow." He sits back on his heels, studying my face. "Can I see them?"

I open my mouth to make some excuse. To explain that I'm not ready to show them to anyone else.

But an image of his doodled dog Gar flashes into my brain. The empty speech bubble extending from his mouth, waiting for words. Filled with vulnerable possibility. I remember how Kevin got choked up telling me about Gar. We hardly knew each other then, but he still opened up to me. He literally opened up his most private notebook of drawings and let me see them.

Maybe that's why I've felt so comfortable with Kevin, from the very beginning. He is such an authentic person. He doesn't wear a mask. He is simply himself.

And the realization hits me, square in the chest: *I want to show him my paintings.*

AND THAT IS HOW, two hours later, after locking up the shop and driving back to campus, I end up leading Kevin through the Alumni Garden to the unobtrusive shed in the far corner.

The door creaks as I push it open. I flick on the lights. My painting blares across the room, a blood-red beacon.

I look at him. He is gazing around, taking it in. His wide eyes remind me of a little kid.

"Wait… so you paint here? In this shed?"

"Yep."

"But there's no lock on the door. Someone could come in and take all your work. Someone could steal it, or destroy it."

I shrug. "That would suck. But what I really care about is creating these paintings. What happens to them afterwards isn't as important." *The process of creating art is what matters, not the end result.* I smile to myself. *Mrs. Muna would approve.*

Kevin notices my half-finished painting, set up on my easel. He walks toward it slowly, as if drawn by a magnet. I walk up beside him and we stand together for a while in silence.

"Wow," he says finally. "Emma. This is…"

The moment hangs there, suspended. I can't breathe.

"…incredible," he says. "The emotion in this painting—it's so visceral, so real."

Tears spring up in my eyes.

"This is stunning," Kevin continues. He takes in my work the same way he took in Basquiat's—his eyes dancing all over the canvas, as if he can't get enough. He leans in closer to examine the brushstrokes. "I don't know what you intend with this painting," he says, "but it makes me feel lonely. Like these legs have been severed, and they can't reconnect. It's beautiful yet devastating at the same time."

"Thank you," I tell him, leaning my head against his shoulder. "Thank you." They're the only words I can say in this moment. These past few months, I have tried so hard to turn myself into a ghost—but now, despite all my attempts to hide, he still sees me.

"Do you have any other paintings here?"

"Yeah. Do you want to look?"

"Heck yes!"

My excitement wells up as I show Kevin the rest of my feet and leg series: my paintings of hips, thighs, calves; bony ankles, slender feet, knotty toes; veins snaking underneath skin; scraggly tufts of hair; blackened toenails. Before long they're propped up all around the small space.

Kevin doesn't rush. He stands in front of each painting, leaning back to gaze at a distance, then stepping closer and peering at details.

Letting Kevin see my underground artwork feels brave and good and right. But deep down, I know that I'm still hiding. I'm still not letting him see all of me.

Because Kevin doesn't know he is staring at the feet of a boy I used to love. He doesn't know I started painting this series after my running-obsessed ex-boyfriend got paralyzed. And he doesn't know that I am responsible for The Accident.

If he knew all of that, would he still be standing here, gazing rapturously at my artwork?

I bite my lip. I'm not ready to tell him about Hunter. Not yet.

Eventually, I glance at my watch. "Uh-oh. We better hurry if we want to make it back to the dorms by curfew."

Kevin helps me stack my paintings and put them away. As I'm closing the shed door behind me, Kevin bends down and picks up a crumpled piece of paper in the garden.

When he unfolds it, I recognize the familiar design. It's a flyer about the student art competition.

"Hey, Em," he says. "You're gonna enter, right?"

"I don't know," I admit.

"You should."

"You think so?"

"Yeah," Kevin says. "I really do. And not your paintings from class. I'm talking about these pieces—your underground artwork."

"But what about Anabelle? I don't want her to get in trouble."

"I'm not the only one who can sniff out Anabelle's BS. I'm willing to bet that Mrs. Post knows exactly who painted those giant feet."

"Well…" I hedge. "These paintings… they were inspired by something terrible that happened. Not to me—to someone else. I can't help but paint them, but I also feel like… I don't deserve to be painting them. Like they aren't really mine to paint."

Kevin studies my face. In the darkness, I can't see him very well, but I can sense his quiet gaze. "These paintings might have been inspired by someone else," he says. "But, Emma—they are clearly about you. This art is bursting with *your* emotion. Am I right?"

"I guess."

"We can be inspired by anything. In my opinion, it doesn't really matter where your ideas or subjects come from. What makes a painting truly great is that the artist pours themselves onto the canvas through each brushstroke." He touches my sleeve. "These paintings are filled with *you*, Emma."

Maybe he's right. Maybe it's time to stop being ashamed of my artwork. Maybe it's time to bring my paintings—my real paintings, my soul paintings—out of my darkened midnight studio and into the sunlight.

"Thank you," I tell Kevin. "Okay, *maybe* I'll enter my paintings in the contest. I'll think about it. But I do have one condition."

"What's that?"

"You need to enter your underground artwork also. Gar's too awesome to be cooped up inside your journal forever."

Kevin gives me a fist-bump. "It's a deal."

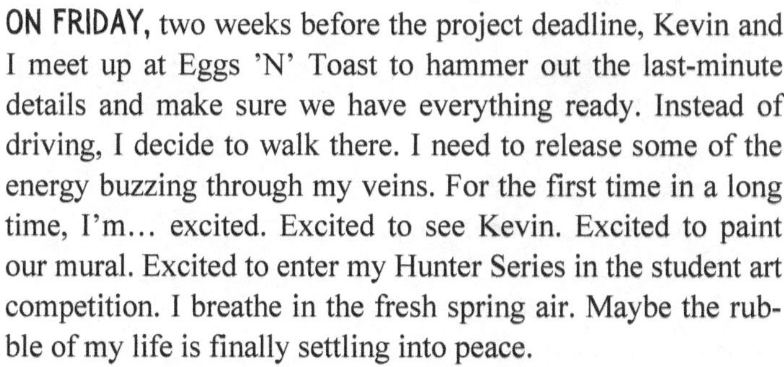

ON FRIDAY, two weeks before the project deadline, Kevin and I meet up at Eggs 'N' Toast to hammer out the last-minute details and make sure we have everything ready. Instead of driving, I decide to walk there. I need to release some of the energy buzzing through my veins. For the first time in a long time, I'm... excited. Excited to see Kevin. Excited to paint our mural. Excited to enter my Hunter Series in the student art competition. I breathe in the fresh spring air. Maybe the rubble of my life is finally settling into peace.

With a few blocks left to go, I glance down at my watch. *Crap. I'm gonna be late.*

I quicken my pace to a brisk walk, then a slow jog, then an all-out run.

Kevin is waiting for me in front of the restaurant. When he sees me, he smiles and waves.

"Sorry I'm late," I gasp. It's embarrassing to be out of breath like this when I ran such a short distance. "Have you been waiting long?"

"No, I just got here. I didn't know you were a runner." He sounds impressed.

"Used to be. Not really anymore."

"Did you run all the way from campus?"

"I mostly walked. I wanted a bit of fresh air."

He holds the door open for me and follows me inside. "A storm's brewing," he remarks.

I glance back over my shoulder. The sky has darkened even though it's mid-morning. The air is dense and electric.

Inside, the booths are filled with people of all ages—elderly couples, parents and young children, truck drivers. The hostess chats with a couple of regulars reading newspapers and nursing mugs of coffee at the counter.

Kevin and I slide into a booth and pick up the laminated menus, smudged with grease. I don't even need to look at mine. I already know what I'm ordering.

"I can't believe you've never been here!" I tease as Kevin studies the menu, his brow creased in concentration.

"What can I say? I lived a dull, Eggs 'N' Toast-less existence before I met you."

"I highly recommend the pancakes."

When the waitress brings our coffee, I order the chocolate-chip short stack with whipped cream. Kevin does the same.

"So how did you discover this place?" he asks.

"Anabelle. We used to come here a lot on the weekends. We'd bring our sketchbooks and laptops and they'd let us camp out in a booth for hours, drinking endless cups of coffee."

"What happened between you two?" Kevin says.

"It's complicated. We were really close last semester, but then we sort of... drifted apart. It was my fault. I ghosted her."

"Why?"

"Pulling away seemed the least harmful option. Long story short, I wasn't a good friend. I did something terrible… something she would never forgive me for."

Kevin frowns. "Well, to be frank, she wasn't a good friend, either—I mean, she stole your painting in class. Was she angry at you? Was that why she did it?"

"No, she doesn't even know I painted it." I shrug. "Whatever. It's water under the bridge. Anabelle has plenty of friends. I doubt she misses me much."

"I find that hard to believe." Kevin fiddles with the salt and pepper shakers. "I'm not asking what you did. That's between the two of you. But it sounds like you're being really hard on yourself. Everyone makes mistakes, Emma. Everyone needs forgiveness sometimes."

"I miss her," I blurt out. Thinking not only of Anabelle, but of Céline, too. "But it's been so long since we've talked. It's too late now."

Kevin shakes his head. "It's never too late. I'm sure she misses you, too."

I sip my coffee, remembering the way Anabelle used to reach across the table—this very table, perhaps—and grip my fingers when she was telling an exciting part of a story or sharing some outlandish idea. She made me feel special, like I was her favorite person in the world, like I could stretch myself to be braver and bolder than I thought possible. Last semester, when I was achingly homesick and wondering if I had made a huge mistake, Anabelle gave me the courage to stay at Wabash. She, more than anyone, made it feel like my second home.

I think of Anabelle's laugh. I would love to hear her laugh again.

But to resurrect our friendship—to *really* be friends—I need to tell her the truth. About what happened to Hunter.

About hooking up with David. About how I was the one who painted those giant ghostly feet. Confronting Anabelle means confronting my own mistakes and regrets and failures head-on. Am I strong enough to do that? And if I try, will Anabelle even listen?

"You should go to her poetry reading," Kevin says.

"What poetry reading?"

"Anabelle and Courtney are hosting a poetry reading for their Community Art Project."

"When?" I ask.

"Next Friday."

"As in, three days before our event?"

Kevin nods.

"I don't know," I hedge. "I'm sure we'll still have a lot to do then. I don't want to flake out on you."

"You won't be a flake. Besides, the reading is only an hour long. I'll come with you. I mean, if you want me to."

I tear off a tiny corner of my paper napkin. "Maybe."

"You should go, Emma." Kevin starts to say something else but is interrupted by a distracting series of beeps blaring from the radio. A hush falls over the restaurant as people quiet down to listen.

"Attention," a computerized voice says. "This is a notice from the emergency alert system. A tornado warning is in effect for the following counties…" I listen through the list of counties, and—yep—ours is one of them. The synthesized voice informs us that the tornado warning will be in effect until two p.m. this afternoon. Another series of beeps, and then the country music comes back on. The restaurant noise swells back up as conversations resume all around us.

I raise my eyebrows at Kevin. "You think we're okay?"

"Oh yeah, I'm not worried," he reassures me. "They give these warnings all the time."

Still, uneasiness gnaws in my stomach. The waitress brings our pancakes, but my appetite has disappeared. I've eaten less than half of my short stack when my anxiety becomes too much. I set my fork down.

"Kevin, I'm sorry. But can we leave? I have a really bad feeling."

"About the tornado?" he asks.

I nod.

He doesn't complain that he isn't done eating or call me a worrywart. He just signals the waitress for our bill.

Outside, the wind shrieks through the trees like the cries of banshees. I'm nearly blown over as we make our way to Kevin's car. As he drives, I stare out the window, watching the tree branches thrash violently in the wind and trying to ignore the giant pit in my stomach. When I first moved to Indiana, I watched videos of tornadoes online, and now I can't help but imagine what one would look like touching down right in front of us. I grip the car cushion tightly. Disaster looms, moments away—the dread is visceral, an elephant sitting on my chest.

As soon as Kevin parks, I leap out and sprint toward the entrance to his dorm.

"No, Emma, over here!" he calls, pointing to the side of the building. "The basement door is here!"

I turn back and together we run toward the basement. The wind tears at my clothes; my hair whips across my face. I'm running in slow motion, like those countless afternoons I bobbed through the pool in my floatie belt, trying so hard to run forward but barely moving through the water. My heart is pounding. A disaster movie soundtrack resounds in my head. I imagine the dark spiral of a tornado touching down right here—ripping roofs off houses, uprooting trees, tossing cars around like Matchbox toys. Leaving nothing but destruction in its wake.

But the tornado doesn't come. The winds are strong, but they are merely winds. Kevin holds the basement door open for me, and I stumble gratefully inside. He shuts the door, bolts it closed, and flicks on the overhead light.

My cell phone rings and I jump at the sudden noise. When I pull it out of my pocket and see MOM flashing across the screen, I answer without thinking twice.

"Mom, I'm okay," I say, adrenaline coursing through my veins. "I'm down in the basement. It's safe here."

"Safe?" her voice sounds distracted. "Why, what's going on? Is everything all right?"

"Oh—yeah. There's a tornado warning here. I assumed you saw on your weather app and that's why you called."

Thunder booms; I shiver. Kevin gently touches my shoulder in reassurance.

"I'm glad you're safe," Mom says. "Is anyone with you?"

"Kevin is," I say. "My partner in that project I told you about." I gaze up through the small, high window. The sky is dark. Angry black clouds roil past.

The connection crackles faintly and I think maybe the call has dropped, but then I hear Mom say, "Emma?" She sounds pained.

"Yeah?" I answer, with an inkling of alarm. "What is it?"

"It's your father, baby. He had a stroke."

22

BEFORE

THE ENTIRE WEEK has been sunny and clear skied, but on Friday—the day of the big rivalry track meet against Santa Barbara—it rains and rains. I sit beside Hunter as the bus rumbles north along the coastal freeway. The ripped vinyl seat is cold against my bare legs, and I wish I'd worn my sweatpants over my shorts. Hunter leans his head back, eyes closed, headphones on. He's listening to his pre-race playlist. His right foot jiggles beneath the seat; before a race, nervous energy always emanates from him like strong cologne.

I turn to the window. Rain streams down the pane, blurring everything. I gaze out at the ocean, waves breaking unendingly against the darkened sand. The pit in my stomach widens to a chasm. I have to tell him. I have to tell him soon, before he hears from someone else. But I can't get myself to say the words. And now is obviously not the right time.

I'll do it after his race. I don't want to upset him before his race, but I'll tell him tonight. My parents probably assume he already knows. They think it's something Hunter and I have discussed. But the truth is, Hunter has no idea that I even applied for the art scholarship to attend Wabash Academy.

When I applied months ago, I tried to tell him. And then, after we almost broke up, I didn't want to tell him anymore. Besides, I didn't think there was a chance that I would actually be chosen.

The school bus pulls into the Santa Barbara High School parking lot and lets us off at the stadium entrance. It's still drizzling and my bare legs are cold and wet as I trudge beside Hunter into the stadium. Everyone helps set up camp under large blue tents in the grassy infield.

It's relatively dry under the tents, but still cold. I'm shivering as I complete my pre-race stretch routine. Hunter barely glances my way. Before a race, it always feels like we're in a terrible fight. It's like he doesn't even register my presence. I know he is concentrating, psyching himself up for his race, but it still makes me feel invisible.

Hunter's first race is the 1500 meters. He takes the lead in the first lap and cruises the remaining three, widening his lead. He looks like an extremely efficient machine, his breathing steady, his arms and legs pumping in rapid rhythm. It is beautiful, watching him run. The drizzle has faded to a mist, and I stand halfway down the final straightaway, clapping and screaming Hunter's name.

Then he appears out of the mist, a shadow solidifying into a sweating, panting person. The crowd in the stands is a blur of noise and cheers. Hunter flies past, sprinting to the finish line. The runner-up is sixty meters behind him. I check and double-check my watch. Hunter has shattered his previous best time. He will be ecstatic.

Maybe I should wait to tell him until this weekend. I don't want to ruin the high from his great race. But I know I can't put it off much longer. A swarm of bees is buzzing furiously in my stomach.

"Emma!" Coach Bill calls. "Time to warm up!" I'm signed up to run the 800 meters. I keep telling myself it's not a big deal, I only need to do my best, that's all anyone could ask—but the calm platitudes from Coach Bill do nothing to soothe my anxiety. I always get nervous before races. Especially today. The big rivalry meet on *top* of my anxiety about telling Hunter my big news. I feel like I'm going to be sick.

I jog with my teammates Lauren and Blair in easy loops around the adjacent baseball field. I try to think about race strategy and goal splits, but all I can focus on is not vomiting my lunch onto the grass.

All too soon, it's time for the 800 to begin. I stand in Lane 5 in my lightweight racing flats. The starter—a woman in a red vest holding the starting gun—explains the race procedures, but I tune her out. There aren't many rules in track. *When the gun goes off, start running. Stay in your lane through the first curve, then begin to cut in. Run until you reach the finish line.* My arms and legs are pimpled with goosebumps and the air is cold and damp against my face. I jump up and down, the way Hunter taught me, to keep my limbs warm and loose.

"Any questions?" the starter asks. All nine of us entrants shake our heads. "Okay ladies, have fun!"

I toe the white starting line, right foot forward, left foot back. Hushed breath. Everyone poised, tense, waiting.

Then... BAM! The gun goes off.

My world narrows to nothing but a string of moments, the seconds ticking by on the clock, my burning lungs, my legs pounding along the track, my heart pumping in my chest. Normally pain is color, intense reds and blues that explode across my vision. Normally I hurt everywhere: pain in my legs, pain in my chest, pain in my cramping stomach. Normally I can never get enough breath.

But not today. Today, I am golden. I'm not running—I'm flying. My mind tells my legs to go faster, and they do. For once it isn't like my different body parts are at war with each other. Today they are all working together, perfectly in sync.

This must be what Hunter feels like every race. No wonder he loves this so much.

I wait for the hammer of pain to hit me at 600 meters, but it doesn't come. Rounding the curve into the home stretch, I only count one person in front of me. *Faster, legs. Faster.* I'm gaining ground. The girl's bright green jersey draws steadily closer and closer.

I'm vaguely aware of whistles and shouts and my name, people are cheering my name, Hunter is yelling, "C'mon Emma, c'mon you can do it, catch her, catch her!" and my legs are pinwheels, careening faster and faster, pushing my body forward, trying to catch up to that green jersey and dark brown ponytail. I could reach out and touch her, almost, almost …

"Second place!" a man yells as I cross the finish line, and another person comes over and unsticks the tag from my jersey.

My legs are jelly. I wobble over to the infield and shake the hand of the girl who won. Then I bend over, hands on my knees, and stare at the grass. My stomach is a roiling mess of snakes. My legs and arms are shaking.

Hunter sprints over, tackling me in a hug. "That was amazing!" he says. "You almost caught her!"

I try to smile, but it is an enormous effort. Even my face muscles are weary.

"You did great, Em! I'm so proud of you!"

I lay down on the grass for a little while, then finally find the strength to stand up and put my arms above my head.

"Your time is one of the best in the county this season!" Hunter says. "Hey, you know what I was thinking—what if you tried out for varsity next year?"

I shut my eyes.

"I bet you could make it, if you really wanted to, Em!"

I am dizzy. I am going to be sick.

"And then we could be on varsity together. Wouldn't that be great?"

"Hunter," I say quietly. More like a gasp, a wheeze. I try to take a big gulp of air.

"What's wrong? Are you okay? Here, let's go sit down." He grabs my arm.

Then, finally, breathing hard, I force out the words: "I got a scholarship. For an art program. In Indiana. And I'm going. To take it."

I can't hold it in any longer. I lean forward and vomit on his lucky racing flats.

23

AFTER

JUNIOR YEAR, APRIL

"IT'S YOUR FATHER," Mom says. "He's had a stroke."

Each word hits me like a punch. All of my thoughts condense into a single burning wish. "Is Daddy all right?" My voice sounds far away.

"I think so. But I booked you a flight home, okay sweetheart? It leaves tonight. Can you be at the airport in an hour?"

I twist a bracelet around and around my wrist. "Yes. I'll see you soon."

We say goodbye and hang up. Blood pounds in my ears.

Kevin's eyebrows knit in concern. "Is everything okay?"

"Um, not really? My dad, um—he had a stroke?" I don't know why I'm talking in questions. "I need to get to the airport? But I feel like I might faint?"

"It's okay, Emma. You're okay." Kevin unfolds a dilapidated lawn chair and guides me into the seat, then kneels in front of me. "Put your head between your knees. Breathe."

I do as he says, and the pounding in my head recedes a little. Kevin places his hands on the rickety metal arms of the lawn chair, as if to steady it, to steady me. I grab onto his fingers. He turns his palms upward and holds both of my hands in his.

When I lift my head back up, Kevin peers into my eyes. "Here's what's going to happen. I'm going to walk you back to your dorm so you can pack a suitcase. Then I will drive you to the airport in time for your flight. Okay?"

"Are you sure? You don't have anything else you need to do?"

"This is more important than anything else."

"Okay. Thank you."

The walk across The Quad to my dorm is a blur. Kevin leaves to get his car, promising to text me when he's parked out front. As soon as I stumble into my room, before I even begin throwing clothes into a suitcase, I press 2 on my speed-dial.

"Céline? It's me."

She does not seem surprised to hear my voice after months of silence. When I choke out that my dad had a stroke, that he is in the hospital, that I'm coming home, she doesn't ask for an explanation or an apology. She simply says, "I'll pick you up at the airport. When does your flight get in?"

I JOLT AWAKE, skin clammy, stomach unsettled. It takes a few moments to place where I am, to remember what has happened. Beneath my feet, the airplane thrums. The older lady sitting next to me snores with her mouth open. Out the window, the sunset blazes bright orange.

I haven't dreamt of Hunter in a while, yet I wasn't really surprised when he came into my dream, strolling toward me with his familiar loping walk and wide smile. He was shirtless, his skin so translucent that I could see the blue veins beneath. I could see his heart, pulsing and very red, throbbing like a wound. He waved at me and strode forward with purpose, as if he needed to tell me something important. But I woke up before he reached me. Before he said anything.

The flight attendant comes by to take drink orders. I ask for chamomile tea, which is one of my "comfort foods"—my mom believes in the healing powers of herbal tea. Growing up, whenever I was stressed or upset, Mom would knock on my bedroom door with a freshly steeped cup of chamomile and a hug. It worked. Inhaling the steam, my dark clouds would recede a little.

The rest of the plane ride, I stare out the window into the scrim of white clouds, remembering a different plane ride. Not very long ago, but it could be another life. If only I could go back in time and tell myself not to break up with Hunter. Or wait and break up with him later, or in a gentler way. Or at the very least I'd tell myself not to go to Robbie Zwick's stupid party. Definitely don't follow that spontaneous impulse to go skinny-dipping.

Above all, it was a mistake to accept the scholarship to attend Wabash Academy. My stomach clenches with regret and shame. What kind of person am I? To choose to leave behind all my friends and my parents, to follow my ambitions instead of thinking about the other people in my life? Obviously it was a mistake to go to Wabash, because look at all the terrible things that have happened since then. Hunter's accident. My fight with Céline. Dad's stroke.

I rub my eyes. Running through my head is a prayer on repeat: *Please let Daddy be okay. Please let Daddy be okay. Please please please.*

CÉLINE IS WAITING for me at Baggage Claim. She looks both different and the same. Her long hair is cut short, and she's wearing a dress I don't recognize. She is standing beside the luggage carousel, looking up at the screen with flight information. Her brow is furrowed, the way it gets when she tries to read something without her glasses.

When I reach the bottom of the escalator, I start to run. My duffel bag thumps against my side and my backpack sags off one shoulder, but I don't care.

Céline sees me and lifts her hand. "Emma!"

Our eyes meet and our smiles do too. What a relief, what a gift, to see that smile on my best friend's face.

I can't even say anything. I hug her fiercely, even though Céline doesn't like hugging. My chest heaves. My nose is clogged and tears smear my face. "Thank you," I say. "Thanks for coming."

Céline's arms tighten around me. Her arms don't feel as bony as I remember, but she smells like herself.

We walk outside together. Daylight is fading from the sky like a bleeding watercolor painting. As the automatic doors whoosh shut behind us, Céline reaches down and links her pinky with mine.

"HERE WE ARE," Céline says. "Room 316." The door is ajar. The only sound I hear from inside the dimly lit room is the gentle murmuring of the television.

I tentatively knock on the door and we stand there together, waiting. My chest is tight. Hard to breathe. I think of the last time I was in this hospital with Céline, visiting Hunter's lifeless body after The Accident.

We barely talked during the drive here from the airport. I think Céline could tell I didn't feel like talking. Small talk seemed pointless. The only thing my mind can focus on is my dad, and I don't know what to say. I don't know what to expect. What news is waiting for me in this hospital room?

"Maybe nobody heard us," Céline says after a moment. "Should we go in?"

I nod and gently push open the door. "Mom?" I say, venturing inside. "Dad?" I watch my shoes take one step forward, then another. Céline follows me into the dim room and it is comforting to have her here.

In the hospital gown, my dad looks like a small boy in a grown-up bed. His body seems shrunken, his head a large weight against the blue-white of the pillow. His eyes are closed. My mom has dozed off in a bedside chair. Neither of them awakens when we walk in. They look like children napping, their faces slack and vulnerable.

Céline sits down in a chair by the door. I tiptoe quietly to my dad's bedside and take his hand. I gently rub the back of his hand with my fingers. The heart monitor beeps steadily.

After a short while, the door opens and a tall woman in green doctor's scrubs comes in.

"Hello, I'm Dr. Hein," the woman says, extending her hand.

I stand up from Dad's bed and shake the doctor's hand. My arm feels weak. "Is he going to be okay?" I ask. "My mom mentioned a stroke on the phone—"

"We're very pleased with how he's doing," Dr. Hein says. Her calm demeanor and warm smile make my stomach unclench a little. "We'll keep him overnight for observation, to be on the safe side."

At the sound of our voices, my mom blinks awake.

"Hi Mom," I say. "It's okay. I'm here. Look, Céline came with me."

"Hi, Mrs. Mason," Céline says, giving a little wave.

My mom beams, one hand at her chest. "Emma, sweetheart! And Céline! Oh my goodness. It's been a long time—it's so good to see you."

Dr. Hein checks Dad's vitals and makes some notations on a clipboard, which she hangs on the foot of the bed. "I'll be back to check on him in a little while," she says. "In the meantime, if you need anything, just push that red Call button." She closes the door behind her, re-sealing the room's dim twilight.

Mom sits up and smooths her hand over the hospital blankets. "They gave him some medication to help him sleep. He was pretty agitated earlier." She sighs. I look at her and, for the first time, I can vividly imagine her as an old woman, wrinkled and gray-haired.

"I'm sorry I wasn't with you, Mom," I say. "I should have been here."

She laughs like I'm being ridiculous. "You couldn't have been here, honey. You live thousands of miles away."

"That's what I mean. I never should have moved so far away. I never should have transferred to Wabash Academy." Tears burn behind my eyes, threatening to fall. I squeeze my dad's hand, half expecting him to squeeze back. But he doesn't.

"Oh, honey. Don't say that." I'm surprised by the fierceness in Mom's tone. "We miss you—of course we do—but we are so amazed by you. You got a scholarship to one of the best art schools in the nation! You made that happen for yourself. You. Made. That. Happen. And we could not be prouder."

All this time I've thought my parents didn't want me to be a painter—that they wanted a more practical life path for me. Is it possible that I've been making assumptions? That I thought they wouldn't understand, simply because they don't make art themselves?

I duck my head, but she reaches over and lifts my chin up gently with her fingers, so I am looking directly into her eyes. "Listen to me, Emma. You have a beautiful gift. Do you hear me? You are an amazingly talented painter."

"Thank you."

"You're welcome. But the thing is, you must pursue that gift with as much passion and bravery as you can muster. Otherwise, you will live with regrets. And regret is a sad way to spend your days on this planet."

I can tell she isn't only referring to my artwork. We've never talked about the breakup or The Accident. I've never told her about the sick regret that has twisted my insides like the stomach flu. I've never told her about how I ruined things with Anabelle by kissing David, or how I've been obsessively painting giant portraits of Hunter's legs and feet—as if I can bring them back to life somehow through swirls of color on a canvas. I've never told her that I blame myself for Hunter's paralysis. But it's as if, somehow, she knows. She knows all of it and she loves me with the same all-encompassing love she always has.

"Your father and I want to be the wind in your sails, nudging you forward. It would make us terribly sad if we were holding you back."

Tears run down my cheeks. I look down at the bedspread, shaking my head. "You're not," I murmur. "I just—I miss you guys. I miss home."

Mom wraps her arms around me. "This will always be your home, sweetheart. And believe me, your father and I are not going anywhere. Dad will be just fine. We're lucky it was a minor stroke. Dr. Hein said he shouldn't experience any permanent damage. He simply needs to rest. Get his blood pressure under control and get lots of rest."

I lean over and kiss Mom's head. Her hair smells of lavender shampoo. "You look tired. You should rest too. Do you want us to get you anything from the cafeteria?"

"No, I'm okay. But their coffee isn't bad—why don't you girls get a cup and visit for a while? Take your time. I'll call your cell if your father wakes up."

I raise my eyebrows in a question at Céline. She nods her answer.

"Okay," I tell Mom. "We'll be back soon." I give her one more kiss, then follow Céline into the brightly lit hallway. I'm swimming up through the deep water, trying to break through the surface into the fresh, clear air.

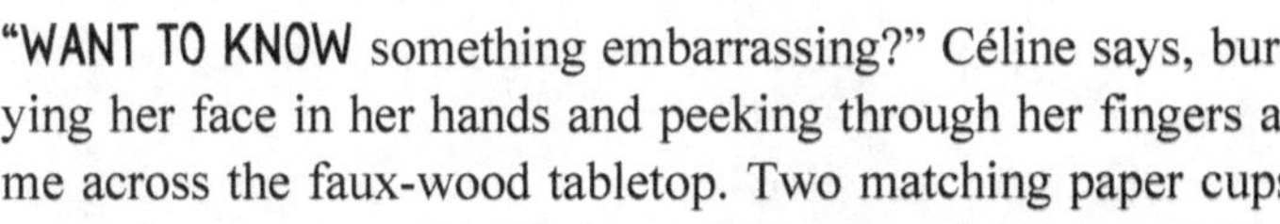

"WANT TO KNOW something embarrassing?" Céline says, burying her face in her hands and peeking through her fingers at me across the faux-wood tabletop. Two matching paper cups steam between us. "I've been stalking your Instagram." She laughs. "Seriously! I scroll through your photos and wonder how you're doing, what you're up to."

"I do the same thing!" I laugh along with Céline and it feels so good. So normal. Inside me, something lights up that hasn't been lit for a while.

"It's still weird not to see you at school," Céline says. "I can't get used to it. Every day, I think of a thousand stupid things I want to tell you."

"Really?"

"Of course! Why do you sound surprised?"

I warm my hands around the paper coffee cup. "I don't know... I guess it seemed, at Hunter's birthday party, that you'd all moved on without me. I didn't fit in anymore. I was like... that awkward uncle at the family reunion. The black sheep of the family."

"Girl, whatever color sheep you are, I'm the same. I'm out there in the pasture right next to you, doing our sheep thing." She nudges my foot under the table. "Seriously, though. School is not the same without you. Like, you know our favorite bench by the English wing? I can't sit there anymore. Not without you. It makes me too sad."

"Oh my god, The Bench. Remember freshman year, how we'd sit there behind the bushes and throw Fritos at boys?"

"That was our idea of flirting! We had no idea what we were doing!" Céline's cheeks are red from laughing.

We sit there smiling across the table at each other, and it feels good—real, not forced.

"So, remember how I've been stalking your Instagram? That Kevin guy is cuuuute," she remarks, with a look that says, *Spill everything.*

"Oh, we're just friends. We're doing this project together." I tell her a little bit about Dana's shop and the mural, showing her some photos on my phone.

"I don't know…" she says, raising her eyebrows. "I've witnessed plenty of awkward Emma Mason pose-for-the-camera smiles to know a genuine smile when I see one."

I almost laugh but stop myself. "This feels weird, C."

"What?"

"Talking with you about a guy who's not Hunter."

Céline shifts in her seat. Her expression is suddenly guarded.

I take a breath. "There's something I need to say. And it's long overdue."

"Okay." She looks down, fiddling with her paper cup.

"I'm sorry," I say. After everything that's happened, I should be all cried out, but new tears burn my eyes. "I'm so sorry for those stupid things I said. I was really upset, and guilty, and I took everything out on you. It wasn't fair."

"No—*I'm* sorry! I've been wanting to apologize to you for so long. I can't tell you how many times I started to call you but then quickly hung up. And the more time that passed, the more impossible it seemed to contact you out of the blue."

"Same."

"I'm sorry I didn't tell you about Hunter kissing me right when it happened," Céline continues. "I should have told you right away. But I never knew how to begin or what to say. It was all so tangled up and complicated—I hoped if I ignored it, everything would go away. But that was stupid of me."

"It wasn't stupid. I proved exactly why you didn't want to tell me when I completely freaked out and yelled at you." I swirl my dregs of coffee around. "Not that it matters anymore, but I've always wondered—Hunter never, like, confessed his love to you before then?"

"He never confessed his love to me, *period*. Emma, listen to me. Hunter and I have, like, zero chemistry. We're not attracted to each other like that."

"But it seems like you're together all the time."

"We only started hanging out more this year because we both missed you so much. He and I were just meant to be friends. You were always the one he truly cared about."

"He probably hates me now." I try to make my tone flippant, but my voice catches in my throat. Embarrassed, I grab a handful of napkins from the metal dispenser.

"Oh, Emma," Céline says, and her gentle tone is almost worse than if she had been condescending. "Of course not. He doesn't hate you."

"He should." I wipe furiously at my eyes. "He's paralyzed. And it's all my fault."

I sense her staring at me but I can't bring myself to look at her as she insists, "It's not your fault. It's not anyone's fault. It was a freak accident."

"No, really. It *is* my fault." I study the dark smudges of my mascara on the napkin. "I'm the reason he got paralyzed."

"No! Don't say that," Céline cuts in. "Have you been carrying that around with you all this time? Blaming yourself for how he drank after you broke up with him?"

"It's not only that." I am a tightly locked chest, its hinges rusted shut. I take a deep breath. "I've never admitted this to anyone. But it's *my* fault he got paralyzed. I'm the one who started the whole thing."

"What whole thing? What are you talking about?"

"It was *my* idea to go skinny-dipping that night at Robbie's house. *I* was the one who yelled it out. *I* was the one who started the frenzy in the pool."

"Oh, Emma," Céline says. The severity in her tone startles me. "It is *not* your fault."

I sigh. "I can't stop obsessing over it. What if I hadn't been there, or what if I had been watching out for him instead of avoiding him all night…"

"Don't blame yourself, Em. It was a freak accident." Céline reaches across the table and holds my hands.

I look down at our hands, clasped together. I look up into my best friend's eyes. "Céline, there's somewhere I need to go. Will you come with me?"

"Of course," she says.

"You don't have anywhere else you need to be?"

"No. This is more important, anyway."

WE TURN LEFT out of the parking lot and drive up Foothill Road, away from the hospital. The houses and street signs crystallize from memory into existence as I drive past. The house at the corner of Dayton Avenue with the big wrap-around porch is still painted a bright yellow. The community college with its crumbling brick walls still looks a little worn down and weary. We pass the turnoff to the post office. We pass Whitney Street; if we turned right, it would take us to Céline's house. We pass the orange groves where Hunter and I used to fool around.

I crack my window open to let the breeze in. As we approach The Keys, I catch the salty tang of the ocean.

Céline parks in front of Robbie Zwick's house. It looks the same. White stucco walls. Terra cotta roof. Twin palm trees arching over the front lawn.

I stare out the car window, at the house where I split in two. Tonight, no bass music thumps from the yard. The windows are dark. Céline and I climb out of the car and walk up the front lawn to the porch. I knock on the front door.

We wait.

Nobody answers.

After a long moment, Céline presses the doorbell.

Still nobody answers.

"C'mon," Céline whispers. "No one's home." She steps down off the porch and heads around the side of the house. I follow.

We unlatch the gate and sneak into the backyard. Palm trees, wooden deck, ornately tiled Jacuzzi tub. And the swimming pool. The scene is so heavy with meaning, it almost seems fake. Like the set of a movie I've watched dozens of times.

The bright chlorine-blue water is the same cheerfully unnatural hue from the night of The Accident. I remember the last time I saw Hunter whole and unbroken, leaning against that palm tree across the pool, chugging beer and refusing to look at me. I try not to think about his body, floating facedown like an eerie, weightless angel.

"You need to see him," Céline says, as if reading my mind. "You won't have closure until you see him."

"I doubt he wants to see me."

"You don't know that."

I cross my arms, then immediately uncross them. "What am I supposed to do? Text him out of the blue?"

"Not necessarily." She winks. "What if you both magically wind up in the same place?"

"How am I supposed to make that happen?"

"Tomorrow's Saturday. I know where he hangs out on Saturday mornings." Céline reaches over and links her pinky with mine, and the chaos inside me settles down a little.

Our wavery reflections are visible in the calm, still waters of Robbie Zwick's pool. Right here, right now, my two selves—Before and After—begin to slowly, tentatively, knit back together.

24

BEFORE

"EMMA," MRS. MUNA says, right after the final bell rings. "Can I talk to you for a minute?"

"Sure, of course." I finish rinsing out my brushes and set them on the rack to dry.

Mrs. Muna is my favorite teacher, and not only because art is my favorite subject. She's young, in her mid-twenties, and only started teaching here at Buenaventura High a couple years ago. In all my other classes, the semester plods along; you can tell the teachers have been doing the same lessons over and over for years. Even when they try to seem enthusiastic, the underlying monotony seeps through. Art class is like stepping into a different universe. Mrs. Muna's fresh energy radiates through the room. Twinkle lights hang from the rafters, sculptures dry on the windowsills, and paintings cover every inch of wall space. Whenever I step into Room 62, my heartbeat quickens and I feel more *alive*.

I meet Mrs. Muna at her desk, which is covered in papers and cardboard boxes and tubes of paint. She rummages through a stack of folders, tucking her magenta-streaked hair behind her ear. "Aha!" she says triumphantly, lifting a bright blue folder in the air. "Here it is!"

I smile, wiping my wet hands on my jeans, as I wait to hear whatever she has to tell me.

"So Emma," she says, her eyes sparking with excitement. "I think you know that you are one of my favorite students."

I blush. I wasn't expecting this.

"I've been your teacher for almost two years now, and you continue to impress me. You have worked so hard to hone your skills. I've been watching you. You come in early and stay late. You have developed your own style. I love getting to see your perspective of the world through your paintings. Your eye for detail is unparalleled, and you are constantly improving and refining your technique in various mediums—watercolor, pastels, acrylics. But even more than that, what I love about you as an artist is your heart. You splay your heart across the canvas every single time, Emma. That makes you truly special."

"Thank you. I, um—wow. I don't know what to say."

"You don't have to say anything. Just consider this." She hands me a brochure.

WABASH ACADEMY FOR THE ARTS is splayed across the top in bold letters. Underneath gleams a photo of an impressive stone building, with a clock tower and ivy-covered walls.

"Have you heard of Wabash Academy before?" Mrs. Muna asks.

"No, I haven't."

"It's a private boarding school in Indiana. One of the top art schools in the nation."

"Wow. It looks really nice." *What does this have to do with me?* I open the brochure. More gorgeous photos of grand halls and stone towers that could be straight out of Harry Potter.

"They offer a handful of scholarships for creative arts students in various disciplines. Public school art teachers around the country are allowed to nominate one student each year. Emma, I would like to nominate you."

"Wait—me?"

"Yes, you."

"Really?"

She laughs. "Really really. Even though we at Buenaventura High would miss you very much, I also think this would be a truly amazing experience for you. I've done what I can for you as your art teacher here. Wabash Academy is an entirely different level. You would have so many resources at your fingertips. Your artwork would grow by leaps and bounds. Have you thought about perhaps going to an arts academy, for college?"

I shift to my other foot. "I, um, I haven't really thought about it." No way my parents would go for something like that. They're both super practical. I'm sure they want me to major in something with clear job prospects, like engineering or accounting.

Mrs. Muna looks at me, her brown eyes round behind her glasses. "You should think about it. You are really talented, Emma. But more than that—you have an artistic spirit."

I gape at her. "Oh, well, um. Thank you."

"You're welcome. So, why don't you take that brochure home and show it to your parents. I know this is a big decision. Since I am only able to nominate one student, I want to be sure you are serious about this opportunity if it is offered to you."

In the brochure, bolded words jump out at me. *Renowned painting professionals. Private studio space. A community of creativity.* I look up and meet Mrs. Muna's eyes. "Do you really thing I have a shot at something like this?"

"Of course you do, Emma. Don't sell yourself short." She reaches across her messy desk and squeezes my fingers. "Besides, I believe there's an element of fate to it. If Wabash Academy is the best place for you to grow and shine, then I truly believe you'll end up there. If not, then it wasn't meant to be after all."

I FIND HUNTER outside the boys' locker room. I can't wait to tell him about my conversation with Mrs. Muna. I think back to our first date, how he called me *an artist* and asked about my paintings. He's always been so supportive and interested in my artwork. Because of him, I feel brave enough to even try for this scholarship.

He is talking with a few guys from the track team that I don't know very well. They're laughing with each other as they lean down, stretching their hamstrings.

"Hey!" I skip up to Hunter and kiss his cheek, awkwardly, like a mom instead of a girlfriend. "I haven't seen you all day. Where've you been hiding?" I mean to be playful, but it comes out sounding a little possessive.

"Nowhere." Hunter turns away. His teammates smirk. "We're starting practice soon, okay Emma? I'll talk to you later."

"Sure. Okay." Have I done something wrong? Last week, Hunter finally got permission from his doctor to start running again, and he's been acting more and more aloof. He hasn't had time to hang out after practice. He takes forever to reply to my texts. He's even stopped calling me "Pea," short for "Peacock"—an inside joke from our first date that always makes me smile.

I don't say goodbye. I don't look back, either. I march across the parking lot and through campus to the pool. It sucks doing water workouts without Hunter. Last month, I returned to running too soon and my shin splints morphed into stress fractures. Now I've been banished to the pool, alone, for at least another month. Coach Bill said he isn't taking any chances this time. "We want to make sure you're fully healed," he told me. "Either that, or you'll join the swim team!" He was joking. I think.

I hate swimming. I hate getting water in my eyes and up my nose. I hate the sharp smell of the chlorine and the limp wet stringiness of my hair. I hate how slow my progress is as I struggle to swim from one wall to the other.

I shiver through another workout of swimming laps and floatie-belt high knees and scissor kicks, ski legs and hammer legs and more laps. By the time I return to the relative warmth of the locker room, sunlight has almost entirely drained from the sky. My phone blinks with a text message from Hunter. I instantly brighten—maybe he isn't really acting aloof, maybe I'm missing him because I got used to spending afternoons together during our pool workouts. I unlock my phone and read his message.

I'm sorry but I need some space to think about things.

The walls of the locker room seem to shrink inward. I peel off my sopping wet bathing suit, rinse it out, and shampoo the chlorine out of my hair. I stand beneath the hot stream of water for twenty minutes, but I still feel frozen. Numb.

Our first kiss flashes into my mind. It was after a pool workout, and we were wedged close together in the small metal shed behind the track where Coach Bill keeps the orange cones and measuring wheel and flotation belts. I was holding both our floatie belts, looking for a place to set them down, when Hunter put his hands on my waist and turned me toward him. Certainty filled my chest as I tilted my face up to greet his lips with mine. Ten minutes later, walking with him down the little hill to the parking lot, my legs were shaking and there was a giddy feeling in my stomach that I wanted to hold onto forever.

Now I feel stupid for thinking it could last.

I'm halfway to the parking lot when I remember Hunter was supposed to be my ride home. Part of me wishes he'll be at his car, waiting for me. Another part of me deflates at the thought. What would I say? What if I start crying?

Hunter is nowhere to be seen, but I do spot a group of his teammates clustered at the entrance to the parking lot. I try to summon an I-could-care-less expression as I stride over in my pullover and jeans and wet hair. They don't glance my way until I'm standing right in front of them.

"Hey, do you guys know where Hunter is?" I ask.

"He left already," Robbie Zwick says. The others laugh, and Brett Javies makes a comment I can't quite hear.

"Oh. Okay. Thanks." I turn away and bite my lip, begging the tears to stay away, at least until I'm out of sight. I try to focus my thoughts on how to get home—it's too far to walk on my injured shin. My parents will both be working for another hour. Maybe Céline will drive back to school and pick me up? Yes, that's what I'll do. I'll call Céline. I'm not ready to launch into the whole story—telling Céline about it will make it real, and I don't want it to be real, not yet—but I don't have to tell Céline about the text message. I can say Hunter must have forgotten he was supposed to give me a ride. I'll play it casual.

I unzip my backpack, rummaging around for my phone, when Brett Javies calls out in my direction.

I look up uncertainly. "Um, are you talking to me?"

Brett nods. His teammates are all staring at me. "You know, he has a thing for your friend!" Brett says. "That girl, Céline. Hunter totally wants to get with her."

My head throbs. Someone is dribbling a basketball inside my cranium and it is the only thing I can hear, drowning out all thought. Just pounding and pain, and that sentence over and over: *He has a thing for your friend. He has a thing for your friend. He has a thing for your friend.*

"We thought you should know!" Brett shouts. Around him, the guys erupt in laughter. Even Robbie, who was my lab partner in Chemistry and was always nice to me, is smirking.

I shoulder my backpack and flee. *Of course. Every guy likes Céline.* Why would Hunter be any different? What if Hunter is only using me to get closer to her? What if every time he kisses me, behind his closed eyelids he is picturing Céline instead?

I jaywalk across the street, leaving the high school and continuing down Foothill Road. If I keep walking and walking, I can follow this road all the way home. The narrow sidewalk is uneven due to the roots of the old, tall oak trees lining the street. I concentrate on physically moving my body forward—like in a race, one stride after another, after another, after another. Waiting at a stoplight, a gust of wind cuts through my pullover. My skin is chilled and clammy and I wonder vaguely if I'll catch a cold. The thought is a comfort. I want to get sick and spend the rest of the week at home. I mean, how can I go back to school? How can I face Hunter or Céline or anyone on the track team? Maybe I should be worried about more than the track team. Does *everyone* know but me?

I imagine girls in class asking me about the homework—or how my weekend was, or what I'm going to do for spring break—nodding and smiling in a fake-pleasant way while behind their smiles a phrase is scrolling by on repeat: *She has no idea, she has no idea, she has no idea.* And later they will mention it to their friends, *Poor Emma Mason has no idea her boyfriend is totally in love with her best friend*, and share a pitying look before returning to their sandwiches and potato chips.

I'm almost to Dayton Avenue, cold tears leaking from my eyes and snot dripping from my nose, when a car drives up from behind and pulls over to the curb beside me.

Hunter? I turn, not sure what I'll say when I see him—but it is not his familiar Honda Civic. It is an old blue Volvo, speckled with dirt and sand, *Buenaventura High School Honor Roll* bumper sticker slightly askew on the back window. I wipe my nose on my sleeve and keep walking.

The driver's window rolls down. It's Matt, Hunter's best friend. "Emma! Hey!"

The wind snaps wet strands of hair across my face. I quicken my pace, pretending not to hear him.

"Emma! Is something wrong?" Matt asks. His car creeps along beside me. An SUV roars around him, blaring its horn.

"Wait, stop!" Matt says. "Let me give you a ride! C'mon, Emma, please?"

Most of me wants to keep walking. But the wind is cold, only growing colder as the sun continues to slip blearily under the horizon, and my feet hurt. My shins are killing me, particularly my left one where the stress fracture is. I am favoring that leg, starting to limp. Still two miles from home.

"Okay," I give in. "But I don't want to talk about it."

"That's fine." He stops the car, leans over, and pushes the passenger door open.

I climb in and collapse on the seat, slamming the door shut behind me.

"Thanks," I say.

"No problem."

I stare out the window at the dry winter hills and shaggy palm trees, speaking only to give Matt directions. When we get to my house, he doesn't pull up to the curb like Hunter typically does. He pulls into the driveway. And instead of letting the engine idle, he shifts the car into Park and turns the ignition off.

"Emma." He studies my face. "You sure you're okay?"

"I'm fine," I say, but the tears come barreling back and it's obvious I am not fine. Everything is made worse by my embarrassment to be crying in front of Hunter's friend. The last thing I want is for Hunter to find out I'm a drippy crying mess over him.

I find a crumpled Starbucks napkin in my pocket. "So, did you know about Hunter and Céline, too?" I ask, wiping my nose.

"What are you talking about?" Matt reaches back to the floor behind his seat and pulls out a box of tissues, which he hands to me.

"You don't have to cover for him. I already know. His friends told me in no uncertain terms that my boyfriend has a thing for my best friend."

Matt laughs. "Who told you that?"

"Brett Javies. Robbie Zwick. A whole bunch of them were there."

"Emma, those guys are full of crap. Nothing is going on between Hunter and Céline. Believe me, I would know."

I blow my nose. I want to believe Matt, truly I do, but I can't get those smirks and jeers out of my mind. *That girl, Céline. He totally wants to get with her.*

"Brett and Robbie love to stir up trouble," Matt continues. "Everyone knows that."

"So, what are you saying—they made it all up?"

"Yes," Matt says. "That's exactly what I'm saying."

"But why?"

"Because they're assholes. They're trying to cause a little trouble for Hunter, that's all. They probably didn't think you'd believe them."

I twist a tissue into frayed knots. "I think Hunter broke up with me today."

"What?" Matt's eyes widen. His eyes are a deep brown, almost black, and he looks genuinely surprised, which makes me feel better. Maybe I'm not the only one blindsided by this.

"He did it over text," I explain. "He said he needed some time. To think. Which is pretty much the death knell for a relationship." Out the window, the trees in my front yard sway, their branches thrashing in the wind.

"Some guys on the team have been giving him a hard time," Matt says. "You know, ribbing him, saying he's 'whipped' and everything, because you two spend so much time together. Typical dumb guy stuff. But I can tell it's been bothering Hunter." Matt runs his hand over his face. "God, he's stupid. To think of letting a girl like you get away."

A girl like you. The way he says it makes it sound like I'm a prize—something worth fighting for, something to be proud of, something to protect.

I shift in my seat. Matt stares back at me. The streetlights have blinked on and the whites of his eyes gleam in the gathering dark.

I imagine Hunter slipping Céline's bra strap off her shoulder. I know Céline wouldn't ever do anything with Hunter, but I can't stop my imagination from running out of control. The images flood my brain.

I lean forward, thinking no further ahead than this moment, here in this small warm car with Hunter's best friend.

Beep! My cell phone. *Beep! Beep!* I reach down and retrieve my phone from my backpack.

Texts from Hunter. The basketball is pounding in my head again.

Emma I'm so sorry. I'm an idiot. I can't stop thinking about you. You're the one for me.

I'm coming over right now.

I love you Pea.

No guy has ever said those three words to me before. I picture Hunter hopping into his mom's car, on his way to my house right now. I remember the first time he held my hand, in front of the zoo exhibit, and how it seemed like my life was a jumble of puzzle pieces finally sliding into place. The night after he first kissed me, I was filled with such jittery excitement that it took me hours to fall asleep.

"Thanks so much for the ride home," I tell Matt. Then I open the car door and grab my backpack off the floor. "Thanks for calming me down."

"No problem," Matt says, turning the key in the ignition. He waves goodbye and backs out of the driveway. His blue Volvo recedes down the street, turning left out of my neighborhood and disappearing from sight.

I sit down on my front steps. I watch the colors fade from the sky. I wait for Hunter to surface back into my life.
But I decide not to tell him about applying to Wabash Academy. It's not like I'll be chosen for the scholarship, anyway. Not in a million years.

25

AFTER

SATURDAY MORNING, I'M up early. I slept surprisingly well last night—as if my body were a tightly wound knot of string that has finally loosened.

Overnight visitors aren't allowed at the hospital. Dad will, fingers crossed, be discharged sometime today. Mom is heading there at nine, when visiting hours begin. I'm happy to see she's still sleeping. I prop a note against the coffee pot.

GOING FOR A RUN. I'LL COME TO THE HOSPITAL AFTER.

Driving Dad's car to the high school, I think about a different morning, in another lifetime, when I drove down this street with Céline on our way to visit Hunter in the hospital.

I park in front of the football stadium. My car—er, Dad's car—is the only one in the lot. This early on a Saturday morning, during the off-season, I guess no one uses the football field or track.

My phone rings. I glance at the screen. *Kevin.*

At the sight of his name, happiness and anxiety surge through me simultaneously. I stare at my lit-up, blaring phone, but I don't answer. I can't talk to Kevin right now. I think about the airport—how I gave him a goodbye wave and fled into the line for security, digging through my purse for my wallet so I didn't have to watch him walk away.

I guess I'm not good at letting go. Or holding on.

The phone beeps—Kevin's left a voicemail. I'll listen to it later.

Thankfully, the gate to the football stadium is unlocked, so I walk down the short hill to the track. It is the same as I remember it, yet also changed. The concrete bleachers still tower over the home straightaway. Palm trees still watch over the far curve like tall, reedy sentinels. But my track—the brown-red dirt with dusty chalk lanes that I practiced on and competed on and watched Hunter race on—has been transformed into a meticulous rubberized surface, springy beneath my feet. A dream track for clocking fast times in races. I knew it was going to happen. The high school has been fund-raising for years to build this track, and construction began during the summer. Now it's finished: brand-new, beautiful.

But part of me misses the tromped-down dirt.

My running shoes are back in my dorm room closet, so I'm wearing my old racing flats. They pinch my toes. After a few steps, I take them off and fling them onto the grassy in-field. I peel off my socks, too. Suddenly I think of the shoes I wore to the Spring Formal, a sparkly silver heel with bows at the toes, the way Hunter tenderly slipped them off my feet that night in the backseat of his mom's car.

I'm not even sure what I'm doing here. Do I think I can change how everything turned out? Do I think I can somehow rewrite what's been written?

The air is cool and damp. Beneath my bare feet, the rubber track has a pebbled texture like a leather basketball. It is perfectly level, smooth and clean, with no ruts or grooves. I begin to run. A slow warm-up jog at first, and then I quicken my pace and lengthen my stride until I am running, running, running.

At Buenaventura High, I was a middle-distance runner. The half mile, 800 meters, was my race. It's the least glamorous of all the running events, but it was the only race I was decent at—the quarter mile required too much flat-out speed, and I didn't have enough stamina for the full mile. So I did the half mile and I won a silver medal at the rivalry meet, when I had that one shining race when my lungs seemed twice as large as usual and my legs had wings, as if weights that had been tied to my ankles for years were suddenly gone. That race, I flew around the track like the runners in those running movies do, with the music crescendoing in the background and triumphant cymbals crashing as I crossed the finish line.

The race lasted two minutes and eighteen seconds. It was the first and only time I ever truly *loved* running.

My bare feet pitter-pat-pitter-pat lightly down the track and I blow air out of my cheeks, trying to find a rhythm in my breathing. After only a lap, I'm already fighting a side-ache.

What I haven't admitted to anyone is that I still feel like I am running after Hunter. Or running away from him. Or maybe I'm not running after all—maybe I'm bent over on the sidelines, lungs clawing for breath, unable to keep going.

Air burns coldly in my chest and throat.

I keep running.

When I think of the track, I don't want to remember this new shiny version. I want to think of Hunter running, red track dust sticking to his sweaty legs. I want to remember the track as it used to be. Our track.

I hear the clank of the gate first. And then I see him coming down the hill into the stadium.

Hunter.

My chest seizes up.

Celine said he would be here. I came here hoping to find him. And yet—I'm not ready. Would I ever be ready to see him again?

My legs keep moving, carrying me around the curve of the track toward him.

His auburn hair ruffles in the breeze. He looks tall, somehow, still—even though he is sitting in a wheelchair. Maybe it's the way he carries himself. His back is straight and his chest is lifted. He holds his hand like a visor over his face, gazing in my direction. After a few moments, he lifts his arm and waves.

I wave back, suddenly self-conscious. This was a horrible idea. Here I am, running, when he can't run anymore. Does it hurt him to watch me?

"Did you forget your shoes?" he calls out when I'm closer.

I smile, gesturing toward the infield. "Too tight—I abandoned them. This feels better."

"You've always been a rebel, Em." He rolls onto the track, and the effortless way he moves in his wheelchair takes me aback. I guess he's had a lot of practice. It's been nearly six months since The Accident. He joins me, matching my pace. Like this is totally normal. Like he's not even surprised to see me here. I wonder if Céline told him I was coming.

The wheels of his chair make a rhythmic whirring. I glance at him out of the corner of my eye. His arms move smoothly, propelling him forward. The movement reminds me of swimming—of the first pool workout we did together.

"I'm so sorry about your dad," Hunter says, and I realize of course it wasn't Céline who told him I was home. It was his mother, informed by my mother.

"He gave us a big scare."

"I'll say. How's he doing?"

"Good—he's being discharged today. The doctors say he should make a full recovery."

"That's great news."

"Yeah."

I'm finding it hard to catch my breath, either because I'm nervous or tired or both. My feet ache. I'm not sure how far I've run—I lost track of laps. The sun is quickly warming the track's rubbery surface. Soon it will be too hot on my bare soles.

"Can we talk for a minute?" I ask, gesturing toward the bleachers.

"Sure," Hunter says in a tone I can't quite read.

I jog over to a bench at the side of the track, and Hunter follows. When I sit down, we're at eye level, and—to me at least—the moment seems heightened. I sneak glances at him. His familiar freckles. His intense green eyes. His lips are a little chapped and his haircut is shaggy. Being here with him is strange and familiar at the same time. We've spent count-less hours sitting side-by-side like this, and yet now everything is different. Hunter isn't sitting on the bench be-side me, holding my hand. He's in a wheelchair. His hands are not mine to hold any longer.

"You're really fast out there," I say, then instantly regret it. Was that the worst possible thing I could have said?

If he's offended, Hunter doesn't show it. "Thanks. My times now are even faster than when I was running. Still getting PRs!" He grins. "Did your mom tell you?"

"Tell me what?"

"I'm gonna race the LA Marathon. Coach Bill put together a whole training regimen for me."

"That's amazing! Wow, twenty-six miles. I can't even imagine doing that."

"I've been lifting a lot of weights, building up my arm strength." He pats his wheels. "And the whole team threw a fundraiser to surprise me with this baby. It's a lightweight racing wheelchair. My normal chair is much heavier and bulkier. This thing flies. It's the next-best thing to running."

I open my mouth to reply, but no words come. The guilt crushes my chest. Heavy bricks. *I need to run. It's not a choice, it's a need.* Even now, he's wearing running shoes. I hate that the soles of his shoes will stay pristine.

We lapse into an awkward silence. Somewhere far above us, a seagull squawks. I take a deep breath, preparing to say what I came here to say, but Hunter breaks the silence first.

"How long did you know?" he asks.

I blink, confused. "Know what?"

"That you wanted to break up with me."

"I didn't know. I mean, until that morning. I wasn't sure."

"Be honest with me, Em."

"I am being honest! I promise. That morning, when I came home, it just—hit me. Like a lightning bolt. Everything seemed all wrong. Didn't it feel that way to you?"

Hunter looks down at his pristine shoes. "I guess I kept hoping that things would go back to how they used to be. That you would come home, and we would feel like *us* again.

I still don't understand what happened. What did I do wrong?"

"Nothing. You did *nothing* wrong, Hunter. I changed. Remember how all semester, you kept saying I was different? You were right. Moving away and living at Wabash made me into… a newer version of myself, as corny as that sounds."

"It's not corny. We all change. I changed, too." He grimaces and pats his wheelchair. "I mean, not only in the obvious way."

I spot my opening and venture toward it carefully. "How are you doing? How is… I don't know, everything?"

Hunter tilts his head back and looks up at the sky. "I'm okay. I'm lucky, I really am. The doctors told me it could have been so much worse. I could have died. I could be totally brain-dead. I could be paralyzed from the neck down—could have lost the use of my arms, too." He thumps his fists lightly against his thighs. "I'll always regret getting so drunk at that stupid party. But for the most part, I'm adjusting. This is my new normal."

Tears flood my eyes. I blink, staring out at the grassy infield. "Hunter, I am so sorry. I'm sorry I broke up with you like that. I shouldn't have sprung it on you out of the blue."

"Naw, it wasn't completely out of the blue. You weren't the only one who could sense things ending between us. You were just braver than I was. I was scared to let go."

"I think about it every day. I wish… I wish I could rewind time. There's so much I would do differently."

Hunter is quiet.

I tuck a loose strand of hair behind my ear. "I'm sorry I made you jealous over David. He wasn't—he didn't mean anything to me."

"Thanks for saying that."

"I never would have cheated on you."

"I know. And the same goes for me, too."

I rub at a smear of dirt on the metal bench. "So you didn't cheat on me, before we broke up?"

"What?" Hunter sounds appalled. "Of course not. Why would you even ask me that?"

"At Robbie's party, Siggy Taylor said you had cheated on me with some girl from Roosevelt."

Hunter chuckles. "And you believed her? Em, you know Siggy. She loves to stir up drama almost as much as Robbie and Brett do."

I remember Siggy at Hunter's birthday party, smirking. *I know nothing could break up Buenaventura High's perfect couple.* Was she happy we broke up?

"Siggy was always jealous of you," Hunter says.

"Of me? Why?"

Hunter's smile is hard to read. "Emma," he says. "I wish you could see yourself the way the rest of the world sees you. You'll always be a peacock to me."

The tenderness in his voice hits me square in the chest. I don't deserve this kindness from him. I take a deep breath, summoning my courage. "It's my fault," I say softly.

"What?" Hunter's brow crinkles. "What's your fault?"

"The Accident. Everything. Not only for breaking up with you. I was the one who started the whole mess in the pool. I was the one who yelled out, 'Let's go skinny-dipping!' It's all my fault, Hunter. I'm so sorry. I'm so, so sorry." My voice breaks and I try to swallow back my tears. I'm not allowed to cry in front of Hunter. Not after all he's been through.

"Emma," he says. "It's not your fault. Don't put this on yourself."

"But—"

"Stop it." His voice is harsh. Fierce. "*I'm* the one who drank way too much. *I'm* the one who dove into the shallow end. Not you."

My cheeks burn with shame. I can't look at him. All this time, have I been contorting the whole situation, making it about me? It wasn't about me. It was Hunter's mistake. Hunter's life. Hunter's fault. Has all my guilt and pain since The Accident stemmed from my ego—my yearning to be important, to be the center of the story?

"Do you remember the giraffe?" Hunter asks, interrupting my thoughts.

"At the zoo? With the crooked neck?" I can see it in my mind, the way its neck made that strange L-shape, as if it had swallowed a boomerang.

"Yep. I've been thinking about him a lot lately. Even dreaming about him sometimes."

"Really?"

"Yeah. When the world looks at him, they only see his crooked neck. But in the giraffe's own eyes, he's normal. His neck isn't a big deal. He's going about his life, chewing his leaves, whatever else giraffes do. His neck doesn't, like, *define* him to himself. You know? It only defines him to the outside world."

Across the track, the palm trees sway in the breeze. A plastic wrapper flutters across the infield.

"I don't want to be defined by the accident. By this chair. When you look at me, Em, I don't want you to only see my crooked neck. I want you to see me as *me*. The same way you've always seen me."

For the first time since we sat down, I look fully into his face. His bright green eyes. Shaggy red hair. Pinprick freckles across his nose. "Hunter." I take his hand and squeeze it. "You will always be you. Smart, funny, determined. The first boy I ever loved. One of the greatest people I've ever met. That's what I see when I look at you."

Hunter squeezes my hand back. "I've missed you, Em. You're one of my best friends, you know?"

"You too."

"I think enough time's passed since the breakup. We could be friends again. Couldn't we?"

I smile at him. "I would really like that."

MY FEET ARE BLEEDING. I wave goodbye to Hunter, gather my shoes from the infield and limp up the hill, through the turnstile, and into the parking lot. I almost turn around for one last look but decide not to.

These past few months, I've desperately wanted to rewind, undo, amend—to go back somehow and fix things. Make different choices. I convinced myself that if I hadn't broken up with Hunter, or if I had broken up with him later, or in a different way... or if I hadn't gone to Robbie Zwick's party, or hadn't yelled about skinny-dipping, or or or... that my life would be perfect.

But life is never perfect. And I'm realizing that life isn't meant to be lived perfectly. Because a perfect life is a safe life. A perfect life means living without risk and spontaneity, without brave leaps or messy uncertainties. Without the growth that comes from heartbreak.

I still wish I hadn't broken up with Hunter over winter break. Because if I hadn't broken up with him, he wouldn't be paralyzed now. And I wish more than anything that Hunter Murray was not paralyzed.

But if I hadn't broken up with him then, I would still have that sinking feeling in my gut. I would still be planning to break up with him. A part of me will always love him, but I'm not in love with him anymore. We aren't meant to be together. My heart was leading me in the right direction. The *fact* of our breakup wasn't a mistake—it's the *timing* I regret.

But no life can ever be truly safe. Sometimes pain barrels into your life with no warning, for no reason, knocking you flat before you've even realized what hit you. Like Dad's stroke.

At the hospital, I embrace Dad gently. Even though he's due to be discharged this afternoon and the doctors say he is going to be fine, he still seems fragile to me. "I love you," I say in his ear.

"I love you too, Em. Always. I'm so proud of you."

"I'm sorry that I wasn't here for you when this happened. I'm sorry that I live so far away. And I'm sorry…" I pull away, looking into his face. "I'm sorry that I broke up with Hunter. I know how much you love him."

"What?" Dad looks bewildered. "Where is this coming from?"

I wipe my nose with the back of my hand. "Just—I know how close you are to Hunter. Sort of like he's the son you never had. And when I broke up with him, I know it changed things. I'm sorry if I let you down."

I am bumbling, losing track of what I'm trying to say, but Dad interrupts. "Emma, I'm the one who needs to apologize," he says. "Yes, your mom and I love Hunter. He's a good kid. Mostly, we loved him because he made you happy. But sweetheart, I'm *proud* of you for following your heart and letting go when things weren't right anymore. That must have been really hard to do."

"It was. I thought that I disappointed you."

"Oh, Emma. No. Of course not." His voice cracks. He puts his hands on my shoulders. "You could never disappoint me. You are the greatest gift of my life. Kind, generous, witty, creative—you make me proud every single day. I'm so proud of the person you are."

By now Dad is crying, and I am too, and this time when we hug each other I forget about being gentle. I wrap my arms around him and squeeze. Mom comes over and puts her arms around us both. I am crammed with love and gratitude—like my insides are bursting with bright light, a light that floods the cobwebby shadows out of every nook and corner.

THAT NIGHT, I listen to Kevin's voicemail for what seems like the hundredth time.

Hey Emma, it's Kevin. I've been thinking of you. Just checking in to see how you're doing, how your dad is recovering. Everything is fine here. Don't even worry about the project. And don't worry about calling me back. But, I mean, you can if you want. I'd really like that. Okay, bye.

I shift on my bed, rolling onto my stomach. My sketchbook falls onto the floor and splays open to the drawing I made of the windmills. I can close my eyes and go back so vividly to that scene: how the windmills spun slowly like Ferris wheels in the icy wind, surrounded by the silent cornfields.

I press the Call icon, twisting one of the yarn ties on my quilt. Hoping he will pick up. Hoping he won't pick up.

"Emma, hey!"

When I hear his voice, a smile spreads across my face.

"How are you?" he asks.

"I'm good. Great, actually. My dad was discharged from the hospital today."

"That's wonderful! I'm so happy to hear that."

"Thanks for your message. For calling me."

He updates me on the final plans for our project that have been squared away. And the results for the Student Art Competition are being announced on Monday. All the entries are being showcased in the Great Hall throughout the week.

"When are you coming back?" Kevin asks.

"Monday."

"Can I pick you up from the airport?"

"That would be really nice. As long as it's not too much trouble."

"Not at all. I'm excited to see you."

"Me too."

A pause, but not an awkward one. The two of us sit quietly on the phone together, and it's peaceful and easy.

"Hey Kevin, can I ask you something?"

"Shoot."

"How come you paint trees?"

He laughs. "You know, Emma, in all of my workshops for all of my tree paintings, no one has ever asked me that."

"Sorry—maybe it's a stupid question. You don't have to answer."

"No, no! It's not stupid. I'm glad you asked. Let me see if I can put it into words…" He pauses for a few seconds. I shift the phone to my other ear.

Kevin clears his throat. "Well, I've always loved trees," he begins. "Even as a little kid. I was always rubbing their bark, touching their leaves. Climbing their branches. Did you ever climb trees as a kid?"

"Yeah, I did! I haven't thought about it in a long time. There was an amazing, massive oak tree at my favorite park.

We would climb all over that thing. It was more fun than the actual playground. I could spend hours in that tree."

"I think a lot of people are in love with trees as kids. And then we grow up and sort of lose touch. Trees have an energy, you know? A life force. A special wisdom. That's what I try to tap into when I'm painting."

I close my eyes and think about Kevin's latest painting— a spindly birch sapling, half bent in the wind. My heart had ached for that vulnerable tree. "What I've always loved about your paintings is that every tree seems unique. Almost like it has its own personality. I wish I could talk to your trees through the canvas. Is that weird?"

"Not at all. That's a huge compliment. Thank you."

"You don't have to thank me. It's the truth."

Another little pause, and then Kevin says, "Can I ask you a question?"

"Okay."

"Why do you paint legs and feet?"

I swallow. Open my mouth to speak. But no words come.

I'm ready. I'm ready. I'mreadyI'mreadyI'mready.

Except… I'm not ready.

Will I ever be ready to talk about it?

"It's okay," Kevin says after a little while. "You don't have to tell me."

"I want to tell you," I say. "I will tell you. Sometime. Soon."

26

BEFORE

I AM WATCHING from my bedroom window when Hunter's car pulls up. He parks at the curb and his tall, lanky form emerges from the driver's side. He is wearing khaki shorts and a collared green shirt with the sleeves rolled up to his elbows. I watch him stride up the brick path to the front door. His hair shines orange-gold in the sunlight. A sliver of bright white sock is visible above the tops of his running shoes. He slides his hands into his pockets, then continues forward out of my sight beneath the roof overhang.

The doorbell rings. My stomach explodes in jittery, first-date butterflies.

"Em-MA!" Mom calls up the stairs in a sing-song voice. "You have a visitor!"

I smooth my hair one last time in the mirror, count to ten, then open my bedroom door and walk slowly down the stairs. I hear murmuring voices—Hunter talking with my parents. God, I hope Dad isn't quizzing him about running. I hope

Mom isn't asking any embarrassing questions. I hurry down the stairs and into the kitchen.

"I'm ready," I announce. I try to act nonchalant, like I don't really care if this is a date, like I'm one of those effortlessly cool girls who don't worry about labels and just go with the flow. I try to channel Siggy Taylor. "Hey, Hunter."

"Hi," Hunter says brightly. He seems calm, but I notice his right leg is jiggling.

"So where are you kids off to?" Dad asks.

Hunter looks at me, as if for approval. "I was thinking, maybe the zoo?"

"In Santa Barbara?" I ask.

"Yeah. Or is that too far away? I don't know, if it's a lame idea we can do something else instead."

"I think that sounds like a fun afternoon!" Mom interrupts.

"Yeah, the zoo's perfect," I say. "I haven't been there in forever."

To be honest, zoos make me sad. All those animals in all those cages, merely so people can gawk at them. Even as a little girl, I wanted to run around the zoo and set the animals free.

Mom ushers us out the front door. "Have a great time, you two!" She winks at me.

I follow Hunter across the driveway to his car. It is an unseasonably warm day for November. The air shimmers with heat.

"I like your car," I tell Hunter as he opens the passenger door for me.

"Thanks. It's actually my mom's."

"It's nice," I say, smiling at him and sliding into the passenger seat. I notice the dashboard has been wiped clean and the floors vacuumed. There is a surfboard air freshener hanging from the rearview mirror that smells like coconut.

"Sorry about that," I say as we buckle our seatbelts. "My parents can be kind of overpowering. It's an only-child thing."

"What do you mean? Your parents are great. It's obvious they're really proud of you."

"Thanks." I can't tell if he's being sincere, or if he just doesn't want me to be embarrassed.

It's a half-hour drive to Santa Barbara on the freeway; forty-five minutes if we take the scenic coastal highway. We take the latter. Hunter turns the radio down low and we talk about everything and nothing. I'm surprised how easily the conversation flows. I learn that Hunter likes horror novels and European techno music. If he didn't spend so much time running, he would be in a band. He can play nearly any corny pop song on the acoustic guitar.

I confess my undying love of Vincent Van Gogh—how "Starry Night" is my favorite painting of all time and one day I'm going to see it in person, the real thing, and when I do I will stand in front of it for hours and hours until the museum closes and the guards push me out the door. This makes Hunter laugh. I flush with a silly sort of pride. I like the way he squeezes his eyes shut when he laughs.

"So tell me about your paintings," he says.

"How do you know I paint?"

"Just a guess." His eyes flicker from the road to my face and back to the road. "From the way you talk about other paintings, it's obvious that you're an artist yourself."

Normally I don't like talking about my artwork—it is too private, too special, and talking about it risks leaking the magic away. I briefly tell Hunter about a couple of paintings I've done this year, the less abstract ones, and how I'm currently working on a beach series. "Sometimes I mix sand into the paint for a gritty texture."

"That's cool. I want to see your paintings." He sounds like he actually means it.

"Okay," I hear myself saying. "I'll show you sometime. If you're nice."

"Who says I'm not nice? I'm always nice." His smile reminds me of some sly animal in a children's book. A fox, maybe. Or a wolf.

At the zoo, heat rises from the cement in thick waves. More than once I escape to the bathroom to splash water on my face and flap my arms, self-conscious about the sweat conquering swathes of fabric below my armpits. Hunter's armpits seem impossibly dry. When I'm standing close beside him and breathe in, he smells like laundry detergent. Fresh and clean.

We pause in front of the giraffe exhibit, hands dangling close to each other but not touching. I want to reach for his hand but I'm too nervous. I almost cross my arms—force of habit—but remember to keep them loose at my sides. Mom says people who cross their arms send the nonverbal cue that they are closed-off and defensive. I want Hunter to think I am open and friendly. More-than-friendly.

My hand is inches from his, right there for the taking.

Most of the animals are out of sight in their cages. They are submerged in their pools of water or resting in shady patches beneath the bushes. The giraffes alone are braving the sunshine, nibbling at the leafy branches of the eucalyptus trees. We watch from behind the enclosure's low brick wall. One of the giraffes turns, ears twitching in the faint hint of a breeze, and that's when I notice.

"Look!" I point. "Its neck—look!"

"Whoa," Hunter says.

The giraffe's neck is crooked, L-shaped, extending straight up from its body before making a sharp left turn, then a right turn, then finally rising up to its head. It looks like it swallowed a boomerang. The giraffe, unconcerned, nibbles at the eucalyptus leaves.

"I wonder how that happened," I say. "Do you think it hurts?"

"Probably," Hunter says. Inwardly, I flinch at his indifferent tone. All this time, I've been imagining that he is different from other guys. I thought there was a sweet gentleness in him, but that must have been my own wishful thinking. My stomach sinks.

Maybe Hunter notices my slight withdrawal, because he smiles tentatively and adds, "Maybe it doesn't hurt. You know what—he looks happy. Seems like he gets along fine."

"Yeah. I think so, too." I smile back, a little.

Hunter drapes his arm around my shoulders and squeezes my body softly against his. I turn my attention back to the giraffe, but my heart is beating wildly.

Maybe I was right. Maybe he is different.

"If you could be any animal," Hunter says, "what would you be?"

I laugh—my standard response when I'm caught off guard and don't know what to say. A parade of animals flashes through my head, but all of them seem stupid. "I don't know," I say, shrugging. "Do you mean my favorite animal? I've always liked panda bears."

"Pandas are cute," Hunter agrees. "But you are definitely not a panda."

"I'm not?"

"No. You're more like… a peacock."

This time, I laugh for real. I am the furthest thing from a peacock. If anyone is a peacock, it's Céline. Not me.

"I'm serious, Emma," Hunter says quietly. "You unfurl your feathers like it's nothing special. Meanwhile, everyone else turns to look at you in amazement. You're dazzling. But you don't even know it."

I duck my head, blushing. No one has ever spoken to me like this before. "Thanks, Hunter. I… well, thank you."

"You don't need to thank me. I'm simply stating the truth."

We stand there together, watching the funny-looking giraffe chew. Even in the sticky heat, I like the weight of Hunter's arm across my shoulders.

"What animal would you be?" I ask.

"A California condor," Hunter says without hesitation. "It's the largest bird in North America. Almost became extinct back in the eighties, but it's making a comeback now. That bird is a fighter."

"Wow. How do you know so much about it?"

"We did a report back in middle school about Native American myths, and I read a myth about the condor. King of the Birds!"

"And that would be you," I tease.

"That would be me. Plus, I've always wanted to fly." He smiles down at me, his eyes dancing.

I like how tall he is. The hairs on his arm tickle the back of my neck.

"You want to go look at the gorillas?" Hunter asks. "Or the lions?"

"Sure. Either sounds good."

Hunter's arm falls from my shoulder, and I wish I'd said that I wanted to stay at the giraffe a little while longer. But then his hand finds mine, intertwining our fingers. I squeeze his hand and he squeezes mine back. Like we are creating our own language. I don't know what it means, but I know it means something.

Right before we turn away, the giraffe with the crooked neck stops chewing and looks in our direction. I try to meet its eyes, but it is looking past me, beyond me, at something I can't quite see.

27

AFTER

AT THE INDIANAPOLIS airport, Kevin is waiting for me at Baggage Claim. When he spots me, his smile is big and pure, tugging at me like a magnet. I walk toward him, quickening my pace.

He opens his arms and wraps me up in a hug. He smells of sunscreen and minty shampoo. I feel overwhelmingly, resoundingly, safe.

"Hi," I say. "Thanks so much for picking me up."

"I'm glad you're back."

"Me too."

Exiting the airport terminal into the afternoon light, the blue sky is heavy, the air warm and thick. I drum my fingers on my thighs. My hands are restless, fidgety; my fingers yearn to hold a paintbrush or charcoal pencil. Aching to create something. Not hairy feet, not underwater legs, not broken pieces, not Hunter. I'm done painting Hunter, for a while at least.

I'm ready for something new.

We are mostly quiet driving back to Wabash Academy. The engine hums and Kevin's hand brushes against my knee when he reaches for the gearshift. I glance over at him—dark hair peeking out under his ballcap, cheeks flushed from the heat, long fingers on the steering wheel—and he catches me looking. We smile at each other.

My thoughts keep drifting to the Student Art Competition. We're heading straight to the exhibition. It makes me a little queasy to think of the judges scrutinizing my three paintings—one of Hunter's feet, one of his injured hip, and one of disembodied legs in a blood-red background—and, well, judging them. What if nobody likes them? What if people think they're weird, or creepy, or just plain bad?

Kevin parks in a student lot and we walk across campus, holding hands. It is nice to hold Kevin's hand—like he is transferring strength from his palm to mine. He pauses outside the entrance to the Great Hall.

"Emma," he says in a serious voice. "Your paintings are amazing. Truly. No matter the results, I hope you know how talented you are. The results won't change that."

"Thank you. The same is true about your Gar drawings." I squeeze his hand and push open the doors.

Inside, the atmosphere is hushed. The room is crowded. Students mill about, looking at the artwork. Paintings, sculptures, collages, pen-and-ink drawings. I spot my paintings displayed at the far end of the room. I want to race over there, but I force myself to walk slowly, making an effort to look at the other pieces as Kevin and I move past them. But I don't really take in any of the artwork. The world around me seems muted.

Before we reach my paintings, a hand touches my shoulder. I turn. Mrs. Post beams at me. "Emma, I'm so proud of you! You found your authentic voice. These paintings are rich with depth and emotion. Stunning work."

Happiness soars inside me. "Thank you, Mrs. Post."

"You should apply for our Master Painting Class in the fall. It's open only to seniors, and on an application basis. I think you would be an excellent fit."

"Really? Okay, yeah. Thank you. I will."

Mrs. Post winks at me and adds, "I always knew that painting of the giant feet was yours. I recognized your style, blooming into life."

Before I can think of a response, she squeezes my shoulder and heads across the room to talk to another student.

I take a deep breath and walk toward my three paintings, all in a row. Hunter's feet, hip, legs. On the wall below them is a placard typed with my name and the title of my series: *Fractured.* As we get closer, I spot something posted on the wall next to the placard.

It is an award.

It is a star.

It is a *gold* star.

FIRST PLACE: PAINTING SERIES.

"First place!" Kevin says. "Awesome!" He gives me a high five.

But a high five isn't enough. I don't care that we're in the middle of the Great Hall with people mingling all around. I embrace Kevin in a tight hug. He squeezes me back.

"Congratulations, Emma," says Sabrina Nichols.

"Kevin, dude—I loved your drawings!" says Blake Nishioka. "You seriously should publish a graphic novel."

I feel numb as the conversation continues to swirl around me. Only it's not the numbness I'm used to. It's not a numbness born from pain or sadness. It's a numbness of disbelief, but a wonderful sort of disbelief. *My artwork... first place?*

A wide, silly grin spreads across my face.

My artwork… first place!

Looking at the paintings I created, I see Hunter's limbs, but I also see more than that. Kevin was right—my paintings aren't really about Hunter. These paintings are about *me*. They are a channeling of my grief and my regret and my anger. My emotions, laid bare onto the canvas. For the first time, when I gaze at my artwork in all its unflinching boldness, I don't feel a hint of embarrassment or insecurity. Instead, a new sensation courses through my veins.

Pride.

Dear Emma,

My sincere apologies for not writing back to you sooner! Your email ended up in my spam folder and I only saw it now. (I guess I need to check my spam more often!) Thank you for reaching out to me with these important questions.

I believe that we, as artists, are conduits for the creative spirit, and part of the mystery–and the magic–is not always knowing where our art comes from. Any subject that you create art about is filtered through you, the artist. It might be about something else outwardly, but in reality it is always about you and your internal landscape. That is what makes each of us unique as creative beings. That is why, in our class, I could assign everyone a still life of the same bowl of fruit, and each painting would be different.

You are the only one who can say what "good art" means to you, but I have found that when I am playing it safe, it means I am painting scared, and that is never when I do my best work. We grow as artists when we stretch ourselves.

It is a normal part of the artistic process to go through periods of doubt, but I hope you know deep in your bones that you are a talented artist with a worthy voice. I know that Wabash Academy must be different than Buenaventura High in many ways, but you belong there as much as anyone, Emma. Don't be afraid to take up space.

I think of you often, and fondly, and would love to see you next time you are home. The doors of Room 62 are always open to you.

-Mrs. Muna

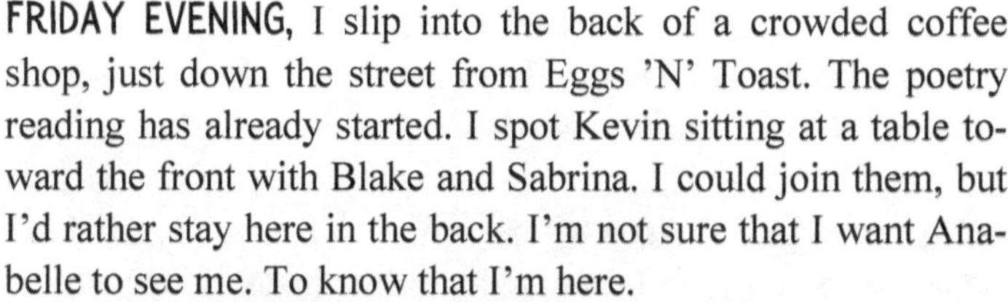

FRIDAY EVENING, I slip into the back of a crowded coffee shop, just down the street from Eggs 'N' Toast. The poetry reading has already started. I spot Kevin sitting at a table toward the front with Blake and Sabrina. I could join them, but I'd rather stay here in the back. I'm not sure that I want Anabelle to see me. To know that I'm here.

The event features community poets of all ages whose poems were inspired by the paintings of a local kindergarten class. A middle-aged man reads a poem about the changing seasons. An old woman reads a poem about a gigantic brown dog. An eight-year-old girl reads a rhyming poem about a peanut-butter-and-*jellyfish* sandwich that receives a standing ovation from the audience.

After everyone has read their poems, Anabelle comes out onto the makeshift stage at the front of the room. I expect her to thank us all for coming, ask us to give one final round of applause for the poets, and send us on our merry way. But instead she says, "Before we go tonight, I have one more poem to share. This one is written by me. It's called Eggs 'N' Toast."

In a loud, clear voice, she begins to read.

I've never been one for sorry
Never like to admit when I'm wrong
Now I have become a matchless sock
That nobody wants, that doesn't belong.

What did I do to make you leave?
Why did you turn and walk away?
I comb through my memories, searching
For evidence in the bright light of day.

I know that nothing lasts forever
Still, I thought we were entwined
Like threads in a woven bracelet
How I wish I could rewind...

Listening to the raw vulnerability in her voice, my heart aches for her. Stupid David. Why did he have to keep stringing her along? I wish, for the millionth time, that I had never kissed him. I was stupid, too. Stupid and selfish and impulsive. But I can't keep punishing myself forever, can I?

I didn't think Anabelle knew I was here. But she looks right at me as she delivers the final stanza.

The truth of the matter is that
Of all the places I love the most
My favorite is laughing across the table
From you, Em, at Eggs 'N' Toast.

Em? Her poem is about me?
Her poem is about me.
Not David.
Me.
She misses me too. Anabelle misses me too.

After the reading ends, I linger for a few minutes, but there are so many people around. Too many people. I want to have a real conversation with Anabelle. Plus, I need time to gather my thoughts.

Leaving the coffee shop, I almost run into a girl drawing in chalk on the sidewalk. *Ephemeral art.* It makes me think of Hunter. And then I get an idea.

Tomorrow is Saturday. I have a hunch where Anabelle might be on a Saturday morning.

EGGS 'N' TOAST IS BUSTLING, as usual. I check my watch. 8:17 a.m.

A waitress leads me to a table and I sit facing the door, so I can watch for her. My legs are jittery, my body buzzing, even though I haven't downed any coffee yet.

8:36. I place an order for chocolate-chip pancakes. "Actually, make it two." The waitress smiles as she jots it down on her notepad.

8:59. The twin plates of pancakes are growing cold, the butter congealing in sad puddles on top. *What if she doesn't come? Maybe this was a dumb idea.*

I cut into my pancakes, pour on syrup. Try to eat. But after only a couple bites, I set down my fork. I'm too nervous to eat.

At 9:11, I'm rifling through my purse for my wallet, when a voice says, "Is anyone sitting here?"

I look up into her cat-eye glasses, relief and anxiety crashing inside my stomach. "No—I mean, I've been saving it for you."

Anabelle sits down across from me. Her hair is pulled back into a bun, a few stray curls escaping to frame her face. Her eyes don't look wary or guarded, like they were when I bumped into her at the art supply store. But her expression isn't especially friendly, either.

"I was at your poetry reading," I begin.

"I know. I saw you there, in the back."

"I loved your poem. I was hoping you would come here this morning, because I need to talk to you. About a lot of things. But mostly, I want to say that I miss you. And I'm sorry. I'm so, so sorry, Anabelle."

Her face crumples open. "I'm sorry too, Emma. I'm sorry I lied and said your painting was mine. I knew it was your painting the whole time."

"Wait—what? You did?"

"Of course I did. You're my best friend. I could recognize your style."

"Then why did you raise your hand that day?"

"Because *you* didn't raise *your* hand!" Anabelle splays her fingers out on the table and studies them for a moment, then looks up and meets my eyes. "It sounds stupid now, but I thought—I thought that I was being a good friend. Giving you some tough love. I wanted to push you, Em. I wanted to make you mad, to force you to stand up for yourself and be proud of your artwork. I emailed Mrs. Post as soon as I got home from class and told her the truth. I didn't want credit for your painting. That wasn't the point."

I shake my head. "I'm still confused. I watched you march up there and sign your name on my painting. I was furious when you did that."

"Good!" Anabelle thumps the table. "That's exactly what was supposed to happen! I thought for sure that you would confront me. I *wanted* you to confront me. I was upset at you for abandoning me at the dance, and for being so distant—I could tell you had all this shit buried beneath the surface, but no matter what I did, I couldn't get through to you. So I got desperate. Raising my hand that day was a last resort." She sighs, her shoulders slumping. "But even that didn't work. Nothing I did could convince you to open up and be my friend, Em."

"It wasn't your fault, Anabelle. I always wanted to be your friend. I just… needed to be alone for a while."

"Why? Because I lied about the painting?"

"It wasn't about the painting. It had nothing to do with you. I created a huge mess all on my own, and I hated myself for it." Finally, I let the words spill out. I tell her about breaking up with Hunter, about The Accident, about her text message that I saved on my phone for months. I tell her about getting drunk at the back-to-school dance and hooking up with David.

"I know about you and David," she says.

My heart thuds in my chest. "You do?"

"Yeah. It was pretty obvious. You're a horrible liar, Em. Your emotions slide all over your face. Plus, I always knew David had a thing for you."

I want to reach across the table and grab her hand, but I'm too ashamed. "It didn't mean anything. I was drunk, and wrecked about Hunter's accident, and I wasn't thinking clearly. It just… happened. But I immediately knew it was a terrible mistake, that I had ruined everything."

"Don't be so dramatic." Anabelle rolls her eyes. "You didn't ruin everything. David is a total player. If I didn't want to be friends with anyone who had kissed David… well, I'd have, like, zero friends."

Our eyes meet. She smiles. I smile. The moment builds, and builds, and then we both burst out laughing. Anabelle throws her head back. I laugh so hard that tears leak out my eyes.

"Oh my god, I missed this so much," I tell her when we catch our breath. "I missed laughing with you."

"I missed this, too." She reaches across the table and snags a bite of my pancake, even though we are eating the exact same thing. "Thank you for forgiving me. I promise to never steal another one of your paintings."

"And I promise to never ghost you again. Or kiss a guy you have a huge crush on."

"Ugh. I need better taste in guys. Oh well! Remember my motto?" Anabelle lifts her coffee mug. "Friends above boys."

I clink my mug against hers. "Friends, always."

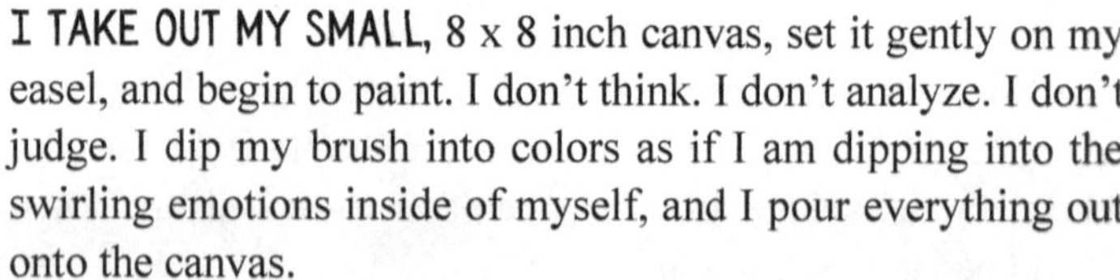

I TAKE OUT MY SMALL, 8 x 8 inch canvas, set it gently on my easel, and begin to paint. I don't think. I don't analyze. I don't judge. I dip my brush into colors as if I am dipping into the swirling emotions inside of myself, and I pour everything out onto the canvas.

I don't know how many hours pass. When I've finished, a calm sense of release floods through my body. I step back and survey my work.

A vibrant sunset, oranges and purples and reds. In the distance stretches the Pacific Ocean, with the Channel Islands marking the horizon. High up in the sky, the silhouette of a giant bird spreads its wings.

Two days later, once the paint has fully dried, I package up the painting and take it to the post office. I don't want to wait until I'm home for the summer to give it to him.

HUNTER,
YOU'RE NOT A GIRAFFE, WITH A CROOKED NECK OR OTHERWISE.
YOU'RE A CALIFORNIA CONDOR. SOARING.
LOVE, EMMA

28

THE BEGINNING

"HERE," COACH BILL says, handing me a faded blue flotation belt and a wrinkled sheet of paper. "You'll be doing pool workouts for the next few weeks, until your shin splints calm down and you can run with no pain. These water workouts will keep your cardio training going strong so you can hop right back into regular workouts when you're healed up. Okay?"

"Um, okay." I squeeze the blue foam. It reminds me of the stuffing inside car cushions. I squint at the unfamiliar words scrawled on the piece of paper. "Wait, Coach? What does this mean—ski legs? Hammer legs?"

But Coach Bill is already halfway across the parking lot, jogging up to the track where the rest of the cross-country team will be running an interval workout. "Murray will be there," he calls over his shoulder. "Ask him, he'll show you."

I nod and make my way across campus to the outdoor pool. The girls' locker room is empty, all the swimmers already in the pool doing laps. I change into my slightly too small one-piece swimsuit, yearning for the familiar comfort of my running shorts and sports bra. The elastic of the swimsuit pinches and the straps cut into my shoulders. This weekend, I'll ask Céline to go swimsuit shopping with me. But for now, this is the best I can do. I wrap a towel around myself, grab the flotation belt, and hesitantly open the door to the pool area.

Outside, I shiver as goosebumps rise on my arms. Fog has rolled in from the ocean. The pool deck is surrounded by an eight-foot-tall metal fence that seems like a cage. The concrete is cold and wet and slippery under my bare feet.

In the pool, the swimmers glide through the water like scissors slicing through silk. Even their flip turns are graceful, with hardly a splash. The swim coach paces the pool deck, barking orders. He is a short man with a bowling-ball belly who looks like he's never been swimming in his life. I hurry past him, feeling wholly out of place.

I love the beach, but I hate swimming. When I was a kid, Mom signed me up for swimming lessons and I cried before, during, and after every one, begging not to go back. I hated getting chlorine in my eyes and water up my nose. I felt horribly clumsy in the water, like a big splashing dog. Mom eventually let me quit and I haven't been in a pool much since then, except for the occasional birthday party where I stay in the shallow end, feet brushing the floor, or in the hot tub, overheating and hoping I won't pass out.

Now I scan the pool deck, looking for someone familiar. Who did Coach Bill say would be here with me? Murray?

In a short time I see him, at the far end of the pool, a tall lanky boy carrying a flotation belt. Hunter Murray. I recognize him, but I don't know him very well. Although we're in the same grade, we don't have any classes together, and he is one of the varsity runners who don't really talk to the slower runners like me. He doesn't seem mean, or even unfriendly. I'm just not on his radar. Mostly, he intimidates me because he is fast—ridiculously fast. Watching him run is like watching what running is *supposed* to be. But Hunter is out for a while, I can't remember why exactly—a torn hamstring? A stress fracture? He still comes to every meet, taking splits for Coach Bill, pacing around like a caged animal in pain. You can tell it is killing him not to be out there running.

I head toward him, watching as he adjusts his goggles. His torso gleams a pale white and I can see the ridges of his ab muscles. He drops his blue flotation belt to the ground, re-adjusts his goggles a final time, and then in one fluid motion leans forward and dives cleanly into the deep, still water. It is a long time before he resurfaces, already halfway across the pool.

I linger on the edge of the pool where he left his flotation belt, holding my own blue foam belt in a death-grip and willing him to notice me. I realize I forgot the paper with my workout written down. Walking exposed like this all the way back to the locker room to retrieve it is a terrifying impossibility. I want nothing more than to hide in the cold, dark water.

Hunter does a flip turn and swims back toward me. I look down at my bare feet, not wanting him to catch me staring. My purple toenail polish is chipped.

"Hey!"

I look up. Hunter rests his arms on the edge of the pool. "You run, right?" he asks, wiping water off his face with one hand. "Are you doing a pool workout?"

"Yeah," I reply, relieved to be noticed. "It's my first time. I don't know what to do."

"That's okay, I'll show you. It'll be nice to have some company for a change. What's your name again?"

"Emma."

"That's right—Emma. I'm Hunter."

"I know."

"Right. Well, we're supposed to warm up by swimming laps first. You can leave your floatie belt right there and come on in."

"*Floatie* belt?" I laugh. "Did you make that up?"

Hunter grins. "That's what it's called!"

I've seen his smile many times before—as he stands on a podium after a big race, a new medal proud and shiny around his neck; when he answers questions from reporters for the local newspaper; as he talks with Mariah Quinn and Stacey Carmichael, the two fastest girls on the team, who both have legs like gazelles.

But this is the first time his smile has been directed at me.

It is blinding.

"Come on, jump in!" Hunter says. "The water's nice."

I hesitate for a moment longer, memorizing his smile, forgetting how much I hate to swim. Life brims with electric possibility. A warm hopefulness expands inside me. Quite suddenly, out of nowhere, the afternoon has transformed into something magical.

I close my eyes, take a deep breath, and dive headfirst into the deep water.

29

THE PRESENT

JUNIOR YEAR, MAY

IT HAPPENS AT A PARTY.

The week before summer break. Sweet Treat Cupcakes. A blue-skied, on-the-cusp-of-humid Indiana day.

Technically, I guess this isn't a party. But it sure seems like one. The cupcake shop is crammed with people, conversation, and laughter. It smells, for once, not of sugar and butter, but of paint, which just might be my favorite smell in the world. Dana curated a special playlist of songs her dad loved, mostly jukebox hits from the fifties and sixties, which plays cheerfully in the background.

Across the large blank wall, the mural is steadily coming to life in vivid color, under the brushstrokes of dozens of hands.

Elementary-school kids carefully paint tufts of grass along the bottom of the wall. A young mom, wearing her sleeping baby in a carrier, paints a garden of yellow sunflowers. A bunch of art students from the public high school paint the river, winding through the mural and all around the shop.

Anabelle helps sponge-paint the sky. Nora and Rachel paint the Wabash Academy clock tower. Mrs. Jenkins chats with Mrs. Post as they adorn a field of tasseled green corn. Even David shows up. He gives me a wave, nods to Anabelle, and then goes over to one of the public high school girls, who kisses him and hands him a paintbrush. I meet Anabelle's eyes, but she only shrugs as if to say, *Don't worry. I'm over it.* Which I hope she is. She deserves someone who is crazy about her. Maybe we can talk through things tomorrow, like we used to—scrutinize and share the ordinary details of our daily lives. We're meeting up for coffee after class. I hope it is the beginning of our friendship, resprouting.

Across the top of the mural, against the bright blue sky, Megha carefully writes in her impressive calligraphy: *IN LOVING MEMORY OF RICHARD RUSH.* Dana paints the cemetery and her dad's tombstone, topped with a small yellow cupcake.

Slowly, steadily, the mural fills in with color and life. Slowly, steadily, the cupcakes get eaten. The music playlist winds down. People wipe their paint-streaked faces with the backs of their paint-streaked hands, stretch their backs and their legs, look at their work and smile proudly.

Everyone crowds together in front of the completed mural for a group photo. Kevin steadies his phone tripod, sets the timer, and runs over to join our gathering. He slips in next to me, like that is exactly where he belongs.

I want it to be exactly where he belongs.

After the photos are taken, people begin to leave. Megha comes over and touches my shoulder. "What a great day! Thanks for inviting me."

"Thank you for coming to help! Your calligraphy pulls the whole thing together. You are so talented."

"Aw, thanks. It's always cool to meet other artists. I saw your paintings at Wabash. They are amazing."

"Oh wow—thank you." I think of Céline, that day back in kindergarten, when she sat next to me on the swings and asked to be my friend. If she were here, she would tell me that making friends isn't all that hard; you only have to be willing to put yourself out there. "Hey Megha, would you want to get coffee sometime before I leave for the summer?"

Megha beams. "I'd love that. Here, let me get your number. I'll text you."

I wave goodbye to David, then chat with Anabelle, Nora, and Rachel for a few minutes—we plan a pre-finals study session at Eggs 'N' Toast for next weekend—and finally make my way over to help Kevin and Dana with the cleanup.

"What are you still doing here?" I chide Dana playfully. "You promised you'd let us handle all the logistics. Go home and rest!"

Dana pulls me in for a warm hug. "Emma, I can't thank you enough for what you've done here."

"It was a huge group effort."

"But you were the inspiration behind it. This was all your idea."

"Actually, *you* were the inspiration behind everything— the stories you shared with me about your dad. Thank you for being vulnerable with me. And thank you for the cupcake that night, when I was really low. You made me feel less alone."

"I know I'm not a stranger anymore," Dana says with a smile. "But if you ever want to talk about anything, I'm here. I'm always happy to listen. That goes for you, too, Kevin."

"Thanks," he says. "But seriously—Emma was right. You need to go home and let us finish cleaning up. That's an order." He tries to make his voice stern, but his grin lessens the effect.

"Okay, okay, I'm leaving!"

But first, the three of us stand side by side, gazing at the finished mural. The river. The clock tower. The windmills. The bronze statue of a lion. The stately sycamore trees. Eggs 'N' Toast. Sweet Treat Cupcakes. It's all here. Larger than life. A vibrant collage of a small Midwestern town that has finally begun to feel like my home away from home.

"Dad would love it," Dana murmurs.

"That's the best compliment you could give," Kevin says.

"Hey Dana?" I ask. "It's totally fine to say no, but would you be open to some company on Friday, when you deliver that Lemon Sunshine cupcake?"

Dana hugs me again. "I would love nothing more."

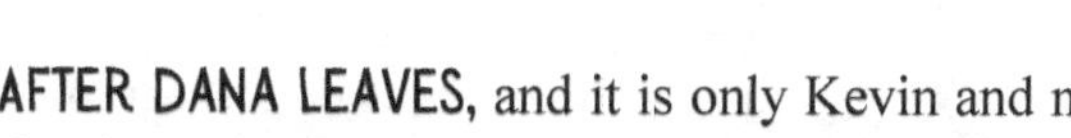

AFTER DANA LEAVES, and it is only Kevin and me remaining, the shop seems especially peaceful. Hushed. Like that feeling you get after a party or a concert, when the music and noise and bustle is suddenly gone, and your ears sink into all that extra quiet.

"We did it!" Kevin says, pumping his fist into the air.

"We did it!" I echo.

We stand there, smiling at each other. This is a heightened quiet, charged with electricity. With possibility. Does Kevin feel it, too?

One beat, two beats, and then our bodies are drawn together like magnets and his arms are around my waist and my arms are around his back and we're kissing. His lips are soft. His stubble grazes my cheek. His hands move up my body, slowly, slowly, until he reaches the back of my neck. He cradles my head, thumbs tracing circles in my hair, such a gentle and intimate gesture. There is a delicious dizzy feeling in my stomach, like I am perched at the very top of a roller coaster, looking down at the ground far below, right before the weightless plunging rush.

No one has ever kissed me like this before.

Breaking away is like resurfacing after being underwater. Kevin opens his eyes and looks at me, a happy astonishment in his expression that I am sure is also written all over my face.

"Whoa," he says, grinning.

"I know," I say, matching his smile.

We finish loading the brushes and paint and drop cloths and other materials into his car. It is a gorgeous evening. The cicadas chirp from the trees and fireflies glow in the grass.

"What are you doing tonight?" Kevin asks.

"Well," I begin. "I've been craving a sandwich from Danny's Deli."

"Oh really?" Kevin says, his eyes sparking. "You mean the turkey-bacon-tomato club?"

"No, I like the ham-and-Swiss."

"Are you sure? Because you really seemed to like the turkey-bacon-tomato club."

I laugh and pinch his side. "Wait, there's more," I say. "After I finish eating my delicious ham-and-Swiss sandwich, I'm going to the Indianapolis Museum of Art."

"Oh yeah?" Kevin says, meeting my eyes.

"Yeah. Do you want to come?"

"What's the exhibit?"

"I don't actually know. I don't even care! I just want to wander through an art exhibit with you, talking about paintings and holding your hand." I grab his hands in mine, look straight into his golden-flecked eyes. "I—I really like you, Kevin."

His smile is huge, like a kid who has finally put a difficult puzzle together. "I like you too, Emma. A lot."

"So will you go out with me tonight? On a real *date*-date?"

Kevin tilts his head, drawing out the moment. "Yes," he says finally. "I would love nothing more than to go on a date-date with you. But can we make a pit stop on the way?"

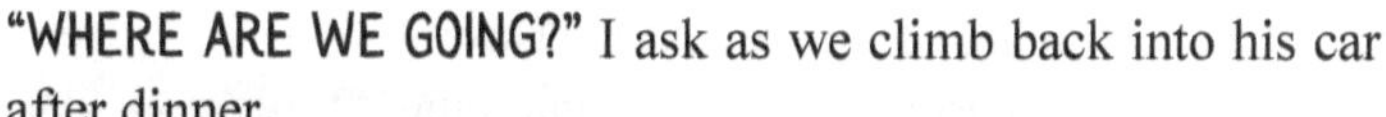

"WHERE ARE WE GOING?" I ask as we climb back into his car after dinner.

"It's a surprise. It's on the way to the art museum."

"Come on, tell me!"

"You don't like surprises?"

"Well, yes, I do. But tell me anyway. *Pleeeease.*"

"Okay…" Kevin says, drawing it out for a couple more beats. Then he says, "I'm taking you to a windmill."

We drive onto Highway 52, slicing through the silent cornfields with the windows down. The breeze is fresh and cool as the humidity fades from the day. During dinner, afternoon fell into dusk, and now the vast sky has become a stunning watercolor painting of a sunset.

The moon is bright, the sky dark, when we reach Benton County. I can't really see the windmills themselves, only their blinking red warning lights to let airplanes know they exist. It is both beautiful and eerie, the sea of red dots in the blackness.

The words rise within me. My truth. The story I need to share.

Kevin, I have to tell you something.
I loved a boy once, and I was certain I broke him.
He is paralyzed, and I thought it was my fault.
And I worried that I no longer knew how to love some-
one.
Kevin, I'm frozen. I've been frozen for so long. But final-
ly, I think I'm thawing.
Now I realize the one I broke the night of The Acci-
dent...was myself.

Suddenly, Kevin veers the Jeep to the right. We jostle in our seats as the wheels bump off the highway and onto the dirt fields.

"You're going off the road!" I shriek.

"It's on purpose!" Kevin says, laughing. "I told you—I'm taking you *to* a windmill."

"You're ridiculous!" I hit him playfully on the arm, laughing too.

"It's what you said, that night. You said you wanted to touch one. Remember?"

I do remember saying that. I wanted to touch one because I wanted the windmills to be something real and tangible. I wanted something steady to grasp onto.

But I don't need that anymore.

I stare at the windmill growing bigger and bigger, taller and taller, as we get nearer and nearer. Its spinning blades remind me of the spokes of Hunter's racing wheelchair, training for the LA Marathon, exhilarated and free. The next-best thing to running. Racing forward, leaving the past behind.

It's time for me to do the same.

The windmill's red light flashes a steady rhythm, on and off, on and off. Like it is warning me to stay away.

Or maybe not. Maybe it is offering guidance, beckoning me forward.

I take a deep, full breath and begin to speak.

ACKNOWLEDGEMENTS

Thank you to the entire Owl Hollow Press team for your unending belief and support in my book. Special thanks to Hannah Smith for seeing the potential in my manuscript and Emma Nelson for making me feel at home from day one. Olivia Swenson, you are magic. Editing this book with you made it infinitely better, helping me see the story with fresh eyes—a miracle after working with these characters for over a decade! Caroline Geslison and Elise Meyer, thank you for championing my book and helping this story reach readers.

Thank you to my MFA professors at Purdue University—Porter Shreve, Bich Minh Nguyen, Sharon Solwitz, and Patricia Henley—and to my friends and fellow writers Shavonne Clarke, Natalie van Hoose, Tiffany Chiang, Terrance Manning, Mike Campbell, Kelsey Ronan, and Chidelia Edochie. Thank you for helping me see that what began as a twelve-page short story might actually have the depth for an entire novel. Special thanks to my MFA thesis adviser Porter Shreve, and my YA literature professor Janet Alsup, for cheering me on during the original drafting of this manuscript.

Thank you to the Creative Writing program at the University of Southern California for helping me build a daily writing routine and find my voice. Special thanks to my professors Viet Thahn Nguyen, James Ragan, Susan Segal, and Richard Fliegel. As always, a big hug of gratitude to Aimee Bender for being my role model as a writer, teacher, and human being.

Writing can be a lonely profession, and I am grateful for the supportive community of my online writing group that formed during the Covid-19 pandemic, especially Robert Aquinas McNally, Katya Cengel, Julia Bricklin, Susan Harness, and Matthew Kerns.

Thank you to Jesse Q. Sutanto, Laura Sibson, Jen Marie Hawkins, Tara K. Ross, Rebecca Bischoff and Genalea Barker for your kind and generous support of this book.

Thank you to all of my teachers, classmates and friends from elementary school onward who have encouraged my writing over the years. Too many to name, but you know who you are! Thank you to my students and clients, who continually remind me of the joy and magic that comes from unleashing words onto the blank page.

Thank you to Amy Davis and her wonderful bookstore Banter Bookshop—such a treasure to have in our community!—for celebrating local authors like me.

Thank you to Jeffrey Dransfeldt for taking such lovely author headshots for me.

Thank you to my family, and to friends who have become family, for your continued love and support: Jess Ahoni Woodburn, Allyn McAuley, Laurel Shearer, Colin McAuley, Kylie Neal, Mary Blasquez, Ann Silvestri, Frank Paschal, Arianna Silvestri,

Amanda Rackley, Julie Hein, Melissa Kaganovsky, Erica Roundy Arbogast, Dana Boardman, Anna Rapp, Lauren Baran-Parks, Carand Burnet, Michael Swaidan, Ben Raynor, Nicole Harrison, Anna Mullikin, Connie Halpern, Susan Goodkin, Kay Giles, Wayne and Kathy Bryan, Barry Kibrick, Julie Merrick, Rima Muna, Patti Post, Shana Lynn Schmidt, Justin and Rose Nishioka, Alicia Stratton, Tania Sussman, Joan Redding, and all of my aunts, uncles, and cousins.

Thank you, always, to my grandma Auden and my dear friends Jewell Butcher and Céline Lucie Aziz for teaching me that love knows no tense.

Special thanks to my aunt Kym Woodburn King for her constant love, staunch optimism, and marathon phone calls that lift my spirits.

Thanks to Grandma and Grandpap, Mary Lou and Gene Paschal, for always making me feel like a best-selling author; and to Gramps, Dr. James Dallas Woodburn II, for the big hugs, phone calls, and mailed cartoons clipped from the newspaper.

Forever gratitude to my mother-in-law, Barbara McAuley, for your fierce belief in me and my writing—and the countless hours of laundry, dishes, and babysitting to give me more time to write!

A big hug to my sister-in-law and favorite librarian, Allyson McAuley, for all the delicious meals, sibling dinners, long conversations, and stellar book recommendations.

Thank you to Holly Mueller, my wise friend and first reader, for being the best listener and cheering me on through the ups and downs of motherhood and life.

Thank you to my brother Greg for the handwritten cards, silly video calls, check-in texts, and for always making me feel loved. Thank you to my mom, Lisa, for the weekend visits, stroller walks, homemade meatballs, and for continually replenishing my stash of TJ's dark-chocolate-covered pretzels. Most of all, thank you for believing in me and my writing—and for giving me the gift of time to pursue my dreams.

To my dad, Woody: I am so joyful and grateful that writing is a love we share. I treasure our conversations, and your feedback always helps me see my work with renewed freshness and enthusiasm. Thank you for being my writing buddy, biggest fan, and constant cheerleader.

To my husband, Allyn: an early draft of this book was the first manuscript I ever shared with you, and I was so nervous. Even though you were in the thick of business school, you read the book in record time, and when you finished you called to tell me you loved it. (I still have that voicemail saved on my phone!) Thank you for being so beautifully, sturdily, wholly supportive of my writing every day since. I am so lucky to be your wife.

To my daughters, Maya and Auden: I love you infinity and am so proud of you, always.

DALLAS WOODBURN'S debut novel *The Best Week That Never Happened* was the Grand Prize Winner of the Dante Rossetti Book Award for Young Adult Fiction. She is also the author of the YA novel *Thanks, Carissa, For Ruining My Life* and the short story collections *Woman, Running Late, in a Dress* and *How to Make Paper When the World is Ending*.

A former John Steinbeck Fellow in Creative Writing, her writing has been honored with the Cypress & Pine Short Fiction Award, the international Glass Woman Prize, and four Pushcart Prize nominations.

When she's not writing, Dallas hosts the podcast *Thriving Authors Podcast*, teaches writing classes for teens and adults, and unapologetically bakes pumpkin-spice everything all year round. She lives in the San Francisco Bay Area with her husband and two daughters.

Find Dallas online:
www.dallaswoodburn.com

#BEFOREANDAFTERYOUANDME